DANGER IN THE DARK

Jovvi was about to call out to Rion, but at that precise moment Naran gasped and wrapped a hand around Jovvi's arm with a grip that was actually painful.

That . . . something different in Naran's mind had flared for an instant, and Jovvi had no trouble understanding what it meant. Rion was in danger *now*, and giving help in another minute or two would probably be too late. Jovvi reached out to initiate the Blending. The Blending formed instantly, and then—

And then it was the entity which had taken over, an entity which was fully aware of the danger to one of its flesh forms. Its senses located three human forms standing in the shadows. One of the three held something in its closed fist, and even as the entity watched, that one opened its hand and flung the contents at the flesh form named Rion . . .

Other Avon Eos Books in
THE BLENDING *Series by*
Sharon Green

CONVERGENCE
COMPETITIONS
CHALLENGES
BETRAYALS

PROPHECY

—✧—

Book Five of THE BLENDING

SHARON GREEN

AVON · EOS

This is a work of fiction. Names, characters, places, and incidents either are the product of the author's imagination or are used fictitiously. Any resemblance to actual events, locales, organizations, or persons, living or dead, is entirely coincidental and beyond the intent of either the author or the publisher.

AVON BOOKS, INC.
1350 Avenue of the Americas
New York, New York 10019

Copyright © 1999 by Sharon Green
Cover art by Tom Canty
Published by arrangement with the author
Library of Congress Catalog Card Number: 98-94801
ISBN: 0-380-78811-X
www.avonbooks.com/eos

First Avon Eos Printing: July 1999

AVON EOS TRADEMARK REG. U.S. PAT. OFF. AND IN OTHER COUNTRIES, MARCA REGISTRADA, HECHO EN U.S.A.

Printed in the U.S.A.

WCD   10   9   8   7   6   5   4   3   2

For Morris Bernstein and Mike Lehman . . . two great friends who really tried to make me understand the device I used so casually. I, alas, didn't understand one word in four, but I still appreciated the effort. There's always been a warm place in my heart for optimists. . . .

Well, we seem to be getting down to the last of it. Some time ago I said I'd tell anyone reading this when we reached the time I'm actually living in, but we're not at that point yet. It's true we're almost there, but there are still some things that have happened which I haven't mentioned yet. I wonder if I'll ever have the chance to put down the very last of it. . . .

No, it isn't a good idea to borrow trouble, not when you have enough of it that already belongs to you. I'm sure you remember that the others and I had finally managed to free some of the Highs and strong Middles who were being used in the empire's army, and that they helped us to defeat the two hundred guardsmen sent after us by the falsely Seated Five. That was a clear and definite victory, which was followed almost immediately by the news that the people of Astinda had finally managed to put together an army of their own—and that army was defeating and destroying ours.

I, personally, had no idea what to do about the situation, but happily my groupmates had no doubts. The Astindan army seemed to be headed for the border between our two countries, intent on destroying our countryside and people the same way theirs had been done. Turnabout is usually considered fair play, but in this instance it would hardly be the nobility, the ones who

1

were responsible for the death and destruction done in Astinda, who would pay with their property and lives. Ignorant, innocent people would be the victims, and there was no one to warn them but us and our new allies. Not to mention getting ourselves out of the path of the avenging army, which outnumbered us ten to one. . . .

And then, of course, there were the personal problems, between me and Vallant Ro and between Vallant and Alsin Meerk. They were small and feeble compared to the rest of what was going on, but it didn't seem like that at the time. For a while it had almost been a game, but then the game stopped being amusing. . . .

ONE

Rion Mardimil rode next to his beloved Naran, extremely relieved that she showed no signs of strain over the haste of their journey. Or no signs that the rest of them didn't show. They'd been on the move for the last day with very little rest, fleeing ahead of the oncoming Astindan host. Lorand was in the lead, this being his part of the country, and he assured everyone that they were almost to the district which had once been his home. Privately, Rion thought Lorand didn't look especially happy over that, but the people had to be warned and their own group could hardly ride from hamlet to hamlet shouting the danger. It would be up to the—Widdertown, was it?—people to pass along the news of imminent attack, and then their own group would be free to continue on in returning to Gan Garee.

Naran gave him a sweet, passing smile which he returned, then she went back to studying the countryside they rode through. The horses of the attacking guardsmen had done well for completing the mounting of their entire force, and those horses the guardsmen had abandoned on the way—the ones which survived having been ridden into the ground, at any rate—were being taken up as they were passed. Having spare mounts never hurt, even though no one but their own rode with them.

Rion took a deep breath, still wondering if the fate of the officers and "prods" who had savaged their new allies should disturb him more than it did. The higher officers had all been nobles, of course, and Jovvi had told him and the rest of their groupmates that the nobles had been incapable of believing they'd be harmed right up to the very end. But that end had been sufficiently long and drawn out to make the nobles believe, not to mention being painful. The former victims had been badly savaged, and their vengeance had been completely in keeping with what had been done to *them*.

And Rion had found himself grimly pleased to hear the screams and suffering of those so-called nobles. Considering the fact that he'd spent most of his life thinking of himself as one of them, his actual enjoyment of their suffering had startled him. He *should* have been highly incensed over peasants treating their betters that way, but the fact was he didn't perceive his current allies as being inferior. To the contrary, he'd discovered that in most ways they were superior to the lazy, pampered drones he'd once considered his peers. It was no longer unthinkable to feel regret that he wasn't truly one of those he'd formerly thought of as useless peasants . . .

"Rion, my love, has Jovvi made any suggestions about what might be done to restore peace between Vallant and Alsin?" Naran asked abruptly in a soft voice, pulling Rion back to the present. "The difficulty between them seems to increase with their very breathing, and if something isn't done there will be a terrible confrontation that none of us will want to witness."

"We all fear the same outcome, my love, but so far Jovvi hasn't said anything," Rion responded, Naran's disturbance affecting him at once. "I'm still not quite clear about how there can be trouble between them over Tamrissa, not when one considers the bond between our two groupmates. Have I missed seeing the obvious again?"

"Yes, and it's one of the most charming things about you," Naran said with shining eyes and a gay laugh, and then her amusement faded. "For some reason Vallant seems to have decided to have nothing more to do with Tamrissa, although anyone with eyes can see that his heart will never belong to any other woman. She, for her part, made an effort to dissuade Alsin's interest in her, but his having noticed Vallant's distance caused her efforts to be wasted. Alsin committed himself to courting her, and Vallant decided to interfere with that intention—without changing his own stance in the least.''

"Oh, dear," Rion said with brows high, sounding to himself a good deal like Jovvi. "Is he truly saying that he refuses to become involved with Tamrissa himself, but also refuses to allow any other man to become involved?"

"I'm afraid so," Naran agreed with her own sigh. "What Tamrissa's thoughts must be like is something I don't care to dwell on, but that's actually only a part of the problem. After Vallant and Alsin had words, Vallant began to . . . take over leadership of our efforts, I suppose you could say. Alsin expected to be consulted, since he *is* supposed to be our strategist, but Vallant isn't doing any consulting. Alsin is now feeling more like an outcast than ever.''

"I'm sure his being a strong Middle rather than a High isn't helping in the least," Rion said, now understanding the glares sent in Vallant's direction by Alsin. "They're both used to being leaders and they both want the same woman; if there are any worse subjects they can disagree about, I can't think of them."

"They don't need any other subjects of disagreement," Naran assured him. "The two they have are two too many, and they really are heading for a terrible showdown if something isn't done. Do you think you might speak to Jovvi and tell her that, and possibly even help to devise something to do?"

"I'll be glad to speak to Jovvi," Rion said, suddenly disturbed in an odd way. "In point of fact you could speak to her yourself, since the others really do consider you one of us. Naran . . . why are you hesitating to speak your own thoughts? Since you seem so absolutely certain, I'm surprised that you hesitate. Do you believe that Jovvi or one of the others would dismiss what you said?"

"Oh, no, my love, of course not," Naran hastened to assure him, the earnestness in her eyes entirely unfeigned. "The others are wonderful and have accepted me fully, but . . . I suppose you could say I'm too shy to speak up myself. At times I've been forced to by the circumstances we were in the midst of, but now . . . I'll just be happier letting you do my speaking for me.''

"Certainly, my love, I'll be glad to take care of it,'' Rion said, reaching over to pat her hand as he smiled. "Anything within my power to make you happy, I think you know that.''

She returned his smile and briefly clasped his hand, and then they returned to paying attention to where they rode. Rion felt a great deal of relief, as he would have been extremely unhappy if anyone had made Naran feel less than completely welcome and one of them. Even though, in all truth, she wasn't. . . .

Lorand looked around as he led the rather large column of former army or potential army people directly toward Widdertown. He was currently in the midst of trying to decide whether to be happy or bothered that he was almost home, but so far hadn't had much luck in making up his mind.

Now that they had left Astinda behind and were back across the border into the empire, there were healthy, cultivated fields to either side of the road. The devastation caused by their army was no longer visible, and despite its being only a few miles behind them, hadn't been visible since they'd crossed back. The nobles had obviously not wanted anyone in the empire really knowing what the army was doing, and so they'd disguised their efforts in the place, close to the border, where they would be most easily seen. Now, that disguising would certainly work against their own group.

"Lorand, would you like to tell me what's disturbing you?'' Jovvi asked suddenly from where she rode beside him, the words gentle and encouraging. "If I can possibly be of help, it would give me a great deal of pleasure to do it.''

"I know that, love, but I don't think anyone can help,'' he replied with a sigh that was part exasperation. "My own mind refuses to stick to the subject bothering me most, so trying to discuss it will probably turn into a conversation about the weather. Do you really want to talk about the weather?''

"If it helps to make you feel better, why not?" she countered with a merry grin. "And it's a rather pretty day, so how can we go wrong?"

"I'm afraid we already have," Lorand told her ruefully. "It's a pretty day right *now*, but in a few hours we'll be in the middle of a chain of thunderstorms. I just hope we can find some shelter before then. . . ."

"So that's what's bothering you," she said softly as they cantered along. "You aren't sure what sort of reception we'll get in your home town. Just because there were harsh words between you and your father before you left, why do you believe everyone else will be just as hostile?"

"The people of Widdertown . . . don't take to strangers very readily," Lorand answered slowly and reluctantly, feeling as though he betrayed his former neighbors by saying that to someone who wasn't one of them. "They're . . . a small, tightly knit community with . . . beliefs and opinions they think everyone should have. They won't enjoy having this horde descending on them, and might not even believe us."

"Lorand, I ache for the hurt *you're* feeling, but if they decide not to believe us, whatever happens to them won't be our fault." Jovvi now spoke firmly and slowly, as though she sought to make him believe. "That means it certainly won't be *your* fault either, even if they fail to survive. When you're dealing with supposedly responsible adults, you can't make their decisions for them. Anyone who refuses to take a warning seriously can't complain about what happens to them afterward."

"Intellectually I know that," Lorand agreed glumly. "If we were anywhere else I would be saying the same exact thing, but we don't happen to *be* anywhere else. We're in the place where I grew up and where my family lives. The idea of them ending up the way so many people we've come across lately have is just too—"

He shook his head, knowing it would be impossible to find the right word to describe his emotions. Everyone in the Widdertown area was *not* like his father, but they did share too many of his attitudes. The idea of not convincing them of the danger terrified him, but it seemed to be beyond him to come up with something that would guarantee success.

Jovvi reached over to touch his arm with clear sympathy and support, and then she let the subject drop. Obviously she'd noticed that discussing the problem was making things worse for him rather than better, and so had left him to his writhing thoughts. But he couldn't bear his thoughts any longer, so he gave his attention to the fields and farmsteads they passed. Everything was alive and thriving and humming with the joy of growth and health, and he refused to think about how soon all of that might end.

It was late afternoon when Widdertown finally lay directly in front of them, with too-familiar neighborhoods safely behind them. There were now farm wagons on the road heading for the same destination, and Lorand realized that luck might be with them. He'd lately lost track of time and days, but the only time the men of the farms came into Widdertown at the end of the day was just before week's end. That would mean that most of the farmers would be there to hear what they had to say, without anyone needing to go and fetch them. And considering the looks they'd gotten from the men in the wagons, word of their arrival would certainly not take its time spreading.

The streets of Widdertown held many more men than women, the women naturally at home preparing the evening meal. Everyone stopped to stare uneasily at their column, pointing at them and muttering to those who stood staring with them. Some also began to follow at a small distance, right into the town square, the place Lorand had decided would be best. The general alarm hung there, and once they reached it he dismounted. Taking up the hammer that was never touched unless a real, true emergency came up, Lorand struck the suspended circle of metal, sending out the harsh and clanging echoes that meant everyone was to come.

By the time Lorand put the hammer down again, everyone who had heard the alarm had come running. Confusion reigned as the newcomers slowed their run and added their stares to those of the people already in the square, and then Ravis Grund finally made his appearance. Ravis was the man who ran things in Widdertown, but not because the farmers and townies had agreed that he should. Lorand had never stopped to wonder why a man who was wealthy only in comparison to most of the people in the district ran things, but now he believed he knew. Ravis Grund was probably the agent of whichever noble claimed the district as private property, and ran it for that noble as an overseer of sorts.

"Who's causing all this commotion?" Ravis demanded as he made his portly way through the crowds, mopping his brow as he came. "Lorand Coll, is that you, boy? What are you doing back here with *that* scraggly-looking lot? And what do you mean by ringing the alarm? You're in deep trouble now, boy—"

"That's enough, Ravis," Lorand interrupted, more than annoyed by the man's attitude. "I'm not the one in trouble, and if you had an ounce of common sense you would have asked *why* I rang the alarm, not decided in advance that I couldn't have had a reason. How much do you know about what the empire's army has been doing in Astinda?"

"I don't know what you're talking about, boy," Ravis denied at once, his gaze shifting furtively to the townspeople around them. Lorand hadn't spoken softly, and everyone but Ravis looked disturbed and confused and had begun to mutter. "The empire doesn't have an army, and even if they did it would be none of your business. Now you take these raggedy drifters and—"

"So you do know all about it," Lorand said with a satisfied nod for the obvious lie, again interrupting the fool. "I'm sure your owners told you, but you never saw fit to pass on the information. With that being the case, I'll do it for you right now, because the information is vital. The empire has more than one army, but the one which has been devastating Astinda is the one everyone needs to hear about. Astinda has finally put together its own army, and it's been destroying all our forces in its path without any trouble. Now that army is heading for the border, and it should be here in much too short a time. The Astindans have obviously decided to return some of the destruction empire forces have caused in *their* country, and Widdertown lies directly in their path."

A chaos of alarm and shock broke out in the crowd,

sustained and encouraged by the fact that Ravis had gone pale and terrified. He'd waxed extremely indignant when Lorand had spoken about his "owners," but now indignation had given way to fear.

"You see?" Lorand shouted over the hubbub, pointing toward Ravis. "If any of you doubt what I said, just take a good look at the man who assured you a minute ago that the empire doesn't have an army. He works for the nobles who bleed you dry and treat you like slaves, so his actions are always in *their* best interests. Now he's willing to let you all die, destroyed under the heels of an avenging army, just to keep his owners' secrets."

"Stop sayin' that!" Ravis screamed, his country accent coming back with the hysteria. "I don't have no 'owners,' I'm a free man! *They* have owners and they know it, but I don't!"

"Too bad we can't say nothin' to deny that," Idroy Welt, one of the district's biggest farmers, said with barely hidden venom. "Those nobles own us body and spirit, an' leave us with almost nothin' to raise our families on. Are we supposta die for them now?"

"Ain't you takin' whut the boy said with a real big grain a salt?" another voice put in, that of Mollit Feldin, another large-acreage farmer standing at the front of the crowd. "I knowed Lorand there since he been a pint-sized hellion, an' everythin's always real important if *he's* in the middle a it. Looks like nothin's changed since he growed, an' I don't fancy runnin' off on just his sayso. If the rest a you think on it, you'll see thet whut he says ain't real likely."

This time the muttering of the crowd was in support of what Mollit had said, the voice of reason drowning out the voice of warning. The fact that they'd known him all his life *was* one of the biggest problems, as no one wants to believe the lie of a possible practical joker and thereby make himself look foolish. Add that to their very understandable reluctance to accept the possibility of their being about to lose everything, and control of the situation was abruptly taken right out of Lorand's hands.

"I've never seen a bigger bunch of damn' fools in my life," Vallant said suddenly and loudly from where he now stood beside Lorand. "They'd rather believe the lies of that fat toady who steals from them in the name of the nobles, so why bother arguin'? It's their lives, not ours, so let's go on to another town where there might be fewer fools."

Everyone took umbrage at that and anger rose in shouts, but the voice of Idroy Welt rose above the rest. Idroy was a big man, hard and tough and respected by his neighbors even if they didn't like him very much, and his booming tone drowned out most of theirs.

"Let's everybody calm right down," he said, looking around in all directions. "This ain't somethin' to believe or not believe right off the bat. Let's invite these here folk to the meetin' hall where we c'n all sit down and hear what they gotta say, an' then we c'n talk about it. Don't know if the meetin' hall's big enough to hold all a them, though. . . . Let's show 'em hospitality an' take care a their mounts too, an' then some of 'em can come to the meetin' hall. By then most everybody oughta be in town."

Mollit Feldin tried to say it was a waste of time and food and effort, but happily the rest of the men there were more inclined to agree with Idroy. They weren't happy about any part of the situation, but at least they were willing to listen. What happened afterward was still up in the air, but at least they'd get fed and their horses would also be fed and rested.

So then, if they were asked to leave after the meeting, there would be nothing but Lorand's memories and regrets hovering in their path out of there. . . .

TWO

Vallant kept silent as their five walked along the dirt street, his thoughts on something other than the meeting they were going to. Having an imagination was rarely an asset to people living in a small town, and those individuals like Lorand who were born with one usually left as soon as they could. The proposed meeting would probably quickly become a matter of the farmers demanding proof and *their* saying there wasn't any—short of waiting around until it was too late. After that "wiser heads" would voice grave doubts as to the wisdom of leaving their homes, and the majority of farmers would listen to them. If this hadn't been the place Lorand came from, Vallant would have been just as happy to simply move on.

But that would have been the only thing he was happy about. Vallant glanced at Tamrissa where she walked on the far side of the group, very clearly and obviously putting as much distance between him and herself as she possibly could. And the way she'd been acting with him. . . . She hadn't turned him invisible in her thoughts the way she'd done once before; this time it was worse. Every time he looked at her his whole being seemed to ache, and she no longer ever looked directly at *him*. He'd gotten the impression he was dead in her thoughts rather than merely invisible, and that brought him more than just a simple ache.

He took a deep breath then, stepping up onto the wood

of the new sidewalk without really paying attention. He and Lorand moved into the lead with the other three behind them, all five apparently sunk into their own thoughts. Vallant had meant to speak to Jovvi, wanting to ask her to explain to Tamrissa that she, Tamrissa, wasn't yet ready for the relationship she thought she wanted, but he hadn't had the opportunity.

The townspeople had stabled as many of the horses as they could and had put the rest in a corral, and then they'd thrown together a meal for the humans. Not that the townspeople had acted friendly or concerned; they were doing what they'd been told was their duty, and standoffish was too mild a word for their attitude. People suffering from disease would probably have gotten a warmer welcome, if those people were considered the villagers' own. Strangers were a good deal worse than disease carriers, and no one even volunteered to help shift the horses which were fed out of the stabling and putting others in their place. The townspeople had supplied the feed and the stabling; let the strangers, no matter how tired they looked, take care of the rest themselves.

Vallant had had to walk among the liberated ''segments'' and calm their anger, telling them that these people weren't worth getting upset about. Lorand had been born and raised among them, and even he was being no more than tolerated. People who were that afraid of change and difference weren't likely to survive the coming of the Astindan army, and maybe that was for the best. When a community gets *too* insular, it starts to decay down deep, where the ruin can't be seen until it's too late for anyone to stop it.

Not like individuals, who were simply trying to keep someone they cared about from making a mistake. Vallant would have liked nothing better than to take Tamrissa in his arms and make love to her again, but it wouldn't have been good for *her*. Was he supposed to forget about that and do it anyway, and ruin any chance they had for a lasting, loving—

''The meeting hall's just up ahead there,'' Lorand said abruptly, pulling Vallant away from the morass of rambling, chaotic thoughts. No matter what he tried to think about, the path always led back to Tamrissa and the last words they'd exchanged. . . .

''Do you think there's any chance of their listenin' to

us?'' Vallant asked quietly, determined to be the master of his own mind. ''The ones who brought that food were colder than mile-high ice, and they don't yet know what we are. What do you think will happen when they find out?''

''I'm trying *not* to think about it,'' Lorand replied, his tone weary rather than sarcastic. ''I keep getting the feeling that someone has dismantled half this town, because I don't remember it being quite this small. And that Mollit Feldin, who wanted to dismiss everything I said. . . . I'm remembering how many others are just like him, uninterested in anyone's opinion but their own. Maybe we should have gone to a different town.''

''If we had, you never would have forgiven yourself—or us,'' Vallant countered, understanding far too well what his group brother was going through. ''And I know what you mean about this place shrinkin', and the people suddenly lookin' like they have blocks of wood for heads. The same thing happened to me when I first shipped out and then came back, and it took some effort to understand that *I* was the one who had changed, not the town or the people. So give your old neighbors a chance, because they just might surprise all of us.''

Lorand nodded with his intensity fractionally lessened, and Vallant was glad that he'd lied. He didn't really expect these people to surprise them, but Lorand would do better believing they might right up to the time they didn't.

The meeting hall was a large building standing alone to one side of the town square, with what looked like a large public bath house diagonally across from it. In the middle of the square was a small fountain with the alarm bar hanging from a post next to it, and people were milling around near the fountain in groups, watching everyone who walked toward the hall. It looked like not everyone had been invited to the meeting, which wasn't a very good sign of progress to come.

Vallant let Lorand walk into the hall half a step ahead of him, a privilege his group brother was more than entitled to. The people who awaited them had no way of knowing just how hard things had been for Lorand, at least as hard as Vallant found walking into the building to be. But at least there were windows lining the big room on either side, windows that could be reached rather easily. . . .

"You been learnin' bad habits in th' big city, boy," the one named Mollit Feldin said to Lorand from where he stood at the front of the room. "This ain't no place fer females, so you jest send 'em on home an' then we c'n get this here meetin' goin'."

"What's the matter, Mollit, are you too old to remember my name?" Lorand countered as they all walked slowly toward where the man and some of the others waited for them. The benches were only half full, Vallant noticed, which meant the people hanging around the fountain in the square had been told they weren't allowed at the meeting.

"Just to help you remember, old man, my name is Lorand," Lorand continued calmly and quietly. "And any man with sense would have asked *why* these ladies are with us, not just told us to get rid of them. So since you've proven you *have* no sense, why don't you sit down and just listen for a change. I know the odds are against it, but you just might learn something."

"You watch yer mouth, boy!" Feldin snapped, his skin darkening at the chuckling some of the others were doing. "I ain't no old man, an'—"

"And I'm not a boy," Lorand interrupted, now standing directly in front of the man—who wasn't quite as big as Lorand. Vallant's groupmate's voice had been strong and hard, showing a self-confidence Lorand probably didn't completely feel, but it was the outer show that Feldin reacted to. The farmer wiped his lips on the back of one hand, glared balefully, but didn't say another word.

"You're a boy compared t' us," the one named Idroy Welt said mildly, drawing Lorand's attention to where he stood, next to Feldin. "We didn't aim to give no insult, Lorand, but you gotta understand—Mollit here's got almost as big a farm as me, so he's entitled to his say. Jest like everybody's got the right."

"An' me especially," another voice said, causing Vallant and the others to look around with Lorand. A big man had stood up among the benches, one who looked very much like Lorand, and Vallant could almost feel the increased tension in his group brother. "I got the right t'have m'say, and I got the right t'call ya boy."

"You gave up the right to call me anything at all, Pa," Lorand said after a very short pause, the words bitter. "When you put your own wants about my life ahead of mine, you stopped being kin to me. You might want to think about what would have happened to the people in this district if I'd done the same thing, and run to save my own neck without giving a damn about yours. There *is* an army heading this way, destroying everything in its path, and if you people choose not to believe it, your deaths will be on your own heads."

"That's somethin' we gotta talk about, but not till everybody's here," Welt said, looking troubled. "Ravis ain't showed up yet, an' we can't start till he does."

"That man Ravis Grund won't *be* showing up," Jovvi put in calmly, drawing everyone's attention. "When he left the square earlier, his intentions were perfectly clear. If he hasn't left the district already, he'll be doing it shortly. He lied about not knowing about the army, and he lied about coming to this meeting. He's getting out as fast as he can with as much as he can, abandoning all of you and running back to the people he works for."

There was a brief but very thick silence, and then Welt said, "Don't mean t'be doubtin' yer word, ma'am, but how could you know thet? Ravis ain't the brightest nor the bravest, but I ain't never seen him run frum a threat."

"An' he's one a *us*, not sum bloody outsider," Feldin added with a growl. "You got a real nerve, girl, talkin' 'bout folks you ain't near as good as—"

"Close your mouth, Mollit," Lorand said in his own growl, one that did more to chill than Feldin's. "Dama Hafford is ten times better than any mudfoot in this room, so you close your mouth and keep it closed. She's also a High talent in Spirit magic, so if she says Ravis is gone, you can bet the farm you don't own on it."

Shocked exclamations sounded around the room, and Vallant saw the expressions of fear and revulsion that accompanied them. For that reason *he* stepped forward, to stand beside Lorand.

"If you're wonderin' about whether the lady is right, you

might send someone over to Grund's house," he suggested, also keeping his voice mild. "But get someone from the street to go, because we're ready to tell you the things you need to know. We'll also probably be leavin' not long after the tellin', because we know that army's real even if the bunch of you refuse to believe it."

"Refe, go grab one a th' boys outside," Welt ordered after a brief hesitation, speaking to a man toward the back of the hall. "Tell 'im t' knock at Ravis's door, an' if he don't get a answer he's t' try openin' th' door an' goin' inside. If he hasta do thet, he's t' hightail it back here fast as he c'n run."

The man addressed nodded and got to his feet, then headed for the door out of the hall. As soon as Welt saw the nod, his attention turned back to Vallant.

"We'll be listenin' to whut you gotta say, but first we'd like them ladies outta here," he said, the words very neutral. "In things like this here, a man don't wanna have t'watch whut he says 'cause there's ladies about t'take offense. We don't mean no insult, but. . . ."

"I'm sorry, but we can't oblige you on that point," Vallant said while Lorand hesitated with a disturbed expression. "And you'd all better sit down, because the ladies are part of the rather long story. You'll want to know how we found out the things we did, and when we tell you you'll understand how everything fits. Are you ready to listen?"

Welt saw that the man Refe was on his way back into the hall from the door, so he nodded before choosing a place on a bench to sit. Feldin hesitated a moment longer, the resentful expression on his face saying he would have preferred to make more trouble, but caution won in the end. He, too, found a place to sit down, as did Vallant's groupmates. But his groupmates sat on chairs on the short dais, leaving the plain, battered old table as a place for *him* to perch. Lorand's father, with an odd expression on his face, had long ago resumed his seat, so there was no reason not to start.

"To begin with," Vallant said, "our empire has been tryin' for some time to take over the countries of Astinda and Gracely. We haven't seen Gracely, but just over the border into Astinda there's nothin' left but destruction and death. They killed the land and murdered the people, and even left some of the people, still alive, hangin' as a warnin' to other Astindans. The army that's comin' here means to get revenge for all that, and we were told by somebody who saw it that they aren't lettin' any of ours live even if they surrender.''

Another mutter arose among his listeners, a very disturbed one, but not everyone was equally impressed.

"So *you* say," Feldin sneered out, obviously prepared to do nothing but cast doubt. "Sounds like a lotta bull t'me, since there ain't no way t'know fer sure 'thout takin' *yer* word fer it."

"There are two ways to know for sure," Vallant countered, showing how unimpressed he was by the fool of a man. "You can talk to a lot of our people, most of whom spent a lot of time bein' forced to work for the damn nobles runnin' the army. They can tell you what sickenin' things they were made to do before the Astindan army forced them to retreat, or you can ignore what everyone says and just stick around. In your case I'd recommend stickin' around, since the world becomes a better place to live every time a damn fool like you gets himself killed."

Feldin surged to his feet bellowing, his fists clenched and ready to do some battering, but suddenly all his rage and insult disappeared. He just stood there blinking and silent, and Vallant smiled faintly.

"If the rest of you are wonderin' what's wrong with him, it should be obvious," he said to the shaken men in the audience. "We already told you that Dama Hafford is a High in Spirit magic, and this is no time to let an imbecile start a fight. Personally, though, I'm gettin' really tired of tryin' to help a bunch of people who are too stupid to know they *need* the help. If you'd rather be rid of us than hear what we have to tell, just say so. Since we mean to leave anyway once the horses are rested and fed, we'll be gone before you remember we're around."

Most of their audience seemed to like the idea of being rid of these dangerous and awful interlopers, but Idroy Welt, despite being shaken himself, stood up and shook his head.

"No, we *don't* want 'em gone yet," he said to his friends

and neighbors, looking around at them. "Mollit asked fer handlin' like she done, jest like usual. He don't think, he jumps, and this ain't no time fer jumpin'. If'n we don't listen, we culd lose more'n our land, so we *are* gonna hear whut they gotta say."

Again most of the audience wasn't terribly pleased, but none of them argued or got up to leave as Welt resumed his seat. Vallant was somewhat surprised, just the way Vallant had told Lorand he'd be.

"All right, then let's get to it," Vallant agreed aloud. "We should start from the beginning, since every one of us up here went through the same thing. It—"

"Please, wait just a minute!" a voice called, and Vallant saw that a man had just entered the hall. He was fairly tall and lean, but what marked him out from the other men in the room was the fact that he wore Gan Garee style clothing, rather than the rough work clothes the others had on. "Forgive me for interrupting, but I only just found out about this meeting. I don't know what's been said here so far, but I would appreciate a word in private with your group before anything else is added."

"And why would that be, Master Lugal?" Lorand asked, getting to his feet again to do it. "Are you afraid that we're going to warn these people not to send any more of their sons and daughters to Gan Garee no matter how strong you say they are? Well, that's just what we do mean to tell them, because of those sent to test for High practitioner, a large number die during that obscene thing called a test. Those who survive at the wrong time of year, like when the nobility has no need of dummy challengers for their Seated Highs, they're drugged and sent as virtual slaves to the various armies. Well, now that they've been told, is there anything 'private' left to discuss?"

Lorand's calling the man Master Lugal told Vallant that the newcomer was the resident Guild man, the one who found strong Middles and potential Highs and sent them to Gan Garee. That would have caused Vallant's anger to rise as high as Lorand's, except for the fact that Lugal had gone pale with shock and now stood holding the back of a bench. The man obviously needed the support to keep from falling, and it took a moment before he was able to shake his head.

"That can't be true!" he denied in a husky whisper, the look in his eyes haunted. "I can't have been sending young people to death or slavery! They would have told me . . . !"

"I get the impression that you aren't lying," Lorand said in a gentler way after a brief moment. "And since Jovvi confirms that, I'll just say how sorry I am for you. I wasn't lying either, and you don't have to take my word for it. Talk to the rest of the people we're with, and they'll tell you the same thing because they also went through it. The nobility has it arranged that way so they won't have any trouble keeping the empire under their collective thumbs."

"What was that you said about dummy challengers for the Seated Highs?" a voice called out from the far left side of the room. "My boy went to Gan Garee two years ago, and if *he* faced one of those Highs, it was no dummy challenge."

This time Vallant joined Lorand in hesitating to answer, touched by the loving pride which had been in the man's voice. It's hard for another man to trample on something like that, but it seemed that women didn't see it quite the same.

"They're *all* dummy challenges, because the Seated Highs are no such thing," Tamrissa said with a sniff of disdain. "I faced the Seated High in Fire magic, unofficially, of course, because he thought I was drugged and helpless. He was no better than an ordinary Middle, and when he tried to match *my* strength he burned himself out. He was a noble, like they all are, so he never *won* his place. They gave it to him, and then they cheated to help him keep it."

This time the muttering sounded more like an uproar in the making, anger and indignation mixed thoroughly throughout. Vallant wondered if the emotions were directed toward the nobility or toward Tamrissa for saying what she had, and a moment later he found out.

"Why ain't I s'rprised?" Idroy Welt demanded of no one in particular, then he eyed the people who sat or stood together in front of the audience. "So th' first lady's a High in Spirit magic an' th' second in Fire magic. Thet mean you men'r th' same?"

"I'm Earth magic, Vallant there is Water magic, and Rion over here is Air magic," Lorand replied after a short but obvious pause. "Do you understand now why the ladies are with us?"

The uproar suddenly quieted, almost as if someone had closed a heavy door on the noise. They did understand— or were afraid that they did—even though Lorand had been gentle in breaking it to them.

"Yes, what you're probably thinkin' is true," Vallant confirmed, again trying to be just as gentle. "We were thrown together by the nobles as a challengin' Blendin', because this was a twenty-fifth year. We lasted until the final challenge, when we faced the last of the five noble challengin' Blendin's, and then, when we began to win, they knocked us out with hilsom powder. But that's somethin' for *us* to take care of once we get back to Gan Garee. Right now there's still that advancin' army to worry about."

Vallant had been trying to take their minds off the fact that they had a real, actual Blending sitting in front of them, and to a certain extent it seemed to work. No one jumped up screaming to run out of the hall, but that might have been because they were too frightened to move. Well, whatever the reason, Vallant meant to take advantage of it. Seeing that the man Lugal had collapsed onto a bench near where he'd been standing, Vallant began the story that it looked like no one would be interrupting again.

THREE

It didn't take as long as it could have for Vallant Ro to tell Lorand's former neighbors about what we'd gone through, but that was only because he glossed over many of the details. These people not only didn't need to know them, they probably didn't *want* to know. Any number of them kept glancing at the rest of us, as though they expected us to go on a rampage of murder and destruction at any moment. At another time I might have been tempted to oblige them, but just now it was all I could do to sit still and pretend that nothing was wrong.

Once again I'd had too much time to think, so my thoughts had gone in the predictable direction. I'd replayed that last conversation with Vallant over and over again in my mind, and the more I thought about it the more upset I became. Jovvi had said he was afraid to become involved with me again, so I'd been trying to soothe his fear the way he'd once soothed mine. I'd resigned myself to the complete lack of progress I'd apparently been making, but then he'd actually come out and said that he had no interest in courting me in Alsin's place.

I moved in discomfort on the old chair I'd chosen to sit on, finding it impossible to make *uninterested* equal *frightened*. I'd been afraid of all men when Vallant had tried to court me, but there had still been that . . . undeniable attraction I'd felt every time I saw the man. My insistence that I felt nothing of the sort had been easy for anyone to see through, which was the major difference between that situation and the one I now had with Vallant. He always moved away from me at the first opportunity, as though he really couldn't stand being near me.

Jovvi stirred in the chair next to mine, and even though she remained silent I understood what was bothering her and tried to get my emotions back under control. The bleakness and desolation I'd been living with lately was quite a lot like the countryside we'd ridden through in Astinda: deliberately spread and impossible to deny. It had to be almost as painful for Jovvi as it was for me, and she didn't deserve to have that thrust at her. It was enough that *I* had to feel it. . . .

". . . so after becomin' aware ourselves of the large number of people headin' in our direction, we then found out who they were," Vallant was saying. "The Astindans have thousands of reasons to cross the border into the empire and give back what they've gotten, thousands of dead bodies and acres of land. They don't know that the people around here had nothin' to do with what the army did, and they probably don't care. They're goin' to do as they were done to, and so far none of our forces has been able to stand up to them."

"Or surrender," Idroy Welt said, sounding and looking more than a little believing and therefore disturbed. "That's what you said, ain't it? That they don't wanna hear nothin' about surrenderin'? So what'r we s'posta do? Jest run, an' hope we c'n stay ahead of 'em?"

"That's a very good question," Jovvi said while everyone in the room made sounds which showed their own disturbance. "It's something none of us have discussed, because we've decided to go back to Gan Garee and take care of the business waiting for us *there*. But our doing that won't stop that oncoming army, or save you and your land and your neighboring towns and *their* land. Does anyone have a suggestion we can talk about?"

"Whut about thet there Blendin' stuff?" someone asked from the back of the room, sounding as though he discussed something dirty but unfortunately necessary. "Cain't you lot do somethin'?"

"You mean like repeating what started all this and destroy them?" Jovvi asked gently but without hesitation.

"It's just possible we might be able to do that, but if we do, what's to stop the nobility from coming back and taking up where they left off? Do all of you *like* being nothing but workers on the land someone else owns even though it's your blood, sweat, and effort that makes it worth owning? I can tell you that the Astindans didn't enjoy being invaded and destroyed, and something like that can happen as easily to you as it did to them."

"No, she's not guessing," Lorand said when a mutter went up that suggested ridiculing doubt. "We came across a farmstead in a hidden place, a spot where people obviously ran away to in order to work for *themselves* rather than the nobility. Guardsmen had been sent after them, and every man, woman, and child—including infants—had been hanged in front of their houses. If those guardsmen were to ride in here to do the same thing to one or more of your neighbors, which of you would be able to stand against them?"

The muttering turned to a shocked silence at that, and then a boy flew in through the doorway. He looked around as he panted, obviously having run to the hall, and the man who had been called Refe stood up near his bench.

"You wus right, sir," the boy said at once, speaking to the man who had stood. "Ravis Grund ain't nowheres around, not him and not none a the rest a his kin. Thet there fancy gold knocker is gone from th' front door too, an' inside everythin's tossed ever' which way."

"So now you know how the nobility and their hirelings take care of the people who produce their wealth," Jovvi said once the panting boy had finished. "They desert them at the first sign of trouble, leaving them to live or die with only themselves to depend on. We've told you everything we know, and it might be best if you share that information with the rest of your neighbors and friends. Excluding anyone now would be more than foolish."

That gave us a reason to stand up and head for the way out, which I joined Jovvi in doing without delay. Those people would probably sit there debating what to do until the army was at their door, and I had no patience for staying there and watching it happen. I wanted *everything* over and done with, including going back to Gan Garee and settling with those thieves Seated on the Fivefold Throne. Only then would I be free to go about living my own life, one which would be nowhere near a certain man who cared nothing about me.

"Excuse me, but I really need to speak to all of you," a voice said, and I looked up to see that man named Lugal. He'd apparently pulled himself together, and now stood in the middle of the aisle between the two sections of benches, blocking our way to the door. "I have a—message I've been asked to pass on."

"A message from whom?" Lorand stepped forward to ask, his expression still less than friendly. "Who could have known we'd be by here, and what could they possibly have to say to us?"

"It's . . . from my colleagues, and I don't think they *knew* you would be by here," the man answered, still distracted to a great extent. "They probably sent the same message to every member of the Guild in this area, hoping one of them would be able to deliver it. As for how they knew you would be coming this way, they're close to Gan Garee and probably get the gossip from there on a regular basis. The message is that they'd like to speak to all of you before you return to Gan Garee. There's a small town called Colling Green about two days away from the city, and they'd like you to stop there first for a meeting."

"To what purpose?" Vallant asked, drawing the man's attention. "Unless they intend to come into this . . . difficulty on our side, they can't possibly have anythin' to say that we need to hear. So why did they think we would bother?"

"You expect *me* to know?" Lugal asked with more bitterness than exasperation. "I'm the one who didn't even know what I was sending the young men and women from this district to—and that's something *I* mean to discuss with my people as soon as possible. I can't believe that *they* didn't know, but they never said a word to the rest of us. . . . Lorand, what about Hat? I was fairly certain that he'd never reach High strength, but I was under orders to send him for testing anyway. Did he. . . ."

"Did he die during that test?" Lorand finished when Lugal's words simply trailed off. "No, Master Lugal, I know for a fact that he didn't. They rescued him and tried to send him home, but the damned fool refused to go. He couldn't give up the dream of being a High, so he got drunk and then got in trouble. The last I saw of him he had just lost the challenge to the Seated High in Earth magic, and the attendants were carrying him out while he shouted and struggled. He must have been sent to a different part of the army than the one we rescued, because there was no sign of him among the others. I meant to speak to his father, but the man isn't here. Will you speak to him for me?''

''It won't be easy, but there's no denying I owe at least that to all of you,'' Lugal muttered, his face now drawn and pale. ''And if you'll excuse me now, I have to see about getting my family ready to leave. Some of those hard-heads will decide to stay right where they are no matter *what* 'fairytales' strangers come up with, but I'm not that stupid. I know the truth when I hear it, so I intend to be on my way out of here as soon as I speak to Hat's father. I wish you good luck in whatever it is you're trying to do.''

The man nodded distractedly to the rest of us, and then he was hurrying out of the hall. If he had any feelings for the rest of the people in the area he would spread the word about leaving, but then I realized that that might just be a matter of wasted breath. The Guild man wasn't really *one* of them, so his opinion might be discounted right along with our warning.

''Let's rejoin the others,'' Vallant Ro said once the man was gone. ''We'll have to discuss this meetin' in Collin' Green and whether or not we ought to go. Somehow the invitation doesn't sound quite right to me.''

''I was thinking the same,'' Rion agreed in a soft voice. ''The man was quite correct in believing that his superiors *had* to know what was being done to and with the applicants he sent for testing, and yet they made no effort to stop sending people. That tells me they're in league with the nobility, so the meeting must certainly be a trap.''

''Maybe we can turn the trap around and make it work for *us*,'' Lorand suggested as we all began to move forward again. ''The five thieves will certainly be behind it, and maybe those who are supervising the trap will know about other traps. It can't hurt to ask them.''

We all agreed that it certainly would not be hurting *us*, and as soon as we got outside I made sure to move as far away from Vallant Ro as possible. Being near him was hurting on a different level, with an intensity not even my flames could produce. He and I would never have a relationship now, not even if we both survived what was ahead of us. Deep inside, part of me cried over that truth, but the rest of me was just too weary to care any more.

Jovvi peeked out from behind the mental barrier she'd been forced to erect, but that quick peek told her that Tamma was still radiating that horrible maelstrom of grief and despair and pain. That meant Jovvi had to keep the barrier firm between them, which happily meant only on the side where Tamma walked just a few steps away. The rest of Jovvi's mind and talent were free to roam all around, but that wasn't the blessed freedom it should have been. There were even more people in the square now, and every one of them was upset to one degree or another.

Not that Jovvi could blame them. She and the others were stared at as they walked past, most of the minds behind the stares hungry to know what had been said in the meeting hall. Rumors were flying all around, making people nervous and frightened, and if the men in the hall didn't call everyone in for a general announcement fairly soon, they would find an angry mob coming after them. The same angry mob that might be coming after *their* group soon, in a mindless effort to deny what they'd been told. Destroy the tellers, and the story could be branded as lies and ignored and forgotten about, many people believed.

Jovvi sighed as she walked, hoping hard that they would not be forced to hurt any of these people. Terror and anger always brought out the mob mentality, which really was a lack of mentality. Denying a problem is so much easier than coping with it, and the group mind did wonders with increasing the individual's ability to ignore.—

"Jovvi, may I speak to you for a moment?" Rion said in a murmur, abruptly walking right next to her. "I'm sure you're aware of all our internal problems, but Naran asked me to make special mention of this one. She seems to fear that if something isn't done to smooth things over between

Vallant and Alsin Meerk, there will be a terrible confrontation between them. Have you given the matter any thought?''

"Of course," Jovvi responded just as softly, trying to pinpoint something odd in what Rion had said. "I've given it a lot of thought, for all the good it did. The only thing I can promise is that if the confrontation comes at the wrong time, I can put Alsin under control to stop it. But beyond that? I doubt if there's much any of us can do. But if Naran is all that worried, why didn't she speak to me herself?''

"Apparently the poor little thing is too shy," Rion replied with a wry smile. "She knows we all consider her one of us, but she apparently has trouble forcing herself to make suggestions unless the situation is critical. Possibly we should tell that to the others, so that we can all encourage her to get over the shyness. But to return to our previous topic, can't we speak to Vallant and Alsin? The antagonism between them would be more properly directed toward our actual enemies.''

"We can try, but I doubt it will do much good," Jovvi said with something of a shrug. "Vallant is being torn in a number of different directions for reasons he hasn't discussed with any of us, and Alsin is feeling more and more like an outsider among us living on our charity. They're both strong men who hate the feeling of helplessness, but there isn't anything they can do about their respective positions. That's why they've turned their aggressions outward, in an effort to let them find release. Something might happen to redirect those aggressions, but we really can't count on it.''

"A pity," Rion said with a sigh. "Vallant is our brother and Alsin is a decent man, and it disturbs me to see them at odds. Have you spoken to Tamrissa about the matter? Naran tells me that she's at the center of one of their disagreements.''

"Frankly, I don't dare mention the thing to her," Jovvi said, beyond sighing. "She's more than just a little upset, and occasionally swings to the very edge of red, unreasoning rage. She's grown so strong that it's almost frightening, but it's also instructive. I believe that her added strength comes from being in constant touch with the power, so I've started to do the same thing. If I begin to strengthen in the same way, you men might consider following our example."

"I believe I'll begin to follow it right now," Rion said with a frown of thought. "After your mention of the matter, I seem to recall that during our last Blending I noticed Tamrissa's increased strength. Once we were no longer melded I forgot the observation, but there's no doubt about my having made it. I feel we should all do the same, so I'll pass on the suggestion to Lorand and Vallant."

"Just don't let any of the townspeople hear you make it," Jovvi cautioned. "When word spreads about what we are they'll be frightened enough, and it would be foolish to add to that. I hope we're ready to leave before anything unpleasant happens."

Rion added disturbed agreement with that sentiment, and then he moved toward Lorand. They were almost back to the large stables where some of the horses and the rest of their people were, so Rion would only have a moment or two in which to speak to Lorand. And then Jovvi saw that he might have even less time than that. Pagin Holter and his Blendingmates had stepped outside, apparently having watched for their approach. They'd made up their minds about something, and Jovvi hoped it wasn't something that would bring even more trouble. . . .

"How did it go?" Arinna asked, standing slightly to the front of her groupmates. She was their Fire magic member, and Pagin tended to push her forward to do their talking. "Are they ready to believe us?"

"They're ready to *talk* about believin' us," Vallant replied with barely covered disgust. "Jovvi threw it all into their laps and got us out of there, otherwise we would probably still be standin' there tellin' them to wake up."

"That's just about what we thought would happen," Arinna said with a nod of sadness. "Too many people are worried about how they look to others, and the idea of looking foolish is something to avoid at all costs. If you believe a lie you end up looking foolish, so they're not quick to believe anything a stranger has to say. But while you were gone *we* did some deciding, and we thought we'd tell you about it before we started to do it. We've decided to use our Blending to try contacting the Astindan army."

"For what reason?" Lorand asked, as bewildered as the rest of their group. "You might stop or destroy a lot of them before you run out of strength, but that will just make them even angrier. Or did you have something else in mind?"

"Definitely something else," Arinna said with a wry smile. "It isn't the Astindan forces we want to destroy, even if that were possible. We were curious about why our army has been unable to stand up to them, so we sent our Blending entity to take a quick look. It's a good thing we were on the very edge of our reach, because we discovered that their army consists of more Blending entities than the two our own group has."

Jovvi joined everyone else in exclaiming in surprise, but that certainly answered a question that had been bothering her.

"Now I understand why it took so long for the Astindans to put together an effective resistance," she said. "If our army was careful, it must have been quite a while before anyone at all knew that their country was being invaded. And then there was the problem of all those small, independent areas actually forcing themselves to work with people they used to consider neighbors and therefore enemies. Then they had to decide on something to do, find people strong enough to be effective in a Blending, and then form and train those Blendings. But now that they finally have it going, they're not likely to want to stop."

"We understand that, but we feel we have to *try* to talk to them," Arinna agreed. "There are a lot of innocent people between here and Gan Garee, and if something isn't done about that army all those innocent people will die. Since we can't live with that idea, we've decided to stay behind and see what we can do to keep it from happening. Five of the link groups have agreed to stay with us, but only if you really think you can get along without them. We don't want to do anything to mess up *your* efforts when you reach Gan Garee."

"That's only twenty-five people plus your five," Vallant pointed out. "If it comes down to it, an extra thirty people won't make that much of a difference in the fightin'. For my part, all I can do is wish the bunch of you as much luck as I hope *we* have.''

Jovvi joined the others in adding their agreement with what Vallant had said, which took a good deal of the tension from Pagin's group. They must have been afraid of what would be said to them, because they'd made up their minds to go on with their plans no matter what. And it really was a good idea, at least to try. If that army could be stopped. . . .

Jovvi sighed to herself as they all began to enter the stables together. Stopping that army was only part of the overall problem, other parts of which weren't quite as far ahead as Gan Garee. Alsin Meerk's simmering anger was far too clear, and the intensity of it said that Alsin was not about to wait very long before he decided to do something about it. . . .

Four

Kambil Arstin found it hard to contain his excitement as he walked into a sitting room in his wing of the palace, the place he'd sent word for the others to meet him. He couldn't wait to tell them what he'd discovered, but seeing only Homin and Selendi brought him to something of a halt.

''Where's Bron?'' Kambil asked as the two stopped their tiresome kissing and touching to give him their attention. ''He should have arrived when you did.''

''I haven't seen him since yesterday,'' Selendi replied with a shrug of dismissal which was both physical and mental. "He was complaining about something or other again, so I paid no attention. He's getting as bad as Delin used to be."

"Unfortunately, I have to agree," Homin said with a shake of his head. "Nothing seems to suit him any longer, and he even suggested that his servants are probably making him miserable on purpose. It might be a good idea for you to talk to him, Kambil, but since Selendi mentioned Delin, I might as well do the same. Isn't he also invited to the meeting?"

"No, Delin's presence isn't called for," Kambil replied in distraction. He hadn't taken conscious note of Bron's behavioral lapses, but that wasn't to say he hadn't noticed them. He'd simply been too busy with his research to bring Bron back into line, but now that the research was mostly finished. . . . "But you're right about the need for me to talk to Bron. Once he understands that acting like Delin will cause him to be confined to a single room in his wing like Delin, he ought to straighten out. We'll wait another minute or two for him, and if he doesn't show up he'll miss out on hearing the great news."

Homin and Selendi made sounds of interest and curiosity, but neither went so far as to ask questions or demand details. Kambil had said that they would wait, and his orders still had first priority in their minds. So he was able to go to the tea service and fill a cup in peace, and just as he turned away from the service Bron stalked into the room.

"I'm late and it's all *their* fault," he growled, heading for the tea service himself. "I wasn't given your message until a couple of minutes ago, which made it necessary for me to come close to running to get here even this soon. As soon as I get back, I'm going to have those useless peasants whipped to within an inch of their lives."

"So it was all *their* fault," Kambil murmured from where he stood, studying Bron through half-closed eyes. On the couch behind him, Selendi and Homin said nothing. That was because he'd taken over their minds and sent them into a . . . waking sleep of sorts. What was about to happen with Bron was nothing he wanted them to see.

"That's right, *their* fault," Bron agreed aggressively,

turning with his teacup to face Kambil. "You're not about to call me a liar, are you?"

Kambil was annoyed with himself for letting Bron get so far out of hand that the man was ready to challenge him for leadership of the group. That should never have happened, and wouldn't have happened if not for those miserable peasants. . . . Well, their turn would come, but right now it was Bron's.

"I'm doing more than calling you a liar," Kambil said mildly while Bron froze where he stood, held tightly in Kambil's mental grip. "I'm saying that you probably gave your servants strict orders not to disturb you while you enjoyed yourself with whichever female you're currently bedding, and they obeyed you. When you finally made yourself available you learned about my summons, and were at least cautious enough not to admit that you deliberately ignored it—by not making word from me the sole exception to being disturbed. Am I right?"

"Of course you are," Bron agreed without hesitation. "I've been more and more annoyed about having to run every time you whistle, so I decided to put an end to it. After all, we *are* supposed to be equals in this group."

"The key phrase there is 'supposed to be,'" Kambil pointed out after sipping at his tea. "To the rest of the world we're completely equal, but in private, with just the four of us, the truth has to be faced. I have the final say among us, no, more, the only say. The rest of you are here to obey my orders and do your parts in the Blending; beyond that you will not under any circumstances make any other effort. Do you understand me?"

"Yesss," Bron said, dragging the word out as his mind was taken deeper and deeper by Kambil's. Down there in the depths was where full control was to be found, and Bron had wandered up and away from it while Kambil was otherwise occupied. Now that he was back to awareness of the people who were supposed to be—no, who *were*—under his control, he would take the time to make sure that this didn't happen again.

Layers of mental bindings held Bron's will tight once more by the time Kambil was through with him. At one point there had been a slight bit of difficulty, but that was only because Grami wasn't there to help. Kambil had had her help in the beginning, when he'd first put his three groupmates under his control, but right now there was no time to send for her. His grandmother was much more practiced at these things, but she'd assured him that one day he would be just as good. That made Kambil proud, not to mention delightedly relieved. She'd hardly be around to help him forever, after all. . . .

"All right, now we can have our meeting," Kambil announced jovially once he'd roused everyone. "But before we begin, I think Bron owes us all an apology. What do *you* think, Bron?"

"Yes, you're right of course," Bron replied ruefully as he took his cup of tea to a chair. "I've been behaving abominably, and I really do apologize. You've all been more than patient with me, and I'll find some way to show my thanks."

"We'll look forward to that," Kambil said as he took his own chair, no longer able to hold back the good news. "But right now I have something to tell all of you. Just by chance I went browsing in my wing's library, and you'll never guess what I found. It's a journal, kept by one of my predecessors in Spirit magic from almost two hundred years ago."

"That sounds interesting," Homin said while the others made polite noises, he being the only one of the three who actually felt a bit of honest enthusiasm. "If the handwriting is still legible, it must make fascinating reading."

"There's a bit more to it than that," Kambil responded, unsurprised that he had to explain things to them. "It details the workings of the man's Blending, and even provides specifics about the exercises they used. There are pages and pages of things no one has known about for more than a century, including an explanation of how those five peasants overcame two hundred guardsmen. The best news is that we can do the same, not to mention add small extras to the various traps we have set up all around and in the city. If they're foolish enough to come here, they probably won't survive long enough to even consider challenging us."

"That's marvelous news," Selendi said with a relieved

laugh while the men sat forward with immediate, sharp attention. "Especially the part about our not being challenged by those awful people. And everything we decided to do is being taken care of?"

"Yes, and that's another reason for this meeting," Kambil agreed. "We all need to know what's happening, so that we can all keep a sharp eye on those who are supposed to be in charge of our safety. If they fail, it won't be *their* necks the knife comes down on."

"Oh, yes it will," Bron disagreed, but dryly and with due respect. "Maybe not a knife, but it will definitely be their necks just before ours if they fail. So what sort of things will we be watching?"

"Part of it is that new system of admission we've put in," Kambil said, listing things in his own mind as he sipped at his tea. "No one gets into the palace without an appointment in advance or a pass signed by one of us, and even so their names are written down in the visitors' register. If someone makes even the smallest effort to *bluff* their way in, they're to be arrested at once and brought straight to us."

"That ought to do nicely in keeping one or more of *those* five from sneaking in here," Homin said with relieved satisfaction. "It should also impress our 'Advisors' and other noble visitors, showing them who's in charge. What's been happening with that business of the hostages Lord Rimen Howser has supposedly been putting together? He has the Earth magic peasant to use against the Earth magic user among that five, but what about any others?"

"Apparently, and to my surprise, I might add, he's doing rather well," Kambil said with amusement. "I'd overlooked the point that Lady Hallina is Mardimil's mother even while I was fully aware of it, but Lord Rimen seems to overlook nothing. Lady Hallina is the second name on his list, so he was delighted to hear that she's been forbidden to leave the city. The third name is that of a merchant Storn Torgar and his wife, who are the parents of our little Fire magic user, Tamrissa Domon. The fourth is a pretty little thing named Mirra Agran, who has been announcing far and wide that she and the Water magic user, Vallant Ro, are due to be married. The only one Rimen doesn't yet have a hostage against is the Spirit magic user, and he considers that only a matter of time. He has guardsmen watching everyone on the list, and if any of them try to leave the city they'll be arrested and brought here.''

"That's really good work," Bron said with a thoughtful nod. "I never really liked Rimen, but I can't deny that he's been doing a job for us. We may never need those hostages, but it's good to know that they're there if we do. What about the latest reports from the west? Is there any good news in among the bad?''

"No, and our so-called military personnel are walking around looking gray and old," Kambil said with a head-shake, now more than slightly disturbed. "Someone finally sent them a message with the true situation spelled out in it, and I had to give them my solemn word that all of them would die painfully if *anyone* else found out. It seems that there's very little left of our army in the west, as the Astindans have put together a force that ours can't even match, much less stop. The invincible Astindans are now marching toward the border, and are expected to begin certain devastations to match the ones committed in *their* country by *our* army.''

"And, of course, it's out of the question to send any warnings to the peasants in the area," Selendi said, looking thoughtful. "We've been telling everyone that the trouble in the west is just something instigated by those escaped criminals in an effort to lure us to a place where we can be waylaid and murdered. So what will we do when word of the true situation starts to come in, carried by refugees fleeing the depredations? We won't be able to laugh and say they're imagining it all.''

"We'll be shocked, of course, and greatly troubled," Homin replied with a faint smile for Kambil. "I also think we ought to have a number of people executed, for giving us misleading information. After that we'll have to send people to study the situation and bring back *accurate* intelligence, without which we can't possibly make any plans. By that time, hopefully, we'll be able to pull the other army from Gracely to meet the Astindans, or maybe by then the Astindans will have gotten all the revenge they want. In either event, any victories will be strictly ours, and any defeats will be the result of incompetent underlings or betrayal by conscienceless enemies.''

"Exactly," Kambil agreed, delighted that Homin seemed to have a talent for subterfuge and circuitous excuses. "We'll be busy directing things from here in Gan Garee, so we won't be able to leave the city to take a personal hand in the problem. And we shouldn't even have stray Highs or strong Middles straggling in to worry about. The Astindans aren't accepting surrender from anyone, most especially not former members of our army. All in all, the only ones who should lose out in this matter are the peasants who are destroyed, and those of our peers who own the land the Astindans will devastate. Does anyone of any consequence own land out there in the west?''

"If they do, it will hardly be their major possession," Bron pointed out, gesturing with his teacup. "And if it is, then they'll be ruined. Is that something we really need to worry about?''

"Since it doesn't involve us, of course not," Kambil said with a small laugh. "Isn't it marvelous that we don't have to worry about the support of fools? There are certain to be complaints by the dozen, but we're the Seated Five. If the complainants leave even angrier than they were when they came, what can they do about it? The only people who knew we had help in winning the throne are no longer among the living.''

"Which is one small thing to thank Delin for," Bron said, still speaking wryly. "There's no way of knowing how long it will be before the confusion over who handled what is straightened out, but at least no one can step forward to announce in ringing tones that we have to *do* something for them because they helped us get what we have.''

"But that means we also don't have those who will support us because it's in their best interests to do so," Kambil warned. "That support, in the form of letting us know what's going on among our peers and in the city, would have been invaluable help, and I've had to substitute a cadre of spies in its place. They should find out what we need to know, and I'll send for the rest of you when one or more of them comes to report.''

"Have you decided when we'll practice some of the

things you found in that journal?'' Selendi asked. ''If they give us more power over everyone, they'll be worth whatever effort we have to put into them.''

''We have nothing scheduled for tomorrow morning, so we'll start then,'' Kambil replied, shifting in his chair. ''Delin will have to be with us, of course, so you'd all better brace yourselves. His hatred and anger have grown quite a lot in the last few days, and most of the time I have to block him out. But I'm actually delighted to see that anger and hatred. If not for them, he'd probably go even more insane than he is. A pity I haven't been able to find a replacement for him as yet. Our former Advisors did too good a job ridding themselves of those of our class whom they feared. Since I refuse to settle for one of the peasants who might have been overlooked, I'll just have to keep searching.''

''You've been using Delin to measure the strength of those you've found, I know,'' Homin said. ''Is it possible Delin himself doesn't know why you're doing what you're doing?''

''I'm sure he's understood each of the three times I used him, but so what?'' Kambil asked as he readied himself to stand and get another cup of tea. ''At the end of each session I ordered him to forget about what went on, and also to forget any conclusions he might have come to. Delin is now the least of our worries, and we still have other things to discuss. I've arranged some traps just outside of the city that the rest of you don't yet know about, so I'll tell you about them as soon as I get more tea. If any of the rest of you need refills, please get them now.''

All three of them got to their feet as he did, so Kambil led the way to the tea service. He also decided that at the next meeting he would bring along one of his controlled servants, so that there would be no need for them to serve themselves while they talked. He and the others were too important for such menial tasks, and it was time that everyone understood that. It was also time for another public audience, and that should be held as soon as possible. After that, news from the west might start coming in, and if it came at an inconvenient time they would have to be unavailable.

A pity, Kambil thought as he stepped aside to let his followers get tea of their own. He did so love public audiences, with everyone bowing and scraping to show who their superiors were. He'd have to make a short list of invitees to the next audience, so that the proper people were seen bowing and scraping. Those he meant to invite would never live down the humiliation of having to show public deference to people they'd once disdained, which would make the whole thing even more marvelous. . . .

FIVE

Delin Moord ran his hands over the arms of the chair he sat in, luxuriating in the silken feel of the fabric. His body also reveled in being held firmly but comfortably, his back no longer aching and his leg muscles no longer stiff from an incorrect height in the chair legs. He allowed himself to sit in that chair only five minutes each day, but he savored those five minutes as much as he'd savored the one decent meal he'd had since Kambil had enslaved him. And he was fairly certain that no one suspected he'd had that one decent meal. . . .

His five minutes being up, Delin rose from the chair and returned to the hard wooden one which had been moved into that tiny sitting room in his wing of the palace. His groupmates still believed that that chair was the only one he could use, just as he was forbidden decent food and a comfortable place to sleep, not to mention use of any other room in the wing. They thought they were punishing him for what they chose to call his insanity, but it wasn't he who was insane—or duped. Kambil was behind it all, Kambil and his Spirit magic having taken over the minds of their other groupmates, making them more slavelike than he'd been able to do with Delin.

"He wasn't able to break my will, so he called me insane and enslaved me with drugs," Delin muttered, letting his hatred of that wooden chair and his condition in general take over his outer thoughts again. "He still believes I'm helpless and can therefore be dismissed from consideration, but he forgets that I've had experience with this sort of thing before."

A small smile curved Delin's lips, the only outward sign of how pleased he was. Did Kambil know that Delin's father had also had Spirit magic? The elder Moord hadn't been nearly as strong as Kambil, but he'd had enough strength that Delin had had to learn how to think out of sight of the man's talent at a very early age. That was why he'd developed that . . . separate inner self, the one which Kambil hadn't been able to penetrate to. It had let him use that foolish female servant to escape, without anyone else knowing that he was free.

Delin's smile widened very briefly at the memory of that female servant. After she'd freed him she'd gone and gotten him that one decent meal he'd allowed himself, and then she'd stood there beaming as she watched him swallow it down almost in a single gulp. When he'd finished every last crumb he'd sent her back with the tray, asking her to tell the cook and the other servants that Delin had refused the meal so she'd eaten it herself to keep it from going to waste. He'd followed carefully behind her, and once she'd made that announcement he'd caused her to have a fatal heart attack. The other servants had fluttered and clustered about, not knowing what to do, not knowing there was *nothing* for them to do. Delin's secret had had to be preserved, and the cost of a single peasant life was a small one to pay for that preservation.

That had been just a few short days ago, but Delin had filled the following time with quite a bit of work. He'd been able to leave the palace only when his groupmates were asleep, but at least he'd been able to use the secret exits he'd learned about that Kambil apparently hadn't yet found.

The man really was an incompetent fool, and all the intrigues he imagined himself in the middle of were nothing but childish dabblings. Delin had been finding out about those things, and he wasn't in the least happy with Kambil's arrangements.

"But I'm not doing anything to change them," he muttered aloud again, still pleased with the actionless course of action. "I intend to be there when all his marvelous plans come crashing down on his head, and it turns out that there's no one to blame but himself. The scene will be pure delight, and he won't even have someone to go to for comfort and support."

That thought made Delin laugh soundlessly, so delightfully delicious was it. Kambil had made the mistake of boasting about the help he'd gotten from his grandmother, the marvelous "Grami" he felt so close to. Well, dear Grami's days were numbered, and in fact were down to a mere few hours. When Delin left the palace tonight, his first task would be settling her hash in the most permanent and painful way. But it would look perfectly natural, and therefore be considered an unfortunate but ordinary death.

"But the same won't happen to Kambil's enemies, no indeed," Delin murmured, watching his hands as he fit the tips of his fingers together in various patterns and poses. Kambil's enemies would not only live but thrive, especially since Delin was prepared to heal them wherever necessary. And Delin knew just who those enemies were, thanks to the scribes who wrote down everything the Five did, even including things said at the most private meetings. That was another thing Kambil didn't know about, the detailed history that had been kept for each and every Seated Five for the last hundred years or more.

Again Delin laughed, finding it impossible to argue the contention that some people just should not drink. It had been at a party right here in the palace some years ago that Delin had learned about the scribes, after starting a conversation with an old man who had been well on the way to being completely in his cups. The old man had sat alone, ignored by the glittering guests at the party, and Delin had discovered that the man was a minor noble and secretary to one of the most important Advisors on the board. He'd

wheedled an invitation to the party, expecting to be treated
as an equal by those who also attended, and had been most
upset that that long-desired acceptance hadn't come.

"It's 'cause they don' know how 'mportant I am," the
old man had mumbled, waving his wine glass at the partying crowd. "Took over th' whole thing all by m'self, I
did, an' made it even better'n it was. The fools don' know
who they're snubbin', an' me th' man who knows every
move th' Five make."

Delin, who had made it a habit to befriend all apparent
outcasts for whatever secrets they might have, had been
intrigued. He'd coaxed and flattered the man to explain
what he meant, and so had gotten the story about the
scribes. The walls of the palace were honeycombed with
service passageways, with no area or room without at least
one. From the time the first chosen Five had been Seated,
nothing the Five did was unknown to the ones who had put
them in their exalted place. Mute scribes were scattered
throughout the passageways in the places the Five frequented the most, and any and all conversation and happenings were written down for the powerful men of the
empire to peruse later.

Which was why Delin had done away with the scribes
watching *him* before he'd dealt with his parents. That Lord
Advisor Ephaim Noll had probably been furious that he
lacked details when he confronted Kambil about the incident, and Kambil had shown his usual stupidity by assuming that Noll had had ordinary spies. No, the spies weren't
ordinary or out in plain sight, and Delin had caused the
new one listening beyond the walls of his tiny room to go
into a permanent paralysis after tearing up what he'd just
written down. That was right after Delin had been freed, of
course, and his skulking around had kept any other of them
from following him to the kitchens where he'd killed the
servant woman with a heart attack.

He'd had to kill only one more of the scribes, the one
he'd forced to bring him all the transcripts of what had been
going on since the new Five had taken over. Those transcripts had been piling up, since the only Advisors who
knew about them were now dead, and Delin had actually
done the scribes a favor by reading them. The scribes could

have gone on until the last one died of old age, piling up pages that no one knew about and therefore could not read. There was no one for the scribes to report to, but Delin had killed the last one anyway, to keep the man from *finding* someone to report to. . . .

So Delin knew exactly who Kambil's enemies were, and of course the fool had left them alive. The man seemed to think that power was for waving in the faces of people you disliked, and then you simply took your power and walked away from those people. It seemed that Delin alone knew that power enabled you to bring before you those who merited death, a fate you gave them after causing them the additional agony of telling them about it beforehand. That way they were *not* left able to store up resentment against you while they plotted your downfall.

Too many members of the nobility knew in their bones that any noble Blending on the Throne had been put there rather than having won to the place, and that despite *their* supposed win. That meant most of the nobility thought of the Five as servants of the empire and therefore of themselves, rather than the rulers of it and them the way Kambil believed. The fool had no idea how many plots were being hatched against him by those he'd exercised *his* kind of power against, and Delin wouldn't have told him even if he'd asked. It would be much more amusing to watch to see which of those plots actually managed to succeed.

But he, of course, would keep himself out of the path of them. If the others of his groupmates were taken down along with Kambil, well, that would just be too bad. They'd all had a hand in adding to his torture, and even though they couldn't really be considered responsible, they'd still had that hand in. If they ended up savaged, Delin would shed no tears of remorse.

And now, he thought as he stretched just a little, *it's time for my evening gruel.* After that he would sit thinking for a while, and then he would go to bed as usual. The new scribe watching him would also settle down for the night, but would stay awake even though nothing would be expected to happen. Delin would put the man to sleep when he was ready to get up again, and would waken him again after he'd finished his night's work.

And he'd have to do the same thing to the scribes watching his groupmates, assuming he decided to present the four with a small gift. If he did, a time would come for Delin to mention those gifts openly, but for now it would be enough that he gave them—if he did. And if he did then one day the four would learn about the gifts, and then it would be Delin's turn to laugh. . . .

Lady Eltrina Razas walked into the small suite in the very exclusive inn she had frequented many times, glancing around to see how the sitting room was furnished. Each of the inn's suites were furnished differently, of course, but the one she usually occupied was unfortunately already taken. This one was a bit gaudier than she liked, but for her purposes it would do nicely.

"All right, I'll just have to put up with it," she said with faint annoyance to the hovering landlord who had followed her to the door of the sitting room, making no effort to turn and look at the man. "Have that meal sent to me without delay, and don't forget that I'm not here tonight if anyone comes looking for me. I've had a ghastly few days, and I need some peace and quiet with nothing in the way of disturbance."

"Of course, Lady Eltrina, you may count on me as usual," the landlord said smoothly, probably with a bow. "I'll have the food brought to you as soon as it's prepared, and in the meanwhile the tea in the service is fresh and hot. Thank you for gracing us again with your presence."

Eltrina made some vague sound that apparently satisfied the man, as he quietly closed the door as he left. That was a great relief, as Eltrina was very tired of either standing in shadow or keeping her face turned away from people. There was only a single bruise on her face, but it wasn't something one cared to advertise the presence of.

A deep sigh accompanied Eltrina's careful lowering of herself into a chair, something she had to do even before she poured herself a cup of tea. She was still in pain, of course, thanks to her husband Grall and his beatings, not to mention the way he'd given her to every male servant in the house. Most of those peasants had been too nervous to do more than enter her before they lost control, but even so the time hadn't been pleasant. But that very unpleasantness had been the key to her freedom, as one of those servants had been the kitchen boy who felt himself madly in love with her. She'd encouraged the boy's feelings out of amusement, never dreaming at the time how important that childish love would turn out to be.

"Torlin, please help me!" she'd whispered when the boy had finally been allowed his turn, having no trouble making tears flow from her eyes. "He means to keep me like this until I die, which won't be long in coming if I cannot regain my freedom. Give me your love one final time, to say goodbye if helping me escape is beyond you. . . ."

"No, m' lady, don't say thet!" the boy had begged, tears in his own eyes. "I'll help ya, 'r die in the tryin'!"

And so Torlin *had* helped her, sneaking back to untie her in midafternoon, not long after Grall had left the house. She'd had trouble moving around, naturally, but hadn't let the pain stop her from doing what was necessary. She'd crept up to her own apartment to dress, and after that had paid Grall's apartment a visit. The man was a creature of habit, and so Eltrina knew that the first thing he would do when he returned would be to pour himself a drink from the excellent wine he kept only for himself in his sitting room. None of the servants was allowed to touch those bottles of wine, so he would serve himself. In the first glass coming to hand, which was also his habit. . . .

"Which means that once he closes his eyes tonight, he'll never open them again," Eltrina murmured, delighting in the thought of that. She'd bought the poison she'd used quite some time ago, intending to employ it once she'd gained a high enough career position, but that time had never come. But the time to use the poison *had* come, and Eltrina had smeared it around the rim of the first glass of the small diamond arrangement of glasses Grall kept near the bottles of wine. He would drink from the glass and swallow the poison all unknowingly, and once he retired and fell asleep, the poison would slow his bodily processes to the point of death and then beyond. And then the poison would evaporate or something, she'd been assured, making it impossible for anyone to know it had ever been present. It was a tool of the great and powerful which she'd managed to wheedle out of an admirer, a tool which most people knew nothing about.

"And tonight I'll feel ill enough to have a pair of serving girls watch me carefully throughout the night," Eltrina murmured as she forced herself erect so that she might get herself the tea she really needed. "It will cost me more than a little silver to have them here to prove I never leave the room, but money is no problem at the moment. Beginning tomorrow, it will never be a problem again."

That would have made her laugh if laughing hadn't been so painful, but at least Eltrina could smile. She really did know the man she'd been married to, and Grall never advertised his problems to anyone who didn't absolutely need to know. For that reason she'd taken a chance and gone to their bank, and had found that withdrawing money had been as easy as ever. The bankers knew nothing about the trouble between her and Grall, which meant he also hadn't gotten around to divorcing her. When he was found dead tomorrow morning and no one was able to prove a charge of murder against her, she would inherit everything that had been his.

"And once his estate is mine, I'll spend every copper of it in order to get even with those peasants—and with the Five," Eltrina said, not shouting but no longer whispering. "What I went through was *their* fault, and I'm *going* to pay them all back. But those peasants aren't available right now, so I'll just have to start with the Five. *Someone* will know how to reach them, someone I can bribe to make sure I have my revenge. And it might even be a good idea to spread the word about how legitimate their Seating is . . . spreading it among the peasants, that is. I wonder what they'll do if the entire city rises against them. . . ."

That time Eltrina did laugh, but the pain was more than worth it.

Six

"What do you mean, you won't be coming back again until you have further word from your men?" Lady Hallina Mardimil snapped to the man Ravence, her patience completely gone. "I'm paying you gold to report to me, so you'll report when *I* tell you to."

"Making the trip to this house just to say that I haven't heard anything more is a waste of my time," the annoying little peasant countered, a dismissiveness in his tone that Hallina was growing to recognize—and detest. "I told you two days ago that my men believed the people with your son are heading for a place called Widdertown, where it's assumed they'll stay for a while. Whether the while is short or long depends on what their plans are, but if there's an opportunity to reach your son, my men will take it. They won't report again until they make the attempt or miss their chance, and that's when I'll be back."

"You haven't yet said anything about the men I asked you to find and hire," Hallina pointed out, refusing to agree to his stance without an argument. "Since *that* matter is still pending, you have more to do than simply wait for a pigeon to deliver a message to you."

"I believe I've already told you that the sort of men you want aren't available through me," Ravence replied, actually having the nerve to sigh. "My business is the confidential settling of private, personal matters, not the hiring of thugs. Even if the thugs are supposed to be 'fearless and capable and adept at all forms of mayhem.' ''

"Are you daring to mock me?" Hallina demanded, feeling her face grow warm with embarrassment at the thought. "For someone whose agents are preparing to abduct my son for me, peasant, you have much too high an opinion of yourself!"

"My men aren't going to abduct your son, they're simply going to return him here," Ravence replied, not in the least disturbed. "If, after he speaks with you, he tries to leave again, they'll do nothing to stop him. I happen to feel that a parent has the right to have one final word with his or her child before that child severs all relations, and for that reason I'm here right now. Otherwise I really would have been too busy to accommodate you."

"I see," Hallina responded, delighted that she hadn't told this detestable peasant her true plans. Once Clarion was in her hands again and back under control of that drug, she'd make certain that he never found it possible to leave a second time . . . unless it became necessary to sacrifice him to save herself. "Well, in that case I won't detain you. Your . . . very important business matters shouldn't be kept waiting."

"No, they shouldn't," he agreed as he rose, straightening the vest which covered part of his paunch. "As soon as I have any word, I'll contact you again."

Hallina sat in her chair and watched as the man bowed briefly and then left, now more than eager to see him go. She'd been counting on the man to find the . . . thugs, as he called them, for her, and he'd failed her. But she refused to give up the rest of her plans, the ones that would begin to take just vengeance on those horrible, ill-mannered children on the throne. She would simply have to find suitable tools elsewhere.

Thought of what the new Five had put her through this last time she spoke with them sent Hallina to her feet and pacing. She'd gone to the palace to pass on the information which Ravence had brought her two days ago, but rather than being admitted at once she'd been made to wait like a commoner. Then, when she'd finally been permitted into the august presences, her information had been thrown back in her face.

"We already know that your son and his friends are in

the west, Lady Hallina," that Kambil Arstin had said dismissively, giving her only a fraction of his attention. "You were supposed to provide information we *don't* have."

"The name of the place they'll soon be is Widdertown," Hallina had replied stiffly, biding her time while pretending not to be insulted. "Unless I'm mistaken, that *is* information you don't already have."

"Yes, you're right, we *weren't* told about that town," the creature had replied, now looking straight at her. "The information may or may not do us any good, but you still have our thanks for providing it. And, if it should prove to be valuable, you'll have more than simple thanks. Now you may leave us."

Hallina had had no choice but to allow herself to be dismissed, something no one had ever dared to do to her before. She'd been determined even before that to teach those creatures a lesson, but after being treated like a peasant, the determination had become obsession. She wanted those five *hurt*, no matter what they were supposed to be capable of doing with their talent. . . .

"If only those peasants I used the last time hadn't dropped out of sight," Hallina muttered as she went to the teacup she'd abandoned when Ravence had arrived. She spilled the cold tea into the pot near the service meant for that purpose, then poured a fresh cup. "Their efforts were more than satisfactory, but my agent feels I may have paid them too much. They've apparently gone off to enjoy all that silver, and probably won't be available again until they've spent it all."

But the man had promised to find others to take their place, so Hallina only had to wait until he did. She'd tried *her* hand at it by speaking to Ravence, but the fool of a peasant hadn't even asked how much she was willing to pay. When peasants pretended to respectability, they were even more tiresome than usual. . . .

A knock came at the sitting room door, and when Hallina gave her permission to enter, one of the servants appeared.

"Your pardon, Lady Hallina, but a note has been left for you," the man said with a bow. "An urchin delivered it, and didn't even wait to be tipped."

"The child was probably too stupid to understand about

tipping," Hallina remarked, holding out her hand. "Give me the note."

The servant did so and then retired, closing the door again behind him. Hallina put her cup aside to unseal the note, and when she saw its contents she was grimly pleased.

"Lady Hallina," the note began. "That private matter we discussed has been partially arranged, all but the very last of it. The men are exactly what you're looking for and are prepared to guarantee results, but insist on a face to face meeting with my principal. I recommend going through with the meeting, as you're unlikely to find others as qualified as these three. If you agree, you're to meet them at The Glowflower Inn at ten tonight. Wear a cloak with a hood so that your face will be covered, as there may well be those at the Glowflower who can recognize you. Until we meet again, I remain, your servant, R."

Hallina was quite put out over the necessity for a meeting with the ruffians she had simply expected to pay, and almost decided against lowering herself to the point of meeting them where *they* demanded she go. Then the thought came that ruffians of the lowest class would hardly know about the Glowflower, which was an inn frequented by those of *her* class. So her agent had arranged the place for the meeting, guarding her standing as he usually did. Very well, then, she *would* go. In a cause as good as this one, a small bit of inconvenience was best ignored.

Hallina dined as usual that night, the service of her household being a bit better than usual after the small difficulty of the day before. One of the kitchen girls had given her a dirty plate, and when Hallina had attempted to discipline her over the matter by docking her pay, the slut had dared to suggest that it was Hallina herself who had dirtied the plate. The cheeky little animal had pointed to the warmed rolls, claiming that one was missing, and that meant Hallina had eaten it. More, the little tart had claimed that the crumbs on the plate came from Hallina's having set the roll there, not from her having been given a dirty plate.

Insubordination of that sort simply couldn't be tolerated, so Hallina had given the girl the choice she usually gave erring servants. The girl would be beaten for daring to talk back, of course, and then she would be dismissed. But, if the girl begged nicely enough, Hallina would order her to be beaten twice as hard and she would *not* be dismissed. The choice had been the little peasant's to make, but Hallina had known which way she would choose. Whenever possible, Hallina hired servants who had families which depended on them. That made them more than a little eager to keep their positions, which in turn produced higher quality service.

The girl hadn't wanted to beg, Hallina recalled with a smile as she helped herself to a buttered roll, and the slut had actually choked on the words while doing so. Hallina had made her repeat those words three times, an abject begging of her mistress for a beating twice as hard as the one she'd originally been meant to have, and then Hallina had granted her petition. Hafner had been brought from the stables to do the honors, and the simpleton had done his usual, thorough job. The cheeky little slut's screams had been quite enjoyable, and by the time Hafner had finished with her she was no longer in the least cheeky.

Hallina lost herself in pleasant thoughts of scenes like that while she finished her meal, and then she went to the library to sip sherry while her resident harpist played for a while. The music was quite relaxing, but rather than go to bed after listening to it, Hallina went to her apartment and let her maid dress her for going out. Annoyance over *having* to go out made Hallina short with all the servants, but she expected to be back rather quickly. She would tell those ruffians what she wanted of them, they would tell her their price, and then the negotiations would be concluded.

Her carriage driver had no trouble finding the inn, even though Hallina had only been to it once before. Quite a lot of her peers did frequent the place rather often, but most of them weren't really members of her circle of friends. They were the sort who flitted about the fringes of true people of quality, having no idea how to join them, half the time not even making the effort. But they did belong to families with standing and power, so they had to be dismissed with a smile rather than with a stiffly turned shoulder. It would never do to insult the wrong person. . . .

An inn servant helped Hallina from her carriage, making

no effort to see her face under the deliberately draped hood of her cloak. The carriage was an unmarked one, of course, a precaution Hallina would have taken no matter the circumstances. Those ruffians might have decided to learn who she was in order to demand gold from her for keeping silent, but she would quickly disabuse them of *that* notion. They would not know who she was, only that she was completely willing to hire others to kill them as easily as she hired *them* to see to her required chore. Once they understood that they were really at her mercy, the negotiations would go a good deal more smoothly.

Hallina walked through the door held open by the inn servant, then had to pause in midstride. She had no idea how to find the men she was to meet, as her agent's letter had provided no details. It was infuriating that the thought hadn't occurred to her sooner, as now she would certainly have to turn around and go home with nothing to show for the time she'd spent—

"Good evening, my lady, and please come this way," a girl's voice said from Hallina's right, startling her. Hallina turned to see an inn servant, but one who was dressed a bit better than the average. The female could well be a hostess for the gaming it was said the inn sometimes provided, and that annoyed Hallina even more.

"I haven't come for your foolish gaming," she snapped, making only a small effort to keep her voice down and her face in the shadow of her hood. "I'm here for another reason entirely, so stop—"

"Yes, my lady, I'm well aware of that," the snip had the nerve to interrupt, although she did do it rather gently. "You've come to meet with three gentlemen, and they're now awaiting your pleasure. If you'll be so good as to follow me, I'll take you to the rooms they've reserved."

"Just a moment," Hallina said, stopping the female in her tracks. "How do you know that I'm the one the three . . . gentlemen are waiting for?"

"I was instructed to look for a regal but unattended lady, one who would be wearing a cloak and hood," the girl responded with modestly downcast eyes. "Is it possible I've mistaken you for someone else?"

"Regal," Hallina murmured, a good deal more than

pleased. Then she raised her voice to add, "No, my girl, you aren't mistaken. Lead me to the place I'm awaited."

The girl curtsied slowly and properly, then began to walk again. Rather than going directly to the main stairs, the girl led Hallina through a long corridor of a hall before they reached a second staircase. This time they went up, and then turned right. The silence all around was unbroken by anything save the soft shushing of their shoes on the carpeting, dim lamplight creating small pockets of shadow along the way. The upper hall was wider than the lower one had been, and they walked past a number of closed doors before they reached the one at the very end.

"This knock will announce your presence, my lady," the girl said as she rapped a bit on the door. "Should you or the gentlemen require anything, the room's bellpull will summon a servant."

The girl performed a second, faster curtsey, then she began to return the way they'd come. Hallina was just as pleased to be rid of her, especially since the door was being opened. Now another knock would not be necessary, nor would the girl have the men's faces to forget. But as for that part of it, the men's faces, that is, Hallina needn't have worried. The man who opened the door widely enough for her to enter wore a leather and silk privacy mask. No wonder the girl had thought them gentlemen. . . .

The room Hallina entered was furnished rather better than the average inn sitting room, the decor obviously expensive but properly subdued. The other two men in it were just as large as the one who had opened the door, and they also wore distinctive privacy masks. The two rose when she entered, actually giving the impression that they were, indeed, gentlemen rather than ruffians, but Hallina wasn't fooled.

"I detest spending my time among rabble, so we will make this meeting extremely brief," she announced once the door was closed behind her, stopping in the middle of the room. "I will tell you the results I'm after, and you may name your price."

"All right, Lady, we're listening," one of the two who had risen from a couch agreed, and oddly enough there was quiet amusement in his voice. "Go ahead and tell us what you're looking for in the way of results."

"I want our precious Five taught a lesson in manners," Hallina obliged, ignoring the possible amusement. "It's true that they're strongly talented, but in all other ways they're just ordinary human beings. You will hire other men to assist you and you will enter the palace unobserved, and then you will separate and render each member of the Five quickly unconscious. At that point their talent will be useless, so you will proceed to beat them so badly that they will need to be carried to bed when they awaken. I don't want them slain, you understand, merely punished."

"That's rather odd," the same man responded, scratching at the bottom part of his cheek with one finger. "There seems to be a plague of people wanting other people punished rather than slain these days. Is this a new style which has recently come into popular favor?"

"You weren't told to be impertinent, you were told to quote a price!" Hallina replied sharply, disliking the peasant's entire attitude. "As soon as we've agreed on that our business will be finished and I'll be able to leave, so get on with it!"

"In the face of such gentle courtesy, how can I possibly refuse?" the man returned in what was almost a murmur, his amusement now clear and definite behind the insolence of his manner. "Our price for doing what you want done would be well beyond the ability of any mortal to pay, as what you ask is foolishly impossible and would mean our lives to attempt. Just because the Five are under constant guard doesn't mean they need that guard to protect them, something anyone but a fool would know."

"How dare you," Hallina growled, entirely out of patience with the useless animal. "Trying to hide your own lack of courage behind pointless insult will get you nothing, not even a common farewell. As we have nothing more to talk about, I'll simply take my leave."

Hallina's chin was as high as ever when she turned to march out of the room, but stopping short became necessary when she discovered the third man, the one who had opened the door, directly behind her. When the buffoon refused to step out of her way she tried herself to walk around him, but a single sideways shift brought him directly into her path again. That brought Hallina's anger out in full force, and she whirled around to glare at the one who had done all the speaking.

"Tell this idiot of yours to get out of my way!" she snapped, outrage almost making the words shrill. "We have nothing more to talk about, and your begging to be reimbursed for the cost of these rooms will simply waste more of my time! You spoke as you wished to *me*, your complete superior, and now you may pay for the disgusting liberty in silver as well as unemployment."

"Ah, but we aren't unemployed," the ruffian replied, a grin now showing on what could be seen of his face. "We've been well paid to do a certain job, and the cost of these rooms was included in that amount. That cost was rather more than is usual at an inn, but that's because these rooms are rather special. The walls and ceiling and floor were formed on a base of resin, and beneath the veneer of the door is further resin. There are also no windows letting into this suite, so that means. . . . Can you guess?"

"It means that no one *outside* these walls can know what goes on *inside* them," the second man said when Hallina merely stood there, staring at the first in confusion—and feeling the very beginnings of a faint apprehension. "We didn't *hear* the knock announcing your arrival, we watched through the provided slit and *saw* your approach. Surely you know what *that* means, now that you've been told the most important part?"

"What you're suggesting is impossible," Hallina informed the man in what should have been a ringing voice, but somehow became less than that. "You can't possibly be considering—"

That was when the third man put his hands to her arms from behind, and then Hallina had breath for nothing but screaming.

Embisson Ruhl sat at his dining room table after having breakfasted there for the first time in what seemed like months. He sipped his tea with full appreciation, and when his son Edmin was shown into the room, he extended a hand.

"Edmin, come join me," he invited jovially with a grin. "If you've already had breakfast, at least have a cup of tea."

"It would be my pleasure to join you for a cup of tea," Edmin said, the startled expression on his face widening Embisson's grin. "I must say, though, that I hadn't expected to find you in such sound physical condition. Were you visited by a new physician?"

"Nothing but a full night's sleep visited me," Embisson said, briefly showing his own surprise over that. "I drifted off last night still in pain, and awoke this morning feeling marvelous. I have no idea where this gift of health came from, but I have no intentions of investigating the matter. I've merely been voicing my thanks on a regular basis, in the hopes that the one responsible will eventually hear me."

"I hear you as well," Edmin said with a faint smile of his own after he sat and poured himself a cup of tea. "This unexpected but delightful outcome won't find itself being investigated by my efforts either. But now that you've given *me* good news, I feel I should reciprocate with good news of my own."

"Don't tell me that your plan involving a certain lady went off without trouble?" Embisson said, suddenly remembering that that plan had been scheduled for the night before. "On top of the way I feel, that would be news almost too wonderful to stand."

"Unfortunately, Father, you'll need to bear up under the load," Edmin said with a small, neat laugh. "That stupid woman got the note I had sent to her, and my paid informant in her house said she never made any attempt to verify the truth of the thing. She merely thought for a moment or two, and then, after dinner, dressed and went out."

"I'm not in the least surprised," Embisson said with full relish as he leaned back in his chair. "The woman was always under the impression that no one knew anything of what she did, as if finding out was impossible. You said your men had no trouble discovering the errand her agent was on, which was also to be expected. And how did she respond to the treatment given her?"

"With full-blown hysterics, I was told," Edmin said, now reaching for one of the sweet rolls still on the table.

"It seems that the lady, despite her advanced age and protestations of parenthood, was still a virgin. That condition no longer obtains in any manner at all, of course, not after my men all took their pleasure. Their report said she screamed throughout the . . . ordeal, and then she managed to scream as well during the beatings. When the three left they took her clothing along with them, all but that hooded cloak. It took more than two hours before she was able to drag herself out of the inn and back to her carriage, with the cloak wrapped tightly about her."

"May she have twice the pain she caused me, and for twice as long," Embisson said, no longer amused. "I detest backstabbers, which she would have been even if she'd been born a man. I must remember to visit her in a few days, when she'll be capable of understanding and appreciating the significance of my visit. And by the way, did she give your men any hints about what she meant to hire them to do?"

"Better than that," Edmin said with a rueful shake of his head. "She actually came straight out and told them what she wanted them for, and that before any agreements or guarantees were in place. It's a wonder that she's managed to survive *this* long . . . but what she wanted: she's searching for men to break into the palace and attack the Five physically. She apparently believes that anyone she hires will have no trouble doing that."

"Once again I'm not terribly surprised," Embisson said with his own headshake and an exasperated sigh. "The woman has no mind, only a rigid determination to have her own way in anything and everything. I knew her father briefly before the man died, and the fool doted on her every word and action. It's *his* fault that she's like this now, but at least now she won't be able to continue with her plans and thereby ruin ours. The last thing we want is for the Five to be warned and become overly alert."

"They won't be," Edmin assured him as soon as he swallowed a bite of the sweet roll. "I've already made arrangements for someone to have a little talk with her agent, and after that the man will send her reports about efforts he never makes. He won't be any trouble, not after it's pointed out to him that he can prove right now that he never sent that note to her. If he *tries* to make trouble for us, evidence proving the exact opposite will come into the woman's hands.''

"And that will be the end of *him*," Embisson agreed with heavy satisfaction. "Yes, that should do to hold him in place. And how are *our* plans coming?"

Embisson had almost been afraid to ask that question, so deep were his hopes for the project. Those freaks on the Throne had taken every one of his rightful titles, and the last time he'd seen them they were even threatening to take his wealth and estates. They needed to be repaid for that, the one who spoke for them most of all.

"Everything is proceeding nicely, just the way it's supposed to," Edmin replied, his smile now small but very sleek. "That new procedure of allowing no one into the palace unless they're sent for or have permission to enter was anticipated, and won't prove to be any problem at all. In fact I already have half my people *in* the palace, and the Five not one whit the wiser."

"Good," Embisson said, greatly relieved. "And now I can help you with the rest of it. We'll go for a stroll in the garden, where we can discuss the matter freely."

Edmin nodded his agreement and reached to his teacup as Embisson reached to his own, both of them eager to get on with finalizing their plans. When those plans came to fruition, he would also be able to be there to see the results. He hadn't counted on being able to do that without pain, but now. . . . Yes, they would have to see if their plans couldn't be hurried a little. . . .

SEVEN

"Rion, I'm so glad you're back," Jovvi heard as they entered the stables, turning in time to see Naran hurrying into Rion's arms. "The next time you go anywhere, I'm going with you. Sitting here waiting and worrying about you is making me a nervous wreck."

Rion laughed gently and began to murmur soothingly to her, but Jovvi's attention had been yanked forcibly to the scene. It was true—*very* true—that Naran was worried, but something about the girl's thoughts was ... different from everyone else's. Most people's worries were vague and formless even when they worried about something in particular, but the same wasn't true of Naran's reactions. *Her* worries were ... formed, Jovvi realized, possibly the best word of description she could find.

"Rion, Naran, excuse me for interrupting," Jovvi said as soon as she made up her mind to find out what was going on. "I've been meaning to talk to Naran for longer than five minutes for quite some time, and now that we seem to have the time I'd like to take advantage of it. Rion, you said you wanted to speak to Vallant and Lorand. Why don't you do that while Naran and I find a place to sit down in peace—while it lasts."

"Yes, my self-appointed errand *is* rather important, and I barely began to speak to Lorand when the other Blending

59

interrupted,'' Rion agreed with a nod and a smile. ''You ladies enjoy your talk while I finish my chore.''

He gave Naran a quick kiss and then walked off, leaving Jovvi and Naran to look at one another. Naran showed a smile of complete friendliness and openness, but Jovvi knew that the girl's mind wasn't feeling what her features showed.

''Please don't be so frightened,'' Jovvi said softly as she put an arm around Naran's shoulders to urge her toward the back of the stables. ''Whatever it is that's bothering you won't change the relationship you have with us, that I can promise you. We all know how you feel about Rion— and how he feels about you, as well—so nothing will be allowed to disrupt that relationship. But we really do have to talk, and we must be honest with one another.''

''Honest?'' Naran echoed, her emotions still ragged despite what Jovvi had said. ''But I've always tried to be honest . . .''

''Naran, please,'' Jovvi said with a sigh when the girl's words trailed off. ''Telling lies isn't the only way people keep from being fully honest. Not telling the *whole* truth is also a form of lying, which I'm sure you know. And we both know that you have a specific worry about Rion, rather than a simple, general unease. Will you tell me what that worry is?''

Naran's eyes had closed briefly, a reflection of the stab of inner pain she'd experienced, but behind the pain was a bit of pathetic eagerness. She *wanted* to talk about what threatened Rion, and only a vast amount of reluctance, fear, and apprehension had kept her from doing so already.

''I—can't give you all that many details, '' she whispered, glancing around to be certain that no one overheard them. ''I just know that people will come out of the shadows to do Rion harm. It can happen at any time, come from any direction. It—isn't simply a possibility, it's just short of an absolute certainty. Nothing is ever absolutely certain, not with everything that might happen to interfere, but some things come closer than others. . . .''

Once again her words trailed off, but through fear rather than because she had nothing further to say. Jovvi had the impression that Naran was afraid she'd already said too much, and in a manner of speaking she was right.

''Then Rion needs to be warned, and right away,'' Jovvi

said, reaching a hand out to grip the twisting fingers Naran held at her waist. "I meant to ask you more than that one question, but I've changed my mind. No one has the right to pry into someone else's privacy, not even when they're as close as we are. Or maybe especially when they're as close as we are. Just remember that if you decide you want someone to talk to, I'll always be willing."

"Do you mean that?" Naran asked, her vast startlement clear. "I've said things. . . . I *know* you have some idea. . . . I was certain you would . . . just continue on with it. . . ."

"A good friend told me that nothing is absolutely certain," Jovvi said with a warm, true smile. "What would be the good of my getting answers to my questions, if the process of getting them shattered you? When you decide that the time has come to give me those answers of your own volition, there won't be any shattering involved. Now we need to get back to Rion, so shall we?"

Naran's nod and trembling smile joined the way she clutched Jovvi's hand for a moment, showing her gratitude in the only way she was currently able to. Speechless with relief would have been a good description of Naran, and if what Jovvi suspected was true it was no wonder. The girl must have been living with her secret for a distressingly long time. . . .

A lot of their people were moving around the stables, so it took a moment before they located Rion. He'd apparently finished speaking to Lorand and was now standing with Vallant, and even as they began to move toward him Vallant nodded, clapped Rion on the shoulder, and then turned to give his attention to something else. Rion, looking and feeling satisfied, also turned away, but not, unfortunately, in their direction. He began to stroll toward the front of the stables, an area that was dim and mostly empty of people.

Jovvi was about to call out to Rion, but at that precise moment Naran gasped and wrapped a hand around Jovvi's arm with a grip that was actually painful. That . . . something different in Naran's mind had flared for an instant, and Jovvi had no trouble understanding what it meant. Rion was in danger *now*, and giving him help in another minute or two would probably be too late.

So Jovvi did something she'd never done before. The

others had no idea of her intentions, but she still reached out to initiate the Blending. She would have sworn it was necessary for everyone to be in agreement—and aware of what was happening—before it would be possible to Blend, but she discovered she was wrong. The Blending formed instantly, and then—

—and then it was the entity which had taken over, an entity which was fully aware of the danger to one of its flesh forms. Its senses located three human forms standing in the shadows of the first stall, which was used as a tack room rather than a place to put a horse. One of the three held something in its closed fist, and even as the entity watched, that one opened its hand and flung the contents at the flesh form named Rion.

But the flesh form was under the control of the entity at the moment, its talent merged into the talents of the others. The fine dust thrown at the Rion form flew out and moved quickly to coat him—but stopped a good two feet away from his form. It was as though the powder had been thrown against an invisible wall, which was just what had happened.

With the wall of solidified air surrounding and protecting the Rion form, the entity was able to get on with seeing to the intruding enemies. All three, wearing wet cloths tied about their faces, began to move out toward the Rion form, their actions more deliberate than hurried. At the same time a fourth enemy form, also with a wet cloth about its face, came from the stall opposite, and would have appeared behind the Rion form's back if the Rion form had turned to face the three. The four had surrounded the object of their attention, and clearly expected to do as they willed with him.

The entity, however, disagreed with that intention. Taking control of the four minds was not in the least difficult, nor was the series of small but bright fire flashes. Ashing something without burning anything around that something was simple, and then it was Jovvi back again and walking toward the five men. The others of the Blending also made their way over, and in a moment they stood staring at the four unmoving men, who remained masked.

"That was hilsom powder we burned up," Lorand commented before stepping forward to pull the masks off three of the intruders. "I sincerely hope that there's not a speck of it left."

"There isn't," Tamrissa assured him, moving to the fourth man to remove his mask as well. "Burning a powder is easier than burning water without producing steam. . . . Well, these four were being properly careful. The wet cloths would have kept them from being affected by the powder along with Rion."

"That means they didn't want to kill him," Jovvi pointed out, making sure to keep a firm hold on the four. "Let's hear what they did intend to do with him. Whichever of you is the leader of this group, answer the question."

"Our job was to bring the man back to Gan Garee," the fourth intruder, the one who had stood alone, responded immediately. "We represent someone who works for his family, and he would certainly not have been harmed. At least not by us."

"What's *that* comment supposed to mean?" Vallant asked, his voice having become a growl. "Did that mother of his decide to have him kidnapped so she could turn him over to that so-called Five?"

"Our employer considered that a possible option," the man agreed with a judicious nod. "He did quite a lot of research before accepting the commission, and therefore came to a different primary conclusion. The noblewoman involved was most likely to have deliberately damaged the man's mind, in an effort to regain what she lost. an obedient child in a man's body. Since the man would then have been more of a moron than a child, chances were excellent that she would have finally decided to give the man to the Five, and then do what she did before."

"What, have another child?" Vallant said, outrage now clear in his voice and mind. "Isn't she gettin' on a bit to keep havin' children?"

"What she did before was take the infant of a dead servant to raise as her own," the man corrected with brows high. "She herself has never borne a child. We were under the impression that you had found that out."

A shocked silence descended on the group, and Jovvi was immediately worried about Rion's state of mind. The shock was greatest for him, of course, but then she saw his delighted grin and felt that his mind and emotions were a perfect match.

"What marvelous news!" he exclaimed, turning to offer an arm to Naran, who hovered just behind the others. "Did you hear that, my love? I'm *not* one of those useless bloodsuckers, not even a half-blood worth. My true mother was a servant, and she was unable to protect me because she had died."

"Yes, my love, I did hear," Naran said after hurrying to him, the relief in her mind as strong as that in Jovvi. "I'm delighted for you, almost as delighted as I am that you're unharmed."

"So what are we going to do with these four?" Lorand asked, looking around at his groupmates. "They didn't come to kill, so giving them death in return might be a bit much."

"If you stop to think about it," Tamrissa answered before anyone else could speak, "what they did come for was worse than simple killing. They knew what Rion probably had to look forward to once he was back in his mother's— his female kidnapper's—hands, but they didn't care. They were still going to deliver him to her, and then turn their backs and forget that they were responsible for putting him *in* that position. For people like this, death is really too easy a punishment."

"I tend to agree," Jovvi said, faintly surprised by how hard her voice had grown. "In some ways their actions are worse than what that woman would have done, and I can't see letting them get away with it. But before we do anything to them, let's ask a few more questions. For instance, are there any more of you around? And if we send you back alive, is your employer likely to send out others like you?"

"At the moment, we're the only ones our employer has sent to see to the retrieval," the leader of the four responded. "We have nothing at all to do with the others, and if we're unsuccessful in completing the chore, whether or not others are sent in our place will be up to the client. As long as she's willing to spend the gold, our employer will probably be willing to send men out."

"Then we'll have to do somethin' about your employer's attitude," Vallant said, but his gaze had turned sharp. "In the meanwhile, I'd like to hear about these others that you have nothin' to do with. Who are they, how many of them are there, and where are they now?"

"We only believe we know who they are," the man responded, now sounding thoughtful. "They arrived in this area about four days behind us, after we'd sent our first report about your group being around here. That means they could have come from Gan Garee if they rode with remounts and didn't stop much along the way. If that was what they did, then they must have been sent by the Five after the client reported what our employer told her. We have no way of knowing that for certain, of course, but the conclusion seems likely. As far as where they are right now goes, they're here in this hamlet, spread out and hiding among the locals, who have been working at ignoring them. Their number? Since we've only seen two or three of them together at once, we really have no idea."

"That's wonderful," Lorand said with heavy disgust, exchanging glances with Vallant and Rion. "Agents of the Five are probably all around us, but we don't know who they are or where to find them. Most likely they're waiting for us to decide to get some sleep, and then we'll find out everything about them."

"Let's see what the entity can do to root them out before we get upset," Jovvi soothed him, also sending a smile. "And speaking of the entity, I really must apologize to all of you for initiating the Blending without telling you first. Rion was in immediate danger, so there simply wasn't time."

"Of course there wasn't," Tamma agreed at once, putting a hand to Jovvi's arm. "All of us would have done the exact same thing if we were able, so stop being silly. And you should have known that without any of us having had to say it."

"Normally I would have, but you have to remember that I'm holding four minds right now," Jovvi said with a small laugh of relief. The men's emotions had agreed with Tamma's so completely that there wasn't any possible doubt. "So does anyone have a suggestion about what we might do with these four?"

"I have a very definite suggestion," Naran said without waiting for anyone else to answer. "Is it possible to make them have to tell the complete truth from now on? That would include situations where people would normally use tact, because tact is a form of socially permitted lying. I don't know how long they would last, but the time would be horrible for them no matter how short or long it was."

"Oh, I like that!" Tamma said at once, delight actually filling her mind. "Naran, you're the most beautifully evil person I've met in a long while. And in case you're wondering, that was very definitely a compliment."

"I agree with Tamrissa," Lorand said with a grin for Naran's blush. "People say men are hard on those who try to harm their loved ones, but we're softies compared to you ladies. Rion, please remind me never to get into an argument with you. I'd hate to have Naran think up something to get even with *me*."

"Since Jovvi's smile says she also agrees, I'm makin' it unanimous," Vallant put in, a sense of satisfaction in his mind if not on his face. "They should never be able to do this sort of thing to anyone else, especially if we make it an order that they warn any potential victims they may be sent after. That will add the icin'."

"It certainly will, so let's do it," Jovvi said, and once again initiated the Blending. She might have been able to give the orders herself and make them stick, but with the entity there was no *might* about it. The necessary demands were fixed in the minds of the four, and then the Blending was dissolved again.

"You men can go now," Jovvi said to them as soon as she released them. "But first tell us what your present plans are."

"We should . . . pretend to leave, but really . . . hang around to see if we can get another chance to . . . complete our job," the leader of the group said, looking and sounding as though he tried to hold the words back. "We. . . . Damnation! What have you done to me?"

"We've thanked you for being completely without a

conscience where other people are concerned," Jovvi told him with a smile that must have shown him exactly how she felt. "Now you'll be causing the same reaction in others, the feeling that they don't care *what* happens to you because of what you say. I hope you enjoy it as much as your previous victims enjoyed what was done to *them*."

All four men looked thunderstruck, and then they simply looked frightened. It must have finally occurred to them that it wasn't possible for ordinary people to do what had been done to them, and that meant they weren't among ordinary people. Almost as one they began to back away, and then they were running out of the stables as fast as they could. For once Jovvi was pleased to see a reaction like that, but unfortunately the pleasure didn't last long.

"Well, now that that's taken care of, we just have to locate the people sent here by the Five," she said as soon as the men were out of sight. "I hope *someone* has an idea about how we can do that, because I surely don't. How are we supposed to pick out an unknown number of enemies who are hidden among all those strangers?"

"It just might be possible," Lorand said, looking thoughtful. "But if it is, it's the entity who'll be doing it. Does everyone want to get started right now?"

"I think we need to set up sentries first," Vallant said, also looking thoughtful. "This is no time to be leavin' our bodies unprotected, not to mention leavin' our people unwarned. Whatever number of guardsmen are out there, they'll do a lot less damage if everyone knows they're there."

"You're right, of course," Lorand told him with a brief but sincere smile. "Let's spread the word, and then we can Blend again. I was looking forward to getting some sleep, but obviously resting is going to have to wait."

"We all wanted to get some sleep, so let's also get a few link groups together before we Blend," Jovvi said, deliberately not letting herself yawn. "Our entity won't do much good if it falls asleep as soon as it forms."

Everyone muttered agreement with that, so they set about making their preparations—before beginning the search for their enemies.

EIGHT

Lorand was more than a little tired after all the moving around they'd been doing, not to mention the tension he'd felt about coming home. He'd actually dreaded running into his father, but when he had—and heard the man trying to get him back under control—something inside him had immediately responded in just the right way. He wasn't the same boy who had left here only a short while ago, and now his father knew it as well as he did. It bothered him that his father had made no effort to speak to him privately after the meeting, but the feeling was more annoyance than hurt. He hadn't expected warmth and welcome, so he hadn't been disappointed when it didn't appear.

He was ready to walk around and talk to various groups of their people, but Vallant called out and got everyone's attention, and then began to explain what the newest problem was. That *was* the fastest way to get everyone alerted, but whether or not Vallant consciously knew it, it was also the worst way for Meerk. The big Middle should have been told first, before everyone else, and when he wasn't his reactions were clear enough for Lorand to read easily.

Which was another interesting thing, Lorand thought fleetingly as he made his way over to where Meerk stood alone. When Rion had made the suggestion that they all touch the power all the time the way Tamrissa was already doing, Lorand had been amused. He'd started doing the same almost two days ago, and he'd noticed differences in his perceptions only hours later. In some definite way the world had changed for him, having grown brighter and clearer and easier to comprehend. That would be the basis of the suggestion he would make concerning the search for their enemies, a way to pick them out from the crowds they were hiding among . . .

"No, Alsin, don't start a fight with him now," Lorand said quickly, having had just enough time to step in front of the man and block his path to Vallant. "I know how angry you are, but you have to put that aside and listen to what's being said. The Five have guardsmen hiding among the people out there, and we need to weed them out and neutralize them."

"How much of this am I supposed to take without saying anything?" Meerk demanded in a hiss, keeping his voice down with difficulty as he glared at Lorand. "I know he's doing it on purpose to show me who the important one around here is, and I don't happen to agree with that stance. It's more than time that he and I—"

"No," Lorand interrupted, before Meerk could work himself up to an even higher pitch. "It isn't time for anything but looking for our real enemies, and you'd better get that through your head. And I know it looks to you as if Vallant is doing things like this just to goad you, but that doesn't happen to be the case. Don't you know he was the captain of a trading ship before he was sent to Gan Garee? Taking charge and giving orders is second nature to him, especially when there's danger in the offing. If he thinks about you at all it's only in relation to Tamrissa, and that relationship doesn't apply right now."

"Of course it does," Meerk disagreed, but with less anger and more control. "He's trying to make me look small in her eyes, like less of a man and therefore unfit to court her. You can't tell me you don't know how these things work—"

"Stop it," Lorand interrupted again, beginning to be more than a little annoyed. "You're just trying to work yourself up again and you know it. It isn't as if Tamrissa has a shining and hero-worshiping picture of you that Vallant is in the process of tarnishing. She knows exactly who and what you are, and Vallant is giving her enough trouble without you adding to it. Don't you think things would be easier for her if she didn't have nonsense to cope with from both of you?''

Meerk made no answer to that, at least not in words. What he did do was frown a bit before his brows went up, as though he'd just gotten an idea. Lorand didn't know what that idea could be, but as long as Meerk's pulse stopped racing and pounding and his muscles relaxed, it had to be considered good rather than bad.

"So can we count on you to help us out while we go searching for those guardsmen?" Lorand pursued, intent on getting Meerk to give his word. "We'll be doing it in our Blending, which means we'll need someone to be in charge while we're mostly out of it."

"Of course, of course I will," Meerk agreed hurriedly, now almost a different man. "But why don't you simply go out and tell those people about the guardsmen, and get *them* to point out the strangers? That way there won't be any mistake."

"I wish we could," Lorand said ruefully—and with a lot of relief. "But think about what we would have to tell them: there are people among you who are representatives of the Seated Five, here to do us harm because we mean to unseat the Five. We want you to betray them to us, even though most of us are strangers to you . . . I really don't think that will work despite the fact that I used to be one of them. And they might even be *afraid* to point out the intruders."

"Yes, I'd have to agree with that assessment," Meerk said with matching ruefulness as well as a headshake. "They'd be more likely to turn on us than help us, especially if they're afraid. But how will you know if you get them all?"

"If we can find their leader and get control of him, we'll know how many there are and where they can be found," Lorand replied, back to thinking about the problem. "The trick will be to spot any of them, leader or not. We've walked past those crowds twice, and nothing about them struck even me as being different or not-quite-usual. I know a lot of those people, but not even *near* all of them. And we'll have to be very careful. The people of this town might consider themselves supporters of the authority represented by those guardsmen, but to the guardsmen they're nothing but hostages and pawns to be used to get what they want. If some of those hostages and pawns don't survive, well, so what? As long as they serve their purpose. . . ."

"Yeah," Meerk agreed gruffly, knowing exactly what Lorand meant. "That's always the way they look at it, isn't it? They're not bright enough to understand that if their bosses run out of pawns to waste, they'll start to spend the guardsmen in the same way. They've been led to believe that they're safe, which is the only thing some people worry about. They don't seem capable of realizing that 'safe' is only temporary at best."

"That's true even with the right people in charge," Lorand said with a nod of his own. "If you have the *wrong* people in charge. . . . Well, I think I'm wanted for the Blending, so please remember what I said."

"I intend to remember every word," Meerk said in a way that seemed odd to Lorand, especially with the smile the man showed. "I've grown to consider you a friend, Lorand, and today you really proved the point. If things turn out the way I hope they will, I'll owe you more than just a favor."

Lorand felt the urge to ask Meerk what he was talking about, but the others were waiting for him to join them so he shelved the question for now. Later he'd have to remember to go back and find out what the man meant. . . .

"We've decided to try something different," Jovvi told him with her usual sweet smile once he stood with the others. "Pagin Holter and his group have agreed to try seeing if their entity can help ours. The last time both of our entities were active, we were at opposite sides of that battle with the guardsmen."

"I wonder if two entities can Blend," Rion said, looking around to see if anyone could answer the question. "If they can't, what about linking? And would that increase our strength the way ordinary linking does?"

"We'll probably find out when we try it," Tamrissa responded with a shrug. "So what are we waiting for?"

"We're waiting to sit down and get comfortable," Jovvi said with clear amusement as she shook her head at Tamrissa. "Standing up will just drain our strength faster, which we definitely don't need. And it ought to help even more if we sit next to our respective link groups.''

Tamrissa put her hands up, palms out, to show she had no intention of arguing, which made Lorand chuckle. Tamrissa was always so eager to get the Blending going, as though . . . Lorand's amusement disappeared as he realized that Tamrissa was always eager to get the Blending going because that was her only escape. The way she moved and held her body shouted that she wanted to be unaware of all personal problems, to *his* senses at least. She had to be a lot more unhappy than she'd let anyone know. . . .

Well, that was something else for later, Lorand forced himself to understand as he took his own place near the link group of Earth magic users. They were all sitting down on the thick bed of straw which someone had spread, and with thirty people arranged in their immediate vicinity— not to mention the other thirty which included Holter's Blending—the formerly wide-aisled stable became a good bit narrower.

The rest of their people stood in their own link groups, ready to defend the searchers if any of the guardsmen came into the stable. With everyone settled in place there was nothing more to wait for, so Jovvi initiated the Blending. Lorand responded to her reaching out with his own talent outstretched, and then—

—and then the entity was there once more, this time for a purpose other than immediate battle. There were enemy flesh forms out among the flesh forms of that town, and those enemies needed to be located. Also, hovering with the intention to be of help, was a second entity. The entity recognized the second as that which had assisted during a recent battle, and therefore welcomed its presence. The strength of the second wasn't quite as great as that of the entity, but perhaps it would indeed be of help. . . .

The entity floated swiftly out of the stables, the second following closely and watching intently. That was proper, of course, for the lesser to follow and learn from the greater, and to be at hand if assistance was required. That foolishness which one of its flesh forms had considered, the possibility of the two entities Blending. . . . Surely even flesh forms were aware of the need for more than two to

Blend. Linking, in the way that was currently done by the flesh forms was also undesirable, for there was a far better and more effective way to accomplish the same end. If such a thing became necessary, it would certainly be done. . . .

Outside the stables there were even more flesh forms than there had been earlier, all of them in a state of agitation. It seemed that those who had met with the entity's flesh forms had come out of the building in which they had been, and now two of them spoke to the throngs which stood about listening. The two were not saying the same thing, the entity realized, and the listeners were agitated because of being urged to two different courses of action. That foolishness could be easily corrected, but later, after the entity's primary aim was accomplished.

And that primary aim might be more easily seen to than the entity had expected. It hadn't appreciated the point earlier, during its two brief appearances, but its senses now felt more . . . sensitive and widespread. The entity was growing closer to the way it knew it really should be, which was extremely heartening. There would be more actions available to it once it had reached its optimum condition. . . .

But for now, the improvement in its senses was very much of a help. Not only was the world about it much clearer, but the flesh forms it was required to examine were also more easily read. Those beings over there were all but terrified, and for that reason were refusing to heed the words of one of the two speaking flesh forms. If those words were heeded, the terror they felt would surely increase, therefore they heeded the second speaking flesh form instead. Denial of the danger was to them a refuge, unlike some of those who stood elsewhere. Those others were prepared to take action against the danger, even if the action were no more than running away.

The entity ceased inspecting those who were read easily, and moved its attention to those who were more difficult. Among this group would its enemies be found, but apparently not immediately. One after the other, the individuals the entity examined proved to be almost the same as the others. Some wore their feelings clearly upon their faces and others not quite so clearly, but all seemed of the same

sort. Ordinary flesh forms, excited to one degree or another. . . .

The entity pulled back from its investigations, momentarily vexed. Right now there seemed to be no difference
between the ordinary flesh forms and those who were enemies, as both groups might be expected to be agitated to
some degree. The enemy did, after all, know that they might
be discovered and destroyed at any time. The objective,
then, would be to produce a different sort of agitation in
the enemy, to mark them out more clearly. With that point
understood, there remained only the matter of constructing
the *manner* of marking them out.

A moment of thought brought the entity a possible answer to its needs. The plan would, in a manner of speaking,
see to solving two situations at the same time, an economy
of effort which the entity fully approved of. With that in
mind the entity floated closer to one of the two flesh forms
who were speaking, specifically the one called Mollit Feldin. That flesh form was very closed-minded, clinging to
its own beliefs no matter the foolishness of them.

"... so we gotta r'member these here strangers ain't our
own folk," the flesh form was in the midst of saying,
speaking to someone in the throng who had spoken first.
"Idroy Welt there'll b'lieve anythin' ya tell 'im, since he
don't care none 'bout lookin' foolish. He *allus* looks foolish, but I don't aim t'do th' same. There ain't no trouble
comin', th' trouble's awready here, an' it's that buncha
strangers. Like as not they'll be tearin' through our stuff
soon's we pack up 'n leave, takin' whut they want without
no one about to say not t'. I ain't been workin' m'backside
off jest t' give whut little I got t' sum slick-talkin' strangers."

"Lorand Coll ain't no stranger," the flesh form called
Idroy Welt countered, but in a way which suggested that
he'd said the same thing many times over. "He's one a
ourn, an' he coulda gone to any town in this parta th' country. But he came *here*, 'cause he still thinks like one a us
an' couldn't bear the idear a seein' us done in. If we don't
tend t' our own backsides an' get 'em an' our fam'lies outa
here, there ain't nobody else gonna do it fer us."

"Hey, shore there is," Feldin responded immediately,

showing nothing of the fact that the entity now controlled what he said. ''We ain't no more alone now'n we been on our farms. If'n there's sum trouble headin' our way, the nobles'll send us all th' help we need. An' why not? Don't they need us t'make their holdin's worth sumthin' more'n jest dirt?''

The babble of voices which had been sounding all around during the speeches of the two men now increased in volume, as they all reacted to what had just been said. Most of those listening knew better than to expect help from the nobility, but some clutched at the suggestion with the panic of desperation. The minds of that sort were suddenly filled with hope, just as the minds of those with a realistic understanding of the world simply dismissed the idea as wishful thinking. Both of those reactions were to be expected from the natives, but the third reaction. . . .

The third reaction was feelings of scorn, or ridicule, or actual outrage, in any combination or even all three. The messages came through clearly from the bodily stances and motions of those who felt the emotions, those who were guardsmen and therefore knew the nobility far better than anyone in the town. The entity was able to scan the throng quickly enough to pinpoint which of the flesh forms these were, but that was simply the first step in seeing to the danger. The second step would have to be finding a way to control so many diverse flesh forms.

Putting them under control a few at a time would be possible, the entity knew, but not highly practical. It floated about examining the various components of the enemy force, seeing how their mode of dress allowed them to blend in with the innocent flesh forms. But now it was also possible to see that they waited for something, were poised to react in a certain way when that something occurred. Their reactions would not be to the benefit of anyone in that town, the entity was certain, therefore something had to be done about them rather quickly.

And then the entity knew exactly what there was to be done. With their brother/sister entity right there, the answer became obvious. So the entity sent the knowledge to the second, which had not been in existence long enough to begin remembering all that the entity did. The second sent its amused agreement, amused because it, too, now remembered what was possible here, and therefore the entity moved to one side of the throng while the second moved to the other, and then it began.

The entity sent its desires radiating out in all directions, but not just at random as it would have done had it been alone. The desires reached the second and were reflected back, intensified as they radiated out again. The entity received this response and also reflected the incoming emanations, which sent them toward the second again. This happened much more quickly than can be described in words as well as over and over again, and when the effect reached its peak, the entity's commands were many, many more times more powerful than they'd been at first.

Those commands reached the disguised guardsmen wherever they were in the crowds, and disobedience simply wasn't possible. They left off speaking to others or simply standing and listening, and began to make their way toward the stables where the entity's flesh forms were. They were now under the control of the true Five, and would obey any and all orders given them. The entity had time to reflect that it hadn't had to discover the whereabouts of these erstwhile enemies to begin with, not with this newly remembered weapon at its command, and then—

—and then it was Lorand back again, suddenly aware that the entity must have borrowed strength from the link groups. He wasn't nearly as weary as he'd been at first, but then he remembered just what their Blending had done.

"Now I know why the nobility is so terrified about having other Blendings running around," Tamrissa said, actually sounding as shaken as Lorand felt. "I had no idea something like that was possible, and I suppose it wasn't—until we had another Blending to work with."

"There are a lot of things we don't yet know about," Jovvi said, looking as disturbed as the rest of their group. "This kind of thing . . . we'll have to be careful not to start using it on a regular basis, or we could end up being worse for the empire than the ones now sitting on the Fivefold Throne."

"I wonder how much of it those approachin' Blendin's from Astinda know about," Vallant said, his disturbance even deeper. "If Holter and his Blendin' are goin' up against them even to talk, this kind of thing—or another—could get them all destroyed. I think they'll need to take one or two of our fledglin' Blendin's along with them, just in case."

Lorand nodded as he immediately saw the sense in that, as did everyone else, so Vallant went to speak to Holter and his group, all of whom looked even more stunned than their own group felt. In a little while, once all the guardsmen reported to them, their personal army would be increased by another two hundred or more, depending on just how many the guardsmen numbered. They'd then be able to spare more link groups for the Blendings which went with Holter, those new Blendings which hadn't done much more than actually Blend. From the point of no one but the Seated Five being able to Blend to having half a dozen or more of functioning Blendings all around. . . .

It was a temptation to stand there and shake his head, but Lorand resisted. The times were forcing all sorts of new things to come into existence, and Lorand didn't quite dread what would happen next. It wasn't *quite* dread, but it also wasn't a wholehearted greeting for the way his world was being turned upside down. . . .

NINE

It wasn't long before their former hunters, the guardsmen sent by the Five, reported to them in the stables. After speaking to Holter and his people, Vallant walked outside for a while to wait for them, or at least that was what he told everyone else. His real reason was that he could no longer bear being inside a building with no windows, with the only exits a long distance between front and back. The hardships of the previous days had been almost a pleasure for him, being experienced, as they were, in the out-of-doors.

It had gotten to be early evening, so Vallant took a deep breath of the air once he stood to one side of the entrance to the stables. Fresh, that air was, with the promise of rain, and clean compared to what was found in the city. But not as clean as what they'd had on the trail, and not as fresh as the air above the seas. It was possible that Vallant's aspect should have been Air rather than Water, and that thought curved his lips into a faint, almost mirthless smile. But air was simply air to him, unless it was in a small, tight building without windows or easily reached doors. Then it was completely unbreathable. . . .

"You're one of the ones we've been ordered to report to," a voice said, one that was clearly used to authority. "But we were told to report *inside* the stables, not in front of it."

Vallant looked at the man who had approached him, a man who was being watched surreptitiously by the others of his command. They'd been told not to converge on the stables in any obvious manner, and were in the midst of obeying those orders. The man himself was at most ten years older than Vallant, with a hardness which comes from exercising not only authority but ruthlessness. That hardness showed in the man's craggy features and dark, unblinking stare, in the leanness of his tall build, in the broad shoulders which seemed incapable of being bowed. He was the sort of man Vallant usually disliked on sight, and it was a relief that he didn't have to *make* himself like—or be pleasant to—this one.

"You'll be goin' inside as soon as you answer a couple of questions for me," Vallant said, deliberately using the tone he'd used so often aboard ship. "The first question is, what's your name?"

"Captain Nome Herstan, at your orders, sir," the man replied in the same tone he'd used all along, that of someone putting up with those who were inferiors.

"All right, Herstan, here's the second question," Vallant continued, ignoring the attitude. "How many men did you bring here, and are all of them followin' you here? Or won't you know until you and they are all inside the stables?"

"All told there are two hundred and twenty of us," Herstan replied without hesitation. "And no, I don't have to wait to find out. Ten of my men are at a farm not far from here, where we left our horses. I've been rotating all of them into the town by that ten at a time, giving them all a chance to rest in turn. We had a long, hard ride getting here, and I want my men at their best when we have to fight."

"Except that you won't be fightin' who you thought you would," Vallant replied with a nod. "All right, you can go ahead on in, but leave the rest of your men out here for now. And don't forget about tellin' the others you have ten men somewhere else. It won't help tellin' me where they are, but there's someone inside who knows this area."

Herstan matched his nod before continuing on inside, but first he held up a hand for a brief moment. That seemed to be the signal to his men to tell them to stay where they were for now, as the men Vallant was able to see just began to loll around as though waiting for nothing in particular. Which suited Vallant perfectly, as he had no real interest in talking to anyone at the moment. What he most wanted to do was brood, since on his way out of the stables he'd seen Meerk talking to Tamrissa. The sight should have only been annoying, but for some reason it was a good deal more. . . .

"Vallant, I need to speak to you for a moment," Jovvi's voice came as she walked out of the stables and saw him. "Do you mind sharing your peace and quiet for that long?"

"I'll never mind sharin' it with *you*," Vallant answered with as true a smile as he was capable of right now. "But shouldn't you be in there with the others, talkin' to that guard captain? There are still ten of his men that we haven't accounted for."

"Lorand and Rion will take care of it," she replied with a smile of her own. "Lorand will know whatever place the man tells him about, and later we can all take care of it.

Right now I need to mention the way you left the stables, as though you couldn't bear to be inside any longer. You're still bothered by your problem, aren't you?''

"Not when I'm part of the Blendin', and that's the important time," Vallant answered with a shrug. "As for the rest . . . well, it's just somethin' I have to put up with since I can't do anythin' about it. If complainin' did any good, I'd be willin' to start doin' it right now."

"Somehow it doesn't seem fair that complaining *doesn't* do any good," she came back with a wider smile. "We'd all be so good at accomplishing it. . . . But some time ago I had an idea about how your problem might be . . . well, not solved but at least settled to the point where you won't be bothered by it at the wrong time. Lorand needs the same kind of help, and if you two are willing I'll be glad to try my idea once we leave here."

"I've been willin' since the first time you mentioned it," Vallant reminded her, trying not to feel *too* much hope. "Even if it isn't a complete cure, I'll still be better off than havin' nothin' done. As soon as we leave this town I'll be sure to remind you."

"Good," Jovvi said with a nod, and then her smile faded. "And now that we're taking the time to talk, I'd also like to ask what you intend to do about Tamma. I would hardly be mixing into your private affairs like this except for a very pressing reason: I'm having a hard time blocking out that horrible disturbance filling you. Since it seems to refuse to go away by itself, I'm forced to offer whatever help I can be."

"As a matter of fact, I'm glad you brought up the point," Vallant said, forcing himself not to back away from the discussion. "I meant to talk to you about it anyway, since it's somethin' that needs seein' to. If you would do me the favor of talkin' to Tamrissa and tellin' her that she isn't yet ready for a serious relationship, I'd really appreciate it. *I* tried tellin' her that, but she didn't believe me."

"Ah, now I see," Jovvi murmured on a gentle exhalation of breath. "That explains a lot . . . but I'm sorry, Vallant, I can't say something like that to Tamrissa—because it isn't true. Are you willing to listen to what *is* true?"

"But of course it's true," Vallant said, his insides beginning to churn again. "In point of fact it's been true all along, otherwise I wouldn't have been sayin' it. I'd be holdin' her in my arms and kissin' her, not spendin' my time *wishin'* I could do those things."

"Vallant, it—isn't—true," Jovvi repeated, speaking the words a lot more slowly and definitely than she had the first time. "And I will say it again: are you willing to listen to what *is* true?"

For a long moment Vallant simply stared down at her, feeling as though he were being threatened by a large group of very big men. It was ridiculous to feel that way, since it was only Jovvi who stood before him. *She* would never do anything to hurt him, even though some part of him didn't quite believe that. . . .

"My dear, *you're* the one who isn't prepared to have a relationship with Tamma, and I can't really blame you," Jovvi said when another minute passed without him saying anything. Her tone was very gentle and filled with understanding, but Vallant still flinched as though he'd been struck. "No, really, you can't be blamed for feeling like that," she added, putting a hand to his arm. "You've been through such an awful lot with her, that it's a wonder you haven't wandered off into the night, talking to yourself. You're still here because you do love her, but a vital part of you can't bear the idea of being rejected by her again. That's why you've been insisting that *she's* the one who isn't ready. It's easier than letting yourself admit the truth."

By then Vallant had closed his eyes, one shoulder leaning against the stable wall to keep him erect. He didn't want to say anything aloud, but somehow the words began to come out in spite of that.

"I—don't know what to do," he whispered, feeling Jovvi take his hand in both of hers and squeeze it tight. "I can't give her up, not when she's the woman who makes me whole, but the idea of facin' that . . . horrible rejection again. . . . Every time she turns and walks away, somethin' inside me dies a little. If it happens even one more time, the somethin' is goin' to die all the way, I know it will. But I won't be lucky enough to have it take me with it. . . ."

The flow of words choked off then, turning itself into a knot in Vallant's throat. Jovvi's grip on his hand tightened even more, and loving, soothing compassion tried to envelop him.

"Please, my dear, you have to believe that everything will work out right," Jovvi urged, her voice striving to match what her mind tried to send. "You're in such a turmoil that you won't even let me ease you a little, which is exactly the state Tamma is in. I think she's given up completely, and hasn't simply walked away only because she knows she's needed by the rest of us. Let me talk to her, and maybe something can be worked out between the two of you."

"What do you mean, she's given up completely?" Vallant asked, opening his eyes to frown at Jovvi. "I haven't seen her behavin' any differently from the way she usually does, and that includes talkin' to Meerk. You don't think she'll . . . do somethin' foolish?"

"Why should she be any different from the rest of us?" Jovvi asked, her expression now rueful. "But no, I don't think there's any *immediate* danger. Later, though, is another matter entirely, and it can't really wait to be taken care of. It's too easy to wait just a little too long, and then you lose the chance to do anything at all."

"Maybe I should be the one to talk to her," Vallant said, still more than a little disturbed over what Jovvi had told him. "I know she doesn't believe me most of the time, but. . . . All I have to do is figure out what to say. . . . No, I'll figure it out once I'm standin' in front of her."

"Vallant, wait," Jovvi said as he began to walk around her and back into the stables. "It might not be the best of ideas for *you* to be the one. Let me start it off for you, and then—"

But Vallant had put a hand to Jovvi's face as he passed her, and then he just continued on into the building. He might be too much of a coward to want to let himself be hurt again, but sooner him than Tamrissa. He'd done his share of hurting her, something he'd sworn he never would, so now it was time to repair the damage. Afterward . . . well, afterward would take care of itself. Right now the woman he would love forever needed him. . . .

TEN

After we dissolved the Blending everyone went in a different direction, and that included me. I wasn't exactly bothered by what we'd done with those guardsmen, it was more a matter of wondering what we would find it possible to do next. I wandered off away from the link groups we'd used, also realizing that we'd drawn strength from them so automatically that the entity hadn't even consciously noticed the action. It was nice to know that we weren't helpless, but how far do you have to go before you cross the line between not-helpless and horribly overbearing . . . ?

"Excuse me," a voice said, breaking into my distraction. "I don't mean to interrupt you while you're so obviously deep in thought, but I'd appreciate a minute of your time. And it really won't take more than a minute."

"I'm going to hold you to that, Dom Meerk," I countered, pausing to look up at him. "I'm not as tired as I was a few minutes ago, but I'm still too tired to listen to—"

"No, there won't be any of *that*," Alsin said quickly, raising one hand and looking serious about what he was in the midst of saying. "I've decided not to keep *telling* you that I'm the better man, but to start showing you. With that in mind, I'm not going to talk bitterly about Dom Ro again, nor am I going to take offense at anything he does. In fact I'm not even going to mention him again, not unless you ask me to. You have enough things to worry you with this

. . . semiprivate war you and the others are waging. You don't need me adding to it.''

He gave me a brief smile and began to turn away, apparently ready to keep his word about only taking a minute of my time. I'll admit I was more than a little surprised, so I raised one hand to stop him.

"Alsin, wait," I said, which did stop him from walking away. "I'd like to know what suddenly brought this on. Only a little while ago you were so angry I thought your blood was about to boil over."

"It was," he replied ruefully, smiling without humor. "I couldn't seem to stop the anger, but then someone told me that my actions were just adding to your unhappiness. Since that's the last thing I want to do, I finally got it through my head that the whole thing had to end—and with me making the first effort. I want you to be able to pay attention to what you're in the middle of, without having to worry about what I'll do next."

"I really hope you can stick to that," I said, letting him know I meant every word. "If you can and do, I'll be very grateful. And there's something *you* need to know: our force has just grown by some two hundred more men. Those guardsmen are now ours, but we can't expect them to be as strong as the rest of our people. Putting them where they'll be most effective is something *you* should start to think about."

"I will, even if it turns out that no one takes my suggestions," he said with a thoughtful nod. "But I have a feeling they probably will, if I'm not yelling my head off when I put them forward. But who's this?"

I turned to look at the man entering the stables, a hard-faced man I'd never seen before, at least not by myself. The part of my memory that covered the doings of the entity recognized him immediately, though, and that told me who he was.

"He has to be the leader of the guard group," I said to Alsin while the two of us watched the man walk closer. "They were all told to report here to us, but only the leader was directed to come inside. Well, we should know for certain in another minute. . . ."

That comment was because the man was now heading

directly for *me*, and when he reached us I found I was right.

"I've been ordered to report to the true Five," he said without preamble, his hard, dark gaze only on *my* face. "I've already spoken to two before you, and now I need to see the others."

"I saw Jovvi speak to him briefly on his way in," Alsin supplied when I raised my brows, clearly knowing what my question was. "And Ro went outside a short while ago, so he must be the second."

"Then he still has Lorand and Rion to meet," I said with a nod. "I'll take him over to them, and in the meanwhile you can do that thinking I suggested. There's no telling when we'll need the ideas."

He matched my nod with one of his own, so I crooked a finger at the guardsman and headed for Lorand and Rion. The two of them were standing with Naran and talking, probably about the activity around Pagin Holter's group. They were getting ready to head out, intending to go back the way we'd just come. They were taking two of the newly formed Blendings with them, but only one additional set of link groups. That was another thirty-five people we would have to do without, and the two hundred we'd just acquired might or might not be an adequate replacement for them.

"Ah, Tamrissa," Rion said when I walked up to them. "Is that the leader of our new forces? If so, he's more than prompt."

"I've been ordered to tell you that there are another ten of my men at a farm not far from this town," the guardsman said, which took Lorand's immediate attention. "I've been rotating them into and out of town to give them all a rest in groups. Which of you is the one who knows the area?"

"I am," Lorand replied, stepping a bit closer. "Tell me where the farm is as precisely as you can."

"The farm is called Arbors, and is on the eastern road," the guardsman replied at once. "It lies approximately five miles—"

"Never mind," Lorand interrupted as he nodded. "I know Arbors, and exactly where it is. How soon are you due to rotate that group out and another in?"

"At midnight," the man replied without hesitation. "But

none of my men were going to be sent there because that was when I'd intended to launch our attack on this stables. I was fairly certain you'd all be here at least that long, but beyond that . . . these farmers are fools, and most of them think they can forget about being in danger if *your* group isn't here any longer.''

''Yes, we'd noticed,'' Rion said dryly. ''But that—and our group—is no longer your concern. We can see to the ten at the farm without much trouble, but I've been wondering just how thorough our efforts were. Do you know as yet whether *all* your men here in town have been neutralized?''

''I haven't had the opportunity to check,'' the man replied, completely unbothered by anything said to him. ''Would you like me to do so now?''

''Yes,'' Lorand said after glancing at Rion and then at me. ''If you find one who hasn't been touched, get him here however you can without doing him permanent damage. We're going to need every talent we can get our hands on once we get back to Gan Garee.''

''Sooner than that,'' Naran said abruptly, startling everyone, apparently including herself. ''I mean . . . it isn't very likely that we'll get all the way back to Gan Garee without running into *some* kind of trouble. In fact, it might be a good idea to keep a sharp eye open while we're still here. I have the strangest feeling. . . .''

''I think we've all learned better than to ignore your feelings, my love,'' Rion said to her while putting his arm around her shoulders. ''So while you're about it, guardsman, set some of your men out as sentries around this town. If there's additional danger in the offing, we'd like to know about it before it turns into a crisis.''

''At your orders, sir,'' the man replied, all but coming to attention and saluting. ''Is there anything else?''

We all glanced at one another, but when no one added any other requirement Lorand dismissed the man with orders to report back as soon as possible. When the man walked away I began to think about sitting down somewhere for a while, possibly even to take a nap, but quickly discovered that I was premature in believing that all the fuss was over with for a while.

"Tamrissa, I need to talk to you for a minute," I heard, but this time not in Alsin's voice. This time it was Vallant who spoke to me, and I didn't even need to turn to know that. To be absolutely honest I couldn't turn, not when that would have put him directly in my sight. I hadn't looked straight at him for quite some time, and probably never would again. . . .

"Please, Tamrissa, it's really important," he said when I neither turned nor spoke. "I don't blame you for erasin' me from your life, but there's somethin' I have to tell you. All this trouble between us . . . isn't your fault. It's completely mine, so there's no sense in you blamin' yourself. You can't give up on life just because I . . . have a problem. I wanted you to know how I really feel about you, which is—"

By then I had pushed between Rion and Lorand and had hurried away, no longer able to bear hearing him talk to me. It didn't matter *why* he wanted nothing to do with me, not when I'd had to admit to myself that I would love him forever. When a feeling like that isn't returned the pain is horrible, but worse, for me at least, would be trying to change his mind. He didn't want his mind changed, and he didn't want *me* anywhere near him. He'd come to speak to me because he thought I needed help, and that had increased the pain. To have someone you love come to help you, but only because he's a gentleman; not because that love is returned in any way. . . .

I hate trying to see through a blur of tears, but simply walking straight out the other side of the stables didn't take much clear vision. Happily no one tried to stop me or speak to me, and then I had stepped outside into the evening air. The street here was quiet, with shops closed down for the day and lamplight visible through the windows of the houses. The people who lived in those houses led quiet, normal lives, the sort of life I'd never be able to find for myself. And to tell the truth, I no longer even wanted it. What's the sense in settling down with someone you'll never feel more for than fondness? The memory of the man you loved with every fiber of your being would stand between you and any other man for your entire life, which would be completely unfair to the second man. No, better to give up thinking about never being lonely again. . . .

I stood listening to the chirp of crickets for a while, also watching the fireflies blink to each other as they bumbled through the air. There was a giant hollow inside me where a small happiness had begun to grow, a happiness I hadn't expected to become very big at all. I'd once told Jovvi that I expected Vallant to get tired of our relationship, and was ready to accept his walking away whenever it happened. I knew now that that had been a lie, that I'd been hoping with all my heart we'd stay together forever. I should have realized that I was hoping, and then I might have had a chance to cope with what was now happening. I *knew* hoping never worked, and now here I was, bleeding into the hollow inside me because I'd forgotten that very important lesson. . . .

I have no idea how long I stood in the dimness of evening, trying to pull myself together. I hadn't quite accomplished that feat when I heard something of a to-do going on inside the stables. By then I was desperate for a distraction, so I went back inside to find that people were moving around and speaking excitedly to one another. It was difficult making my way through the throng, but I managed to get to Lorand and asked what was going on.

"The guard leader, Herstan, was just finishing setting up the sentry positions we'd asked him to establish, when one of the ones he'd already posted toward the west came to report." Lorand's frown was clearly one of worry, a reflection of the expression on everyone else's face as well. "The sentry has Spirit magic, and he noticed the large number of people approaching just a matter of moments before they reached here. By the time he got to Herstan, the town was already under attack."

"Attack?" I echoed, shocked to hear the word. "But the Astindan army couldn't have gotten here *already*. It would be impossible even for an individual to move that fast, so an army couldn't possibly do it."

"I know it isn't likely to be the Astindans, but it *is* someone," Lorand returned, disturbance as clear in his voice as it was on his face. "Once we put the Blending together we should be able to find out who the someone is, or should I say someones? There are more than a few of them, and

Herstan has gone to check with his men, whom he's formed into some sort of defensive effort. They're trying to delay the attackers until we can find Jovvi and Vallant. Vallant left the stables from the other door after you went out that one, and Jovvi went out after him.''

That probably explained Rion's absence, I thought. He'd gone looking for Jovvi and Vallant Ro, and I couldn't help wondering why she'd gone after *him*. Then it came to me how difficult it must have been for Vallant Ro to force himself to talk to me, and that told me why Jovvi had gone to help *him* rather than coming to join *me*. His sense of upset must have been worse than mine, and to add to that, Jovvi had said she couldn't reach through to me. Right now I wished rather fervently that she could have, but then I remembered that wishing was very much like hoping. . . .

And then my own private problems were pushed aside by the problem we all had. Screams and shouts sounded in the distance, as though people in the middle of town were in a panic, and various people rushed into the stables. Some of those had to be guardsmen being sent with word, as one of them spoke quickly to Alsin before running out again, and then Alsin hurried over to Lorand and me.

"The attackers have formed into link groups, and our guardsmen can't do anything against them but retreat," Alsin reported at once. "Whoever they are they're stronger than the guardsmen link groups, and if it comes to a face to face fight our guardsmen will lose. The townspeople are running in a panic and getting in everyone's way, because the leading link group of the attackers is of Fire magic."

"Where can Jovvi and Vallant be?" Lorand demanded, looking completely frantic. "If Rion doesn't find them fast and bring them back here, there won't be a town left for us to defend."

"What about our own High link groups?" Alsin asked, almost as seriously concerned as Lorand. "They should be able to do a better job than those guardsmen, none of whom can be anything but a Middle at best. If we can get *them* out there—"

"We'll just have a war between our side and theirs," I interrupted, knowing I was right. "It seems to me that the better idea is to *stop* a war, not contribute our own effort to one that's started. I'll go and see what *I* can do, and as soon as Jovvi and the others get back she can form the Blending. We don't all have to be together, remember, so standing around waiting while things get worse doesn't make any sense.''

Both Lorand and Alsin tried to talk me out of going, but they were men worried about a poor, helpless little girl. I, on the other hand, was a woman worried about the coming destruction of a town, so I didn't let their silliness interfere. I left them still painting horrified word pictures about how hurt I would get, and hurried out of the stables.

The street outside was filled with pure insanity. People ran every which way as they shouted and screamed, as though they had no idea where the danger was coming from. Lorand had said it was the sentry on the western approach who had first sounded the alarm, so that had to be the direction the attack was coming from. I remembered our route into the town well enough to retrace it on foot, fighting to get through the insanity without being killed by accident, and after the first couple of streets there were fewer people in my way. That had to be because the attackers weren't very far off, something the flicker of flames suggested rather strongly.

I had to be very firm about not letting my hands tremble as I drew even nearer, and then the scene I came on made me forget all about being afraid. Anger rose as I saw a link group of guardsmen stagger back from a wide gout of flame, one which was allowed to spread to a nearby building. The gout shrank back to nothing but the building began to burn, and those who caused destruction so easily laughed as they swaggered forward. They laughed at the guard link group and they laughed at the fires burning behind them, and it was all just one jolly good time—at least for them.

For my own part, I'd gone past being angry and was well on the way to being boiling mad. I've heard it said that everyone would be a bully if they thought they could get away with it, but that doesn't happen to be true. Bullies pick on people who either can't or won't fight back, and that will never be something I'd enjoy. Intimidating the weak isn't the way to prove yourself strong, but sometimes it's all right to show off a little to people who think it is.

The fire that was beginning to get a good hold on the building to my left lit the darkness more than the lamps on poles which lined the street at intervals of twenty-five feet or so. I can't say I minded having the extra light, but it was time to make the point I'd come out here to make: this town wasn't wide open to anyone who cared to march on in. If for no other reason, Lorand wouldn't have liked it, so I reached to the flames with my talent and . . . slid around them, so to speak, protecting the wood of the building from their ravening. The flames flickered a bit in an effort to continue burning, found nothing to consume, and a moment later died out completely. That left me in a pool of shadow from which I could see those approaching, but probably couldn't be easily seen myself.

"Hey, did you see that?" one of the five coming toward me said to his friends, his voice sounding disturbed. "Our fire went out, just like that. Did one of you put it out?"

The other four voiced their denials pretty much all together, and then one of them laughed.

"I bet one of those piddling Middle groups got together and smothered it," the laughing one said. "We weren't encouraging it, after all, so they'd have had no trouble doing it. Let's start it again, and this time make sure their pitiful efforts won't do any good."

The others in his group agreed with laughter, and then they linked up and sent their considerable talent toward the building. I felt every movement and nuance of their effort, and in fact had to open to a bit more of the power to counter them. But counter them I did, keeping them from doing even so much as singeing a square inch of the building. Their efforts increased just a little, most of them straining to do it, and then the attempt died out completely.

"Something's going on," that first one said once their effort ended, his tone now faintly worried. "I don't know what it is, but I don't like it."

"The Astindans couldn't have gotten ahead of us, so it can't be anything to really worry us," the second replied, no longer laughing but not sounding as concerned as the first. "The others aren't that far behind us, and we can always go back or wait for them here. If we really have to."

"Oh, sure we can," a third put in, his voice filled with sarcasm. "And when they ask us why we didn't keep on going, we'll just say we're too shy to go into a strange town alone. They'll understand."

"Okay, let's not start to bicker," a fourth man said when the second and third began to argue. "I agree that something odd is going on, but we can't afford to stand here wasting time. The Asties aren't that far behind us, and the last thing we want is to find them catching up. Do any of you want to get rolled over the way the rest of our section was? No? Then let's get on with scaring the piss out of these townies so they'll give us what we need without argument, and then we can move on."

The other four men of the group agreed with nods or single words, ready to follow the very sensible suggestion of the one who was obviously the group's leader. But now that I knew who they were, I also knew what my next move had to be. For that reason I stepped forward just a bit, to a place not far from one of the street lamps. That let them see me, and when they did they relaxed rather than tense up even more.

"Well, will you look at that," the first, loud-mouthed one said with a small laugh of delight. "The townies have decided to try distracting us. I don't know about the rest of you, but it's starting to work with me."

"Be quiet, Gall," the one who was their leader said as the others laughed out their agreement. "Can't any of you fools tell that she's a lady of Fire? If the rest of you have forgotten what happened just a couple of minutes ago, I haven't."

"Come on, Listle, you can't be seriously suggesting that *she's* the one who kept us from burning that building," the man Gall returned with a snort of ridicule. "There are five of us and only one of her, so you have to be wrong."

"He isn't wrong," I said, and my voice was satisfactorily even. "And even beyond that, I'm in command. That means you now have to take my orders without question."

All five of them stiffened when I used the keying phrase for segments of the army, the same phrase we'd used to free our own groups of former army segments. They should have responded with immediate promises of obedience, but instead the man Listle just shook his head hard.

"No, I know that isn't true, so it isn't going to work," he said, now looking at me with hatred in his eyes. "I don't know who you are, girl, but my commander you are *not*. That particular fool is dead, so I never have to be a slave again. All right, you idiots, together with me *now*!"

And just that quickly I was under attack, defending myself from their efforts to burn me alive. There was hatred and loathing on all of their faces, obviously from whatever memories tortured them, and then their expressions were blotted out by the sheets of fire meant to consume me. Frantically I reached for more of the power, currently having only enough to keep myself untouched. The plan I'd counted on to work hadn't, and now I had to try to defeat a link group of five High talents all by myself.

The sweat that began to cover me was more the result of my efforts than of the walls of fire, and the outpouring increased as I realized that although I could hold off the five, I couldn't seem to attack in return. I had the distant impression that I *should* have been able to attack, but the knowledge I needed to do it just wasn't there. Where that left me I didn't know, but before I had the time to become more than just a little frightened—

—it was no longer just me alone. Suddenly I was part of the entity again, but this time the part that was *me* wasn't lost amid the rest. The entity's thoughts now merged with mine, bringing me the realization of how much more strength I now had to draw on. With that in view I reached out to the five who worked frantically to destroy my flesh form, and repeated what I had said just a little while ago.

"You were mistaken in what you said, for I *am* in command," I told them all in their minds, forcing the keying phrase in deep. "As you can see, you are no match for me even together. Stop your attack before you force me to retaliate—which will surely destroy you."

"I obey, I obey," the man Gall babbled, just as the others said the same. Their attack also ceased immediately, which pleased me quite a lot. To waste these flesh forms would have been a pity, as they were needed to fight on *our* side.

"Very well," I told them. "You will wait here until the

others of your section join you, and in the interim you will see to putting out the fires you started. Once you are all together again you will proceed to the stables in the middle of town, and there you will report to me and my associates. Is that clear?''

"We hear and we will obey," the five said together, now firmly under my command. Then they turned and began to see to the fires they'd started, leaving me free to . . . float in the direction from which the rest of their section was to come. My flesh form remained where it was, but *I* floated away. . . .

. . . and in a moment found the location of the rest of the section. They were only a short distance behind the group of Fire, and there were approximately seventy-five of them. All of them looked as bedraggled and shabby as the first five, and most of them were more worried and disturbed than lighthearted and carefree. It was the work of moments to visit each of their link groups and establish control over them, then order them to rejoin their Fire link and report to the stables. And then—

—and then it was me alone back again, actually more shaken than I'd been when under attack. I had no idea why the Blending had suddenly become something different, and that was bad enough. Worse was the knowledge that my groupmates were all waiting to talk to me, but possibly talk was the wrong word. They were furious that I'd put myself in a position where I really could have been hurt or killed, and once I was within screaming distance of them again. . . .

Knowing what was coming made me flinch, but short of taking off alone into the night, there was no way of getting out of it. Maybe taking off alone wasn't such a bad idea . . . at least it would probably prove safer. . . .

ELEVEN

Everyone around Jovvi was shouting and nearly frothing at the mouth, but for once she made no effort to stop it or change the mood. In point of fact she shared that mood, and possibly even led the others in being rabidly incensed.

". . . told you that that could happen, but did you listen to me?" Lorand was in the process of shouting at a flinching Tamma. "No, you did not listen, and you were nearly killed!"

"And for no reason!" Rion added his own high anger, Naran standing beside him and looking only slightly sorry for Tamma. "At the time you left here, I was already on the way back with Jovvi and Vallant. There was absolutely no reason for you to do as you did, and should it ever happen again, I'll—I'll—"

"No, *I* will," Vallant interrupted to growl, his own emotions so incredibly wild that it was a wonder he hadn't burst into flame himself. And the way he stared down at Tamma with a gaze as hard as steel. . . . "I don't care if you're the strongest Fire talent in the entire world. If I ever catch you doin' somethin' like this again, I'll put you over my knee and show you just how I feel about it!"

"And I'll help him!" Jovvi couldn't help adding in much too high a voice, her nerves still jangling over how close Tamma had come to being hurt or killed. "You're just lucky there isn't any privacy around here, or I would be helping him do it right now!"

"All right, you've all yelled at me and have hopefully gotten it out of your systems," Tamma said, finally bristling up at Vallant's threat—and Jovvi's support of it. "I know you were all worried about me, so I haven't pointed out that I wasn't in danger of being hurt—just of not being able to retaliate. And I *should* have been able to fight back, I know I should have, but there's no one around to teach us how to handle our talents properly. Why don't you direct your anger at the nobles, who are the ones who created that situation? Not to mention all the rest of this insanity . . ."

"It wasn't the nobility who sent you out there to face those five men alone," Naran pointed out without her usual hesitation when the men didn't immediately argue Tamma's statement. "And you may not have been in danger at first, but once your strength began to drain out you certainly would have been. It was a very unwise thing for you to do, Tamrissa, and I think you know it."

"Of course she does," Jovvi confirmed, still trying to calm down. "She's just too stubborn to admit it. But she's right about one thing: now that we've all had our say, we'd better get to the rest of what needs to be done. If we don't, we'll never get any sleep tonight."

"Do we have to examine *all* those segments tonight?" Rion asked, sounding more tired than annoyed. "Since we have them firmly under our control, why don't we leave the rest for tomorrow?"

"I agree with that," Lorand said, sounding just as tired. "Some of those people went along with what the others were doing simply because they had nowhere else to go and no one to go with. We can probably end up trusting that sort, but as for the others. . . . Can we take the chance of having them around even fully under control? If our enemies regain control of them, they'll fight against us as quickly as they'll fight against the Astindans or anyone else."

"If we don't keep them with us, there's only one other thing we can do with them," Jovvi pointed out when everyone else made sounds of agreement with Lorand. "We certainly can't leave them behind, to take advantage of the people of this town and any others they may come across. If you haven't thought about that part of it, I suggest you consider it now. But since you'll need *time* to consider it,

I suppose I ought to agree about putting off working with them until tomorrow.''

That idea seemed to meet with everyone's approval, and Jovvi was just as glad. Once her anger at Tamma began to fade, the rest of her strength started to flow out along with it. Leaving one of the new Blendings on guard along with the guardsmen they'd acquired would let the rest of them sleep, so that tomorrow morning they'd be able to do whatever needed doing.

"What about what happened in addition to my risking my poor little neck?" Tamma said just as everyone began to turn away. "Isn't anyone going to mention *that*? Or don't the rest of you know about it?"

"Know about what?" Jovvi asked, more than aware of the fact that Tamma wasn't making something up just to get back at them for yelling at her. "I didn't notice anything else happening."

"I really don't think it was my imagination," Tamma said when the others made sounds indicating they also had no idea what Tamma meant. "It was when we Blended. . . . I was drawn into the entity as usual, but this time it was through *my* point of view instead of the entity's. And none of you noticed that?"

"I certainly didn't," Lorand said, his tone showing his disturbance. "I also know you believe you're telling the truth, so I wonder what it means. Is it a step forward, or a step back?"

"Since the entity was still there, it can't be a step backward," Rion pointed out reasonably, a comment Jovvi happened to agree with. "I just don't see the benefit in it as a step forward."

"I can think of two possibilities," Vallant said, sounding thoughtful. "The first would be the obvious, that the entity is too . . . nonhuman for our taste at times. That may allow for distancin' it and us from what's bein' done, but that isn't necessarily a good thing. The second possibility is that at times we *need* one aspect more than the others, so this may be a way of gettin' it. If it isn't one of those two, it can be just about anythin'.''

Jovvi was about to say that that made sense, but was kept from uttering the words by a sudden flurry of activity from a newly arrived group of people. In the front of the group were Idroy Welt and Mollit Feldin, the two men who had disagreed about the news they'd been brought. They led half a dozen others who looked more than slightly upset, and when they saw the members of the Blending they made straight for them.

"You said them furriners wusn't gonna be here this soon!" Mollit Feldin shouted at them as soon as he was close enough. "Half th' town's burned, an' it's all *yer* fault!"

"You can stop that right there," Lorand countered in just as loud a voice, looking at Feldin with disgust. "Since you're the one who insisted there wasn't danger of any kind coming, you have nothing to complain about. You're just as much of a fool as you've always been, Mollit, and if you're the one leading these people, you can lead them right back out of here."

"No, Lor, he ain't leadin' nobody," Idroy Welt said quickly, giving Feldin the same sort of look. "We din't even want 'im comin' in with us, but he shoved in anyways. Just don't pay 'im no mind, but I'd be obliged if'n ya told *me*: what in the name a th' Highest Aspect *wus* all that?"

"Those people are from *our* army, and they're running away ahead of the Astindan army," Lorand explained, doing as Welt said and ignoring the now-sputtering Feldin. "Some of them aren't very nice, but we have them under control now. Nothing else will be burned because of *them*, but that doesn't mean the town will stay untouched. There have to be other groups like them, and after the groups will be the Astindan army."

"So we don't have nowhere near as much time's we thought," Welt said with a nod while his neighbors paled and muttered to each other. "Don't know 'bout nobody else, but I'm gettin' packed up t'night an' leavin' with first light. My woman's got kin somewheres in th' east, so us an' th' kids's headin' out. Your bunch gonna stick around a while longer?"

"We're also leaving in the morning," Lorand replied with a headshake, which comment silenced the people behind Welt. "We'll appreciate being able to take as much food with us as possible, as we'll be quite a few in number.

We're willing to pay for the food, and selling it to us will be better than leaving it behind to rot.''

"Ain't nobody in this here district gonna charge you nothin' fer th' food," Welt said belligerently, turning to scowl at his neighbors. "This town'd be ashes if your bunch gave back what you been gettin' frum us, so I don't wanna hear nothin' different. Ever'body's gonna bring what they can't carry 'n use themselves. Ain't that right, men?"

"We'll see t' it," one of the group said quietly, the others nodding in the same way. "We feel shamed fer th' way we follered th' babble Mollit kept spoutin', like none a us got minds t'think with. Men git stupid when they git scared, folks say, an' now *I* c'n say I know it's true. But it ain't gonna be true no more."

"Is there anyone who's willing to stop at the surrounding towns and spread the warning?" Lorand asked after nodding soberly at what the man had said. "Whoever goes may well get the same reception we did, but with pieces of the army running around ahead of the Astindans, the danger is a lot closer and more immediate than it was."

"When they sees us passin' through in smaller r' bigger groups an' not stoppin' t'argue, they oughta know it ain't no joke," Welt said after taking a deep breath. "If'n they don't, they c'n stay 'n find out like we done, th' hard way. Well . . . gotta leave now 'cause I got things t'do, so I'll jest wish ya luck wherever yer goin'. Got a feelin' ya'll need 'er. . . ."

Welt let his words trail off as he held out his hand to Lorand, and Jovvi was able to feel Lorand's disturbance as he took the hand and shook it. The other men—except for Mollit Feldin, who had stalked out of the stables a pair of moments earlier—also came forward for handshaking, and for a wonder Jovvi and Tamrissa weren't excluded. Jovvi's hand was pumped more gently, though, and then the group of men left.

"Alsin is working with the guardsmen and our own people," Lorand said after the men had gone. "He's organizing rest for those who haven't had any, and food for the new segments we just brought in. I think he also ought to be put in charge of the food that will be coming, and that's something we can use the Low level talents for: keeping the food fresh as long as possible. It won't be easy feeding almost five hundred people on the way to Gan Garee.''

''It also won't be possible to move very fast,'' Tamma pointed out. ''I think we ought to leave them all to come at whatever rate of speed they have to use, and go on ahead alone. We can use the time to . . . look around while they're catching up.''

''Whether or not that's a good idea depends on what we'll be . . . looking at,'' Rion pointed out dryly. ''It isn't likely that our enemies won't have large groups of guardsmen waiting to pounce on us, not to mention other things we won't have thought of. We won't have the strength to handle all that alone, so why, dear lady, should we put ourselves in jeopardy for no reason?''

''Rion's right,'' Vallant said, once again looking directly at Tamma—who was deliberately not returning the look. ''Headin' out alone would be foolish, and we'll be doin' enough foolish things without needin' to search for more. If we take things one step at a time, we may even live to take care of other matters once this business with our enemies is over.''

Tamma made no response to that, partly because, as Jovvi could tell, she knew that the suggestion had been less than practical. Jovvi wanted to speak to Tamma, had been wanting to since they returned to the stables, but Lorand's sudden and intense inner stiffening took her attention. When she turned to look at him she saw that he was staring toward the front of the stables, where a husky man stood partly in shadow. The man, who wasn't one of theirs, was alone, and Lorand stirred where he stood.

''It . . . looks like I have a visitor,'' he said softly to Jovvi without taking his gaze from the newcomer. ''Will you walk over there with me?''

''Of course,'' she replied at once, slipping her hand into his. Lorand was both reluctant and eager at the same time, which meant the stranger had to be his father. He'd felt the same exact things in the meeting hall, where the man had first shown up.

Lorand's fingers closed gently but firmly over hers, and then they walked together toward his father. The man actually came forward a few steps into a patch of lamplight, and when they reached him his gaze was locked to Lorand's.

"Wasn't gonna come here, but felt I hadda," the man said, sounding as unsure as his emotions showed him to be. "When you left—when I throwed you out—I knowed I wus right 'cause you wus jest gonna throw away th' life you shoulda bin usin' fer yer fam'ly. Now . . . now I c'n see you had somethin' more waitin' on you, an' I shouldn't never have—done whut I did. Jest needed t'say I'm proud a you, boy, comin' back after gettin' whut you said you wus gonna. Me an' yer Ma an' th' boys is headin' out now, 'cause I went back home soon's I heard whut you had t'say. It took half th' town burnin' t'make them fools see reason, but I knowed th' truth soon's I heard my boy say it. We's gonna be awright—thanks t'you."

Jovvi knew Lorand wanted to speak, but the lump in his throat kept him from doing it. He released Jovvi's hand to step forward as his father did the same, and the two men hugged in that half-embarrassed way men sometimes have a habit of doing. But they didn't hurry, and when they finally parted they were smiling at each other.

"Now then, boy," the elder Coll said with a hoarseness that suggested a smaller but similar lump to the one Lorand had had. "I gotta be leavin' soon, but first you gotta let me meet this here beautiful lady. You two holdin' hands fer a reason?"

"Pa, this is Dama Jovvi Hafford, the Spirit magic member of our group," Lorand said, and Jovvi had no trouble telling how carefully he chose his words. "She and I love each other, and if we happen to survive what we have ahead of us, we'll probably be married. I—wasn't going to mention that part about surviving, but I think you have a right to know. It won't be easy, but for everyone else's sake as well as our own, we have to try. A man shouldn't have to slave all his life to make profits for people who never lift a finger to help."

"Ain't thet th' truth," Coll muttered, his expression now troubled. "It also makes a man say stupid stuff, 'cause he's afeared he won't have help enough to do what he's gotta. But it ain't worth yer life, boy, not t' *my* way a thinkin'.

You watch yer back—an' this here lady's back—an' when it's all over you come home an' bring yer lady. Yer Ma'll wanna meet 'er. . . ."

The two men hugged again, and then the elder Coll turned to Jovvi for a hug. She gave him one, relieved that the big man did nothing but squeeze her carefully for a moment, and then he turned and left. He looked back once when he reached the exit, and then he was gone into the night.

"I have to admit I never expected him to do that," Lorand said softly once his father was gone from sight. "Not come here to speak to me, and not believe me so completely that he's already ready to leave. It's fairly clear that I misjudged him."

"You just didn't know what pressures he was under," Jovvi pointed out, moving closer as Lorand put his arm around her shoulders. "And he didn't understand the need driving *you*. Now the two of you see things a bit more clearly, so everything will be fine—assuming we do survive."

The only reply to that was the sigh Lorand gave, so they turned and went back toward the stalls that they would use to sleep in. They all needed sleep rather badly, because the morning would find them starting back to Gan Garee for real. And come to think of it, Jovvi decided that leaving *before* dawn might be the best idea. With all those other people who would be fleeing the town, the road would be more crowded than they would be easily able to ride through.

Jovvi voiced her own sigh, knowing she would have to pass on that idea before she could sleep. And those who stayed up arranging things while everyone else slept. . . . They would have to be given places in the food wagons so that they, too, might get some sleep once they were all on the road. There were so many things that would have to be taken care of. . . . Maybe Tamma had been right to suggest that leaving everyone else behind would be the best idea. But no, that just wasn't practical. There might be a practical compromise, but Jovvi was too tired to think about it. Tomorrow . . . tomorrow would have to be soon enough. . . .

TWELVE

"That was really very delightful," Kambil heard Selendi say as they all took chairs in Kambil's private meeting room. "I feel less tired now than I did before we began."

"It was more than just delightful," Bron said in partial agreement after sipping at the tea he'd taken. "It added to my strength in a way I never thought was possible. It's really a lucky thing you found that journal, Kambil."

"And I, for one, would like to know what else it contained," Homin said, also looking fully satisfied. "If the rest is anything like drawing from link groups, we all need to know about it."

"And you all *will* know," Kambil said with strong approval for their enthusiasm. "Drawing strength from link groups is only the first, most all-around useful trick I discovered, and easily explains how our adversaries overcame all those guardsmen we sent against them. Once they freed those first segments from the caravan, they had *their* strength to call on."

"But the caravan contained strong Middles and Highs," Homin pointed out, now faintly disturbed. "We used members of our palace guard, who are mostly Lows with a few ordinary Middles. If we gained so much by drawing on low grade link groups, how much more are our adversaries gaining?"

"Actually . . . not as much as we did," Kambil said, breaking the news to them with a grin. "The journal spoke about using single link-groups, and said that that wasn't as effective as using link groups arranged in tandem, the way ours were. When you hook in a second group after the first, you get more than double the strength from the arrangement. But you have to know the proper way to hook them in, or you get a jumble instead of additional strength. Unless our adversaries have read the journal—which I strongly doubt—they don't know about that particular trick.''

"What a shame!'' Bron crowed out with a laugh, Selendi and Homin joining him in his amusement. "They don't know about the trick, so they can't use it. What else aren't they likely to know about?''

"Well, there's the matter of how vulnerable our bodies are when we're Blended,'' Kambil said after sipping at his own tea. "I discovered more than one way around that problem, and the first is relatively simple. Instead of stopping at a distance from where we want to be and sending our entity out ahead, we move ourselves in close and let our entity stand guard over our bodies. That way nothing can get past it to harm us.''

"That's so obvious, we should have seen it ourselves,'' Homin said after blinking in surprise. "It goes against our instincts to stay out of harm's way, though, so that's probably why we missed it. But can't our link groups protect us, as well as feeding us additional strength?''

"That's another simple way, but not the best,'' Kambil agreed with a nod. "If we use our link groups as buffers between us and any danger and something happens to them, we also lose our extra strength. After thinking about it I believe I prefer a different way, the way suggested by the writer of the journal. He said that once we practice a bit with the tandem link groups, we'll discover that we can . . . *project* an image of ourselves in a place other than where we are. Our enemies can fight like madmen to reach our poor, vulnerable bodies with the intention of destroying them, but it won't do them any good. They'll have reached an illusion, and we'll be somewhere else entirely.''

The others laughed aloud again, the idea as enjoyable to them as it was to him. But there were other things they needed to discuss, so the laughter would have to wait until later.

"I've ordered a celebratory meal for tonight, so let's save

any further discussion of this topic until then," Kambil said, causing the mirth to wind down and dissipate. "Right now I'd like to hear about the chores I've assigned to you, a report on the progress—or lack thereof—that you've made. Bron, will you begin?"

"Certainly," Bron agreed, sober again. "The army in Gracely has been recalled, which at first annoyed its commanders no end. They were making more than adequate progress, with little or no opposition. I made sure that they weren't told about how strong the Astindan army is supposed to be, just that they would be a punitive expedition sent to assist our forces—who aren't being capably led. I think they began to preen when they heard they were to punish the leaders of *our* force as well as the upstart members of the Astindan force. That secretary was right when he said the commanders of the Gracely force felt slighted and insulted that they hadn't been given commands in Astinda. They've already crossed the border back into the empire, and they're marching directly west."

"Good," Kambil said with a smile of approval. "I knew we'd find *some* secretaries and assistants who knew what they were doing. Just make sure that that army is adequately supplied, otherwise they might begin to live off the countryside. That sort of thing is fine in someone else's country, but if we allow it to happen here we'll have delegations of our former peers screaming for blood. And don't forget that some of the countryside they'll be passing through now belongs to *us*. What about the last guard expedition sent West?"

"That's something *I* was looking into," Homin said, his expression and the disturbance in his emotions telling Kambil most of the story. "They stopped communicating with us as abruptly as all the others, but this time there were independent watchers sent secretly after them. The watchers reported that instead of being destroyed, they've been . . . taken over in some way by our adversaries and are now working only for them. And that town they're all in was attacked, but not by Astindan forces. The attackers were former members of our own army, without commanders and therefore uncontrolled. Our adversaries gained control over them as well, and ended the attack almost before it began. Now all the townspeople and farmers are getting ready to run away, obviously wanting to be gone before any other attackers appear.''

"Chaos take them!" Kambil growled, more than simply annoyed. "We needed the shipments of food they would have sent right up to the time the Astindan forces appeared, and now we'll have to do without them. If those interfering fools hadn't stopped to warn them. . . . Make sure that the new Advisor in charge of the farms in that area is made aware of the situation, so he can coordinate provisioning Gan Garee from other areas. And tell someone to keep an eye open in case an opportunity to punish those farmers comes along. If we let them get away with leaving their farms—for any reason—then others of the peasants will try to do the same. Who's next?"

"I am," Selendi replied, her thoughts even more annoyed than they had been. "I've been receiving reports from Rimen Howser on that matter of hostages against the adversaries, and he's really done an incredible job. In addition to that gardener he showed us who's supposed to be a good friend of the Earth magic user, the parents of the Fire magic user, and the fiancée of the Water magic user and *her* parents, he now also has the former sponsor of the Spirit magic user. The sponsor had been sent to one of the deep mines because of an attempt to kidnap the Spirit magic user, but Rimen brought her back here anyway. The Spirit magic user was supposed to have been really broken up at the sentence given her former sponsor, and now can be expected to feel all sorts of guilt—especially when she sees what the mines have done to the woman."

"And we have the mother of the Air magic user, in the person of Lady Hallina Mardimil," Kambil said with a certain amount of brightening. "Yes, Lord Rimen *has* done a good job, which we'll certainly have to reward him for. Or has he already begun to receive part of his reward?"

"I've given him the first part," Selendi said with a shrug that was nevertheless filled with satisfaction. "The rest of it, naming him a High Lord, is for you to do. I'm sure you know that that's what he's after, and it isn't his fault that Lady Hallina is not in the best condition possible. She *is* still alive, although she's making the most awful fuss.

You'd think that what happened to her was something to get upset about."

"Something happened to her?" Kambil asked, his interest piqued. "What a terrible, awful shame. Was it something painful, I hope?"

"*She* claims so," Selendi replied with a sniff of disdain, and then she grinned. "She went to the Glowflower Inn, that place that caters to those with . . . different tastes in entertainment, and ended up getting raped by three men. She refuses to say why she was there or how she came to be in the rooms the three men took, but has demanded of the guard that the three be found and arrested and executed. She took to her bed immediately and has had a physician in attendance, but no one is taking her wailing seriously. She's always wailing about *something*, and after all, how serious can it be? It was only three men, for pity's sake."

"Have they found any trace of the men?" Kambil asked, more amused by Selendi's reactions than by the story. Despite all the adjustments he'd made in her personality, Selendi would have enjoyed being the one who had had that . . . experience with the three men. She'd probably never admit it aloud unless ordered to, but her emotions made the matter perfectly clear to Kambil.

"No, the men have apparently disappeared off the face of the world," Selendi replied. "And they wore masks, so even Lady Hallina can't give a full description of them. Of course, she *should* be able to tell everyone what their bodies were like, and then the guard could go around making the peasants strip down for inspection."

Everyone laughed at that, everyone, that is, except for Delin. He sat in his place as silent and fumingly angry as ever, a good sign as far as Kambil was concerned. He'd been afraid Delin's mind would begin to crumble to uselessness, but so far it hadn't. If only he, Kambil, could have some luck in finding another High talent in Earth magic, he'd never have to waste time thinking about Delin again. . . .

"But there *is* some bad news," Selendi added, quieting the laughter. "Lord Grall Razas, that man you had such high hopes for us to make use of, is dead. He died at night, I was told, and when a physician was summoned the next morning by Lord Grall's staff, it was far too late to do anything for him. They think it must have been a seizure of some kind, as there wasn't the least indication of foul play."

"Are they absolutely sure?" Kambil asked, once again back to being extremely displeased. "With the former Lady Eltrina in the same house, how can they be so certain?"

"They're certain partially because she *wasn't* in the house," Selendi replied at once with a headshake. "She must have charmed or paid someone on the staff to free her from the chains Lord Grall had her locked up in, and as soon as she was free she disappeared from the house. Investigation showed that she went to an inn she'd frequented many times before, easily producing the gold to pay for her accommodations. She also seemed to be . . . under the weather, the investigators were told, as she asked for and got two of the inn's ladies' maids to sit with her all night. The maids reported that her sleep was interrupted with moans of pain and various nightmares causing her to cry out, but she never left the rooms."

"So she couldn't have gone back and somehow murdered him," Kambil grumbled, knowing any investigator would have Spirit magic enough to be aware of when he was being lied to. If the maids' story was accepted, then they hadn't been lying. "But I think I know where she got the gold to pay for her night's stay. It's probable that Lord Grall neglected to speak to his bank about cutting her off, so they gave her whatever amount she asked for. Well, have her arrested and returned to that house in chains again, this time under the care of someone *I'll* appoint. I don't want her to be running around loose—"

"Kambil, I've already tried that," Selendi interrupted, now looking and feeling annoyed. "I knew you didn't want her free so I sent a contingent of guardsmen to arrest her, but she'd already left the inn. That was after the management told her her husband was dead, and she did go back to the house. But she stayed only long enough to have some of her clothing and belongings packed, and then she left again. Where she is now, no one seems to know."

"I'll give you odds that wherever it is, she stopped at the bank again on the way," Kambil growled, beginning to be really furious. "If Grall never bothered to cut her off from his funds, it's certain that he also never went through the process of disinheriting her. Since they never had any children, she's now his sole heir and entitled to do as she pleases with his gold and property. What she most likely pleased was to carry away as much gold as she could conveniently handle."

"You have to admit it took nerve if she did that," Homin said, his chuckle showing how impressed he was with that sort of behavior. "She must have known she was in danger of being arrested again otherwise she never would have disappeared, and yet she stopped on the way to complete freedom to collect her belongings and pick up spending money. We could make good use of audacity like that, especially if we make it clear that serving us loyally will let her keep Grall's estate."

"But I don't *want* her to keep Grall's estate," Kambil said slowly and clearly, so that Homin would have no doubts about how he felt. "Grall and his multitude of connections would have been of much more use to us, and I seriously doubt if that Eltrina piece could ever be trusted. She won't inherit his business ability and his lines into all those closed groups even *we* don't have access to, so what good would she be to us? Brazen, mindless nerve can be found anywhere, so I want the guard to be on the alert for her. And when she's found, I want her brought here, to the palace, not put in another place she'll have no trouble getting out of."

Selendi nodded to show that she'd take care of it, both she and Bron ignoring the way Homin now tried to pretend that he'd never said anything to anger Kambil. If Homin had known women a bit better, he'd never have suggested anything that ludicrous to begin with. . . .

"And, finally, we come to Embisson Ruhl," Selendi said as though there hadn't been any interruptions. "The man is slowly mending, or at least his body is. I'm told that his mind is rather shaky now that he's no longer even an ordinary lord, not to mention a High Lord. He's suffering just the way you want him to, and his son has been visiting him more and more often, in an attempt to get him to pull out of his funk. Dom Ruhl, however, has been resisting all attempts, and it's been suggested that he may eventually even turn to suicide.''

"Good," Kambil pronounced, leaning back in his chair. "If he does kill himself, make sure I hear about it right away. I'm thinking about having his body hung up in front of the palace, to show people what happens to those who work against our best interests. It's time we—Yes, what is it?''

That last was for the servant who had knocked quietly and then entered the room, one of Kambil's trusted servants. The man was completely under control, of course, which was why he was so trusted. And he also knew better than to interrupt a meeting of the Five without good reason. . . .

"Excellence, please excuse the interruption, but a note sent by your father has been delivered," the man said with a bow, holding up an envelope. "The servant delivering it said it was most urgent.''

"All right, bring it here," Kambil directed, wondering what his father could want. Nothing of importance was going on which would involve *him*, so what could be so urgent? The envelope was brought over to Kambil and he opened it at once, and then he nearly fell unconscious after reading those terrible words. The room swirled around and around and voices sounded from very far off, and then it was Bron, Selendi, and Homin who were clustered around his chair and speaking all at once.

"Kambil, what's wrong?" Bron's voice broke through the others, worry making it sharp. "You almost went off the chair and onto the floor! What does the letter say?''

"It . . . it says that . . . that Grami is . . . is dead," Kambil forced out, not believing the words even as he spoke them, the room still turning a bit. "It can't be. . . . It isn't true. . . . I know it isn't. . . . I have to go home. . . .''

"Of course you do," Homin said, his tone and mind filled with sympathetic understanding. "We'll send for your private guard, and they'll take you home. Do you want the rest of us to go with you?''

"No . . . no . . .'' Kambil said, pushing them out of his way so that he could get to his feet. He swayed unsteadily for a moment, and then his servant had taken his arm to support him, which let him stumble toward the door. He wanted nothing of the presence of his groupmates, they who were such . . . blatant tributes to Grami's work. Just in case it was true . . . which it couldn't be, please, don't let it be. . . .

THIRTEEN

High Lord Embisson Ruhl—still a High Lord despite the attempted actions of rude young interlopers—sat in his study all alone. He wore the shabbiest clothing he had, and spoke little or not at all to his household staff. Everyone professed to be deeply concerned about his "depression," a part of the plan which was his own contribution. He knew well enough that he was being watched, and common sense dictated that he give the watchers something other than planning and machinations to observe. A cup of cooling tea sat on a table near his elbow, but his slumped posture changed not at all until Edmin was shown in and the door closed behind him.

"Please, Father, you really must pull out of this," Edmin said in a fairly loud voice, to satisfy the ear which was certainly at the door. "If you don't, you'll surely make yourself ill."

Embisson said nothing to that, as should have been expected, and a moment later Edmin turned his attention from the door and nodded.

"He's gone now," Edmin said in his usual, sober way. "Off to tell whomever he tells that nothing seems to have changed. How are you really feeling, Father?"

"Quite well, actually," Embisson replied as he stood and took the opportunity to stretch. "The main drawback of this charade is the way I must slouch around, ruining my back. Let me get you a cup of tea while you tell me what brings you here at this unscheduled time."

"I came to tell you that our plans for tonight have to be delayed," Edmin replied, causing Embisson to stop short on the way to the tea service. "That celebration dinner the Five had planned for tonight has been canceled."

"They became suspicious?" Embisson asked sharply, the first reason for such a disappointment to come to him. "How could that possibly have happened?"

"It wasn't suspicion," Edmin hastily soothed him, one hand held up. "It seems that Arstin received word of his grandmother's passing, and he hurried to his father's house to join the man in grieving. Quite a few people are grieving, as the woman was a renowned poet."

"The woman was too . . . smooth for my tastes," Embisson said, no longer alarmed as he returned his attention to the tea service. "And her poetry seemed to mock people and life rather than describe them. So now we must wait, but hopefully not too long. Do you think the man will grieve more than the single day?"

"Arstin was apparently quite attached to the old lady, so there's no telling," Edmin replied, coming forward to take the cup of tea Embisson had poured. "A forced wait such as this frustrates, I know, but our plans are merely delayed, not destroyed. As soon as Arstin returns to his place among the rest of the Five, those plans will go forward again. In the interim, I have the latest on Lady Hallina."

"Ah, yes, I did mean to ask," Embisson said at once, if not distracted then at least diverted. "How *is* the dear, sweet lady?"

"Not too well, I'm afraid," Edmin said with the faint smile which indicated his strong amusement. "I'm told she continues to remain abed, wailing loudly in pain, ceasing only when demanding that the guard find the blackguards and hang them. She seems to have no idea of what they'll be able to tell the guard if they're caught, something she should be extremely aware of."

"She would need to have a mind to be aware of that,

and she most certainly does not," Embisson reminded him, gesturing Edmin to a seat while he returned to his own. "Acting without thought of the consequences is something she has always done, which is why she finds herself in this fix to begin with. Has she any idea that it wasn't the actions of those three alone which brought her to this pass? Is she at all close to learning the truth?"

"She believes she has already found the truth," Edmin said after settling himself and sipping at his tea. "That agent of hers, the one she believed set up the interview and the one we had begun to use for our own purposes, had a terrible accident a short while ago. The guard initially believed that it *was* an accident which took his life, but one of my people disabused them of that notion—anonymously, of course. They now seek the man who was named to them, and once they find the cutthroat they will also find who paid him to do the deed. The lady may soon learn that ignoring consequences is the pastime of a fool."

"No, she'll never learn that," Embisson said with all the satisfaction he felt. "Her whims have been indulged her entire life, and she'll go to her own execution still outraged that someone would dare to cross her. And they'll *have* to execute her, if only as an example to teach others to be more circumspect if they decide to indulge in premeditated murder. Once she's been condemned then *I* mean to step forward, letting her know the truth for the short time remaining to her. She'll have no opportunity to do anything about it, and the knowledge will be excrutiatingly painful."

"I wager she'll be no more than outraged, and will probably appeal to the court," Edmin said with the same quiet smile. "Her stance will be that she had the wrong man killed, and therefore she should not be punished for it. I really do hope to be there to see that."

"Hopefully we'll both be there," Embisson said, his mood darkening again. "If our plans go the way we hope they will, we should also be in a much better position politically. Those five upstarts must also be taught a lesson, which is that it was *others* who placed them on the Fivefold Throne. Most of those others are now dead, and not a single man I know doubts that the upstarts are responsible for every death. Some of the fools are going out of their way to placate the interlopers, hoping to be ignored the next time a bloodletting is in the offing. The rest are meeting quietly in shadowy places, desperate for a plan to remove the uncontrolled danger. Have you looked about as I suggested?''

"Yes, certainly, and you're quite correct," Edmin confirmed. ''Once we have the place our plans will achieve for us, we will only need to step forward and claim the leadership of those groups. They will be more than happy to follow our lead, and by the way, it's possible you may be able to add one more name to the list of those the Five have done away with. Lord Grall Razas, who established the most powerful of those groups, was suddenly found dead. It's being said that the tightrope he walked, pretending to serve the Five while working for their downfall, finally plunged him to his death.''

"That's really too bad," Embisson said with a frown. ''I knew Grall well, and he was most effective at making people believe he supported whatever stance *they* supported. But the upstarts aren't ordinary people, and he must have misjudged—''

Embisson fell silent at once at Edmin's sudden, sharp gesture, knowing immediately what it meant. Someone was approaching the room they sat in, and it would certainly not do for him to be speaking and acting normally. For that reason he slumped again in his chair, staring down at the carpeting, and Edmin began to speak coaxingly, as though he'd been doing the same all along. A brief moment later there was a knock on the door, and Edmin was the one who called out permission to enter.

"Please pardon the interruption, my lord," the servant said from the doorway. ''There is a lady here who demands to see High Lord Embisson, but one who refuses to give her name. Shall I send her away, or—''

"No, I'll see her," Edmin said, decision clear in his voice. ''If she needs to be sent away, I'll see to the matter myself.''

"As you wish, my lord," the servant said with a bow, and then the man stepped aside to allow a cloaked figure into the room. The figure was clearly a woman's, and Embisson saw, out of the corner of his eye, that her hood was drawn down to shadow her face. He was intensely curious about who she was, but not to the point of being willing to abandon his pose.

"And now, Dama, you will kindly remove that hood," Edmin said to her once the door was closed again. "And then you may have five minutes to speak of your reason for being here. If the reason lacks importance, you will then be ejected."

"My reason for being here lacks importance for neither of us, Lord Edmin," the woman replied, reaching to the hood. "We have mutual enemies, your father and I, and I don't mind speaking of the matter in your presence. I've heard that your father is succumbing to depression over the way he's been treated and I can't blame him, but I've come to tell him not to despair. There *has* to be a way to overcome those vermin, and together he and I shall find it."

"Lady Eltrina, you surprise me," Edmin said when the woman's face was revealed, and he did indeed sound surprised to Embisson. "I'd heard that there were some ... difficulties between you and Lord Grall, brought about by some matter having to do with the Five. Have the difficulties ended because of your husband's death?"

"Hardly," Eltrina returned with a sniff, moving toward the chair Edmin indicated she could take. "Because of those five vermin I found it necessary to escape from my own house as though I ran from a prison. I was rather ill during the following night, and when I awoke I was told that Grall was dead. So I returned to my house to collect some of my things, visited the bank, and then found a place of refuge. The vermin are hardly likely to stand by and simply watch me inherit Grall's estate, not when my ... difficulty was at their instigation to begin with. You see that I speak frankly to you, and have also placed my freedom in your hands. If you were to hold me here and call the guard, there would undoubtedly be a reward from the vermin themselves."

"Undoubtedly," Edmin agreed with a sober nod as he studied her. "However, I feel I must point out that if you were promised your inheritance in return for ... enticing innocent people into a plot against the Seated heads of our empire, you would say the same words and behave in precisely the same way. For that reason, as well as the fact that those of us in this household are loyal and without treasonous notions, I really must ask you to leave. In deference to your being a woman and an acquaintance of long standing, I'll delay informing the guard until you've had a chance to leave the area.''

"You can't turn me away!" Eltrina protested, disturbance now visible even to Embisson in the depth of her eyes. "I'm not here working for *them*, I would *never* work for *them*! Don't you know what Grall did to me because *they* were so terrified? It was considerably worse than what was done to your father, even though it was for the same reason.''

"Really, Lady Eltrina, I would love to continue this discussion but find it discomforting in the extreme," Edmin said, his expression unchanged. "I have no idea what you're referring to, and what's more don't *want* to know. You—''

"Oh, but you do know, unless your father keeps secrets from you, which I don't think he does," Eltrina interrupted intensely. "I was there at the final competition, just as he was, and I know—just as he does—that our vaunted leaders were about to *lose* the competition to the peasants. Their Blending was stronger than our wonderful Seated Five's, and if not for the help the vermin were given they would now be sitting in their various homes, nursing their wounds. I'm a witness to the way the peasants were betrayed, and unless I can find another way to get even with those vermin, I'm ready to spread that story far and wide. You were at least entitled to a warning, and now that you have it I'll be glad to go.''

"Wait," Edmin said as she rose to her feet, her hands already reaching to her hood. "If that story gets around, none of us will be safe from the rioting it will cause. Nobles will be attacked simply because they're nobles, and you yourself will not be exempted. I'm able to tell that you're sincere in what you say, and for that reason I advise you—''

"Sincere!" she echoed, staring down at him with chest heaving and eyes blazing. "I'm not sincere, I'm rabid! Do you have any idea what I was put through because of those sickening little freaks? I want to see them utterly destroyed, and if I must be destroyed along with them, then so be it. If they get their hands on me again my life is over anyway, so what's the difference? This way it's more likely to be a quick end than the slow one *they* would provide. You and your father were my last hope for finding a different way to exact my revenge, but now I realize that there's no way for me to convince you of my . . . sincerity. Good day, Lord Edmin, and good luck. . . .''

"Lady Eltrina," Embisson said as the woman reached to her hood again, once more straightening in his chair. "You have convinced *me* of your sincerity, therefore I will admit you to the knowledge of my little charade. Deception rather than depression is what obsesses me these days, and I ask you not to put your own plan into effect until all hope of formulating a more efficient plan is gone. Will you agree to that?"

"Gladly," the woman said at once, her eyes lighting with formerly lost hope. "And I'm delighted to see that you're your old self again, Lord Embisson. It was shattering to believe that those vermin had beaten you down so low."

"When your enemy considers you helpless, they may even go so far as to turn their back on you," Embisson pointed out, paraphrasing an old saying. "When it comes to my enemies, I have no compunction against using a back as my target. Would you care for a cup of tea, Lady Eltrina?"

"Thank you, no," she replied, also not resuming her seat. "I must be on my way very shortly, else whatever spies the vermin have in your household will certainly take note. Tell me quickly what you mean to do, and how I can be of help."

"At the moment, we are nearly done with gathering information," Embisson told her smoothly, meeting the intensity of her gaze with calm. "Knowledge is power, after all, and once we have all the data we need, we will then be prepared to formulate a workable plan. Are you completely dedicated to being a part of that plan? If we're discovered before we can put it into effect, our end will be as horrible as our enemies can make it."

"I'm prepared to take that risk," Eltrina replied, her chin

rising with the challenge. "And if you should happen to need gold to make the thing workable, let me know at once. Grall's account at the bank was extremely full, and my expenses these days are minimal. How soon will it be possible for me to return? How soon do you expect to have all the data you'll need?"

"We'll have it in two days at most, so return here then," Embisson replied. "But first I must ask: how safely are you hidden? If you should be taken by the guard now, we could well be taken up right after you."

"I'm in a place where no one will find me, so don't worry about that," she said, this time completing the action of replacing her hood. "And as for betraying you if I'm taken, that, too, has been considered and planned for. If they find me, only I will suffer. But I don't intend to be found, so I'll be back in two days."

"You'll forgive me for not rising," Embisson said, in fact returning himself to the slumped position he'd been using so often of late. "And as far as anyone is concerned, we never spoke."

"Lord Edmin, I do hope that your father will soon be feeling well enough to be himself again," Eltrina said, no longer even looking in Embisson's direction. "I'll return to find out if he is, and until then I bid you a good day."

Edmin nodded to acknowledge the wish, then saw the woman to the door. The servant who had brought her waited a short way up the corridor, and when Eltrina was escorted away toward the front door, Edmin closed the door to the room and returned to his father.

"I hope your actions were wise, Father," Edmin said, his expression faintly troubled. "I'll admit that the woman wasn't pretending to feel what she wasn't, and yet to allow her into our secret. . . ."

"Into only one of our secrets," Embisson pointed out as he straightened again. "And that much was necessary, to keep her from doing what she threatened to. I'm of two minds about her, Edmin, and must think a while before I decide which road to take. She could well be extremely valuable to us, and yet I know from past experience that the woman isn't to be trusted. Her ambitions are far too exalted for a female."

"Her current ambitions run the same course as our own," Edmin said as he resumed his seat. "I believe I'll look into her story in the next day or two, and whatever I find out should help you to make up your mind about her. My own opinion is valueless, as I merely knew her to nod to. Perhaps, in two days when she returns, you may have decided to let her in on our other secrets."

"Perhaps, in two days when she returns," Embisson corrected slowly, "we may be fortunate enough to have something of true interest to share with her. If our plans go properly, and if she proves to be what she claims. . . . It would be pleasant to have allies again. . . ."

Ruthless allies, Embisson finished in his own thoughts. Edmin was one such and certainly the best, but there was always strength in numbers. And even if their plans went perfectly, they would still require as many allies as they could find. . . .

At least until they had the upstarts firmly under their control. After that their allies could be put into the position of followers and servants, where they would more properly belong. . . .

FOURTEEN

Lady Hallina Mardimil jumped at the sound of her bed-chamber door opening, but it was just one of her serving girls. She'd become a nervous wreck ever since that ghastly experience at that so-called respectable inn, and having paid back the fool who was responsible for her going there hadn't helped in the least. The fool was dead, but *she* still shivered in bed, jumping at the least sound.

"Excuse the interruption, my lady, but the physician is here to see you," the serving girl said, her expression one of deep concern. "May I show her in?"

"It's a waste of time, but go ahead," Hallina muttered, not at all pleased. Anyone would have thought that another woman would have understood exactly how much she was suffering, but that fool of a physician. . . . She'd tended Hallina's bodily hurts and claimed to have gone a good distance toward healing them, and hadn't believed Hallina's denial of that. She was in *pain* for chaos's sake, and words telling her she couldn't be weren't of any help at all.

"I understand that you refuse to leave your bed," the physician, Lady Sislin, said as soon as she entered the room. "That isn't good for you, Hallina, and I must insist that you rise and go back to your usual life."

Sislin, an older woman who had grown to be a bit bent over, looked more like a crone than a powerful noble who enjoyed dabbling in other peoples' lives. Hallina stirred at what she'd said, but that was as far as she was prepared to go.

"I can't rise as long as I'm still in pain," Hallina said clearly, staring at the older woman. "You've done something wrong, Sislin, and now you're trying to cover it up by saying I'm imagining things. If you can't stop the pain *this* time, I'm going to call another physician."

"Another *dozen* physicians will tell you the same thing I have," Sislin countered, looking not the least unsure as she stopped beside the bed. "It's the *memory* of the experience that continues to give you pain, not the injury itself. If you rise and resume your normal life, the memory will fade and so will the pain of it. As long as you remain lying there, it has little chance to fade."

"You sound as though you know exactly what I've gone through," Hallina said bitterly, aware of the undertone of dismissal in the other woman's voice. "You don't know, Sislin, can't know unless you've had the same thing done to *you*. Have you had that experience, that you now presume to give me advice?"

"My husband indulged in that sort of thing all the time,"

was the surprising reply, this time spoken stiffly. "And yes, I was beaten as well, so I do know what you're going through. You're doing what I did at first, weeping helplessly and asking why it had to have happened to you. Your poor little pride is shattered, and all you can do is snivel."

"And you think there's something else to do?" Hallina demanded, but shock dulled the edge of her words. Sislin, having the same thing done to *her* . . . ?

"Of course there's something else to do," the woman said, ignoring the chair which had been drawn up beside the bed for her. "You figure out exactly who is responsible for what you've been made to go through—and that one *isn't* you—and then you take steps to see that it never happens again. Once that's been done, the memories fade and you're able to live again."

About to protest that she'd already done exactly that, Hallina stopped herself with an unsettling thought. Her agent Relsin may have been immediately responsible, but the ultimate reason the entire problem began was what that ingrate of a son of hers had caused to happen. If not for him, she never would have been put in the position of having to look for those who would get her own back from those disgusting children on the Throne. . . .

"The one who is responsible, yes," Hallina murmured, finally seeing the truth. "Take care of *that* one, and you never have to worry again. But what do you do if that one is out of reach? How can you stop the nightmares if you can't get to the one who is ultimately responsible for them?"

"You wait until that one *is* in reach," Sislin said very simply, giving Hallina a glimpse of horribly determined patience. "When that happens you strike, and the waiting time can be used to make very sure that your strike will find its proper mark. Leave nothing to chance, and then chance cannot betray you."

"No, only people betray you," Hallina said with a slow nod, now understanding exactly what she must do. "To give them another chance at betrayal would be foolish, so you give nothing of the sort. Yes, I believe I *will* get up now."

Sislin smiled her approval and turned away to summon

one of Hallina's girls to assist her, but Hallina needed no help. She did still suffer from twinges of pain, but now she no longer wanted them gone. They were a reminder of the betrayal she'd suffered—and a goad to make very sure that the betrayer failed to live long enough to betray her again. . . .

Delin Moord sat in his chair with no expression on his face, but his mind writhed with hatred and a desire for freedom. Those feelings were pure camouflage, of course, as he actually had all the freedom he needed at the moment. Freedom enough to do what needed to be done, at times when no one knew they were being done by *him*. . . .

"Kambil, are you sure you're really in the mood for this?" Homin asked the one Delin hated the most. "It was only yesterday that your grandmother died, after all . . ."

"Grami would have been the first to say that life goes on," Kambil replied, obviously forcing himself to that philosophical outlook. "And we've earned a celebration, so there's no real reason not to have it."

The others made sounds of support and gratitude, something Delin was glad not to have to join in. They all sat at a relatively small table for dinner in Kambil's wing of the palace, a table meant to be used by the Five together with no one else joining them. For the first time since Delin had met him, Kambil looked less than totally sure of himself. That could well be because he no longer had his partner in control, his beloved grandmother.

Delin had taken very great pleasure in bringing about a stroke in her, which had left her aware of her condition but helpless to do anything to change it. She'd actually tried to reach him with her Spirit magic, to control him the way she and her grandson controlled the others of the Five, but the stroke hadn't allowed her to do that. As an Earth magic user, Delin had known that a stroke would rob the old woman of her ability, and he'd taken great pleasure standing in her bedchamber and laughing at her. Then he'd arranged for the second, fatal stroke to hit after a number of hours, and he'd left to return to the palace.

And there had been nothing of blackouts, nothing of anyone else doing the deed. Delin felt the deep-down pleasure of that, of knowing he was truly free of all interference.

When the proper time came he would tell Kambil all about it, laughing while he described the old woman's frustration over her helplessness. When she felt his second touch she must have known she was going to die, but not knowing when—or if she would manage to alert someone to her plight—would have added to her torture. She could have been saved—if a good physician had been called soon enough. She must have struggled to the very end to get someone's attention in that household of sleeping people. . . .

The servants began to bring in the food then, and Delin's mouth watered with the aroma of it. Kambil's cook was even better than his own, and Delin hadn't had real food to eat since that one time after he'd been freed by the servant woman. He would have preferred being nowhere near the other four of his group, but for a real, true meal. . . .

"Oh, that's to be given to Lord Delin," Kambil's voice came, and Delin looked up to see that he spoke to a servant who carried a large bowl of something. "Lord Delin has taken some sort of vow, so he won't be joining the rest of us in what *we're* eating."

As soon as Delin had seen the bowl, he'd known what Kambil was up to. The bowl would contain the gruel he'd been forced to eat all along, but this time he would also be forced to watch the others feast as he choked it down. Hatred for Kambil flared in Delin's mind, and Kambil smiled to show that he was fully aware of it. The others chuckled quietly to indicate their own awareness, but no one said anything else.

Delin was lost to seething fury for a while, which carried him to a land of bright red blood and severed bodily parts. When he finally returned it was to see the others well begun on their meal, and his own fare beginning to turn cold. For that reason he reluctantly turned his attention to it—but stopped abruptly in the midst of reaching for a spoon. There was something about the gruel which felt different and wrong, and all thoughts of hunger departed as he gave his full attention to discovering what that was. Kambil couldn't have known what he'd done, but that didn't mean the fool wasn't up to *something*. . . .

It took Delin a surprising number of minutes to discover

just what was different and wrong. If he hadn't been so completely familiar with the gruel's composition he might well have missed the first signs of difference, even though the dish was basically pure and simple. The . . . addition to it was so subtle that Delin wasn't able to figure out exactly what it was, but it certainly had nothing to do with Puredan. And after a moment, when it occurred to him to check the dishes the other four were consuming with such gusto, he was only just able to notice the same substance. If he hadn't had the gruel as an example to use, he never would have been able to see anything in the food at all.

Well. Delin slumped back in his chair, pretending to brood while he thought furiously behind his facade of safety. It was fairly obvious that someone had put something into all their food, but just what that something might be was the most pressing question. The second question, of course, was what to do about it, aside from not ingesting any of it himself. If it was a poison it was already too late for the others, seeing how much of the food they'd already eaten. Even he was able to see nothing of it in their systems, which meant that no physician would be able to neutralize it to save them.

So saying anything about the substance would achieve nothing but letting his enemies know that he was no longer under their control. Delin's lifelong habits refused to let him do that, even if the other four would soon be dead. But there was nothing to say for certain that they *would* be dead, so the habit of silence remained strong and unbreached. His only option seemed to be to sit and watch and wait, letting the passage of time determine what would or would not happen to his groupmates.

The others spent the rest of the meal stuffing their faces, chatting to one another and undoubtedly enjoying themselves even more at the knowledge that someone at the table had been denied the enjoyment of joining them. When they finally sat back, replete satisfaction clear in all their faces, Kambil looked over at him.

"Oh, Delin, what a pity," the man drawled, looking at him as someone else might look at an insect. "You've apparently lost your appetite, as you haven't even touched your meal. Well, don't fret about it. The next time we have

something to celebrate, I'm sure you'll join us completely—
by eating your own fare. You can't very well earn a pardon
with good behavior, after all, since your behavior isn't your
own choice. And since the rest of us are ready to leave the
table, you may be excused to return to your own wing.''

Delin rose immediately to his feet with an inner growl,
hating the way he'd been sent to his rooms like a small,
naughty child. He let the hatred carry him out of the dining
area and into the corridor, and then all the way back to his
small, single room. Even once there he gloated only beneath the raging anger, and then sat down to wonder what
was in store for the four who had laughed so well as he'd
left their presence. Hopefully it would be painful rather than
fatal, and then *he* would take his turn to laugh. . . .

He'd already undressed and lain down on his cot, but
wasn't yet asleep when the knocking came at his door.
Rather than waiting for his acknowledgement to enter, a
servant burst in looking wild and ragged. The man held a
lamp which he raised to examine Delin, and his relief was
immediately obvious.

''Excellence, thank the Highest Aspect that you're all
right!'' the man blurted, no more than a short step from
showing terror. ''The others of your Five . . . they're terribly ill and the palace physicians are helpless to aid them!
Will you . . . come and see what *you* can do?''

Delin nodded with feigned concern, but made no effort
to race out of his wing as he was. He stopped to dress first,
and although it only took a brief moment or two, the servant was nearly beside himself. The wing closest to Delin's
was Selendi's, and when he entered the incredibly ornate
bedchamber there were more than half a dozen people
standing around staring at her where she lay. Or, rather,
where she writhed on the bed, screaming out her pain. She
took no notice of any of the people so concerned about her,
the sweat drenching her hair and covering her body suggesting why.

''How long has she been like this?'' Delin softly asked
the servant who had brought him there. ''And is she as
unaware of us as she seems to be?''

''It's been nearly an hour since her screams woke her
servants, and yes, she does seem to be completely unaware

of us," the servant replied, his gaze fastened to her writhing form. "The others are in a like state, and we simply don't know what to *do*!"

"I want to see them before I try anything myself," Delin said, more interested in seeing his tormentors in agony than in trying to end that agony. It had been perfectly clear from the first that Selendi wasn't on the verge of dying, at least not yet. She had quite a long time to suffer before she reached her end, a result which thoroughly delighted Delin. If he hadn't known better, he would have thought *he'd* been the one to arrange such a marvelous situation. . . .

The servant nodded jerkily and hurried out of the bed-chamber and into the corridor, probably heading for Homin's wing, which was the next one in line. Delin followed him at his own pace, but when they reached the public corridor which led to all the wings, he was stopped by one of the palace guardsmen.

"Excellence, this was left at the front gate by a man wearing a privacy mask," the guardsman said, handing over a small package. "The guard who took it was told that the Five would send for it when they needed it, and then he walked away. After that it was a good two hours before the furor began, and that was when the gate guard sent the package in here. It's only a slim chance, but maybe there's something in it to help . . ."

Delin nodded when the man's words trailed off, having the impression that the guardsman was more frightened than concerned. The servants were undoubtedly the same, as it had been *their* job to make sure the Five were safe and comfortable. If the rest of the Five recovered then only the guilty would be punished, but if they died then the Advisors would probably have them all put to death.

Delin's curiosity was strong as he opened the small package, although he had a definite suspicion about what might be in it. He tore away the paper covering a small box, and inside the box were five slim glass vials and a note. That made Delin smile as he withdrew the note and opened it.

"Greetings to the Seated Five," the note began, its tone downright jolly. "If you're reading this, then you've already been given the contents of the enclosed vials and have come back to yourselves. Isn't it delightful when pain like that ends?

"Well, of course it is, so we're sure you'd like to make certain that the pain stays ended. You may accomplish this by doing exactly as we wish, a state of affairs you will be more fully informed of in due course. For the moment you must understand that if you fail to receive regular doses of what the vials contain, the agony will return and will eventually kill you. If you use any of the vials to experiment on to discover *what* they contain, the one who lacks the contents will be returned to the agony and eventually sent to his or her death. Experimentation *will* eventually tell you what you need to survive, but by then one of your number will be beyond the need for the knowledge.

"So we fully expect you to choose the course of wisdom and make no effort to discover who we are or what you've been poisoned with. The next package of vials—along with more detailed instructions—will be found tomorrow in a place you will be informed about. Until then, we remain, your loyal subjects."

Delin snorted wry amusement at the way the note had been signed, almost appreciating the jibe. And there was nothing in the way of traces on the paper, showing that the writer had probably been wearing gloves. He closed the note again and replaced it in the box, then looked up at the guardsman.

"Yes, this is something that will indeed be of help," he told the man with a smile. "And sometime tomorrow another note will be delivered. When it arrives, it's to be brought to me at once."

"Yes, Excellence, as you command," the guardsman acknowledged with a salute. "May I perform any other service?"

"Not at the moment," Delin said with a headshake, then turned his attention to the servant who had been leading him along. "We'll go to Lord Kambil's wing now, rather than Lord Homin's. As he's the most important of us, I'll begin my efforts with him."

The servant bowed to acknowledge the command, and then began to lead the way to Kambil's wing. It was something of a walk to reach Kambil's bedchamber and the room was just as filled with servants and physicians as Selendi's had been, but Delin took care of that by chasing them all out. They left unwillingly, but refusing the orders of one of the Five was something they weren't prepared to do. Once he was alone with Kambil, Delin walked closer to the magnificent bed and looked down at his groupmate.

"What . . . ohhh . . . help . . . me," Kambil mumbled as Delin found the pain centers of his mind and partially numbed them. Kambil had been screaming and writhing just the way Selendi had, but now that the pain was being dulled he was able to return to himself just a bit.

"Why, certainly, Kambil, of course I'll help you," Delin said pleasantly with a smile. "We're groupmates, after all, and groupmates always help one another. Haven't you gone out of your way to help *me*?"

"Delin . . . don't be . . . a fool," Kambil panted out, looking up with very little worry. "You . . . *have* to . . . help me, that's . . . an order. You can't . . . refuse my orders . . ."

"Oh, but I can," Delin told him brightly, his smile widening. "Did I forget to mention that I'm no longer under the control of the Puredan? Well mercy me, how silly to be so forgetful. I'll bet I also forgot to mention that I'm the one who ended your precious Grami. It's your turn next, my friend, but not right away. First you have some suffering to do, and I'm going to enjoy every minute of it. And just as you're dying, I hope you remember that I could have saved your life—if I'd felt like it. But I don't feel like it, so goodbye old friend, we'll miss you terribly. . . ."

Kambil screamed then, but not from the poison he'd been fed. It was agony of the mind which took him first, just what Delin wanted to happen. And then Delin felt Kambil's efforts to touch his mind and take him over, so he released his hold numbing the man's pain centers. That brought back the agony and the screaming over *that*, which Delin stood watching for a few moments before turning with a smile to leave. He would tell the servants that Lord Kambil should be fine in a little while, and then he would go and save the others of his group. Their Blending would be almost as effective without Kambil as it was with him, possibly even more so once Delin explained the changed circumstances to the others.

For now Delin would be in complete charge, and if any of the others tried to give him trouble they would scream in agony for it. Whatever the vials contained *he* would be the one to find out, and that would put him in complete control of them. They would obey him or they would scream for a time, and as for those stupid peasants who were their enemies. . . .

Kambil had been too soft on them, but Delin would not make the same mistake, *that* was for certain. . . .

FIFTEEN

Vallant held his hand up to stop their shortened column when they were within sight of the town of Colling Green. Coming to this place was, in his opinion, a mistake, but Jovvi had insisted and, strangely enough, Naran had agreed with her. Naran, of all people, putting forward an opinion before it was asked for. Vallant thought it was about time Naran began to act like a full—or almost full—member of their group, but he wished she could have found something other than the idea of stopping to support. They didn't have many allies in the empire, and there was no reason to believe that the Guild was an exception to that. But they were still going to the town where the leaders of the Guild wanted them to.

Their group of thirty-five—thirty-six with Naran—came to a halt behind him, everyone craning their necks to see what they could of the town. They'd brought five link groups and one of the new Blendings, hoping that that would be enough to counter any traps the Guild might have decided to set out for them. The rest of their company, almost five hundred people, were coming more slowly with the provision wagons they'd filled in Widdertown.

They'd had to stop once to refill those provision wagons in a town along the way, and they'd paid gold for the meat and flour and fish and whatnot that they needed. They'd also tried to warn the people of the town, but everyone there simply smiled and nodded and then went on about their business. They were too far from the border to take the idea of invasion seriously, even if refugees from Widdertown and its surrounding area were coming through from time to time. If other people were silly enough to take wild stories seriously, that was none of *their* concern.

So they'd simply described the situation to as many people as they could and then they'd moved on. At least that way people would *know*, and if they chose to disbelieve then that was their problem. Vallant had problems of his own, and stopping in a place he thought was a trap was only one of them. A bigger headache was the fact that Tamrissa flatly refused to talk to him at all about anything personal, but hadn't done the same with Meerk before they left him and the rest of the group behind.

Vallant sighed as he joined everyone else in looking down from the gentle swell of the hill to the town only a few miles away. All he'd wanted to do was tell her not to be so reckless, not to risk herself as though she had nothing of much value to lose. Her sudden unconcern over danger wasn't a good sign, and he hadn't needed Jovvi to tell him that. But almost as bad was the way she'd actually spent time with Meerk, as though the man had grown more . . . attractive to her for some reason . . .

"Sitting here won't help us to find out what the Guild wants," Jovvi's voice murmured from his right, where she sat her horse. "And I have to admit that the prospect of being able to take a bath is an even stronger incentive to hurrying. It's a good thing that last contingent of guardsmen had gold with them so that they could pay for whatever they might need. Our baths and meals and accommodations in real rooms will be through the courtesy of the Seated Five.''

''Why would a small town like Collin' Green have an inn large enough to accommodate all of us?'' Vallant asked, partially distracted by curiosity. ''And for that matter, what makes you think the Guild people won't already be takin' up all that room? Assumin' their trap lets us get anywhere near the inn to begin with.''

''If there does happen to be a trap, the idea of being able to get a bath once we're past it should let us destroy it without the least effort,'' she returned, laughing at him with her eyes. ''As for why they should have an inn large enough to accommodate all of us, I'm told that they have three inns large enough. Colling Green is a hunting preserve set up by wealthy merchants and very minor nobility about twenty years ago. Since it's less than two days' normal travel from Gan Garce, it's in the perfect place for those people to come to in order to show what great hunters they are. The place began with no more than an oversized hunting lodge, and proved so popular that now it has three large inns and a good-sized town to support the businesses which have also grown up there.''

''And you were told about all this,'' Vallant said, trying not to let the words come out sourly. ''Do I need to ask who did all this tellin'?''

''Tamrissa's parents brought her and her sisters here a few years ago,'' Jovvi replied with a shrug that said he'd guessed right. ''They came at the invitation of a business associate of her father's, and apparently he even went out hunting a time or two. She also told me that there are dress shops and tailor shops which will produce single outfits in one day. Apparently some people are foolish enough to take all their luggage with them when they go hunting, instead of leaving most of their possessions in an inn room. Then some catastrophe strikes, like a flash flood or some such, and the fools are left with nothing to wear. Guess where she and Naran and I will be going once we've had our baths?''

''I think I've suddenly changed my mind about goin' into that town,'' Vallant said, finding it impossible not to smile at her. ''Rion and Lorand and I need new clothes as badly as you ladies do, and this would be the perfect time to get them. We ought to look our best when we reach Gan Garee."

"First we really do need to find out what the Guild wants," Jovvi said, no longer jokingly. "I know it isn't very likely that they'll be on our side, but if for some unknown reason they are, we could make good use of the support."

"How much support can talentless people give us?" Vallant countered, also losing the momentary good humor. "Even if they're willin' to do everythin' they can for us, how much is that likely to come to?"

"Don't forget that talentless or not, they have a large, widespread organization," Jovvi reminded him. "If nothing else, they can gather information for us about what's waiting in Gan Garee. Finding out about traps in advance will prove easier than finding out by walking into them."

"That's *if* they're willing to support us," Vallant pointed out, not terribly heartened. "I can't help rememberin' the Guild member who was in charge of gettin' me to Gan Garee. She was one of the most poisonous females I've ever met, tryin' her best to send me off in chains with a guard escort. Judgin' the rest by the one I know is only natural, and I also can't help askin' *why* her group would support us when they've been workin' for the nobility all along."

"But we don't know that," Jovvi countered reasonably. "We're assuming they've been sending people to their deaths because they know what the testing entails, but what if they *didn't* know? What if they've been working for the nobility to keep from being ostracized by our society as freaks, and don't have any idea about what happens to applicants once they reach the testing centers? For all we know, they may hate the nobility even more than we do."

"For usin' their desperation against them," Vallant said with a grudging nod. "All right, I grant you that it's possible, but I'm not goin' to count on it. Be ready to initiate the Blendin' at the first sign of trouble."

"Always," Jovvi agreed, and on that note they continued on down the hill and toward the town. As they drew nearer Vallant was able to see the large, pretty houses the town boasted, situated as they were on the main road leading into the town. Those houses told people that gold wasn't as scarce here as it was in most places, so they'd better be ready to dig deep if they wanted to stop. Well, he and the others had the gold, and no matter what the Guild people wanted they *were* going to stop for a while, at least until the rest of their little army caught up. . . .

When their group rode directly into the town, they were given a few curious glances by the passersby but no one stopped to stare or point or take to their heels. That was only faintly comforting to Vallant, who turned to nod at the Spirit magic member of the second Blending with them. The man returned Vallant's nod and then took on the distracted air of someone turning his attention inward, which meant he was initiating his Blending the way he was supposed to. He and his five had learned to brace themselves in their saddles, with their entity having their mounts under full control. They would take the first look around, giving anyone who watched the impression that Vallant's Blending approached with nothing in their hearts but trust.

The town had large, pretty shops with wooden walks in front which were well taken care of. And their main street was cobbled, showing that they were just as prosperous as the rest of the rather small town suggested. The locals seemed to hold themselves with pride and satisfaction, and everyone appeared to be well dressed. At the end of the first street was a fountain, an intricate thing composed of dancing children and animals, and the street beyond it contained more shops and houses. The group was just passing the fountain when the entity of the second Blending touched Vallant's thoughts.

"Nothing here seems to be out of order," the entity told him silently in his head. "This being has found a fairly large group of those who do nothing but wait, but much of the group is composed of flesh forms who appear to be less than Low talents. Touching them was somewhat disagreeable, and yet that was not because they harbor hidden thoughts of attack and destruction. They sit with the others in a dwelling not far from here, and some of the group have grown depressed from the boredom."

"Just where is this place where they're waitin'?" Vallant

asked aloud, knowing the entity would be able to hear him. "And what do those flesh forms look like? Are they composed mainly of men who remind you of the guardsman part of our group?"

"This being is reminded of none of those who are part of our larger group," the entity replied in Vallant's mind. "The flesh forms are mainly too well fed, which includes those who are slender in physical appearance. The place where they wait is located to the left, two of these divisions from the crossing you now approach."

"Thank you, and you may now return to your own flesh forms," Vallant said, then turned to Jovvi. "Our reception committee is waitin' a couple of streets away to the left, so we'll turn at the next corner. And they sound like merchants or nobles from the description I was given."

"I prefer that to having them look like guardsmen," Jovvi said wryly, obviously having heard what he'd said to the entity. "So if this is a trap, it can't be an ordinary one."

"I wouldn't be surprised if it *was* other than ordinary," Vallant countered, part of him refusing to be anything other than sour. "They could be a bunch of merchants waitin' to sell us things, and ready to badger us to death if we don't buy. That would be one way of gettin' rid of us."

Rather than answer in words, Jovvi made an odd, strangling sound. When Vallant looked at her he realized that she was struggling not to laugh aloud, knowing how little his current mood would enjoy a reaction like that. He appreciated the attempt, but his being aware of it ruined the reason for it in the first place.

"All right, no need to hurt yourself swallowin' the laughter," he grudged after a moment. "I suppose the comment *was* on the funny side. . . ."

That seemed to tickle her even more, and her delighted laughter rang out even as she touched his hand in thanks for his understanding. She was a beautiful, wonderful woman, and Vallant was only sorry that he and Lorand hadn't switched their interest right from the beginning. Jovvi would never have given him half the problems Tamrissa did. . . .

That settled the sour mood even more firmly on him, so Vallant led the way to the left at the next cross street without a comment. A glance had shown him that the second Blending had dissolved their entity and were now back with them, their members looking a good deal more relaxed than they had. They were clearly convinced that no danger awaited at their destination, which Vallant found almost disappointing. He would have enjoyed a good rousing fight right about now. . . .

Two streets farther down was an odd arrangement, the likes of which Vallant had never seen. Most inns were either in a town—and not far from taverns and eating parlors—or standing alone along the road and *containing* places to eat and drink. What they now approached was an enclave of sorts, with the three very large inns standing in the midst of green lawn and trees. Each building was surrounded by lawn as if it were a ship on the ocean, and only at the very edge of the lawn area, back out of easy sight, were other buildings. The three inns appeared to be alone in their togetherness, if such a thing could make any sense.

"That's really quite lovely," Jovvi murmured, her amusement having disappeared some time earlier. "The balance is so perfectly fitting along with the landscape, an artist must have designed the arrangement. But the inn on the right has a large number of people, while the other two can't have more than staff members present. Do we pay our respects first, or register first?"

"I'll enjoy registerin' a lot more if we get some questions answered first," Vallant replied, not in the least unsure. "Maybe we'll get lucky and they'll try somethin', and then we won't feel guilty about not payin' after we take care of it. If we do have to pay, the gold we have with us may not be enough."

"Yes, it does look rather expensive, doesn't it," Jovvi agree with a sigh. "Just sitting on that lawn would be pure relaxation, especially facing that circular drive. Its curves are all part of the design arrangement . . . and now I want that bath more than ever. But I also have the distinct feeling that after we bathe we won't be as impressive to the people waiting for us as we are right now."

"You mean we can use lookin' like desperados for our own purposes," Vallant said, understanding the point immediately. "I think you're right, and it's a good thing—

because that's what I meant to do anyway.''

This time Jovvi only smiled, and then they were approaching the curving, circular drive which led to the three inns in turn. But the drive didn't link the three buildings, not directly at least, with those sweeping curves. And there, off to the right, behind a stand of screening trees, seemed to be immense stables. They wouldn't be visible from any of the three inns, and were only just visible from the foot of the drive.

Vallant led the way to the first of the inns, but he wasn't happy about it. The closer they got to Gan Garee the more . . . trapped he felt, the more surrounded and outnumbered. He wouldn't have minded so much for himself, but the others were riding toward the trap right along with him. If these people waiting for them *did* prove to be helpful in some way, that would only bring the time closer when their five would have to enter Gan Garee again.

And that could very well end their lives, all their lives, whether or not misunderstandings were straightened out and hurts were soothed. Their Blending was stronger than that of the Seated Five, but it would be foolish to assume that facing those five enemies again would be all they had ahead of them. Their enemies knew who was stronger, so they could be counted on to avoid a direct confrontation until no other option was open to them.

So Vallant had a decision to make while they were waiting for their army to catch up, and it would prove to be the hardest decision he'd ever made in his life. . . .

SIXTEEN

When they reached the inn Lorand dismounted, then moved around to the right side of his horse to help Tamrissa dismount. There hadn't been much conversation between them as they'd ridden, but once they'd reached Colling Green Tamrissa had . . . come back to herself a bit more, Lorand realized. She'd commented on the town—at least on the amount of it she remembered—and seemed to be making a firm return from the withdrawn and determined stranger she'd been during most of the ride.

Lorand sighed to himself as he helped Tamrissa to the ground, agreeing with Jovvi that they were interfering, but also knowing that he and Jovvi had no choice but to interfere. She had spent her time with Vallant while Lorand stayed with Tamrissa, and later on, once all danger of attack was over, they would change places. They'd hoped to ease the ever-widening rift which was growing between Tamrissa and Vallant, and Lorand hoped that Jovvi had had more success than he had.

"Why is the damn fool stopping?" Tamrissa had muttered when Vallant had halted their group at the brow of the low hill to look down at what they meant to approach. "If a trap is visible from this distance, then those people are idiots and we have nothing to worry about from them."

"Most people seem to want to look at the place where they're going before they go to it," Lorand had answered lamely, trying to defend Vallant on the one hand and hoping to avoid disturbing Tamrissa on the other. "He's probably just trying to give everyone a chance to do that. Why have you refused to hear anything he has to say?"

"Why should I listen?" she countered, making no effort to turn her head to look at Lorand. "He never says anything worth hearing, a fact I can testify to from personal experience. On top of that, I'm tired of being asked to listen when *he* wants to talk, and at all other times being expected to accept his silence without question. And I also don't care to hear excuses for his behavior from every second or third person. To be truthful, I don't care to hear about him in any way from anyone at all."

And at that point she *had* looked at Lorand, in a way which had ended the discussion right there. Lorand knew that Tamrissa would never hurt him, but the hint of flames in her gaze was now an almost constant thing. If her temper flared then her talent might do the same, before she could consciously halt it. Lorand had overheard two High talents in Fire magic discussing Tamrissa's strength with awe in their voices, and therefore was doubly anxious to avoid all possibility of an accident.

"We'd better move up with the others," Lorand now said to a Tamrissa who currently stretched the aches of the ride out of her back. "Since we're the ones they want to see, it's only right if we walk in there first."

"It's also the place for the strongest among us," Tamrissa said in agreement. "Any traps should be set up to neutralize *us*, and will hopefully overlook completely the second Blending we have with us. If there's something in there that we can't handle alone, our second will help us to get out of it."

"I certainly hope so," Lorand muttered, but only to himself. Master Lugal hadn't known why his superiors wanted to talk to them, but the fact that they'd been told about it in *his* former home town made Lorand feel personally responsible for whatever would happen. Intellectually he knew that the decision to come had been a group effort, but that knowledge did nothing to alter the set of his emotions.

Rion and Naran were already on their way to joining Jovvi and Vallant, so Lorand and Tamrissa brought up the rear.

But that was only the rear of their own group. The five link sets and the second Blending formed up in the true rear, pretending that they were only casually grouped. Their mounts formed a solid line all along the front of the very dignified-looking inn, a barrier that would hopefully keep any hidden attackers from approaching very quickly from behind them.

Lorand glanced at the sky as they moved in a body toward the entrance to the inn, seeing the clouds already beginning to roll in. There would be rain by nightfall, which gave them even more incentive to take care of whatever lay ahead of them. They no longer had wagons to take shelter under when they camped for the night, so it would be either stay at one of the inns or sleep in the dripping wet. They'd all had more than enough of roughing it, so it would take quite a lot to keep them out of clean, comfortable beds tonight.

Vallant led the way inside, making no effort to let Jovvi walk in ahead of him the way he normally would have. Lorand felt grateful for that deliberate lapse in gentlemanly behavior, and that despite the fact that Jovvi was more than capable of taking care of herself. Until they found out what the Guild people wanted, their ladies would *not* be put in a position where they would be the first to face an attack. Rion and Naran entered behind Vallant and Jovvi, and then Lorand and Tamrissa walked in to look around.

The inn's entrance area was carpeted almost up to the double doors, with thickly upholstered furniture and beautifully carved tables carefully arranged across it. Half a dozen people sat in some of that furniture, and now they sat staring at the newcomers. From their expressions of stunned shock Lorand gathered that Jovvi had been working to keep these people from being aware of their approach, which was a really good idea. An older man among the group stood shakily as he looked briefly toward a boy and gestured at him, and as the boy ran off the man offered an awkward bow.

"Unless I am very much mistaken, gentles, you are certainly expected," the man said in an unsteady voice, his gaze moving back and forth among them. "May I ask who succeeded in sending you here?"

"It was master Lugal, in Widdertown," Lorand supplied

when no one else spoke up. "How many others did you leave your . . . request with?"

"Why, with everyone," the man responded, showing his surprise. "We knew you had escaped from Gan Garee, but we had no way of knowing which direction you would take. So we sent messages by pigeon in every direction, knowing that *someone* would come across you. . . . The others will be here in just a few minutes, but I'm afraid there aren't chairs enough for your entire escort. If the five of you will seat yourselves, I can see about having more chairs brought out and having refreshments served . . ."

"Thank you, but until we find out what this is all about, we prefer to stand," Vallant said in a hard and grating tone that made the poor man flinch. "I'm sure you understand that we've had to learn caution."

"Oh, but there's no need to be cautious with *us*," the man responded, again looking startled. "We know, you see, and we've known from the very first. Surely you must have expected *someone* to know?"

Lorand saw Vallant exchange glances with Jovvi and Rion just before he himself exchanged a glance with Tamrissa. He didn't need to be told that the man spoke what he considered the truth, but just what that truth was still hadn't been made clear.

"Why don't you tell us what it is that you know," Jovvi suggested gently to the man in her friendliest voice, possibly even using her talent at the same time. The man automatically returned her smile and relaxed a bit, but that didn't have to be talent, just a normal response to the woman who was Jovvi.

"Why, we know the truth," the man supplied willingly enough. "You five are the Chosen Blending, the one spoken of in the Prophecies, and the only way the nobles could have won the final competition against you is with cheating. We consider it our duty to stand beside you when you return, so that—"

"Ensor, enough," a stronger voice interrupted, and Lorand looked up to see a group of men and women following the boy who had run off only a moment earlier. All those people must have been close and together, Lorand realized, or they couldn't have gotten here this fast. "The Chosen don't need to be burbled over, not when they're obviously so tired. Let's at least see them seated and fed before we pester them.''

"I was merely answering their question, High Master," the man called Ensor replied, but in a quietly respectful way. "And now that you and the others are here. . . .''

He faded back without finishing his sentence, ceding his place in front of the Blending with what looked to Lorand like a great deal of relief. The newcomers quickly made up for that by crowding forward—in a reserved way—and the man addressed as High Master smiled around at them.

"I'm Lavrit Mohr, and we're delighted to have you here with us at last, Excellences," he said with a bow. "Accommodations have been prepared for you, and as soon as you've had your meal you can all—"

"Just a moment, Dom Mohr," Vallant interrupted the flow of the man's words, his tone as dry as Lorand's would have been. "There seems to be some sort of misunderstandin' here, and we need to get it straightened out before we go any further. We do happen to be the ones who would have bested the new Seated Five in the final competition if their people hadn't cheated, but that doesn't make us the Chosen ones spoken of in the Prophecies. I've never put much stock in the Prophecies, so—"

"But Excellence, of course you're the Chosen ones," Mohr interrupted with a small laugh, looking around now to see that the entire Blending agreed with what Vallant had said. "How can you possibly doubt it, when each of you witnessed the first sign yourselves?"

"What sort of sign were we supposed to have witnessed?" Jovvi asked gently—and rather quickly, probably to keep Tamrissa from telling the man her opinion of him. Tamrissa had opened her mouth with an impatient expression on her face, but Jovvi's question kept the second woman from speaking.

"Yes, I'd like to know that as well," Rion put in, supporting what Jovvi had asked. "I recall nothing in the way of signs, and it was merely happenstance which threw us all together. We could just as easily have ended up as members of different challenging Blendings."

"But Excellence, of course there were signs," Mohr protested, having lost his air of ecstatic delight. "All of the Guild members who sent you five to Gan Garee reported on them most completely, so there can't possibly be any doubt."

"If you're talkin' about Guild members supportin' what you're sayin', now I know you're mistaken," Vallant told him with what was almost a snort of scorn. "The—lady who was in charge of sendin' *me* to Gan Garee tried her best to see that I made the trip in chains, with guardsmen as travelin' companions. I don't know why she felt such . . . almost hatred for me, but she made it perfectly clear that she did."

"Yes, I'm aware of the incident, Excellence," Mohr replied, his nod quiet and his expression just short of amused. "Raina Santray had . . . a bad experience with a young man from a monied family, and so developed a certain prejudice. She confessed what she'd done in her report, and also confessed that she hadn't had the heart to apologize afterward, when she realized the truth. If she'd faced you again she would surely have blurted out what she knew, and all Guild members were warned against speaking about the signs when they came. The nobility was also watching for those signs, you know, and we had no wish to let them learn that the first had manifested. It could well have meant your deaths."

"So you kept quiet and thereby made sure we were all perfectly safe," Tamrissa put in, the sarcasm in her voice much too clear to miss. "Or could it possibly be that no one noticed these 'signs' until we nearly won the last competition? Then everyone looked back and lo and behold, there were the signs they'd missed the first time around. How convenient for everyone involved."

"Your skepticism is somewhat puzzling to me, Excellences," Mohr said, his brows having risen after hearing what Tamrissa had to say. "We were delighted to discover that no one noticed the signs but our own people, but now you're saying that they were missed by your Five as well. Since I know that that can't possibly be true, the answer must be that you've forgotten. With everything which happened to you afterward, that's perfectly understandable. Would you permit me to remind you?"

"Yes, why don't you do that," Tamrissa said very dryly, speaking as Lorand might have if he hadn't been taught to be polite and mannerly. These people were obviously entirely mistaken, but it might be worth their while to pretend to believe them—at least until they'd all had a few solid meals, a nice long bath, and a good night's sleep in a bed. . . .

"It would be my pleasure," Mohr replied with a bow that was more courteous than sarcastic. "And it's most fitting that the request should come from the lady of Fire. Inasmuch as the first sign was the appearance—from out of nowhere—of an attacking fireball. Surely you all remember now. . . ."

Lorand felt the clang of shock as he suddenly did remember that fireball, the one which had attacked him on his way to the coach going to Gan Garee. He hadn't known who could have been responsible for sending it, but he did remember how . . . intense master Lugal had been after the incident. He'd had to use his talent to put the thing out, but surely that applied only to him. . . .

And then the shock grew more intense as Lorand noticed the same expression of shock on the faces of his groupmates. It couldn't be, not them too . . . but that would mean. . . .

SEVENTEEN

Jovvi had to shield herself completely for a moment, so resoundingly strong were the feelings of shock coming from her groupmates. That wouldn't have been so bad, though, if her own feelings hadn't been sending the same message: this is all a mistake, it has to be a mistake. *We* can't be the ones spoken about in the Prophecies. . . .

But Jovvi could remember the fireball vividly, and judging from the reactions of her groupmates, they all had memories of the same sort. Realizing that brought an odd weakness to Jovvi's knees, as though as strange as it seemed, there might be something to what the man had said after all. . . .

"Ah, the silence speaks volumes, as do your expressions," Lavrit Mohr said, his smile more benevolently pleased than triumphant. "May I assume that you now remember the incidents to which I referred? Each of you was threatened, and each of you met the threat and bested it."

"But . . . surely that must be some sort of coincidence," Rion tried, his voice less than steady. "Or possibly it was the doing of some of *your* people. You required a group you might call 'Chosen' to rally your members behind, and so you put everyone sent to Gan Garee through the same thing. No matter which of us ended up in the final competition, you would still be able to say that they were Chosen because of the sign."

"Yes, that sounds reasonable," Vallant immediately agreed, and so did the others. Now it was relief they showed on their faces, and Jovvi could understand that. The only problem was, the man called High Master now laughed gently at what he *knew* wasn't the truth.

"The Prophecies also say that the Chosen will not know themselves at first," Mohr supplied, still speaking gently. "And I think you've all apparently forgotten that none of my members could possibly have caused that fireball, because none of us can do magic the way everyone else can. Our talent is entirely different and, as you should know, revolves about being able to know a magic user's strength. That particular talent tells me you're currently standing with others who can easily be considered High practitioners. Why don't you ask *them* if they were attacked by fireballs when they were first sent to Gan Garee by my people?"

Jovvi found it impossible to keep herself from turning to look at the members of the link groups and the second Blending. They all stood there behind the people they considered their leaders, but their expressions and emotions had now changed to a large extent. Awe colored their thoughts, and any number of them shook their heads to answer the question that none of Jovvi's group had been able to put.

"I'm suddenly feeling something of a chill," Tamma muttered, wrapping her arms about herself. "But I also still agree with Rion; this can't possibly be true, so why are we continuing to discuss it?"

"We're still discussing it because we need the truth, not our own pet theories," Jovvi told her, but made certain that her tone was completely gentle. "I know exactly how you feel because I feel the same way, but there are too many unexplained facts that we can't simply dismiss. *Is* it true that the rest of you were attacked by a fireball in the same way I was?"

"I certainly was," Lorand replied with a sigh, the expression in his dark eyes troubled. "The thing almost burned me to cinders, and Hat was no help at all. I had to stop the thing myself, before it killed me and then set the whole town on fire."

"With me, it nearly ruined my favorite hat," Rion said, and Jovvi could tell that he grasped at tiny details to keep the shock from returning. "I was outraged, of course, but when the Guild member with my coach ticket showed up, I denied all knowledge of what had happened. He himself seemed to have missed the incident."

Now Rion looked rather closely at Lavrit Mohr, as though he'd found a flaw in the man's story. It so happened that Jovvi had also denied all knowledge of the fireball attack, so she joined Rion in listening for Mohr's answer.

"Allow me to assure you that Lord Astrath missed not a single minute of it," the High Master replied to Rion, still looking completely unruffled. "None of your Guild members missed the incidents, but they were trying to find out what *your* reactions to the attacks were. If one of you had had a friend who was prone to playing practical jokes, for instance, the incident would have become much less certain. But no one lurked around snickering afterward, and there were only the five reported incidents. That helped to convince us that we weren't wishful thinking. . . ."

Jovvi contributed to the flood of disturbance coming from the others until she shielded herself again, and then it was only her own disturbance which she had to worry about. The whole thing seemed to be impossible to believe, and they really needed to discuss the matter alone.

"I . . . think we ought to accept the hospitality we've been offered here," Jovvi said after a moment, looking at her groupmates. "I don't know about the rest of you, but I'm too tired—and dirty—to think clearly. Let's get a meal and some rest first, and then we can talk about this again."

"Yes, please, we insist you accept," Mohr said when the others hesitated. "This inn has been prepared for you and your companions, while my own people and our allies have been quartered at the other two. I meant to introduce you to them all, but later, at dinner, would be a much better idea. Right now it's not much past lunchtime, and if you'll honor us by taking the meal here in the dining room, we'll have the rest of it ready for you as soon as you're through."

"The rest of what?" Jovvi couldn't help asking, despite the picture her mind insisted on putting forward of her sitting down at a table again, as though she were a civilized woman instead of a hunted fugitive. "What else have you . . . prepared for us?"

"Well, we arranged to have some clothing made for you," Mohr said, and now he sounded a bit hesitant. "We knew your approximate sizes, after all, and knew you probably hadn't been able to take any clothing at all when you escaped. But we only had four outfits made for each of you, which is certainly not enough to clothe your entire group. If the tailors and seamstresses in the town are permitted to take measurements, though, and the extra outfits made for *you* are distributed, we may well be able to clothe everyone by tonight or tomorrow morning at the latest."

Everyone began to murmur over that, and this time the surprise was a pleasant one. Every one of them needed new clothing rather badly, and the idea of being able to get into fresh new things after bathing had an attraction that couldn't be ignored. So that meant they weren't going to refuse what had been done for them, but Jovvi also had no intention of just relaxing and enjoying it all. Their Blending entity would have to have a good look around as well as a talk with some of those so-called supporters of theirs before that happened, and maybe not even then.

"I think we ought to apologize for being . . . less than grateful for all these marvelous things," Jovvi said to Mohr with a smile meant to dazzle. "I'm sure you know we haven't had an easy time of it, and after being attacked almost every time we stopped somewhere, it was hard to imagine being in a place where there would be help instead. We really do appreciate everything you've done for us, and especially for offering the members of your Guild as our supporters."

"I . . . think I ought to mention that not all of our members mean to support you," Mohr said, the admission obviously embarrassing and needing to be forced out. "One faction of our people seems to be rather firmly on the side of the nobles, and they claim that if we really give the nobility our support instead of just pretending to it, we'll be rewarded the way we should be. They want what the nobility has within its power to give, you see, and refuse to admit that no one whom that monied group considers a freak will ever be granted any of the largesse. But we made certain that that faction knows nothing about this meeting, so their opinions and views won't touch you in any way at all."

"That's a relief," Lorand said, clearly trying to support Jovvi's preferred attitude of grateful weariness. "It will feel good to get back into the habit of not wondering about every stranger I see. Ah . . . which way did you say we can find that meal you mentioned?"

Mohr and his people hurriedly volunteered to escort everyone to the dining room, and promptly began to do so. Once everyone began to move in the proper direction, Jovvi turned to look at Ramis Foll, one of the Highs in her link group. Ramis was also looking in her direction the way he was supposed to, so Jovvi nodded slightly with a matching smile. Ramis echoed the nod, then turned to speak to the others in his link group. Certain plans and signals had been arranged before their group reached the vicinity of Colling Green, and Jovvi had just set one of those plans in motion.

The dining room was a rather large and formal place a short distance toward the back of the inn, and enough place settings had been arranged on the round, generous-sized tables to accommodate a good sixty people or more. Seating arrangements made very little difference to Jovvi and the others, as they'd all practiced enough with their link groups—and the link groups with their own members—that it didn't matter where anyone happened to be. If trouble suddenly erupted they could all link up in seconds to take care of it, so they spread out and claimed whatever table and place happened to appeal to them.

Except that Jovvi and her groupmates all moved rather briskly to their places, then lost no time in sitting down. Ramis and his people, along with members of the other link groups, were occupying their hosts by stopping them to ask various questions. That was to give the primary Blending time to form their entity, which would then search the entire inn and the food in particular. If there was nothing wrong with the meal and it *was* being given freely by those who were on their side, it would be a shame to court indigestion by not knowing that in advance.

So Jovvi and the others arranged themselves as they'd agreed to do, pretending that they were more than a little tired. They *were* weary, but their positions were meant to suggest that they were taking a moment to rest—rather than letting the Guild people know that they were no longer in their bodies. Vallant sat with his legs stretched out straight and his head back, one hand to the back of his neck with his eyes closed. Rion had lowered his head to his folded arms on the table, and his eyes, too, were closed. Beside him Naran leaned on his shoulder, eyes blinking slowly but still open, hopefully distracting any observer from noticing that Lorand leaned back with an arm across his eyes, which effectively closed off *his* sight.

Tamma had put her elbows on the table and her hands to her face, the ends of her fingers pressing against her closed eyelids. As soon as Jovvi had made sure that everyone was in the proper position, she lowered her face to her hands, her elbows braced on her own thighs, and then she initiated the Blending.

And then the entity was there, moving as quickly from place to place as it possibly could. Everything in the inn's various rooms looked perfectly normal, as did the workers in the kitchens. The entity first took over one of the people who were involved with the Guild, and asked about their intentions. As far as the man knew, Lavrit Mohr had spoken only the truth, and really and truly did want to help and support them.

After wiping the man's memory of the episode, the entity floated quickly to the kitchens and took over the mind of the kitchen mistress. It asked a few direct and pertinent questions, removed all memory of its presence once it had its answers, and then it was Jovvi back again. Their hosts had given orders for more than one day of meals for the newly arrived guests, and had also promised bonuses to the staff if the service turned out to be perfect. Their hosts were *very* anxious that their visit be a pleasant one, and were apparently willing to spend gold in order to make sure that it was.

"I still don't quite believe it, but for the moment I'm through arguin' about trust," Vallant said softly as he straightened in his chair again. "If they want to pamper us, I'm willin' to be pampered."

"They think we're the Chosen spoken of in the Prophecies," Lorand pointed out, and Jovvi could tell that he, like Vallant and Rion as well, was also not completely convinced of the sincerity of their hosts. "With that in mind, what else *would* they do? I'd just like to know what will happen if they find out they're mistaken, and discover we're not at all who they think we are."

"They would probably explode, in disappointment if nothing else," Jovvi replied, also sitting straight again. "But we still haven't gotten to the bottom of that claim yet, so let's leave a discussion of it for a time when we're not so hungry and tired."

"I'm finding it very hard to open my eyes again," Tamma said into the grudging silence put forth by Vallant and Lorand, who seemed to want to discuss the matter right here and now. She still hadn't removed her fingers from her eyes, and her speech had slowed down quite a bit. "If I fall asleep before the food comes, I don't know whether to ask to be awakened or to be allowed to stay asleep."

"If you fall asleep and miss the meal, you'll also miss taking a bath afterward," Jovvi pointed out with a small bit of amusement and a great deal of shared understanding. "Remembering that was what let *me* open my eyes again."

"An excellent point," Tamma said, slowly but definitely pulling her head back from her hands and forcing her eyes open. "There, see? It worked for me, too. Now if I can just keep this going until the food is brought out. . . ."

That might have been a problem for Jovvi as well, but just then servants began to appear with trays of dishes. Ramis Foll and the other Highs had already ended their distraction of the Guild people and had found a table of their own, so Lavrit Mohr and his associates approached the table where Jovvi and the others sat.

"Your meal is about to be served, so we'll leave you to enjoy it," the man said, looking around at all of them. "Unless, of course, you would prefer to have one or more of us taste the dishes before you do. We're perfectly willing to do that if it will ease your minds."

"Thank you, but that won't be necessary," Lorand said, answering for all of them. "I made very sure to check all the ingredients of every dish, and there was nothing to show that the composition of any of them has been changed or added to. Every drop of it was fully identified, so if you'd like the recipe for any of the dishes, just ask me."

"Some of us just may accept that offer," Mohr said with a chuckle that only a few of his associates shared. The rest were startled and even faintly disturbed, as though they hadn't stopped to realize that they were dealing with actual High talents. "But for the rest of the day until dinner, we won't be disturbing you. A few of our younger associates will be on hand to run errands and give directions and help you all to get settled into rooms, but they won't impose on your time or patience. Until dinner, then."

Jovvi joined the others in thanking the man as he and his friends bowed before moving away, leaving them to the promised privacy. And the servants were already beginning to put steaming dishes of deliciously smelling food on the table, which Jovvi couldn't wait to dig into. They hadn't realized they'd neglected to include any decent cooks with their thirty-five until they'd camped that first night after leaving the larger group. . . .

"Jovvi, Naran has had a marvelous idea that just might make things better between Tamrissa and Vallant," Rion murmured from Jovvi's left as a servant moved between Jovvi and Vallant on her right in order to put a dish on the table. "We'll come to your and Lorand's rooms later, and tell you about it."

"Yes, do," Jovvi murmured back before the servant no longer blocked Vallant from easy seeing and hearing. Her curiosity was now aroused, but it wasn't possible to ask for details with Vallant sitting right next to her. And they certainly needed *something* to get those two stubborn mules to listen to reason. For supposedly fearless fugitives, Tamma and Vallant were too afraid of what might happen if they gave themselves another chance together. There had to be a way to make them really bold, to lessen the chances of someone else coming between them if for no other reason.

Jovvi sighed as she reached for the serving dish nearest her. The performance of the Blending didn't *seem* to be affected by the small, private war, but the way things were continually changing with the entity, there was no certainty that the Blending *wasn't* being affected. And while they'd traveled, Jovvi had taken the opportunity to work with both Vallant and Lorand and their individual problems. It remained to be seen whether or not her idea would be effective, but Naran had said that they would soon need everything they had to stay alive. Jovvi knew that herself, and that time was very quickly running out.

So that idea about how to get Tamma and Vallant back together had better be a good one. If it wasn't, it could well mean the difference between victory and defeat for them. Or life and death, which it would certainly come down to. There was less than two days of travel in order to reach Gan Garee, and the rest of their people were less than two days behind them. Four or five days could well see them in the thick of things, and as necessary as the confrontation was, Jovvi was *not* looking forward to it. She'd had the strangest premonitions of disaster . . . but hopefully it would just turn out to be her imagination. . . .

EIGHTEEN

"Does everyone have a cup of tea?" Jovvi asked as she looked around at us. "There's only about an hour or so until dinner, so we really do need to talk."

Up until then we'd been sleeping, and I, at least, felt a good deal better for it. Lunch had been excellent and the bath marvelous, and then, with plain but new, clean clothing waiting for us, we'd all taken naps. Or almost all of us had napped. Our second Blending had stayed awake and on guard, and now that we were up again they were getting their turn at sleeping. We meant to give them as much time as possible before we woke them, so that they'd have no trouble standing guard for the rest of the night. We were supposedly among friends, but even if that were completely true, there was nothing to keep enemies from sneaking up on us while we relaxed. Nothing, that is, but our own vigilance.

Our sleeping chambers were all grouped together, and right now we were in a private sitting room meant to serve the occupants of those chambers. A tea service and cups had been waiting when we'd come in, another indication that the staff was determined to earn their bonus for excellent service.

"We've needed to talk ever since that Mohr fellow told us what he and his friends believe," Lorand said, shifting in the chair he'd taken. "We agree that we all did have that fireball experience and none of the other Highs with us went through the same, but that doesn't mean we're the ones spoken of in the Prophecies. There are just too many questions left unanswered, like where did those fireballs come from in the first place?''

"The Prophecies never say where these things are supposed to come from," I contributed when no one else offered a suggestion. "The point was never brought up in school, where they taught about the Prophecies, and even skeptics like my father never noticed the lack. I suppose most people assume that they're sent by the Highest Aspect or something."

"I'm afraid I can't quite accept that," Jovvi said, her expression faintly disturbed. "The fireball *I* faced was much too solid and real to be any sort of manifestation from the Highest Aspect. It's much more likely that someone real was responsible, but I have no idea who that could be."

"Well, we know it wasn't these Guild members," Vallant Ro put in, his expression tinged with a sourness that was apparently becoming permanent with him. "There's no doubt about their not bein' able to use magic of any aspect, but that's not to say they didn't hire someone. But why *us*, and what about the other signs that are supposed to manifest? When the Guild man gets around to askin' about that, I'll have to tell him that there honestly haven't been any."

"Those other signs are supposed to manifest in privacy, 'out of the sight of the enemies of the Five' or some such," Lorand put in with a nod. "I don't remember anything like that either, and I'm sure I would have."

"All I remember is a practical joke or two," Rion said, adding his own agreement. "And one of those jokes had to be from my own subconscious mind, since it involved Air magic. The other was accomplished with Water magic, which at the time meant either Vallant or Pagin Holter. Both of them were in the residence, and they were the only ones with strong enough Water magic."

"Oh, yes, I remember that practical joke with Water magic too," Lorand agreed, and then he grinned sheepishly. "I was feeling so out of place at the time, that I thought I was the only one the joke was being played on. So I decided to show I was sophisticated enough to ignore the prank, while privately hoping that I was ruining the joke for whoever played it."

"That someone had to be Holter, because it certainly wasn't me," Vallant Ro said with a snort of remembered annoyance. "I thought at the time that he might be tryin' to challenge me or somethin', but nothin' ever came of it."

"Are you saying you were a victim of that practical joke too, Vallant?" Jovvi asked softly after she and I had exchanged a glance. Personally I also felt a chill, and I had a suspicion that Jovvi shared that with me. "It's odd, but I was also treated to that same practical joke, and from her expression and emotions, I'd say Tamma makes the fifth victim."

"All of you?" Naran said, looking around at us. The men were now wearing expressions that probably matched my own, odd twists of the face that reflected the confusion and muddiness of their thoughts. I remembered thinking at the time that the stupid joke had to have been done by Vallant Ro, and I'd been furious when I gave him the chance to apologize for it but he hadn't. Now . . . if all of us had had the same experience *again*. . . .

"And now that we're talking about practical jokes and odd happenings, I remember something else," Jovvi went on, looking at each of us in turn before turning her attention to Rion. "You mentioned something about a joke involving Air magic, but had decided that it was your own mind playing the trick. What specifically was involved with that, Rion?"

"It . . . wasn't at all like the other occurrences," Rion answered slowly and carefully, his expression grave despite his having Naran's hand in his own. Usually when they held hands, he seemed very much at peace with the world. "Years ago I fashioned a . . . number of different shapes and forms out of hardened air to . . . help me with my exercising and working out. After I received one of Mother's—that woman's—letters, I happened to need those shapes and forms to work off my anger. Finding it right there in front of me to satisfy the need must have been nothing more than my own mind seeing to the matter. . . . Wasn't it?"

The plaintive note in his voice was perfectly clear, but with my hand over my eyes I could no longer see his expression. Not that I needed to. Once again it must have been a lot like mine, as I remembered an invisible net swing that had to have been made out of hardened air too. Lorand groaned and Vallant Ro made a sound deep in his throat, and then Jovvi sighed.

"To answer your question, Rion," she said, "I wondered at the time how you knew about the refuge I'd had as a child, and also how you knew I needed it so badly right then. It was exactly the proper shape and size but it was invisible, so I concluded it was made of hardened air. With you being the only Air magic user in the residence...."

Rion voiced a groan like the one Lorand had produced, and I took my hand away from my eyes to see that everyone else was also looking around. And looking drawn, which was very much the way I felt.

"That's Fire, Water, and Air magic accounted for," I said, hating the way some sort of noose seemed to be tightening around us. "I'm going to mention something reluctantly, and only because it falls into the realm of Earth magic—in a way. If no one else had a similar experience, please say so right away as I happen to need the reassurance rather badly."

"Of course we will," Jovvi said encouragingly with a smile. "Go ahead and tell us."

"All right, it was at the mastery tests," I said, wishing I could feel more foolish about discussing what *had* to be a flight of fancy. "I ... was more than a little unsure and nervous, especially since there were two of the Adepts and I was alone. I didn't like being alone, so I ... pretended that a bird was ... giving me encouragement and company, a bird which didn't seem to be afraid of the fire I used...."

"Oh, that's marvelous," Jovvi cut in, her smile now wide and relieved. "I don't remember anything at all about a bird, only about a spider which happened to be in the testing building with me. This is a definite break in the pattern, which has to mean the pattern isn't really there at all. We're all just—"

"Jovvi," Lorand said abruptly, sounding as though he'd had to force himself to speak. "I really hate to say this, but ... the bird ... it was there for me as well."

"And me," Vallant Ro said in a lifeless voice, a perfect match to the way my heart sank. "I felt like a fool thinkin' it was there to give me support, but that's just what it seemed like.''

"And Jovvi, about your spider," Rion said, his body slumped back in his chair. "I had a spider companion as well, there in the testing building. That means there were birds out of doors and spiders indoors, with both falling under the aspect of Earth magic. What were you saying about a broken pattern?"

Jovvi simply shook her head, the relief she'd shown completely gone. But at least she'd felt it for a little while, and I envied her that. . . .

"Why are you all looking as if the world was in the process of ending?" Naran demanded, her bewilderment tinged faintly with exasperation. "Everything you've been saying simply supports the contention that you five are the Chosen mentioned in the Prophecies, and that's wonderful! You're *meant* to be on the Fivefold Throne, so you will be.''

"Naran, dear, I don't quite know where to begin the answer to your question," Jovvi said, sighing as she groped for the proper words. "For me, at least, this all began as something which circumstance forced me into, and then, considering all the people who were being hurt, it became something that had to be done by me because I had the necessary strength. I'm fairly certain that my groupmates felt the same way, but now . . ."

"Now someone is telling us that doing this is our destiny, that it's what we were born for," I took up the explanation, too . . . upset to just sit there. "Choice isn't involved in something like that, and you don't dare even think about failure, not when you've been *chosen* to do the thing. I hate being told that I have no choice, but even more I just keep remembering that I'm a plain, ordinary woman who has made more than her share of mistakes. How can I think of myself as *chosen*, when I'm certain to make even more of them, probably at the worst time possible?"

"And when you're *chosen*, people expect things of you," Lorand put in in agreement. "I have enough self-confidence not to mind when people expect ordinary things from me, but something like this? When not only my life and future depend on how well I do, but everyone else's along with mine? How am I supposed to live with that?''

''But . . . if you're Chosen, all you have to do is continue on the way you've been going,'' Naran protested, obviously still not understanding. ''For anyone else that might not be enough, but for you it has to be. If it wasn't, why would you be the Chosen ones in the first place?''

''Naran, my love, it isn't quite that simple,'' Rion said, trying his hand at it. ''When I was a small boy, one of my nurses taught me a poem. It was a simple thing and I learned it quickly, and then I spent a good deal of my time reciting it over and over. One of those times my mother— that woman—heard me reciting, and she thought it was the most marvelous thing. The next I knew, she was dragging me in front of a group of her friends and telling me to recite the poem. With everyone watching and listening so closely, the words completely disappeared from my head. I could have recited the poem in my sleep or standing on my head, but with everyone listening and watching I couldn't do it at all.''

''That sounds like the time I had to be certified as capable of bein' an officer aboard ship,'' Vallant Ro put in with a nod. ''Two members of the certifyin' board shipped with us, since a skipper's word about a member of his crew is never accepted without support—especially when the crew member is also the fleet owner's son. I knew every one of my duties cold and could have *commanded* that vessel rather than just bein' its lowest officer, but you'd never have known that to look at me. Bein' watched made me so nervous it's a wonder I didn't fall overboard and drown.''

''And we're not talking about just a few people here,'' Naran said with a nod and a sigh. ''Once the word begins to spread, you'll have everyone you pass watching avidly. Whether or not you want to do this thing, everyone will insist that it's your duty and destiny. Yes, I think I finally understand.''

''Let's not forget about the people who will be watching and hoping that we *fail*,'' I said, wanting to round out the picture properly. ''Some of them will be people who don't believe in the Prophecies at all, and some will be those who believe in them utterly—and don't want any ordinary humans cluttering up their picture of ideal perfection. And then, of course, there will be those who just like to see people fail, not to mention the members of the nobility, who will be *praying* that we fail. . . ."

"So you see that we're not in a very enviable position," Jovvi summed up, closing the circle. "Until now we were just a group of people out to make as much trouble for our enemies as we possibly could. Now . . . everyone will *know* what we're supposed to do and how, and most of them will tell us about it. Some of our supporters will try to direct our actions, being convinced that they know the proper way to handle this thing. Others will try to direct us because they don't want us to win, not when their fortunes and/or loyalties are tied up with the other side. Once all that nonsense starts, we'll be lucky if we reach Gan Garee in time for next year's competitions."

"You're right, and that means we can't allow it to start," Vallant Ro said, suddenly looking more alert. "That army comin' behind us from Astinda won't take that long to get here, and they'll be destroyin' things every step of the way. We can't turn to face *them* until we know our backs are secure, and that means takin' on and bestin' those five on the Throne. We'll just have to tell our new allies that they're wrong, and then we can get on with what has to be done in peace."

"Simply telling them that won't work," Lorand disagreed with a grimace. "They know about the fireballs, which is what led them to us in the first place. That happening is a fact, and unless we can come up with a good, logical reason for that happening other than the one they believe, we're wasting our time with denials."

"How can we possibly come up with another reason?" Rion asked, vexation strong in his voice and manner. "We can't simply say that that sort of thing happened all the time in our respective home towns, so another episode simply means nothing. They know better than that, as will anyone else who hears the excuse."

"Why can't we just offer a suggestion?" I asked slowly as the idea came to me. "What I mean is, we suggest a different interpretation of what happened, and then leave it to them to think up the logical reasons. For instance, if we said we thought that someone arranged for those fireballs to make people believe we're the Chosen when we aren't, that would make them stop and think. The reason would be to take the support away from the *real* Chosen in order to make the real ones fail, or maybe to protect them."

"And since the fireballs are the only evidence *they* have, they'd have to consider the idea seriously," Jovvi agreed at once as she brightened. "They don't believe that the nobility knows about the fireballs, but how can anyone prove that they don't? If someone caused the fireballs to appear in order to misdirect people, they'd also make certain that the nobility knew about it."

"They chose us because we were all heading for Gan Garee at the same time for testing," Lorand jumped in with enthusiasm. "They knew we were strong enough to justify belief in the claim that we're the Chosen, and that's why they picked us. The real Chosen are probably among the group of people coming here more slowly, and are perfectly safe as long as everyone is looking in *our* direction."

"And considering the fact that we're simply pawns in their plan, we don't even have to know who they are," Rion said, delight putting a grin on his face. "We can leave the speculation to the Guild people, and simply get on with our own affairs."

"We may even be able to get their help in Gan Garee," Vallant Ro said musingly, his mood lightened as well. "If the real Chosen are among those followin' us, helpin' *us* will be helpin' them. We can say we're meant to protect them and get them where they're supposed to be, and that's why we're leadin' this bunch."

"Now, this is what I call a decent solution," Jovvi said with a laugh. "Not only does it get us out from under, it even lets us make use of the assistance we need. Let's just make sure not to give anyone a reason to doubt the story, and we ought to get away with it. And who knows, if we're very lucky, the story may turn out to be true after all."

We all made some sort of comment agreeing with that last part, and my own agreement was extremely fervent. I'd been chosen for enough things in my life by my parents; to now find out that I was chosen by people centuries dead would be close to the last straw. Anger rather than dread was beginning to rise at the thought of that, but also an intense curiosity. All those hundreds of years ago . . . how could they possibly have known? And how could they now be causing the things we'd all experienced? It all made very little sense, and I knew I'd have to find some time to think about it.

But not now, when voices and footsteps down the hall said we were about to have some company. . . .

Nineteen

Rion heard the sound of voices and footsteps in the hall approaching their sitting area, which meant they'd found their solution to the problem just in time. That it wasn't a true solution to the actual circumstance couldn't be thought about right now, not when the truth would put them in an extremely untenable position. Or at least what seemed to be the truth. For some reason believing in something special about another person was a good deal easier than believing the same about oneself.

"Ah, I think we're about to have company," Jovvi said in a normal voice, one which was certainly heard by those in the hall. "See, I was right. It's Dom Mohr and his friends."

"We bid you a good evening, Excellences," the man Mohr said with a bow as he looked around at them. "I thought this might be the perfect time to introduce you to my associates, but if we're intruding. . . ."

"Not at all, Dom Mohr," Vallant assured him when the man's voice trailed off. "There's no question of intrudin'.

There are certainly enough seats in here for all of us, so please join us."

"But I'm afraid we have some bad news for you," Lorand put in as the four men bowed and began to make their way to the empty chairs. "We've been discussing this matter of being Chosen, and we've discovered that that incident with the fireball was the only one of its kind. Since there were definitely supposed to be more signs, we've been forced to conclude that we're not the ones—but we may know who *is* Chosen."

"If not you five, then who?" Mohr asked, stopping in front of a chair rather than sitting in it. "And it's always possible that you missed the other signs, since they're supposed to manifest in private. You must think back to any odd incidents you may have been involved with, but dismissed at the time. You—"

"We've already done that, sir," Rion interrupted, forcing himself to sound friendly rather than curt. "There just isn't anything of that sort, but we've thought of a reason why that is. *We* aren't the Chosen ones, but they must be among the hundreds of people following us. Someone wanted to protect them, so they made it seem as though *we're* the ones."

"So that the enemies of the Chosen will try stoppin' us instead of them," Vallant added, rounding out the explanation with a smile. "It makes a good deal of sense, and we don't mind in the least. We'll blaze the trail, so to speak, so the real five can simply walk in and do what they're meant to."

"I . . . don't think it's meant to work in quite that way," Mohr said as he slowly seated himself. "Have any of you actually read the Prophecies, and I mean as they were written down? Not heard about them or had someone paraphrase or interpret them for you, but actually read them? And for that matter, how familiar are you with the ability of Guild members?"

Rion exchanged looks with the others, but none of them spoke up to say they'd read the Prophecies. *He* certainly hadn't, nor had he ever heard anyone else say they had. And as far as being familiar with Guild practices went, everyone probably knew just what he did.

"It seems that our education is lacking in more than one way," Rion told Mohr ruefully, speaking for them all. "It's fairly obvious that none of us has read the actual Prophecies, and we also know almost nothing about the Guild. Your members are unable to use magic yourselves, but you're able to judge the use of it in others—or so I interpret the matter."

"Your interpretation is correct, if incomplete," Mohr replied with a smile and a gesture of his hand. "But that subject may be left for later, after we've discussed the Prophecies. In point of fact there is just one Prophecy, with more . . . minor supporting statements which are also called Prophecies. The major statement is as follows: 'Beware and be warned. In three hundred years will come a time of greatest crisis, a time when the teachings of wisdom are no longer followed. This will presage the reappearance of the devastating evil of the Four, which nearly destroyed our empire.' "

"Just a moment," Jovvi interrupted the man, clearly as surprised as Rion felt. "That isn't precisely what everyone claims the Prophecy says. There's a difference between the reappearance of the Four, and the reappearance of their evil. Most people claim that it's the Four themselves who are supposed to reappear."

"I'm of the opinion that those who first interpreted the Prophecy were possessed of overactive imaginations," Mohr said with a smile more wry than his previous one. "That or secret believers in the supernatural, which would certainly color their thinking. In point of fact the Prophecy reads exactly as I've quoted it, a matter I made sure of personally."

"What about the rest of it?" Tamrissa asked, her brow furrowed with disturbance. "Is that also imagination?"

"The rest of the major Prophecy says, 'In this time of crisis there will appear a Chosen Blending, and there will be no doubt of their identity. They will stand against the reemergent evil, and will do their utmost to triumph.' " Mohr looked around at all of them again, and his smile softened. "That part *I* interpret as there being no doubt to the Guild."

"Which means what?" Lorand asked, taking his turn to

speak for all of them. "Why would your people in particular have no doubt?"

"That goes to what I said earlier about our ability," Mohr replied, and Rion noticed that two of Mohr's companions were paying very close attention, as though what was being said was new to them as well. "Those of us who are of the Guild are actually able to see the strength of those who practice in the various aspects, and we have a scale we use for our own private files. Each level of strength, Low, Middle, and High, can be broken down into first, second or third level of intensity, with first level being the lowest. When people—other than Guild people—talk about a strong Middle, they're usually referring to a third level Middle."

"I'd be curious to know how the present Seated Blending was rated," Jovvi said, her expression neutral except for a . . . gleam of sorts in her eyes. "Or hasn't the Guild been allowed to rate them?"

"It isn't a matter of 'allowed,' " Mohr replied with a shrug. "As long as one of us is within range of them, they're rated whether they want to be or not. And to answer your question, they've been rated as third level Highs."

"And we must be rated the same," Lorand said musingly. "But one thing I don't understand is, why hasn't the Guild come forward before this? Surely you and your people knew that the various Seated Blendings over the last hundred years or so haven't been more than Middles? Why didn't one of you tell someone?"

"To what end?" Mohr asked, his face set in lines of seriousness. "Most people, noble or not, consider Guild members freaks, so who would have believed us? If you and these others hadn't tried your hands against the current Seated Blending, would you have taken my word for the fact that you're much stronger than they are? In the beginning we wouldn't have been believed, and in these latter years the nobility would have kept us from spreading the word very far. Most of us would have been killed, and only those of us too frightened to disobey them—or those more than willing to work for them—would have been spared."

"You now touch on a question *I've* had, High Master," one of the three men with Mohr put in, drawing his attention. "In the past the Guild has done nothing but perform its job, but now your people move through Gan Garee, spreading the word that the Seated Blending was seated through trickery rather than through honest endeavor. Why have you suddenly changed tactics?"

"Surely you jest, Dom Ambor," Mohr replied with a short laugh. "With the changed situation in Gan Garee. . . . But forgive me. I meant to introduce everyone as soon as we entered, and the matter simply slipped my mind. Excellences, may I introduce Dom Gorlin Ambor and Dom Mirist Koln, the chosen representatives of the merchants of Gan Garee. The third gentleman there is Master Holdis Ayl, my second in command in the Guild."

Rion joined his groupmates in nodding politely to the three men, also joining them in noticing that Mohr still addressed them as "Excellences." Clearly they hadn't yet convinced him of their . . . decoy status, which surely meant they must work harder at doing so.

"I'm familiar with the names of two of those gentlemen," Tamrissa said to Mohr, showing an odd kind of satisfaction. "My father considered them his greatest rivals and yet completely unworthy of being his intimates, which is the best recommendation they can possibly have as far as *I'm* concerned."

"Your father, lady?" Gorlin Ambor said, surprise in the question. "I wasn't aware that we knew your father."

"Oh, you know him all right," Tamrissa said with a very unladylike sound. "His name is Storn Torgar, and my late husband was Gimmis Domon, who *was* worthy of being his intimate."

"You have our deepest condolences, lady, on both accounts," Ambor said after exchanging a glance with Mirist Koln. "No merchant with the least amount of integrity— or the slightest amount of self-preservation—would ever have considered doing business with either of those two. They tend to prey upon those who are unfamiliar with their practices, a group which is unfortunately rather large. But I would appreciate your returning to my question, High Master. What has the changed situation in Gan Garee to do with the change in your Guild's behavior?"

"That should be rather obvious, Dom Ambor," Mohr

said with more amusement than chiding. "With so many of their members dead or missing, the nobility is very much in a confused uproar. Oh, their agents still prance around pretending that everything is the way it used to be, but that's utter nonsense. Most of the really powerful nobles are gone, and the majority of their heirs aren't up to truly taking their places. Even the competent ones are having trouble finding out everything their fathers were involved in, and that sort is in the minority. The majority of the heirs are simply spending the gold they've come into, without worrying about how they're going to replace it. Their lackeys are busy trying to educate them, so there's no one watching us as closely as they used to. We are, after all, no more than freaks, and who cares about what freaks do?"

"And now the people are believin' you?" Vallant asked, a point Rion had meant to put if no one else did. "If your people are still freaks to them, and the trouble the nobility is havin' shouldn't change that, what makes the difference?"

"The whispering campaign makes the difference," Mohr replied with satisfaction. "Right after the last competition we started the rumor about the Seated Five having cheated, and spread it all over the city. We waited a short while to let the rumor be spread, and then we staged 'forced admissions' in a number of places. Two of our people would go into . . . say, a tavern, separately, of course, and then the first would 'recognize' the second as a Guild member. The first would then demand to know if the rumor was true, and the Guild member would reluctantly admit that it was. Then the Guild member would look frightened and leave quickly, and that would convince everyone who heard him."

"Now I understand why I noticed so many angry . . . mobs, I suppose you would have to call them," Koln put in, the first words the man had spoken. "That was just before we left the city, and now I wonder if they've tried to do something about their unhappiness."

"If our plan is working properly, they haven't," Mohr said, again speaking soberly. "We've also spread the word that ordinary people haven't got a chance if they go up against the usurpers alone, and they need to wait for the

Chosen to lead them. That part of it will hopefully save lives, because most of them really don't have a chance against the usurpers, not by themselves.''

''They should make an impressive force once we get the real Chosen into the city,'' Vallant commented, obviously making an attempt to reestablish their stance. ''With enough ordinary people—and, hopefully, members of the guard—behind them, it might even prove possible for them to oust the usurpers without any fightin'. There have been enough lives lost in this, and we mustn't forget about the army comin' from Astinda. Takin' over in Gan Garee won't help any of us if that army follows us in and pulls it down around our ears.''

''Then there really is an army?'' Holdis Ayl, Mohr's second, asked, his face having paled. ''Messages have come in by pigeon from some of our people, but they seemed disjointed and were hard to read. We were hoping it was just a rumor without any validity behind it. . . .''

The man's voice trailed off in partial questioning, but Vallant's headshake killed the faint spark of hope.

''No, unfortunately it's no rumor,'' Vallant said heavily. ''Our own army—which we weren't supposed to have— has been destroyin' large parts of Astinda, and now their army means to return the favor. We've learned that they have more than one Blendin' in it, so we're goin' to need all the help we can get to keep our country from bein' completely destroyed.''

''But we have to settle matters in Gan Garee first,'' Jovvi added as the four men exchanged disturbed glances. ''When the time comes for the Chosen to turn and face the intruders, we don't want them to have to worry about what's going on behind their backs.''

''I think it's time I returned to that explanation of what the Guild actually does,'' Mohr said with a sigh, apparently ignoring Jovvi's comment. ''It should help to clarify matters. . . . Well, as you know, we begin to examine what talent people have when they reach the age of five. No five-year-old has ever come anywhere near his or her potential, of course, but there are certain . . . echoes of what that potential will be which become obvious to the trained Guild member. The echoes are examined carefully while the children are put into one of the five categories—or six, if you count the ability of Guild members, but certainly not seven. Those who have unfortunately been born nulls are . . . eased away from their parents and sent to one of the preserves, where they're taught to live as normal a life as is possible for them.''

Rion looked down at his hands in discomfort, a reaction everyone else in the room undoubtedly shared. It was considered very much in bad taste to discuss the crippled, those who were born without any ability whatsoever. That sort was quickly sent to a place where normal people would not be disturbed by their lumpish, talentless presence, and that was very much a kindness for them. To do otherwise would have exposed them to taunting ridicule from their peers while they were children, giving them pain over something that couldn't possibly be considered their fault. Even sweet Naran tightened her grip on Rion's hand, showing her disturbance at the topic under discussion, and Rion patted her hand encouragingly.

"Now, those echoes I mentioned are only hints," Mohr continued, his expression showing he was partially lost to distraction. "They *suggest* what the child might become as he or she matures, letting our people know who should be watched most closely over the following years. We have files on every third level High in this empire, files which have been updated as the Highs grew older and more adept. Over the years it's been possible to detect and delineate the upper level of every single one of them—except for you five. We were looking for the Chosen, you understand, so we were extremely careful and thorough. That's why the Chosen can't be among those following you; there are any number of Highs who have approached your strength, but none have ever matched it. If you five aren't the Chosen, Excellences, then no one is.''

Rion added his silence to that of his groupmates, also refraining from exchanging glances with them. Mohr seemed to have them trapped, but there might still be a way out for them. The plan of Naran's which Rion had mentioned to Jovvi and Lorand, the one they hoped would bring Vallant and Tamrissa closer together again . . . possibly that could now be used for a double purpose. . . .

"Excuse me, sir, but I believe you're deliberately over-looking something rather important," Rion said into the awkward silence. "Those minor Prophecies you mentioned earlier, which you never went into fully. Unless I'm mistaken, I *have* seen something in writing referring to them, and one segment has stuck in my memory. It's the part about the Chosen blending in their ordinary lives as well as they do in the Blending of their aspects. Is *that* part, at least, accurately recorded?"

"Yes, it so happens it is," Mohr replied cautiously, as though he had no intention of agreeing to anything which would destroy his beloved theory. "But I'm afraid I'm missing the point. I've seen your group interacting, and there's been nothing to indicate that that condition doesn't exist."

"Unfortunately, sir, that doesn't happen to be the case," Rion said, this time glancing briefly at Jovvi and Lorand, whose sudden alertness told Rion that they knew exactly what he was in the midst of. "Most of us are quite close and friendly, but two of our number are having . . . difficulties of a personal nature. Not that anyone can blame *him*, of course. She's being quite unreasonable in all ways, giving him no choice but to respond as he does."

"I'm afraid she's rather more than unreasonable." Jovvi took up the explanation smoothly, exactly as Rion had hoped she would. "She's deliberately torturing the poor man, callously ignoring his feelings as she tramples all over them. And he simply accepts the cruelty of her treatment, making very little protest. I've been feeling terribly sorry for him . . ."

"Yes, we all feel sorry for him, but there's nothing we can do to change matters," Lorand put in, deliberately speaking heavily. "She's completely heartless and cruel, but she *is* one of our Blending so we have to try to overlook that. Changing the composition of our group now would be extremely difficult."

Mohr looked close to being shattered at the news, especially since the stricken look on Tamrissa's face and the shock on Vallant's told their own stories confirming, in a way, what had been said. Tamrissa had turned mute with the weight of what she'd heard, just as Rion had hoped she would, and that should do it as far as convincing Mohr went. The discussion would continue after they'd gotten rid of their "guests," and then Vallant would hopefully respond the way they all expected him to. But not now, not when they were so close to convincing Mohr and the others that they were mistaken—

"No!" Vallant suddenly shouted, surging to his feet and causing Rion to groan. He *wouldn't* respond to the ploy *now*, not when they were so close! Surely he wouldn't . . . !

TWENTY

Vallant had tried his best to help the others to convince the man Mohr that he was mistaken, but it didn't seem to have worked. Mohr's explanation of what the Guild people did, something which had obviously gone unmentioned until now, stopped them all in their tracks. Vallant was in the middle of racking his brain for another idea when Rion spoke up, mentioning part of the minor Prophecies. Then, when Mohr agreed that what Rion had said was true, Rion continued in a way that at first made Vallant believe he was hearing things.

"Unfortunately, sir, that doesn't happen to be the case," Rion said, referring to Mohr's agreement on the relationships the Chosen were supposed to have. "Most of us are quite close and friendly, but two of our number are having . . . difficulties of a personal nature. Not that anyone can blame *him*, of course. She's being quite unreasonable in all ways, giving him no choice but to respond as he does."

Vallant immediately decided that Rion had chosen to lie about Tamrissa in order to throw Mohr off the scent, which was a reasonably good idea. But Rion *did* sound awfully convincing, and then the shock worsened when Jovvi spoke up.

"I'm afraid she's rather more than unreasonable," Jovvi said, also sounding completely believable. "She's deliberately torturing the poor man, callously ignoring his feelings as she tramples all over them. And he simply accepts the cruelty of her treatment, making very little protest. I've been feeling terribly sorry for him. . . ."

Sorry for him. The phrase clanged in Vallant's mind as a faint echo from his own thoughts agreed with the sentiment, but that was pure nonsense. Tamrissa wasn't callous or cruel, it simply wasn't in her to behave like that. Jovvi must be doing nothing more than agreeing with what Rion had said, supporting his try to—

"Yes, we all feel sorry for him, but there's nothing we can do to change matters," Lorand put in, the heaviness of his tone telling Vallant that the man spoke reluctantly—but was supplying what he considered the truth. "She's completely heartless and cruel, but she *is* one of our Blending so we have to try to overlook that. Changing the composition of our group now would be extremely difficult."

For a brief moment Vallant couldn't move, let alone speak. Naran, who sat beside Rion as usual, wore an expression of complete agreement, supporting what had been said without using the words. That was bad enough, but Tamrissa, the woman Vallant loved with every ounce of his being—

Tamrissa looked absolutely devastated. She, too, had seen that everyone was apparently speaking what they considered the truth, and the painful bewilderment in her beautiful eyes brought Vallant a stab of agony. Their groupmates were horribly wrong in what they'd said, and someone had to set things straight—right now!

"No!" Vallant shouted, rising to his feet with the intensity of his feelings. "None of that is the truth, and you all should know it! *I'm* the one who's responsible, the one who's too afraid to say even a single one of the words he should. Not even knowin' she might be in danger from actin' too recklessly has been able to make me tell her she's the most important thing in the world to me. If she refuses to listen, the way she has every right to do—and the way she probably will, knowin' me for the coward I am—I'll never be able to go on. It isn't *her*, you fools, it's *me*—''

Words abruptly failed Vallant, and were replaced with an overwhelming need to be alone. For that reason he strode out of the sitting area with the idea of returning to his room, but that was a place he'd be expected to go. If someone decided to follow him and tried to talk about what had happened. . . . No, he'd never be able to stand that, so he'd be wise to find a different temporary refuge.

At a time so close to dinner, the inn's entrance area was completely deserted. Vallant strode through it and then outside, barely pausing even when he realized it was raining. Realized it consciously, that is. He'd known about the rain even before it had started, and had been thinking that it was a good thing their sentries didn't have to stand outside in order to keep watch. The second Blending had had an early dinner, and by now were probably fast asleep. He and his groupmates were available again to take their place. . . .

A large and leafy tree stood not far from the inn's front entrance, and Vallant walked slowly through the dripping rain until he reached the partial shelter of its branches. It had turned cool and a sheet of rain tried to mist his face and clothes, but he'd already removed the dampness from himself and now disallowed a return of it. The moon was invisible behind the thick dark of the rain clouds, a perfect match to the mood now on him. Dark depression, self loathing, a mewling helplessness. . . .

Vallant only just stopped himself from throwing a fist into the hard and uneven trunk of the tree. Even after the scene he'd just been a part of, his mind still attempted to avoid thinking about the whole thing. He loved Tamrissa more than life itself, and therefore knew that if she refused and rejected him one more time it would destroy him. Too many people were counting on him for him to let that happen, so he'd gone out of his way to avoid touching on the question of their relationship. Except for that one lapse, when Tamrissa had gone out against that Fire link alone. . . .

But after that he'd deliberately let the matter lapse. He'd simply told himself that she was better off without him, and the truth of that couldn't be denied. So for the past few days things had gone along uneventfully, but now—

Vallant's head suddenly came up, a reaction to what he'd felt rather than heard. The inns' stables couldn't be seen even from where he stood beside the tree, screened as they were by the heavy row of trees to the right. But someone over there had just used Water magic, and not simply to dry himself after coming in out of the rain. There had been far too much strength behind the effort, as though someone had used the aspect in some sort of attack. All their own people were inside the inn, most of them getting ready to go to dinner. It couldn't have been Mohr's people, not when they weren't able to use magic, so who . . . ?

Rather than waste time speculating, Vallant left the shelter of the tree and made his way toward the stables. He'd also dropped his shield, letting his very plain but brand-new breeches and shirt get wet, preferring that to announcing his approach. He was no longer able to release the power, not after the last few days, but hopefully not *using* the power would help to keep from betraying him. It was possible nothing at all was wrong, but he preferred to go and see that for himself.

After a few moments, Vallant stood among the trees which no longer shielded view of the stables. They were really very large, meant for the use of all three of the inns, and a long row of buildings directly opposite were probably for the servants and guardsmen of those very important people who usually frequented the inns. Not a single flicker of lamplight showed in any of the windows of the building, but lanterns hung along the outer stables wall and shone dimly from within. Everything looked peaceful and quiet beyond the backdrop of the rain, but inside the stables. . . .

Inside the stables Vallant could detect the masses of water which represented their own horses and those of the men who had come to meet them, but that wasn't all. There were smaller groupings of water which represented human beings, and there were more than a dozen of them. As large as the stables were, having that many stablemen made no sense at all. Their own horses had been taken care of hours ago, so nothing else should have been required that would bring so many people to the stables.

Which meant that something was definitely wrong. Squinting against the mist of rain, Vallant shifted his attention to the row of buildings opposite the stables. It would have been understandable to detect a small number of people in them, but most of the servants working at the inns would be *there* now, getting ready to serve dinner. And most of the servants—and stablemen—were undoubtedly locals, with their own homes to go to when they weren't working. There shouldn't have been at least forty indications of human beings, clustered together in one section of the buildings, as though they were part of a force getting ready to attack.

"Chaos take 'em," Vallant muttered angrily when it became clear that that was exactly what they had to be: an attacking force which wanted no one free left behind them when they actually got down to the attack. The smaller part of their group must be taking care of the stablemen on duty, either killing them or tying them up. Considering that burst of Water magic used earlier, it was more likely they were killing rather than tying.

"And they chose the perfect time to come at us," Vallant muttered to himself, knowing he should have expected something like this. The second Blending had come off watch when his own had awakened from their naps, and the comfort and apparent safety of the inn—not to mention that contention that they were the Chosen—had worked to keep his group from taking a precautionary look around. In a little while everyone would be expected to sit down to dinner, which meant they would definitely not be Blended. The attack would come without warning, and the intruders' relatively small numbers suggested they had more of a plan in mind than simply trying to overwhelm them.

So it was time for Vallant to get back to the inn, to join the others in an attempt to defend against these people. He knew he could be there quickly, but sight of the men coming out of the stables made him pause. There were eleven men coming out, and the rest remained unmoving inside the stables. A moment after they appeared there was movement at the section of building where the larger force was, and then *those* men were emerging to join the ones from the stables. They might not see Vallant as he ran back to the inn through the dark and rain, but they would be much too close behind him.

So Vallant knew he *couldn't* go back, at least not physically. All that left was an attempt to reach Jovvi with his mind, and Vallant was fairly certain that that would work. But it would also undoubtedly warn the intruders, letting them know that someone lurked in the trees and watched them. As fast as the Blending entity came into being, it still took *some* time for the being to form once the Blending was initiated. That brief moment might be all the intruders needed to locate and kill him, since the very act of Blending would turn him helpless. Death held no particular fear for Vallant, especially not now, but his death would mean the end of the Blending. Without him it would be incomplete, and therefore unable to defend itself and the others. So what was he supposed to do . . . ?

That frustrating question had only just formed in his thoughts when the strangest thing happened. He felt Jovvi's familiar touch in his mind, causing the automatic reaction of his reaching out to his other Blendingmates, and then the entity was formed and there. But rather than being submerged in the group consciousness which was the entity, his own personality and awareness were left to direct matters. That had never happened before, at least not to him, but thinking about it would have to be left for another time.

The intruders had brought their two groups together in the open area between the stables and the buildings, and the Vallant entity counted quickly. Fifty-one men dressed all in black, with just one of them speaking to the others. That one would most likely be the leader of the group, and the leader was the one the Vallant entity wanted to contact. So the entity floated a bit closer, and reached out to take control of the man. As soon as his mind was tightly held, the Vallant entity inserted words in the man's thoughts.

"Tell your men to stand where they are," the Vallant entity whispered to the man in its grip. "And when you respond to my questions, do so in this manner. Speaking aloud is unnecessary."

"I'm . . . not supposed to respond to this sort of thing,"

the man replied silently, and oddly enough his mind fought a bit to free itself. "I'm . . . supposed to be protected, but it doesn't seem to be working. And if it doesn't work they'll kill me, then go on to do the job we were sent here to do."

"I take it the Five told you you would be protected," the Vallant entity said as it examined the man's mind. "Yes, I can see indications of where they had you under control, but their strength still can't match mine. What plan were your men supposed to follow?"

"There are two link groups for each aspect," the man replied with less hesitation, no longer struggling very hard. "Both sets of groups are under orders to attack the fugitives at the same time, aspect to aspect without giving them a chance to Blend. We were told by freak informers that they would be here, and that this would be the best time to attack. We're the first group of—"

The man's words ended abruptly as he screamed, a re-action to the knife which had been thrust into his body. One of his own followers had murdered him, and now the ten link groups stood together and braced, their minds flaring out in an attempt to reach and destroy the entity. The Vallant entity actually staggered under the load, which certainly shouldn't have happened. The entity should have been stronger than *all* those minds combined.

But that, the Vallant entity suddenly realized, was incorrect. A memory now resurfaced, one which belonged to none of its flesh forms. It was part of the data which the entity had somehow lost, and was now only partially re-gaining. It had something to do with two link groups acting in tandem, which more than doubled its strength. Yes, that was it, but how did the required response go . . . ?

The Vallant entity staggered again, feeling itself losing ground against the onslaught. At the moment it was able to shield its flesh forms from the attack, but soon its strength would be drained and the attack would reach them. That could certainly not be allowed, but the proper response con-tinued to elude it. The answer was on the tip of its mental tongue, perfectly obvious if one only looked at matters in the correct way. The enemy had obviously regained more of the lost knowledge than the Vallant entity, which was extremely annoying. What *was* that response . . . ?

"Ahhh," the Vallant entity breathed as it staggered for the third time. The response *was* completely obvious, and now it was also remembered. But it would require the use of its own link groups, which hadn't been assembled before the moment of crisis. To contact them would be more than awkward, as part of the shielding effort would need to go into the contact. What to do . . . ?

And then surprise touched the Vallant entity, as it realized that its own link groups were assembled after all. How that had come about was something to be left for another time; right now there were enemies who needed to be vanquished. And vanquished they would be. . . .

The Vallant entity now looked carefully at each link group, searching for the weakest member in each link. And there always *was* a weakest member, no matter how close their strength was one to the other. Drawing on the strength of its link groups let the Vallant entity divert part of its efforts into the search, and then the ten weakest were located and marked. The next step was to draw even more power, which, for some reason, made the Vallant entity briefly uneasy, but it was necessary so it was done. And once done. . . .

And once done, that additional power was poured into the weakest members of the ten links. Those members died without making a sound, falling to the sodden ground in lifeless heaps, and then the ten link groups were link groups no longer. Five was the required number for the utmost in efficient output, and they no longer had that. Which made it possible for the Vallant entity to touch each group of four with its own aspect, burning to ash the Fire magic users, completely dessicating the Water magic users, stilling the hearts of the Earth magic users, and taking the breath of life from the Air magic users. Those with Spirit magic had all sense of balance withdrawn, which left them nearly mindless in their forced insanity. Some of them screamed, some cried, some sat down and raised their faces to the rain, and some wandered away. All, however, were beyond ever using their talent again, and the proposed attack was over.

"And now it's completely me again," Vallant muttered

after the Blending had dissolved, once more looking at the scene through his eyes alone. The rain mixed the ash of burning with the dust of dessication, all of it joining the mud of the ground. Motionless bodies alternated with those which were mindlessly humming or sitting silently, and around the fringes there were dark forms wandering aimlessly about. ''And this is the worst it's ever been.''

With which words Vallant turned and hurried back toward the inn, needing to get away from the sight of what he'd just helped to do. But queasiness couldn't be allowed to rule him, not when the entity thought that the Five had regained some of those ''memories'' that *it* still lacked. And that leader of the group had been about to tell them how many other groups like this had been sent after them just as he was killed. Now they'd probably only be able to get the number after the other groups attacked them.

And worst of all, being part of the Blending again had given him a much more intense understanding of Tamrissa's pain. The memory of that wasn't likely to leave him very soon, and he didn't know what to do. Coward that he was, he simply had no idea what he could possibly do. . . .

TWENTY-ONE

Delin slept late before coming out to breakfast, a sumptuous meal he had served in his private dining room. As this was only his second day of returning to normal eating, his mouth watered as all his favorite breakfast dishes were uncovered by the servants. He would not be able to finish any of the dishes, that he'd discovered the previous morning, but as the time passed and his normal eating habits were allowed to return, he would make better and better progress.

But the first step necessary before eating was examining the food with his talent. He'd been lucky enough to miss being poisoned with the others, and wasn't about to overlook the possibility that someone would try again. In the last day and some he'd grown really proficient at separating out and identifying the various components of his favorite dishes, all the way down to any water which might have been added as well as the butter in which the rest had been fried. He also knew how much salt, pepper, taragon, thyme, paprika—any seasoning—had been added, which was something of a pity. At one time it had been one of his small pleasures to try to guess the various ingredients.

And yet now he had other things to give him pleasure, both small and large. Real food was one of them, of course, but once the meal was over he rose to go to a far greater one. He'd called a meeting of the Blending for this morning, *ordering* the others to be there. They'd spent most of yesterday recovering from their ordeal, but they weren't unaware of the fact that Delin was the one who had ended their agony. Now it was time for them to find out about the rest.

When Delin walked into the large, formal sitting room, Bron and Selendi and Homin were already there. The sitting room was one of the largest in his wing, and they were already there because he'd had them come a good twenty minutes before *he* intended to show up. They still looked somewhat pale and drawn, but more than that they looked impatient.

"It's about time you got here!" Bron snapped at once, glaring at Delin from the chair he'd chosen. "You had no call to keep us waiting like a bunch of begging peasants, and—"

"That's enough," Delin interrupted, not raising his voice but letting the coldness inside him come through clearly. "What I *expected* to hear was how all of you were feeling. Any unexpected side effects from the . . . balm I provided?"

His three groupmates exchanged furtive glances, hating to be reminded that they had *him* to thank for no longer being in pain. It had come as a shock to them, of course, an unexpected and unpleasant surprise that apparently they still hadn't adjusted to.

"If this is supposed to be a meeting of our Five, you can't start it yet," Selendi put in sullenly, her stare extremely unfriendly. "Kambil isn't here yet, which is rather wise of him. He didn't have to sit and wait the way we did. . . ."

Her words trailed off in an attempt at admonishment, but by tone rather than by browbeating as Bron had tried. Delin found that rather amusing, showing as it did that if she didn't yet respect him, at least she did fear him.

"Kambil won't be joining us this morning," Delin told her and the other two, his tone still easy. "For some reason he isn't responding to the counteractive the way the rest of you have, and is therefore in no condition to be away from his bed."

The three of them looked seriously worried, not knowing the half of it. Delin had been *that* close to letting Kambil die, when he realized that the man could be allowed to die anytime. There was no need to make a hasty decision in the matter, when feeding Kambil half the dosage of the counteragent kept the poison from killing him. It did very little to relieve the agony, of course, but that was only Kambil's misfortune, not Delin's. Once Delin decided on how to control the man completely—and if he really wanted to—then that would be the time to settle the thing.

"In the meanwhile, we have important matters to discuss," Delin went on, regaining the attention of his small audience. "The first and foremost thing on everyone's mind is this poisoning business, which you need to know the details about. Those who fed you and Kambil the poison intend to control our group, but you'll be pleased to hear that there's no longer a danger of that."

"Why not?" Bron demanded, but with less bluster than usual. "We still need to take their damned counteragent, don't we? And while we're discussing it, how did *you* manage to end up in control of this whole thing? My servants tell me that you weren't affected at all, and that made me the least bit suspicious."

"Suspicious that I'm the one who caused all this?" Delin

said lightly, making no effort to avoid the accusation. "To be perfectly honest I wouldn't have minded being the one, but it so happens that I'm not. Here's the note which came with the first delivery of the counteragent."

He produced the note and handed it over, and Homin held it while the other two read over his shoulder and along with him. When they'd all finished and looked up again, Delin gestured to the note.

"You'll notice that they expected all five vials of counteragent to be used up, but that turned out not to be necessary," he told them. "The poison must have been administered in the food of our 'celebration,' the food I wasn't permitted to share. Pure luck made me too depressed to eat my own meal, so I was saved what the rest of you went through. But more importantly I had no need to *use* my vial, so its contents were available for analysis. I now know what the counteragent consists of, and I've personally made up a batch of it. You all had some of it this morning, and if it hadn't been properly done you would be back in pain right now."

"So we won't have to take their orders, whatever those orders turn out to be," Homin said, relief clear in his manner. "We won't even have to have the vials picked up, which ought to tell them exactly where we and they stand."

"But we don't *want* them to know where we and they stand," Delin pointed out sharply as the others agreed with Homin. "We want to know what they're after, and also who they are. And as long as they believe their plan is working, we won't have to worry that they'll think of something else to try that we *won't* know about. The second package of vials was left for us, so I had it picked up as though we really needed it. Here's what the accompanying note says."

Delin drew out the second note and opened it, then read aloud, "Greetings to our illustrious leaders. We trust that you're feeling much better now, but there's no need to thank us in words. We have only your best interests at heart, as all loyal citizens should. For that reason we ask you to show your thanks by naming certain people to the Advisory Board. These men are all strong and capable, and will guide you properly in the running of our empire. The

Advisors you have now are nothing but incompetent fools, who take orders rather than give sound advice. You five are in no position to give those orders, as you have no experience at all in running an empire.

"At the moment, only a very few people know that your Seating was made possible more by the efforts of others than by your own. It happens to be in our own best interests as well as yours to keep this fact private, but arrangements have already been made to spread the word far and wide if any attempt is made to discover who we are. We expect you to learn the composition of the counteragent fairly soon, which is why we now tell you about our other preparations. One thing, however, won't be learned from the counteragent: the fact that the *antidote* to the original poison is of another composition entirely. If anything happens to us, your five will need to take the counteragent for the rest of your lives in order to remain free of the pain—and eventual death. We suggest that you ponder these matters well before you take any action against us.

"Our next missive may well contain the names of those we wish put on the Advisory Board. Right now we are in the midst of compiling that list, which is far from easy. Most of our really capable brethren have . . . disappeared, in one way or another, which was rather foolish of you. An empire like ours cannot be ruled through the efforts of any five people, no matter the strength of their talents. The various shortages now suffered by those in this city ought to have taught you that we speak the truth. Our hopes in that are sincere, and we remain, your loyal supporters."

"The nerve of those bastards!" Bron growled, mirroring Delin's own feelings. "Trying to tell *us* what we can and can't do! And now we do have something else to worry about besides the counteragent, a couple of somethings. I don't like the way these people always seem to be a step ahead of us."

"They're a step ahead of us because they know what will happen to them once we find out who they are," Delin pointed out, a growl in his own voice. "They'll die in worse pain than what they gave to you three, you have my word on that. And all we have to do is wait for that list of names. Theirs will be on it, supposedly buried among all the rest, but knowing that they're there will let us find them. After that they're ours.''

"What about those other minor points they mentioned?" Selendi asked, her expression furious despite the faint pallor she'd developed. "They know we didn't really win that last competition, and the counteragent won't do anything to get the poison out of us permanently. If the list of names they supply turns out to be only the *first* list and we arrest all those people, we may never be truly free again."

"And even if their names really are on the list and we get them," Homin added, "there's nothing to say that they won't kill themselves before we can find out what we need to know. And that business about spreading the word about our Seating. . . . We'll have riots on our hands the likes of which this city has never seen. We'd better speak to Kambil about it, and find out what *he* thinks."

"Kambil doesn't think anything, because he's in too much pain," Delin snarled, hating the way the other two immediately agreed with Homin. "And that means *you* three can't think either, doesn't it? Is that the way it used to be? Don't any of you *remember* how it used to be?"

"What's that supposed to mean?" Bron asked, trying for brash and certainly not finding it. "Are you suggesting we're different from the way we used to be, the way you tried to suggest it once before? Of course we're different, we told you so at the time, and we happen to like the difference. We're more efficient and capable now, and we have Kambil to thank for it."

"You have Kambil and his grandmother to thank," Delin corrected, letting the venom enter his tone. "The old woman was the one in control of Kambil, and she helped him to become the one in control of you three. One of the things he made you believe is that you're better people now, but are you really? Efficient and capable people get to make decisions, but what decisions have *you* three made since we were Seated? Name even one that has nothing to do with your own private wings, and I won't mention the fact that you've been taking Kambil's orders ever again."

All three of them actually started to answer him, but all three discovered at once that they really had nothing to say. Their expressions suggested that they were searching for an example to give him, to support their Kambil-induced belief that they were independent parts of the group, but none of them could find even one example of independent decision. Everything had been decided for them by the one in control of them, and suddenly they weren't able to deny that.

"Kambil told you that *I* couldn't be 'helped' the way you were because I was insane," Delin continued, pressing the point as hard as he could. "The truth of the matter is that I'd developed a . . . block of sorts from having grown up with my father, and Kambil and his grandmother weren't able to breach that block. That's why he used Pure-dan to control me, and why he hated me so much. I'm the only one those two couldn't reach, and they detested the idea."

"But . . . where does that leave *us* now?" Selendi asked, her tone and expression wavering. "I still can't bring myself to believe what you said, but—I also can't argue your claim, even though I want to."

"You want to because Kambil's talent is still influencing you," Delin soothed her, privately delighted that his guess had been correct. These three *were* more susceptible to suggestion now than they had been, courtesy of Kambil's efforts. But Kambil wasn't here now to take advantage of the situation, and *he* was. . . .

"All three of you will have to work at it," Delin continued, "but in a little while you should be able to throw off Kambil's strangling influence. Then you'll be your own people again, and we'll be able to formulate a plan against our newest enemies that will gain us everything we need. Everything *you* need. I'm not involved in that part of it, but you can be certain I won't be abandoning you. I know that the way you treated me was all Kambil's fault, so I hold no grudges against you."

"That's decent of you, Delin," Bron muttered, still obviously rather unhappy. He also hadn't met Delin's gaze, just as the others were avoiding looking directly at him. Their feelings of guilt were most likely rather faint, not at all as strong as their realization that they needed him in order to be pain-free. And to figure out some way to save their lives and positions. And Delin meant to do exactly that, although possibly not in the way they were expecting. . . .

"All right, enough about this for now," he announced, trying to brisk them up. "We have other things which have to concern us, and the first of them concerns a journal I found in Kambil's bedchamber. Considering what we began to practice, I take it Kambil told the rest of you all about it?"

"Maybe not *all* about it," Homin said, the words grudging. "You know he told us a few things, but he was the only one who read it."

"That's about to change," Delin said, and now they all looked at him again. "I've read through it already, so the rest of you can take your turns. But more than that I've had a search started, and a like journal has already been found in my own library. Chances are excellent that there are other journals to be found in *your* libraries, but until they are we'll concentrate on the two we already have. And I need to be brought up to date on what's been happening out in the world. We can't be an effective team if one of us is forced to stumble through the darkness of forced ignorance."

They all nodded at that, their expressions having turned somewhat impressed, and Delin smiled to himself. Before very long they would be taking *his* orders in the same way they'd done with Kambil, and being just as unaware of it. Yes, Kambil had prepared things nicely for Delin, and now was the time for him to begin making use of that preparation. . . .

TWENTY-TWO

High Lord Embisson Ruhl was far from happy. Agitation made him pace back and forth in his study, at least until he heard footsteps out in the hall. Then he immediately slumped into the nearest chair, and only just in time. A single knock brought the servant into the room, to announce his visitors.

"My Lord, Lord Edmin and his companion are here to see you," the servant said, sounding as concerned as he always did. "You do wish to see them, do you not?"

Embisson turned his face away as he'd taken to doing of late, pretending that he wished to have nothing to do with the world or any of its happenings. Also as usual Edmin thanked the servant and dismissed him, and when the sound of the door being closed came, Embisson turned to look at Edmin. Edmin's hand was up, showing that the servant was still close enough to hear what was said in the room, so Embisson remained silent. Edmin, though, began his usual attempt to jolly his father into having some interest in life again, and then Edmin's words abruptly changed.

"All right, Father, he's gone now," Edmin said, looking at Embisson with a frown. "I can see that you're extremely agitated about something, so please tell us what's happened."

"Your chief agent was unable to reach you, so he came to me instead," Embisson replied as he stood, watching Eltrina Razas lower her hood. "We've been talking about celebrating how well our plans have gone, but a celebration would have been premature. One of your agent's spies has gotten word to him that only four of the Five were affected by our little gift to them. The fifth, Delin Moord, apparently never ingested it at all, and now he's been able to duplicate the counteragent. Why did it have to be the Earth magic user who was unaffected?''

''The possibility of that happening was always there,'' Edmin said with a shrug that wasn't entirely unconcerned. ''It's the major reason we chose the poison we did, one which requires an entirely different antidote. They know all about that after having read the second note, but what they don't know is that the counteragent will soon be insufficient to hold off the poison's effects. If they don't give us some indication of being willing to deal straightforwardly with us, we'll just sit back and let them die.''

''A result which will be extremely pleasant, but one which will leave us out in the cold,'' Embisson grumbled, his agitation still rather active. ''We need to have those five little nothings firmly under our hands, else control of the empire will still elude us. And what if they feel secure enough to start searching for us? The fact that we made certain to know almost nothing about the poison and its antidote won't stop them from trying to rip the information out of us.''

''They won't use torture on us, not at the beginning,'' Eltrina said, and her certainty was clear and unfeigned. ''They'll have their Spirit magic user force the answers from us, or they'll feed us doses of Puredan. All they'll get out of *that* is the knowledge that we're in touch with the people who have the answers they need, but we don't know where they are. At the least sign of something being wrong, those people will disappear out of Gan Garee, and that will be the end of our beloved Seated Five. We'll have to explain that in the next note we send, but in the interim there's another problem we need to find an answer to. One of our secret holds on those five little vermin is no longer a secret.''

''Do you remember our first conversation with Lady Eltrina, Father?'' Edmin asked as he made his way toward the tea service. ''She was rather upset at the time and spoke of her intention to spread the word about the cheating at the final competition, but we made her understand that that course of action would have been most unwise. Rather than continue on with it she joined our own plans, but now it seems that someone else has been talking about that particular subject. The word has spread all over the city, and everywhere one goes there are large groups of people listening to various agitators and shaking their collective fists."

"We're not feeling as lighthearted about it as Lord Edmin's words might suggest," Eltrina put in at Embisson's startled exclamation. "We've just come from a meeting of our peers, which is why Edmin's agent wasn't able to reach him. Things are rapidly getting completely out of hand, and we've been trying to formulate ways to put an end to the trouble."

"Which is not working as easily as Eltrina has made it sound," Edmin added as he turned away from the tea service with two cups in his hands. "Most of our peers are either frightened out of what little wit they possess, or insist on being totally outraged. Their agents have made some few, pitiful attempts to collect what's due them, but the peasants have been too busy listening to those agitators to run the businesses the way they're supposed to. And the growing shortage of food has added to it all, and there have been certain incidents."

"He means that certain of the shops in our part of the city were broken into the other night," Eltrina supplied as she took one of the cups from Edmin with a brief smile of thanks. "They were all food shops—and half a dozen eating parlors—and every scrap of food meant for *us* was taken. Those groups of guardsmen who were on duty tried to stop them, naturally, but the guardsmen all ended up either badly beaten or dead. There were just too many of the peasants, the survivors said, and now everything they took is hidden away somewhere on *their* side of the city."

"And now no one knows what the peasants will decide to do next," Edmin said, again taking up the narrative as he seated himself near the woman. "Eltrina and I have been discussing the matter, and we'd like your opinion on the conclusions we've come to. To begin with, considering these latest happenings, just how much good can we expect to get out of controlling the Five?''

"Why, quite a lot," Embisson began, but then he paused to rethink that conclusion. The desire to control those little nothings as well as the empire had burned in him for quite some time, but now . . . now things had changed from what they once were, and personal safety would soon become a man's first concern.

"You know, Edmin, I believe you're correct," Embisson said as he walked to a chair of his own and sat. "We've been through this sort of thing with the peasants before, and no matter how ragingly destructive they get they eventually quiet down and let us all go back to the way things were. Since the Five are responsible for *this* set of disturbances, their deaths ought to quiet everyone down. And with many of our peers gone, we'll be in the perfect position to be the ones to hold the next set of competitions. The new Five will be ours from the very first, and we won't have to worry about whether or not they intend to destroy us."

"So you're willing to simply sit back and watch the Five die?" Edmin asked with an expression of qualified approval in his eyes. "Are you certain about that, Father? I know how badly you wanted to repay them for humiliating you, and I would dislike being the one who takes that satisfaction from you."

"There will be satisfaction enough in knowing how agonizing their deaths—or the deaths of four of them—will be," Embisson said after considering the matter for a moment. "Under other circumstances I might have decided differently, but with everything else occurring. . . . No, Edmin, I would be a fool to insist on personal satisfaction. But I'd like to know how Lady Eltrina sees it. Her difficulties, as she once pointed out, were far more intense than my own."

"Knowing the agony they suffered before they were given the counteragent did quite a lot toward making me forget my own pain," Eltrina replied with a smile which showed exactly how pleased the knowledge made her. "It also helps to know most of them will feel the same again before they die, so I'm also willing to let the matter of controlling them drop. But I should tell the both of you that I'm meeting with an agent of my own tonight, who's been doing some oblique checking around for me. That peasant Five is still on the loose, and we need to know what they're up to.''

"Yes, I'd nearly forgotten about them," Embisson replied with a frown. "They aren't at all as important as the doomed Five made them out to be, but they certainly could become a nuisance. We'll have to find out what precautions against their return the little nothings have taken, and then do our best to improve on what will certainly be uninspired planning. But you still haven't told me what everyone's decided to do about our outraged citizenry.''

"Various plans are even now being put into effect," Edmin said, and the way he exchanged a glance with Eltrina confirmed Embisson's earlier opinion: he was undoubtedly sleeping with the woman. As a diversion that was perfectly all right, and Embisson made a mental note to speak privately with Edmin to be certain that it *was* no more than a diversion. Before one made a permanent liaison one paid attention to the political aspects of the match, and with Eltrina Razas there no longer *were* any. The woman was nothing but annoyance and difficulty in skirts, and as soon as their current undertaking was over, so would their relationship be.

"The first of those plans is a set of daytime and nighttime curfews," Edmin continued. "Gathering idly on street corners listening to rabble-rousing will no longer be permitted, and anyone found on the street, day or night, without a legitimate reason for being there will be arrested by the guard. If anyone tries to resist arrest, he will be put down like the lawless animal he is, which will certainly be a lesson to the others.''

"Yes, that sort of thing always impresses the peasants," Embisson said with a judicious nod. "Fear is the key to controlling them, fear in regard to their personal safety, fear for their families, fear of being dismissed from whatever position earns them their daily bread. The guard won't find it necessary to put down more than a very few of them, and after that there won't be any more violators of the curfews.''

"Yes, everyone was very aware of that," Edmin agreed. "The second rule will be that anyone who is arrested for unsocial behavior will be joined in his detention by the rest of his family. There are always fools who will risk their own lives and freedom to show their displeasure, but not many are also willing to risk the lives and freedom of their families. We've also set a bounty—in gold—on the heads of any agitators, and those who collect the gold will be given 'positions of trust' as well. That should make them think we'll be appointing them as agents for some of us, but of course we won't do anything that foolish. Traitors are traitors and can never be trusted."

"Some of our peers also intend to begin demanding a larger percentage from those who run their businesses," Eltrina put in, her expression unsure. "They feel that that will force the peasants to spend more time working in order to feed themselves and their families, but I'm undecided about how good an idea that is. If you reduce a peasant's means of livelihood without actually taking away his responsibilities as well, you trap him in a place he might decide to escape from. It doesn't force him to go back to doing what he always has, it changes his refuge of normality. Do you understand what I mean?"

"No, to be truthful, I don't," Embisson said without hesitation, but for Edmin's sake he spoke gently. "Peasants are peasants, and will accept the new circumstances as normal whether they like them or not. They may *want* to protest, but when protest brings horror they'll swallow the words and feelings and return to what's expected of them. But is that all everyone's decided to do?"

"Oh, there will be the usual public executions of agitators once they're betrayed to us," Edmin said, his head moving in a gesture of dismissal. "That will add to it only a little, as most of those witnessing the executions won't be the sort to become agitators. But it will rid us of those who might lead the sheep to revolt, and so will be a worthy end in itself."

"There's one thing we *haven't* discussed," Eltrina said, and now she appeared to be more than slightly concerned. "The poison will take care of four of those five disgusting pretenders, but what about the fifth? The fact that he'll be left alone without the others isn't particularly comforting when one remembers he's a High talent. He'll still be able to make difficulty for the rest of our peers, and us in particular if he discovers we're behind the deaths of his groupmates. We really need to do something definite to send him quickly after the rest.''

''I agree,'' Edmin said before Embisson could poohpooh the woman's unfounded fears. ''We once spoke about people who are foolish enough to turn their backs on their enemies, and because the Five did that, most of them will die. If we do the same in *our* turn, we won't be able to complain if we meet the same fate.''

''All right, you may have a point,'' Embisson agreed, not as reluctantly as he would have at first. ''We need to find something which will be effective against Moord, but we'll also have to be extremely careful. Shortly after the Five were Seated, Moord's own parents disappeared under rather mysterious circumstances. If he was ungrateful enough to do away with his own parents, we can't afford to take any chances with him.''

This time Edmin and Eltrina were the ones to agree, so they all began to discuss ideas. Embisson meant to settle for nothing less than a failproof plan, which he was confident they could come up with. But he would also bring up the matter of another note to the Five, which he had now decided would be completely unwise. Every additional contact with that group increased the danger that they would be found and unmasked, so simply dropping the whole thing right here and now would be best. And then, in a matter of a month or less, four of their five problems would be gone.

But that fifth one would have to be taken care of, not to mention the problem of Lady Eltrina. Edmin was eminently practical, but practical men had been taken in before. *Ah well, these things did happen*, Embisson admitted to himself. If necessary Eltrina could be seen to a good deal more easily than the man Moord, and if Edmin were in danger of becoming too deeply involved with her, Embisson knew he would not hesitate a single heartbeat. . . .

*   *   *

As they left the High Lord's house, Eltrina Razas let Edmin Ruhl fuss over helping her into the carriage as much as he wanted to. In point of fact it felt good to have a powerful man fuss over her, something Grall had never done at any time. And Edmin was considerably more interesting in bed than Grall had been, not to mention younger and just as wealthy. Under certain circumstances Eltrina would consider marriage again, but first there were other, more important concerns to pay attention to.

Like the fact that those five peasants could well be on their way back to Gan Garee. That was the preliminary word she'd been given by Grall's searchers, with a more detailed report due tonight. Somehow, some way, she *had* to get them under her hand, at least for a short while. She had a score to settle with that Domon bit, and a lesser one with the man Ro. Both of them would be sorry they'd ever involved themselves with crossing her, that was a vow Eltrina had taken. They *would* be sorry. . . .

And it might become necessary to make High Lord Embisson just as sorry. Eltrina hadn't missed the way he'd looked at her, as though she weren't at all good enough for his precious son. It was fairly certain he meant to make a fuss, so it was time to prepare Edmin in the proper way. Then, no matter what his father said, Edmin would refuse to listen. Yes, it was certainly time. . . .

TWENTY-THREE

Once Jovvi dissolved the Blending, I just sat there with my thoughts whirling around. Not that they hadn't been whirling before we Blended; now they were doing the same, just a bit more intensely.

"Well, that takes care of *that* problem," Lorand said with the same relief we must all have been feeling. "It's a good thing you tried to check on Vallant, Jovvi. If you hadn't, we would have known nothing about all those men waiting to attack this place."

"And it's an equally good thing we arranged that alert-signal with the link groups," Rion said in agreement. "If they hadn't been there to add their strength, we would have had a serious problem."

"Yes, my guiding Tamma's ability to where the link groups were and having her show a thick flame worked really well in telling them we needed them to link up," Jovvi said, one hand to her forehead. "But what bothers me about the whole thing is that tandem arrangement *their* link sets were in. We would have had a great deal of trouble standing against them alone, not to mention trying to fight back. If we hadn't . . . 'remembered' the best way to defeat something like that. . . ."

"Excuse me, but would you mind telling *us* what just happened?" Mohr put in, trying to be polite despite the agitation obviously filling him. "We could see that you took care of the trouble—whatever it was—but *how* did you do it? Your fifth wasn't even in the building.''

"He didn't have to be," Jovvi explained, calmly smiling a bit at the four men. "We've discovered that once a Blending has had practice working together, the members of it don't have to be in the same place in order for them to Blend. But before you decide that that's another bit of proof for your argument about us being the Chosen, you have to understand that all our Blendings can do the same, as can our link groups. Thanks to the nobility we've lost most of the knowledge we ought to have about these things, but we're beginning to regain some of it.''

"And you *fought* from *here*?'' Ambor asked shakily, while his colleague Koln just sat there looking stunned. "We had no idea you'd be able to. . . . I mean, the *power* something like that gives you . . . !''

"It's something the usurpers can do as well, and probably already have," Rion pointed out, speaking just as calmly as Jovvi had. "We're not certain as yet, but even less powerful Blendings should be able to do the same. You do realize that once the nobles are overthrown, it will no longer be illegal for people to form their own Blendings? It's something that normal life should contain for all of us, but we've been deprived of it so that a certain select few might own and rule us. You would hardly be as upset as you apparently are if you were a member of a Blending yourself.''

"Us?'' Koln said in a high, wavering voice while Ambor took his turn at sitting and staring openmouthed. "Us as members of a Blending? But that's only for—''

"Yes, that's right, it *was* only for the one Blending allowed to be formed," Jovvi agreed with a better smile when the man's words broke off. "Once we're rid of them, the way to Blend will become common knowledge. Don't you think it's about time?''

"So that's what you intend to do when you win," Ambor said, and suddenly the sober, practical, successful merchant was gone behind the shining eyes of the converted. "You mean to give everyone the gift of Blending. I think I can honestly say that no one else I know would do something like that, would . . . hand over for nothing the precious knowledge that they might easily keep for themselves. And you still claim you aren't the Chosen? I'll admit I wasn't quite sure if the High Master was right, but now my doubts have disappeared.''

''You feel that way only because we've decided to do something you consider noble,'' I put in, trying not to let the disturbance inside me color the words. ''If you were to stop to think about the matter unemotionally, you'd realize that our intentions are really rather selfish. If we keep the details about Blending to ourselves, the entire burden of doing what it takes a Blending to do falls completely on us. By sharing the knowledge we also share the burden, and the real Chosen Blending apparently sees the matter in the same way, because they haven't made any attempt to change our minds.''

''Maybe that's because there *isn't* any other Blending of that sort,'' Koln said, apparently in complete agreement with his brother merchant. ''It seems to me that if you aren't the Chosen, maybe you ought to be.''

''Just that easily?'' I asked with the sound of scorn I couldn't hold back on. ''You like our point of view, so we ought to be put forward as the Chosen? Is there anything in the Prophecies that says the Chosen are Chosen by popular opinion? If so, then I withdraw my name from the nominations.''

''You still seem disturbed by that . . . scene so recently enacted with your absent member,'' Mohr commented, an odd expression in his eyes. ''He defended you rather vigorously, I recall, just before he left so hurriedly, but his effort apparently failed to please you. Is that the reason why you would . . . withdraw your name?''

''That part of my reason happens to be private, and won't be discussed with strangers,'' I told him coldly, refusing to allow the intrusion. ''But the concept itself does well as an illustration of the rest of my objection. If you hadn't decided that we were your precious Chosen, would you have had the incredibly bad manners to discuss a subject that was obviously private between two people you don't really know? *You* tell *me*, Dom Mohr. Would you have?''

He flushed at the accusation and didn't reply, but his attitude was answer enough.

''I take your silence to mean you would never have done so boorish a thing,'' I said, aware of the way his companions shared his embarrassment. "But you *do* consider us the Chosen, so you feel free to intrude as you like. Most people seem to view the matter as you do, that people in what you consider *our* position belong to them completely. For your information I belong to no one but myself, and after that to my Blending. Beyond that no one has a call on me, and I mean to keep matters unchanged from that position. Anyone interested in arguing had better be a good deal stronger in Fire magic than I am."

Even as I stood up I could see all of them pale, especially the two Guild men. They claimed they knew exactly how strong each of us in the Blending was, so they understood my threat as clearly as I wanted them to. It would have helped if I could have stalked back to my bedchamber to underscore what I'd said, but I was far too hungry to do that. Those intruders had drained quite a lot of our strength, and I needed to replenish some of it with food.

People were already beginning to take their places at tables in the dining room, and it wasn't long before Jovvi, Lorand, Rion, and Naran joined me at ours. No one commented about what I'd said—or about what had happened earlier—and the food began to come rather quickly, but there were fewer people to serve it than there had been that afternoon. It seemed that part of the staff had been appropriated to help clean up the mess we'd made near the stables, and those servants who remained fell into two categories: Some were happy and relieved, but most were very nervous and jumpy. They hadn't known who they were supposed to give their best service to, but there was no doubt that they knew *now*.

After a short while Vallant Ro joined us as well, but no one said anything to him beyond a quiet question asking if he was all right, and his only response was an assurance that he was fine. We all paid attention to eating rather than talking, and in that way the meal was quickly over. I drained my last cup of tea and was getting ready to rise and leave, when Jovvi changed that intention.

"Tamma, wait just a minute," she said quietly, looking directly at me. "We have to talk about one part of that attack, and we'd better do it now. We'll go back to that private sitting area."

Since I knew what she was referring to, I couldn't very well argue the need. So I settled back in my chair until everyone was through eating—only a matter of another couple of minutes—and then we all went back to the private sitting room. Once again we all chose chairs, and when Jovvi had settled herself she looked around at us.

"Those link groups were in a tandem arrangement we haven't seen before," she said without preamble, knowing we would all understand what she meant. "Were any of you able to catch *how* they linked?"

"I didn't," Lorand replied, sounding just as worried as Jovvi had. "I was *almost* able to see it, but the details were just a bit beyond me."

"What about you, Tamma?" Jovvi asked after Rion and Vallant Ro simply shook their heads. "I'm in the same position as Lorand, where I *almost* saw the arrangement. Did you get even a single hint we can use?"

"I saw the braided pattern clearly among the Fire magic users, and only slightly less clearly among the others," I answered with more than a hint of surprise. "Since we were all Blended, why didn't the rest of you see the same?"

"Probably because we haven't been constantly touching the power as long as you have," Jovvi replied seriously, obviously considering the matter. "And possibly also because your strength is greater than ours. Does anyone else remember 'hearing' our entity think that we were *almost* to our optimum condition? That could be at least part of what it meant."

This time I joined the others in nodding, also remembering the thought Jovvi meant. With all the power our Blending had shown, there was still more our entity expected to be able to do. . . .

"Tamma, can you describe the patterns you saw?" Jovvi asked next, and now everyone was paying very close attention to me. "A description may not help all that much, but it's better than nothing."

"I think I can *show* you the patterns," I answered with a frown, trying to get them clear and separated in my mind. "Lorand, see if this makes any sense to you."

I then drew in the air with fire the pattern I'd seen the Earth magic people use, which had been possible only because I'd been part of the Blending—I thought. There was, after all, no other way for me to see the doings of people of another aspect, but that still left the question of why *I'd* been able to see it but Lorand hadn't.

"Yes, of course!" Lorand said with eagerness as soon as he saw what I'd drawn. "It makes perfect sense. But if *you* were able to perceive it, why couldn't I?"

"The situation suggests that it's individual strength which controls perceptions in the Blending," Jovvi said slowly after I'd shrugged to indicate my ignorance. "Tamma used your senses to see the patterns, but her own strength to detail them. But now that we know she saw them accurately, we'd better get the rest of them from her."

I nodded and produced the pattern for Spirit magic, then Air magic, and lastly for Water magic, all of it carefully drawn in the air with thin lines of fire. No one did more than nod with an "Ah!" of satisfaction, and when it was over Jovvi leaned forward again.

"Now I can't wait until the others join us so we can show it to all the link groups," she said, smiling at me. "That pattern is so obvious I should have seen it myself, but I've felt that about a lot of things which are currently beyond my reach. But this is only part of why I asked for this meeting, and the rest of it concerns someone who is one of us but not completely one of us. Naran? Do you agree that it's time?"

"I wish I could say no, but I can't," Naran answered with a sigh while the rest of us—including Rion—exchanged glances of blankness. What could there possibly be about Naran . . . ? She looked pale and nervous and very unhappy, but her decision was more . . . fatalistic than reluctant.

"Then you know that it definitely *is* time," Jovvi said to her with a gentle, supportive smile. "Don't worry. They'll be surprised at first, but they won't react the way you're afraid they will. I'll start it off by saying that I didn't just happen to check on Vallant and thereby learned about the presence of the attackers. I was warned that something was wrong, warned by Naran when she came over and whispered to me. Why don't you take it from there, Naran?"

"I—think I'd better start from the very beginning," Naran answered obliquely as she watched her fingers twist about each other. She looked at none of us, not even Rion—or possibly I should say *especially* not at Rion. He sat very still and straight, his expression touched with a shadow of terror, obviously afraid of what he was about to hear. Naran made no effort to offer her hand to him or ask for his, and that must have been what frightened him so badly. They *always* held hands, especially when Naran was upset, and Rion must have been convinced it was about to be over between them. . . .

"I—didn't have the sort of childhood that other people do," Naran said, and now her words were reluctant. "My mother loved me very much, and for that reason she and I kept moving around until I was eleven or twelve, when she died. After that I was alone, but by then I was able to look after myself—because of the reason we *had* to move around so much. You see . . . when I was five, I was classified as a null."

A heavy chill touched me at that, the sort I always felt when I heard the term *null*. That's what they'd said of one of our neighbor children when I was small, a pleasant, round-faced little boy I occasionally played with when my parents weren't watching. He'd been very sweet and never rough when we played our pointless child-games, but after they said he was a null he disappeared and I never saw him again. His parents had seemed more embarrassed than upset that he was gone, but then they *had* been friends of my own parents. . . .

"So that's why you never commented about the strength of any of our group," Rion said softly to her, his expression filled with pain. "I thought you were simply being circumspect . . . my poor love, carrying around the burden of that for all these years. Please—will you give me your hand so that I might know you're still beside me? It almost feels as though you've left. . . ."

It wasn't possible to miss how horrible an idea Rion thought that was, that Naran had left and was no longer beside him. She looked up with the most pitiful relief I've ever seen, and then she quickly gave him her hand. He took it and folded it in both of his, and Jovvi chuckled.

"I told you that Rion would never react the way you were afraid he would," Jovvi said to a glowingly radiant Naran. "As a matter of fact, no one here is reacting that way. Everyone is shocked and horrified, but only at what you must have been put through—and are still going through. Would you like to continue now, and explain that that first assessment of you was wrong?"

"My mother and I didn't realize that for quite some time," Naran went on, now holding tightly to Rion's hand. "All she knew was that she wasn't about to let a bunch of strangers take me away from her, so we left our house in the middle of the night, and didn't stop running until we were quite a long way away from our town. My father was dead and so were my grandparents, and so my mother had nothing to keep her there. We eventually reached Gan Garee, where it was easier to hide among the crowds of people. I later found out that my mother had stolen a blank certification form before we ran away, and then she forged our Guild woman's signature classifying me as a very weak Air magic user. Her own aspect was Air magic, and more than once she covered for my complete lack of talent in Air magic."

"But Jovvi said they were mistaken," Lorand put in with a frown, asking the question I was just about to. "What did your aspect actually turn out to be?"

"It's . . . not what you're expecting," Naran replied, once again looking uncomfortable. "I *don't* have any of the usual five talents, but I do have *something*. . . . For instance, I didn't find out where Tamrissa was by having someone tell me. I . . . *knew* where she was, without any doubt, and also approximately when she would leave that house. And it isn't the first—or last—thing I knew."

"What do you mean, you *knew* it, love?" Rion asked, apparently as confused as I felt but in no way reluctant to continue touching Naran. "Or am I the only one who doesn't understand?"

"No, Rion, you aren't alone in not understanding," Jovvi assured him, then she looked at Naran again. "You'll have to explain it to them, my dear. Just say it straight out and then it will be behind you."

"Yes, you're right, of course," Naran said with the most

. . . reluctant agreement I'd ever seen. "I do have to say it aloud, don't I . . . ? Rion, my love, what I meant was . . . I knew it because I can often . . . see the future."

And with *that* revelation, all my own problems somehow . . . faded into the background.

TWENTY-FOUR

The room all around them was as silent as death, but Jovvi flinched at the uproar coming from everyone's mind. Shock clanged and emotions echoed, and all of them seemed to want to speak without knowing what to say. The reactions were expected ones, and so was the comment Vallant was finally able to make.

"Surely you're jokin' with us, Naran," he said, letting his expression fall into one of tentative amusement. "No one knows what the future holds, and if they did they would be owned by the nobility. You're probably just good at seein' the most likely possibilities. . . ."

"Sometimes I wish that's all it was," Naran replied, her expression—and thoughts—finally determined to have the entire truth come out. "But at other times I'm very glad I have this particular talent, because it helped my mother and me to survive, and then helped me alone when she was gone. When I was young I had to see a place before I knew whether it was safe or dangerous for us to stay there, but once I got older I . . . knew in advance that the place would be there. I also used the talent to find places to work, without wasting time going where I would be refused."

Naran hesitated then, but the subject was purely personal.

That was proven when she turned the hesitation toward Rion.

"My talent *told* me I would meet the man I would love forever if I went to a certain place," she said, speaking as though the two of them were alone. "It turned out that the tavern was short one girl for their upstairs rooms, something I also knew would turn out to be. I was there deliberately to meet *you*, my love, and I left shortly after we parted. I also found you that second time on purpose, only pretending that our meeting was an accident. Can you ever forgive me for . . . lying, yes it was lying, but I'd do it again if I had to. Are you badly bothered by that?"

"Am I bothered by the fact that the one woman I'll always love with every fiber of my being came to search me out?" Rion responded with a grin as he leaned closer to her. "Oh, yes, my love, I'm terribly wounded, but not mortally. I think I'll get over it."

Naran's relief was clear to everyone as she laughed and did her part in leaning closer to Rion, so Lorand was the one who asked the question that Jovvi had been thinking about herself.

"Naran, if you *know* all these things, why have you been so uncertain about telling us about them, and most especially about how Rion would react? If you *know* things, you should know about these things as well."

"The best I can tell, my own emotions get in the way at times," Naran responded, looking away from Rion with a sigh. "When I'm afraid of what an answer will be to something, I seem to . . . block out that answer. And there's also the fact that I don't see *everything*. Every once in a while something will happen that I haven't had the least idea about, and it will come as a complete surprise. Why that happens I don't know, and I'll probably never find out."

"But all the rest of the time your talent is working to *our* benefit," Tamma said, the words thoughtful. "You've already been absolutely invaluable, and I'm sure you will be again. It's just too bad that you can't Blend with us. It would make us—"

Tamma stopped speaking abruptly as she realized what she'd just said, but Jovvi—and the others—were already ahead of her. They exchanged startled glances with their brows raised, so Jovvi put the question in all their minds.

"Why *can't* Naran Blend with us?" Jovvi demanded, looking around almost belligerently. "If she has a talent, and she most certainly does, it should be able to Blend with ours."

"But that would make our number six rather than five," Vallant protested, sounding more unsure and confused than disagreeing. "Isn't that goin' against what everyone knows the prime number to be?"

"As little as everyone 'knows' about Blending and the talents, how can we be sure?" Jovvi countered, feeling more strongly about the matter by the minute. "At one time people thought that the prime number was four, and then the first fivefold Blending came into being. If Naran's talent is something new, and that seems likely since no one apparently knows about it, how can anyone consider a sixfold Blending? Anyone but us, that is."

"The only drawback I can see is that Naran won't have link groups to back her up," Lorand said with a nod of agreement. "But we really should try to see if Blending with her will work."

Jovvi could tell easily that everyone was in agreement on that point—everyone but Naran. The poor girl was somewhat in shock over the idea of joining them completely, and her lack of self-assurance was horribly clear. Her mind thrashed around trying to find the proper words of protest, but not because of reluctance. Jovvi knew exactly what the problem was, so she leaned forward a bit.

"Naran, my dear, you can't think that way," she said gently with the warmest smile she was able to produce. "I know you've felt the outsider for all of your life, but you can't let that interfere with what we want to try. If it works then things will be much more interesting, and if it doesn't then things will remain just the way they've been. You can't possibly lose any standing with us, so why not relax and have some fun?"

Naran's expression and thoughts lightened with that, and once she looked around to see that all the others agreed with what Jovvi had said, her smile was more than just tentative.

"Relax and have some fun," she repeated, her smile

widening. "You're absolutely right, Jovvi, it *could* be fun. All right, let's try it."

"Now, let's not count too heavily on its working," Jovvi warned the eagerness she could feel in everyone. "It may not decide to work until our second or third try, the way it sometimes goes with ordinary Blendings. This will be our least significant effort, so I want *everyone* to relax. Are you ready?"

The others all smiled and nodded, but no one actually relaxed. They pretended to for Naran's sake, but Rion, especially, yearned for success in the experiment. It would make his beloved really and truly one of them, rather than just a member of their group because of him. Jovvi knew that as well as he did, which meant delaying the effort would simply cause more discomfort.

So Jovvi reached out to the others as she usually did, but this time she reached toward Naran as well. There was an odd . . . emptiness that wasn't really an emptiness there, but it still remained one she couldn't penetrate. Full Blending was being held off as the others reached toward Naran as well, all of them experiencing the same trouble. They were being stopped dead in their tracks—until Jovvi got a sudden idea.

Rather than trying to reach Naran directly, Jovvi . . . *slid* through Rion's awareness of Naran and approached her at the same time and in the same way that he did. It was a mini-Blending of sorts, and at first it didn't seem to make a difference. Then, slowly, the emptiness became filled with *something*, a something that was being held back by automatic fear. Jovvi reached out and touched the fear, soothing it away to a large extent, and then—

And then the entity had again come into being, an entity that sighed with the sensation of being complete. It wasn't quite up to its full strength as yet, but that would come as its flesh forms matured and flowered to the point where they were supposed to be. And all of the bonds weren't as close as they should be, but that, too, could be easily seen to. What mattered more at the moment was the Sight the entity had gained. Or regained, as it had been at one time in the distant past.

A clearer awareness of the future now lay before it, a

future it already knew would be fraught with danger. Perhaps a better description would be to say that the *picture* was blurry with multiple possibilities, but the awareness of those possibilities was a good deal more clear. It was faintly possible that they would reach and enter Gan Garee without difficulty, just as it was faintly possible that they would not reach the city at all. The stronger possibilities were that they would get there with more or less fighting, and the same for entering the city. Beyond that was the near certainty that they—or some of them—would face the usurping Five, but the results of that confrontation simply weren't visible. For some reason there were more possibilities of various outcomes involved there than in what went before, and making sense of them just wasn't . . . possible.

The entity chuckled to itself, not in the least disturbed by the lack of clarity around the confrontation. Considering the number of variables which surrounded even the smallest happening, it wasn't unexpected that the confrontation would be rife with this-or-that possibilities. The closer they came to the actual event, the clearer the picture would become. And there were other things to concern them before they reached the time of that event.

For instance, the rest of their flesh forms would arrive the next day, most likely shortly before noon. It suddenly became obvious that a group of guardsmen would attempt to ambush them as they rode into Colling Green, a group much like the one which had earlier attempted to take its own flesh forms unawares. That group was not yet in position for the ambush, nor would it be until shortly before the column was due. And it would be larger than the one attacking earlier, significantly larger.

The entity, no longer amused, paused to consider the matter. There had been difficulty before the previous attackers had been vanquished, and there had been danger to its flesh forms. It had managed to recall the manner of countering the enemy's more complex kind of linking only just in time, but now that was clearly insufficient. Something more intensely efficient would be needed for tomorrow, as well as for those battles they would certainly have to face before finding it possible to enter Gan Garee. There *was* something which would serve, but at the moment the memory of the something escaped it. Perhaps, when it next came into being, it would find it possible to recall the method. . . .

At that point Jovvi returned to herself, having dissolved the Blending as the entity seemed to want her to do. She put a hand to her head, the least bit shaken, and not simply from having seen a picture of the future. The entity had *never* acted that way before, and Jovvi couldn't help finding it somewhat disturbing.

"Well, now we know it works," Tamma said, also looking a bit on the shaky side. "Is that what you see all the time, Naran? How do you stand it?"

"It's . . . never been quite like *that* before," Naran replied, clearly breathless from the experience she had just gone through. "But now I understand why the five of you are so close. It isn't possible to put that . . . blending and meshing into words for an outsider to follow. But I'm not an outsider any longer, am I?"

"No, you certainly are not," Rion agreed with a laugh for her sudden, blooming delight. "You're completely one of us, and more, the entity told us that *it* knew about your talent. It thought about the way things *used* to be, which apparently indicates that its memories stretch all the way back almost to prehistory. No wonder it was having trouble remembering the best way to face tomorrow's attack."

"I hope it remembers by tomorrow," Lorand said, sounding as worried as Vallant looked and was. "That was a really large force it . . . *saw*, and it will do our people a lot of damage if they're caught unawares. If it comes down to it, we'll have to send someone to warn them."

"That probably won't work," Vallant said with a shake of his head. "They know enough about where we are to send a group to attack, so they've got to be watchin' us. If they see any of our people headin' out in the direction the rest will come from, they'll know immediately what's goin' on and will stop him. We'll have to think of somethin' else."

"We'll Blend again early tomorrow morning," Jovvi said, the decision easily made. "If the entity hasn't remembered what it needs to, we'll have to use it to sneak someone out past whatever sentries they have set up. In the meanwhile, is there anything else?''

"Of course there is,'' Rion replied, his arm proudly about Naran's shoulders. "I'm sure all of you recall the entity's thoughts about the bonds to Naran not being as close as they should be, so that needs to be taken care of. Naran, love, you do recall what I told you about that, do you not?''

"Yes, certainly, love,'' Naran answered with her usual sweet smile, the thrill of having Blended still strong in her mind. "The rest of you have already done it and it's necessary, so I'm fully prepared to do the same. After all, Lorand and Vallant are part of *you*.''

"They certainly are,'' Rion agreed with a happy smile, giving her a brief kiss before looking toward the other two men again. "So which of you is to be first to lie with her?''

Jovvi felt the mild shock and odd discomfort in both Lorand and Vallant, and felt amused herself by it. As well as they knew Rion, they still didn't completely understand that his main thought patterns and habits had been developed among all of *them*. He loved Naran so much that he wanted to share her with his brothers, the brothers he loved almost as much. He would certainly kill any other man who might ever attempt the woman of his heart, but his brothers were another matter entirely.

"I'll be first,'' Lorand said after he'd exchanged glances with both Jovvi and Vallant. "And I'll also be honored. Naran, are you certain you understand completely and don't mind?''

"Of course I understand,'' she replied, her mind finally serene. "And how can I mind when I now know you as well as Rion does? This is a family I *want* to be a part of, even more now than before we Blended. There can't possibly be five finer people in the entire world.''

"Six finer people,'' Tamma corrected with a gentle smile of her own. "We know *you* a bit better now too, and if we were fond of you before, the feelings are much stronger now. Right, Jovvi?''

"Absolutely,'' Jovvi agreed, meaning exactly what she'd said. "But I have a suggestion I think we all need to consider. We're all delighted with this brand new development we've accomplished, but I believe we ought to keep it to ourselves for the time being. Our . . . hosts haven't been entirely convinced that we aren't the Chosen, and hearing about this might clinch the matter for them. And besides, I've heard it isn't wise to let people know about *everything* you have up your sleeve."

"I agree with Jovvi," Vallant said at once, but he needn't have bothered. The others were all nodding their own agreement, not one of them uncertain. "This is a strong weapon in our arsenal, and if people don't know about it, they can't prepare against it or try to take it away from us. If nothin' else, we have to think about Naran's safety."

That was the ultimate deciding factor, of course, and no more discussion was called for. Lorand rose from his chair, went to Naran, and bowed as he offered his hand. She took it with a grin and let him help her to her feet, then held to his arm as they began to leave the sitting area. Rion rose as well, his mind humming with happiness, and he went over to walk with Vallant, who was already standing. Tamma waited quietly near her own chair, pretending not to notice who it was who now left the area, but her reluctance to leave at the same time that Vallant did gave Jovvi a chance to speak to her.

"Tamma, please wait just a moment," Jovvi said softly when Tamma was about to take her turn at leaving. "I really do need to talk to you about what happened earlier. I can see how agitated you still are, and—"

"No, it's all right," Tamma said wearily, turning to look at Jovvi. "I was in shock for a minute or two when it seemed as though all of you were against me, but then I understood what you were doing. You were all trying to make Vallant Ro respond, but things didn't turn out quite the way you wanted them to, did they?"

"How can you say that?" Jovvi asked, honestly surprised as she got to her feet. "He told you exactly how he feels, which isn't at all what you thought he did. He loves you, Tamma, so much that he's afraid to do anything more about it."

"Yes, you said he was frightened, and you were right about that part of it," Tamma said ruefully, reaching one hand up to her hair. "At first I didn't know how to feel, but now my mind seems to have . . . made up its mind, so to speak. I expended a good deal of effort to show that man how *I* feel, but he ignored all that because of the possibility that we might sometime have words again. I consider the idea completely ludicrous, but *he* was right about something as well: I do detest cowards. I'll love him to the day I die, but if he finds it impossible to get over his fear, I'll never have anything to do with him again. And now that I'll be able to sleep, I'd like to go to bed."

Jovvi stood with brows raised as Tamma left the area, and it finally came through to her that Tamma *was* relatively serene in her mind. Indecision no longer tormented her, and it was now up to Vallant to act to change the situation as it stood. Could Jovvi *force* Vallant into it? Could anyone? If not. . . .

TWENTY-FIVE

Rion entered the sitting area after breakfast the next morning feeling very satisfied. He'd not only enjoyed the meal, he was also enjoying the way Naran now walked among the others as a complete equal. Her former hesitancy had vanished entirely, and in its place was a . . . wholeness, a fullness of spirit which had not been evident before even in his presence alone. Oh, they both considered themselves half of a single whole, but this was more than that very personal relationship. It was a complete sharing which he'd never been able to hope would ever come about.

But it *had* come about, and Rion still chuckled to himself

over the discomfort his brothers had tried to hide the night before. They seemed to think that Naran was *his*, not in the mutual "ownership" he and Naran practiced but in an exclusive and all-encompassing way. It continued to be a bit beyond him how anyone could think they were entitled to rule the life and doings of another person, especially a person they loved. That sort of relationship was no relationship at all, and it pleased Rion that his brothers seemed to be getting over the outlook. But, of course, there had still been a problem of sorts the night before. . . .

Rion sighed as he remembered what Naran had told him after she'd been with both of his brothers. Lorand hadn't had any trouble sharing his life and love with her, but Vallant had been a different story. Oh, he'd succeeded in strengthening the bonds their Blending needed, but Naran had told Rion sadly that only Vallant's body had been involved. His mind and heart had been another place entirely, and Naran had ached for his very obvious pain. And that confrontation between Vallant and Alsin Meerk also still hovered on the horizon. . . .

"Let's take seats and get started quickly," Jovvi said, bringing Rion's attention back to his surroundings. "I got the impression that High Master Mohr and his friends intend to come by again in a while, and I'd like to be through before then. And even more importantly, we need to know if we'll have a solution to the problem of the ambush, or if we need to think of one ourselves individually."

It wasn't possible to argue with that, of course, so Rion chose a chair next to Naran's and arranged himself comfortably. A moment later he felt Jovvi reaching out to him, and then—

And then the entity was formed again, this time much more quickly and easily than the last. The one who completed it was no longer fearful and hesitant, and the bonds to the others of its flesh forms had been properly strengthened. Now for the problem of how the attackers due later this morning might be met and bested. The memories. . . .

The entity breathed a silent sound of satisfaction to itself, now knowing what must be done. There had been confusion the last time because the problem was properly two problems, not merely one. The first part was that there were insufficient link groups with the entity's flesh forms for an effective defense, and the second was that the approaching allies knew nothing about how they would be attacked. They needed to be told not only of the impending attack, but also how to resist it and reply to it. Once that was done, there would no longer be a problem.

And now the entity knew exactly how they might be warned and informed, with the enemy having no idea that the effort was being made. It was an old technique which would solve the difficulty, and was also the one the entity had been attempting to remember. Clarifying the problem had brought the memory back at once.

And with the thought the entity floated quickly out of the inn, knowing precisely where it was going. The allies of its flesh forms would already be on the road, albeit still some hours away. They would surely have been out of reach to the entity, were the link groups with its flesh forms not warned and already formed. It was necessary to draw heavily on their strength, but speed and . . . solidity were essential.

The speed was there, and the entity made good use of it. Far faster than the fastest horse might have galloped, it floated back along the road its flesh forms had taken until it reached the allies, who were moving at their own best speed. The entity slowed to a stop at a point on the road somewhat ahead of the column, and then manifested a representation of its six flesh forms. It was meant to seem to the allies that the flesh forms were there in the road, and so it did.

"Look, the five of them are back!" someone at the head of the column shouted, and those in the column pulled their mounts or wagon horses to a halt. "Why have they come back?"

"There must have been trouble," the one called Alsin Meerk replied, speaking over his shoulder as he urged his horse on ahead. "Stay here and get the column stopped, and I'll find out what's wrong."

"The trouble is not here, but ahead of you," the entity said into the Meerk flesh form's mind once he had reached what seemed to be the six flesh forms. "We are not here either, but have come to give you warning. Send for members of the strongest link groups, for there is something they must be shown.''

The Meerk being hesitated a moment in uncertainty, but then he turned his mount and rode back along the column. It took several moments, but at the end of the time there were five other beings with Meerk before the entity's representation.

''As our strength is limited, this must be done as quickly as possible,'' the entity said to the five in their minds. ''There will be a large force of enemies who attempt to ambush you as you come to the place called Colling Green, and this is the way they must be fought.''

Into each mind the entity placed the woven pattern of his or her aspect which would form the much stronger tandem link groups, and then they were all given the method of defeating such tandem groups. As High practitioners they all nodded their understanding with smiles of delight, so the entity returned its attention to the Meerk being.

''The enemy's presence will undoubtedly be shielded by their Spirit magic members, therefore must you all be prepared beforehand,'' the entity sent. ''Allow only one Blending entity to be on the alert for your group, and caution it not to draw on the strength of the tandem link groups. This entity means to draw on them once all of you are close enough, and before then will do what it may to protect your column. That may prove to be very little, so be prepared to ward off sudden attack.''

The Meerk being nodded and began to open his mouth in questioning, but the entity ran perilously close to the end of its strength. For that reason it withdrew even more rapidly than it had gone out, and then—

And then it was Rion back again, but one who felt completely drained and hollow. Looking around showed Rion that the others were in like condition, and Jovvi shook her head.

''Every time the entity does something new, I find myself standing with my mouth hanging open,'' she said, sounding as weary as Rion felt. ''But this time I'm sitting like that, because I haven't the strength to stand. And I think I need another breakfast.''

Rion joined the others in agreeing to that, then turned

his full attention to Naran. A glance had shown him that she was even more drained than the rest of them, undoubtedly because she'd had no link group to draw strength from.

"Naran is definitely in need of more food, and I think we all need some rest," Lorand said as Rion put his arm about Naran in an attempt to lend her a bit of strength. "First we'll eat, and then we'll get the second Blending to stand guard while we get a few hours of sleep. If they watch for the arrival of both the attackers and the column and wake us when one or the other is sighted, we should be all right."

Once again no one felt the urge to argue, so they all rose and made their way back to the dining room. The staff was more than startled to see them returning for a second meal, but not nearly as startled as the man Mohr and his friends. They'd apparently been waiting until breakfast was over before approaching them again, and seeing the six of them—plus the link groups—back at tables and demanding food brought the Guild men and merchants a good deal of confusion. They hovered for a moment, as though expecting the matter to be a ploy of some sort to avoid conversation, but when the food was brought and everyone tore into it as though starved, the four men retreated to rethink their position.

The second Blending, which had gone to bed after standing watch all night, was roused and told what was going on, and then they were left to keep watch again while all the rest of them got some sleep. Once the link groups awakened the second Blending would be able to share their strength, as Rion and the others hoped to draw strength from the approaching allies. A question fleeted across Rion's mind at that thought, but in the face of his weariness and his concern over Naran, it was quickly gone again.

It seemed as though they'd barely closed their eyes before they were roused again by the second Blending, letting them know that the column would soon be approaching. They hadn't yet located the enemies who meant to attack, but that wasn't surprising.

"They're almost certainly hiding behind their Spirit magic members," Rion said to Naran after sitting up in bed and rubbing at his eyes. "We'll be fortunate indeed to locate them ourselves before they attack. You still seem close to exhaustion, my love. No one will think any the less of you if you remain here and regather your strength in additional sleep.''

"I know that, my love, but it isn't possible," Naran replied with a strengthless smile that was nevertheless filled with confidence and assurance. "I know now that the lack of my talent will make the entity less than it needs to be, so I must be there with you. Possibly the entity will find a way to strengthen me even without my having a link group to call on.''

"It may indeed be possible," Rion agreed, rising to his feet and waiting until Naran circled the bed and joined him. "We'll ask the others when we reach the sitting area.''

They left the bedchamber then, and found the others leaving their own bedchambers at the same time. They'd had less than three hours of sleep, but some small measure of strength seemed to have been returned to all of them.

"The column is less than half an hour away," Vallant said once everyone had gotten cups of tea and found seats. "The second Blendin' kept searchin' all around, but still can't locate the attackers. I think we need to see if we can reach those special tandem link groups in the column now.''

"And we also need to find a source of additional strength for Naran," Rion added after everyone's immediate agreement about trying to reach the groups in the column. "Our last excursion exhausted her, and there *has* to be something our entity can do.''

"We'll make that a priority even before we search for the attackers," Jovvi said after putting her teacup aside. "Having Naran collapse will do no one but our enemies any good, and the entity will certainly understand that. Is everyone ready?''

Rion belatedly put his own teacup down, and then Jovvi reached out to all of them. Once again there was no difficulty in Blending, and then—

And then the entity looked about, knowing precisely the reason for its being there. Those attackers, the ones who meant harm to the entity's flesh forms' allies, hadn't been located. It would be necessary to make the effort to find them at once, which ought to be possible for *it* despite the failure of the second entity. And perhaps now that the column was so close. . . .

The entity reached out rather than floated, and a moment later found just what it had been hoping for: the approaching allied link groups, formed in tandem in the new way. The additional strength available was tremendous, and the entity immediately allowed it to spread out in its being. *Now* it would be able to accomplish something!

Floating swiftly out of the inn, the entity began to look around. It was able to see the possible places of concealment for the enemy to use, of course, therefore it began to go over those places first. The three least probable locations proved empty of life, as did the second most probable. The first most probable, however, was where they were, a fact the entity frowned over. Those who led the enemy should have known better, which could well mean that those leading them were less than the best strategists and tacticians available. Although it could also mean that they attempted to lull the entity into a false belief concerning their ability. Best would be to keep an open mind. . . .

The enemy was indeed well hidden behind the ability of a tandem group of Spirit magic users, but now the entity was able to pierce the screen of their power. There were one hundred and fifty of them, three sets of tandem link groups, and they were poised ready to attack as soon as the column came within reach. The level of their strength was a good deal more than normal, but not in comparison to the strength of the entity's tandem link groups. In point of fact the enemy was now almost helpless in comparison, which meant they needn't be destroyed.

With that in view, the entity floated away to make contact with the third Blending entity, the one on guard for the column. It shared with the third the knowledge that it might now partake of the strength of the second tandem grouping with the column, and also what it might do to aid the entity. Taking over the enemy forces as it and the second Blending entity had done in the place called Widdertown would be simplicity itself, and there might even be information gathered from their new prisoners which would aid them.

Therefore did the entity and the third begin to radiate

power back and forth between themselves, their intention being to convert all of the enemy at the same time. They had nearly reached the point where it would become possible, when something entirely unexpected occurred. The enemy, apparently able now to perceive the use of that power, suddenly screamed as though in great pain, and then there was a . . . gap of some sort where they had formerly been. The entity, filled with confusion, broke off its effort with the third entity, then floated to where the enemy had been. Was it possible that they had found a way to escape? Or perhaps they merely shielded themselves. . . .

It took no more than a moment to discover that the enemy had neither escaped nor found a way to shield themselves. Bodies lay everywhere in the place of ambush, to both sides of the road, and not one spark of life remained to be found. This event puzzled the entity, and after reporting the fact—and the location—to the third entity and leaving it and its tandem link groups to continue looking about for further enemies, the entity dissolved—

—to thunderstruck horror, at least for Rion. His hands trembled as he looked about at the others, to find that they all appeared as drawn and shaken as he felt.

"Knowin' they were about to be taken over signed their death warrants," Vallant said hoarsely as he ran a hand through his hair. "Those five lowlives must have done that, preferrin' to see them dead to havin' them under *our* power. Strengthwise they were completely unimportant, those bastards must have known that, but they made them die anyway."

"Just to deny them to *us*," Jovvi said in agreement, her face pale and sickness in her lovely eyes. "Something like that goes beyond cruelty, and shows just how unimportant the lives of people are to them, even the lives of their own. How many more times are we going to have to go through something like that?"

"As many times as necessary," Lorand replied with a frown, but his expression wasn't for what had happened to their former enemies. His attention was on Naran, and Rion turned with sudden concern to see that she sat bonelessly in her chair with her eyes closed. "No, it's all right, Rion, she's just fainted from exhaustion. Once she gets a lot of sleep she'll be fine, but this leads to a very important question: why didn't the entity even try to find a way to strengthen her as well as us? We all wanted it to be the first concern, but the entity didn't even consider it.''

''Since she's definitely one of us, it doesn't make any sense,'' Tamrissa said, having left her chair to bend to Naran. ''But whatever the answer turns out to be, we'll have to continue on to Gan Garee as soon as possible. Staying here makes us nothing but targets, and the sooner we dispose of those five pieces of garbage, the fewer people will die.''

Rion heard the murmurs of assent as he lifted Naran into his arms, at the moment concerned only with *her* well-being. Lorand's question *might* be answered at some time in the future, which meant that the situation would probably not change for the next time they Blended. Perhaps he'd be able to persuade Naran to refrain from joining them, but the likelihood of that wasn't strong. She would give her life, if necessary to assist them, but that Rion would never allow. He would *not* lose her because of this, he would *not* . . . !

TWENTY-SIX

Delin strode toward the meeting room he was to get together with the others in, his mood rather foul. Things weren't going at all the way they should have, and his efforts so far hadn't done anything to change matters. He didn't understand *why* his methods weren't working, not when everything inside him said they should have been completely successful. Could someone be working against him in secret, someone he didn't know about and therefore couldn't be expected to suspect . . . ?

"Oh . . . Delin," Homin said as he walked out of the corridor leading to his wing, the words no more than an acknowledgement of Delin's presence rather than a greeting or the preliminary to a question. "I'm on my way to the meeting."

"You should already *be* at the meeting," Delin pointed out as he slowed his pace, forcibly keeping himself from snarling. "Why are you only just on your way?"

"I became . . . involved with something," Homin replied, looking around rather than meeting Delin's gaze. "It made me lose track of the time, but there's no harm done. After all, you haven't gotten there yet either."

Delin nearly choked on the words that would have told Homin he was supposed to have waited for Delin, just the way all of them had at the last meeting. He *was* their leader now, but it was far too soon to rub their noses in it. A better idea might be to hand out the medication they needed to be free of pain at the meetings, then no one would even consider being *tardy.* . . .

"Oh, by the way, Bron won't be with us," Homin said, his manner reminding Delin of the way Homin used to be, which was a bit slow, more quiet than not, almost completely unreliable, and with very little personality. "He sent one of his servants to tell me that so I might pass it on to *you*, and that he would reschedule the meeting for a more . . . convenient time. I wonder how he'll know what's convenient for the rest of us."

This time Delin stopped short, so outraged he could barely contain it. *Bron* had sent word to *Homin* that *he* would reschedule a meeting *Delin* had called? Just as though *he* were their leader rather than Delin? Not in *this* lifetime!

"You, come here!" Delin snarled to a servant who stood ready to get the Five anything they desired. "Go to Lord Bron's wing and find him no matter what he's doing, and tell him I said that if he isn't at the meeting in two minutes, he won't be getting anything to drink tomorrow morning. No, don't worry about what that means, just tell him!"

The servant bowed hastily and then took off at a run, which made Delin feel a small bit better. At least there was *someone* around there who took his position seriously. . . .

"Would you really do that?" Homin asked from the place where he, too, had stopped. "Withhold Bron's medication, I mean. Would you really do that to him?"

"If you can think of a reason why I shouldn't, I'd be curious to hear it," Delin said, seeing the faint worry in Homin's eyes. "I'm the only one who knows the composition of that counteragent, so if Bron decides he can do away with me and not have to worry about consequences, he's as wrong as usual. Or don't you agree?"

"Oh, of course I agree with you, Delin, just as I always have," Homin hastened to assure him while glancing around in an uneasy way. "It's just that . . . Bron probably doesn't realize that he's inconveniencing you, since he seems to have reverted quite a long way toward what he used to be. And Selendi has barely said a word to me lately, not to mention indulging in . . . other things. I don't understand what's happening. . . ."

Delin frowned at Homin, seeing the lack of ease and self-confidence that used to be so evident at all times. Homin was also clearly reverting, and the reason for that added to Delin's disturbance. Kambil had had the three of them under control, and they'd behaved just the way they were supposed to while actually obeying Kambil's orders. Delin had expected to walk into the position Kambil had previously held, had expected his three groupmates to take his orders without argument, but once again things weren't going as planned. The constant pain Kambil was in the grip of must have loosened his hold on the three, letting them revert to what they'd been before Kambil and his grandmother had put them under control. . . .

Delin cursed under his breath as he resumed walking toward the meeting room, Homin trailing silently after. Obviously someone *was* working against him, and he meant to find out exactly who that someone was.

When they reached the meeting room, Delin saw that Selendi had obviously only just arrived. A servant was in the process of pouring her a cup of tea, while she sat staring at herself in a hand mirror. That vapid, mindless expression she'd always worn was back, and although she knew Delin and Homin had come in, she made no effort to acknowledge their presence. Delin's first urge was to snap at her, but then he held the words back. He'd wait until Bron arrived, and then he'd have to say it only once.

It took more than twice the two minutes he'd specified to the servant in his message to Bron, but the Fire magic user did finally stalk into the meeting room. His expression said he was furious, but before he could speak Delin reached out with his talent and touched the man's heart.

"Yes, it hurts, and if you try to use Fire magic on me it will hurt a good deal more," Delin said as Bron gasped and staggered, needing to keep erect himself as there was no servant in the room to help him. "And even if you decide the pain is worth it to turn me to ash, you'll change your mind tomorrow, when the counteragent isn't available to hold off the agony of the poison. Do you understand that thoroughly and completely?"

Bron nodded convulsively as he tottered to a chair and fell into it, so Delin also nodded and released his hold. Homin stared silently from where he sat—as close to Selendi as he could manage—and even Selendi had looked up from her primping in the mirror.

"As for you," Delin said to the stupid girl, "you won't ever bring a mirror to a meeting again. You'll all show up *on time*, and you won't send excuses or bring other things to do. Is that clear?"

"How could it be anything but?" Selendi demanded with a very unladylike snort, sending hatred to him with the daggers of her gaze. "You have a hold on us, so you're going to use it. What a surprise."

"Well, I'm glad you liked that so much," Delin said, keeping the edge out of his voice. "Since you did, I'll add something to it just for *you*. From now on we'll have a meeting every day, at a time and place I'll decide on shortly before the meeting. Once I decide I'll send servants to tell the rest of you, and that meeting will be where you'll be given the counteragent. The last one to arrive, though, will have to wait until the meeting is over before he—or she— gets to drink the counteragent. I'm sure everyone will be really grateful to you, Selendi, for making me think of that.''

The hatred in her gaze increased, but at least she had the good sense not to say anything else. She and the others could spend the rest of the day wondering just *when* the meeting would be, as they would have to wait until then for the counteragent. Delin decided to make it somewhat later in the morning than the three had been taking the counteragent until then. That way the pain would be starting again by the time they reached the meetingplace. . . .

"Are you through pushing us around, Delin?'' Bron asked, his skin still pale from the near heart attack Delin had caused him to experience. "Because if you are, you might like to hear why I was late getting here.''

"Are you seriously going to tell me her name?'' Delin asked with a snort of his own. "Do I look as if I *care* what her name is?''

"The name is of a man, and he's the commandant of the city guard,'' Bron replied with disgust dripping from the words. He still wasn't able to sit straight in his chair, but his air of contempt came through clearly. "He came to report to the Five about the disturbances in the city, but you were 'unavailable' and the others were too. That's why I saw him alone, and he was just finishing his report when that servant showed up with your ridiculous message. Next time it would help our image if you found out what I was doing before you threatened me in public.''

Delin stood silently for a moment, trying to decide whether or not to believe Bron. It would be just like the man to make up a story like that to embarrass him, to emasculate him before the others. Well, it wasn't going to be done quite as easily as that. . . .

"So you had a visit from the commandant of the city guard,'' Delin said after the pause, having decided to call Bron's bluff. "Why don't you tell the rest of us what he had to say.''

"I'll be glad to, but first I have a question,'' Bron had the nerve to answer. "We were supposed to get another letter with a list of names in today's delivery of the counteragent. Was the list picked up? None of the palace guards could tell me.''

"We . . . haven't received word as yet about where the package and letter have been left," Delin admitted, hating to voice one of the things that hadn't gone as he'd expected it to. "The delay probably doesn't mean anything beyond the fact that our enemies have grown cautious, so I wouldn't worry about it."

"Of course you wouldn't," Bron replied, finally forcing himself straighter in the chair. "You aren't one of those who need the counteragent in order to stay free of pain and continue living. But that's really beside the point, isn't it? *We* don't need their help either, but they're not supposed to know that. My guess would be that they do know that, so they've abandoned their schemes for good."

"Are you saying they have a spy here in the palace?" Delin demanded, the assertion too close to his own thinking to be nothing more than coincidence. "The same idea occurred to *me*, but no one is supposed to be able to get through our guard security. If there *is* a spy here, how did he get in?"

"If it's someone who's been here all along, there would be no question about how he got in," Bron said, his attitude now somewhat brooding. "I've been thinking about it and about how they managed to poison us in the first place, and that looks like the only answer. They've been here all along, and we simply didn't know. And, at this point, we have no way to question that army of servants and expect to find the guilty ones."

Delin felt the barb of that accusation, even though it was only suggested. With Kambil completely out of it, they'd have to question each and every servant one at a time in order for Delin to be able to tell if the one being questioned was lying. That would probably take years, when they couldn't even count on having weeks.

"Our lacks at this point can't be helped," Delin said after a moment, making his counter about Kambil as oblique as Bron's accusation. "Happily we don't need the enemy in order to have the counteragent, so we can put that problem aside for the moment. Did the guard commandant come with a problem that *can't* be put aside?"

"I'd say that was an accurate description," Bron agreed with a judicious nod. "If Homin will be so kind as to get me a cup of tea, I'll find it easier to tell all of you about it. . . . Yes, thank you for agreeing, Homin. Now to the problem: There's been trouble all over the city, and the guard commandant is complaining that he doesn't have enough men to handle it. It seems that too much of his force has been sent *out* of the city, and none of it has returned yet.''

"The peasants are making trouble?" Delin asked with a frown, ignoring Homin's scurrying to the tea service on Bron's behalf. "Why haven't we been told about this before now?"

"That was my question, and it took a bit of doing before I had an answer," Bron returned, back to looking sour. "It seems that our peasant population has been told about the . . . 'help' we were given to win the final competition, and very few, if any, are doubting the truth of the accusation. Our noble peers decided on a course of action and gave the orders for it, just to keep us from being disturbed, you understand. The fact that no one had the insides to mention the matter to us had nothing at all to do with it.''

"Of course not," Delin agreed dryly, fighting to keep from screaming at the stupidity of their so-called peers. "If someone *had* mentioned the matter to us, we could have shown those lowborn fools just how much help we need *now*, but our people were protecting us. So why have they come to us at *this* time?"

"Because matters have gotten out of hand," Bron said very simply. "Curfews were instituted to keep the peasants off the streets and away from the ranting of agitators, and those who defied the curfew were arrested. Gold was offered for the names and locations of agitators, and two were betrayed to the guard.''

"That doesn't sound like matters getting out of hand," Delin pointed out, shifting in the chair he'd taken a pair of moments earlier. "It sounds as though matters are well *in* hand.''

"They only began that way," Bron disagreed, thanking Homin with a nod for the teacup the smaller man had brought over. "The arrests of the peasants and agitators should have quieted the rest of the noisy fools, the way it's done in the past. This time, however, the places of detention were attacked and the peasants were freed, and the traitor who was paid gold for betraying the agitators was found hanging outside one of the guard posts. During the attacks the defending guardsmen were beaten savagely, and one or two, who had been teaching the peasants under arrest better manners, were killed. Now large numbers of peasants are defying the curfews, and the commandant's men are reluctant to make any more arrests.''

"We'll have to find more men for him to use," Delin said as he stood and began to pace. "If we let the peasants get away with doing as they please, they'll start to do even more. Once he has the men, we'll tell him to kill the peasants rather than arrest them. That way there won't be anyone for the others to rescue, and they'll get the message that the same could happen to any one of them. That will make them toe the line again, just wait and see if it doesn't.''

"Where are we supposed to get more men for him?" Bron had the nerve to ask after sipping at his tea. "The guard has always recruited from the peasants, and in the last week or two the number of applications from possible recruits has fallen off to almost nothing. We've had no word at all from *any* of the guard groups sent to take care of those five peasant upstarts who escaped from the city, and I doubt if we *will* hear from them. With that in view, killing any of the peasants out of hand will just make the others insanely angry and push them into retaliating in kind.''

"We may have to show more of the guardsmen how to link in that new tandem way," Homin ventured before Delin was able to reply to Bron. "If we do that, we won't need more guardsmen. Kambil didn't want to, I know, but it looks like we may have to do it anyway now.''

"Kambil had a reason for not wanting to show any of the local link groups," Bron said to Homin with a headshake. "That special tandem link makes them a *lot* stronger than normal, and he didn't want a bunch of them getting ideas about taking over from *us*. Now that we're . . . less than full strength, there's even more of a reason to keep the knowledge from them.''

"But that's only a possibility, while the lack of enough

guardsmen is a reality,'' Selendi said, startling Delin. ''With going up against the rabble ourselves the only alternative to doing nothing or showing them the new linking, what choice do we have?''

''We *can* go up against them ourselves,'' Homin mused, no longer hesitating the way he had. ''After all, we're far from strengthless as far as our abilities are concerned. They won't know the difference between High talents, they'll only know that we *are* Highs. That might even do the job of squashing most of those rumors about us. What do *you* think, Delin?''

''Are you suggesting that I let Kambil rejoin us?'' Delin asked, aware of those three pairs of eyes staring at him. ''That may seem like a good idea to *you*, Homin, but not to me. Kambil won't be Blending with us ever again, but we really don't need him. The four of us can do the same without him.''

''And let everyone know that there's serious trouble among the Five?'' Bron asked, derisive again. ''That would bring *more* problems, not solve the ones we already have. If we can't go out complete, we can't go out at all. What other suggestion do you have?''

''Why do I need another suggestion?'' Delin demanded, pausing in his pacing to glare at Bron. ''Because *you* say so? Well, the point may be difficult for you to grasp, but you're not the leader of this group!''

''I never claimed to be the leader, Delin,'' Bron returned, much too calmly to suit Delin. ''What I am, though, is someone who remembers that there's a prophecy out there claiming that the evil Four will return. If we go out in public without Kambil, people will start to say that *we're* the evil Four, come back in different bodies to enslave everyone. Right after that they'll start to attack the palace here, and we won't have to worry about finding the spy among the servants because most of them will either be gone or will be attacking us along with everyone else. Is that really what you want?''

Delin stared his hatred at Bron, but the words which would have put him back in his place refused to come. Everyone knew about the Prophecy, and even people who had till now refused to believe in it would be forced to change their minds if a Four showed up in public instead of a Five. Delin couldn't argue that, but he also couldn't think of anything else to do.

"What I want is to have those troublemakers put down as quickly as possible," Delin finally answered, glaring at all three of them. "I have the beginnings of a plan in mind, and I'll tell the rest of you about it as soon as I have all the details straight. In the meanwhile, Bron, tell the commandant to carry on as best he can. But remind him that we can't let the peasants get away with doing as they please."

"What about the antidote for the poison we were given?" Bron called after him as Delin headed toward the door. "If we've lost the chance to find those people, we've also lost the chance to get rid of this poison permanently. What are you going to do about *that*?"

Delin hurried out of the room, refusing to acknowledge hearing the question. He had no idea what to do about that, just as he had no idea what to do about the peasants. He wanted to kill them all, but then who would do all the work that a city needed doing? Maybe if he had half of them killed, the other half would change their minds about making trouble. Yes, that might work, and he would have to think about it . . . along with the fact that those five peasants who had almost defeated them in the competitions were on their way back.

Peace would have to be restored before they arrived, but how were they going to achieve that? Delin didn't know, and he hated not knowing. But there was a way to find out, if he handled things exactly right. Yes, it could be the right time to try that. . . .

TWENTY-SEVEN

Eltrina Razas let Edmin Ruhl hurry her into his father's house, no longer finding his concern amusing. Edmin had reason to be concerned—just as they all did—and nothing about the situation was amusing.

"The High Lord seems much better today, Lord Edmin," the elderly servant said as soon as he shut the front door—which took longer than it should have. "If you'll be good enough to give me a moment, I'll conduct you to him."

"Don't bother, Rishlin, I know the way," Edmin said at once, most likely to keep the trip to the back study from taking an hour, Eltrina thought. "You may see to your other duties."

"With most of the staff gone, not many duties are being seen to," the old man muttered as Eltrina and Edmin began to walk toward the back of the house. "It's a blessing that my wife is able to cook, else the High Lord would likely starve. Don't know what this world is coming to...."

"It seems to be trying to come to an end," Eltrina murmured to Edmin, knowing the old man wasn't likely to hear her. "Can he and his precious wife really be trusted?"

"Rishlin was born to parents who served my grandfather," Edmin replied in a soft voice. "He grew up serving my father, who is only a few years younger than him, and married just as he was directed to. My father had hoped he would produce a son to serve *me* the way Rishlin served *him*, but there were no children from the union. If that old man can't be trusted, no one can be."

The comment did well to describe Eltrina's feelings, that no one *could* be trusted, but she refrained from saying so out loud. In these new times it would be necessary to *pretend* to trust those she was forced to associate with, as they were done for if they began to bicker among themselves.

Edmin knocked on the door to his father's study and then walked in, and for the first time since Eltrina had been coming to that house the High Lord was on his feet and looking like his old self. His high color also said he was more than slightly put out, both of which meant he knew exactly how many servants he had left in the house.

"Edmin, you're late," Lord Embisson said, more a comment than a criticism. "Were you attending another meeting?"

"No, we were slinking through the streets, actually, trying not to be noticed," Edmin replied, not joking in the least. "My household is as bare of servants as yours is, more so in that I don't have even a single couple to see to it. Most of the servants everywhere have picked up and left, and our peers are frantic."

"Or irate, I imagine, just as I am," Lord Embisson growled, looking around for something to glare at. "Even my agents have missed their scheduled meetings, but just you wait. When those lazy ingrates try to come back to their jobs, they'll find they have no jobs to come back to, agents and servants alike. I'll turn them all out to starve, damned if I don't!"

"Father, there's every indication that none of the servants *intend* to come back," Edmin said after seating Eltrina, his voice gentle in an obvious effort to break the news in the nicest way. "Some of my people felt loyal enough to make final reports to me, and that's what I've been told. The peasants have begun to follow a plan of some sort, and that's part of it."

"What sort of plan can they possibly have?" Lord Embisson demanded, watching Edmin at the tea service. "If they leave their jobs and don't go back, they'll all starve while living in the streets. No plan can possibly change that.''

"One can," Edmin denied, turning with two full cups when he finished filling them. "Where it comes from no one seems to know, but it does address the problem rather efficiently. Your agents haven't been by to see you because most of them have been ejected from the city. Those who used to run various business enterprises for us have taken over ownership of those businesses, and will no longer turn over our percentage of the earnings. Instead they'll use the gold to feed that horde of unemployed servants, while the ex-servants spend their time building housing for themselves and others. The land being built on used to belong to various of our peers as well, people who had no wish to see the land littered with housing for the lower classes. Now they no longer have a say over the property, and once the new housing is built the ex-servants will find employment among their own kind—financed by gold which was supposed to be ours."

"But that's outrageous!" Lord Embisson exclaimed while Edmin took a seat after giving Eltrina her cup of tea. "How can they expect to get away with it? The guard will. . . . Come to think of it, the guard should have stopped this already. Are they all just standing around watching what's happening without lifting a finger against it?"

"The guard, apparently under orders from the Five, made an effort to regain control early on," Edmin replied after sipping at his tea. "Ah, I needed that after our rather lengthy walk. But about the guard: When this new attitude among the peasants first began, a platoon of them was sent to make examples of individuals and to send them all back to where they belong. They marched out intending to obey their orders—and found three times their number of peasants waiting for them. Their link groups immediately tried to disperse the crowds, and only then discovered that even more laws were being broken. The peasants had formed their own link groups, and the confrontation turned into a rout for the guard. After that an unfortunate number of guardsmen deserted their posts and joined the rabble, who have now taken it upon themselves to police the city. The guard commander pulled the remainder of his force back into our sections, but they're far too few to keep out anyone at all. Which is why our walk over here was far from pleasant.''

"This is a nightmare," Lord Embisson muttered as he dropped into a chair, apparently beyond pacing. "Our ancestors never had this trouble keeping the rabble down . . . but why did you have to *walk* here? If your carriage drivers went with the rest, you could have driven the carriage yourself. Doing that may be undignified, but not as undignified as walking.''

"Yes, Father, I certainly could have driven the carriage— if someone had hitched the horses to it," Edmin told him with as little ridicule as possible. "All those straps and harnesses and things. . . . I looked them over carefully, and discovered that I hadn't the first idea of what went where. Then I tried to saddle one of the horses, but found it impossible to tighten the girth strap far enough. The fool horse kept puffing out its belly, that is, when it wasn't throwing the saddle off to begin with. I believe I once heard someone say that there's a difference between carriage horses and saddle horses, but *I* couldn't see a difference. They all look like horses, and all of them were most uncooperative.''

"I see," Lord Embisson said, clearly not seeing anything but his own position and fortune disappearing from the world. "Well, there seems to be only one thing left for us to do. You'll stay here while I complete preparations, and then we'll go to Bastions, my estate in the east. It's completely self-sufficient with a full complement of servants, and we can stay there until this nonsense blows over. Rishlin tells me that his wife has had trouble getting food at the market lately, which is why I began my preparations to leave. Now I think we'd better get going as quickly as possible.''

"That's the only plan you can come up with?" Eltrina blurted, helpless to keep the words inside. "Abandon everything and just run away? What about those five disgusting peasants our own Five are so afraid of? They're definitely on the way back to the city, and are expected almost at any time. They're the other half of the source of all our troubles, and we owe them the same kind of vengeance we meted out to those vermin in the palace! If we run away now, they'll have won."

"My dear Lady Eltrina, allow me to state the obvious," Lord Embisson returned, not in the least out of control. "I've lived far more years than you have, and I've learned one very important lesson: the winner of any particular confrontation is the one who survives it. Whether that survival is brought about by fighting or running makes not the least difference, as long as survival is achieved. If those peasants also survive, which at this point is no foregone conclusion, we'll then be able to see what might be done about them. If not, then *we'll* have won without needing to lift a finger. You're perfectly welcome to accompany Edmin and myself, but if you feel you must remain here in the city, only a blind fool would agree to stay with you."

Eltrina glanced quickly at Edmin, and caught the faintest trace of a flush of embarrassment in his complexion. She'd learned that the one thing Edmin couldn't abide was the thought of looking like a fool, and of course his father would know that. By speaking to *her* rather than to Edmin, Lord Embisson had made his opinion a general statement rather than a direct criticism against his son. Edmin could well respond to that, despite the work she'd done to bring him over onto *her* side.

"I'm afraid I don't agree with your comment about staying," Eltrina tried, keeping her voice as steady as Embisson's had been. "Survival is, as you said, the most important thing, but at times one's survival depends on being in the right place at the right time. Staying here to strike against those peasants could mean the difference between surviving as a potentially penniless outcast, and helping things to go back to the way they were. With that in mind, how can you even consider running away?"

"Rather easily, child," Embisson replied, standing up from his chair to stretch. "I've seen to my business affairs carefully over the years, and to be very frank I've enough gold to keep me in comfort even if I live to be two hundred and fifty. Edmin is almost that well off, and once I'm gone he'll have the balance of my estate to add to his own. Much of our gold is hidden at Bastions, to be handy in an emergency like this one. And there's one other, very important point to consider.''

Lord Embisson took two steps toward her, and stood looking down with as serious an expression as she'd ever seen him show.

"It would destroy me if anything were to happen to Edmin," he said, the words simple and open. "There's no longer a society here to protect him, a society of guardsmen and servants and those who would support him against the rabble. By his own admission he cannot even saddle a horse, so what good would his remaining in the city do? The best-conceived plan in the world would be useless without those to carry it out, and we no longer *have* those to carry it out. Remaining in danger when there's something one might do is heroism; remaining when one is helpless is not. But Edmin is a grown man, and more than capable of making his own decisions. If he wishes to remain behind, I'll . . . somehow find a way to cope without him. I do, after all, have Rishlin and his wife.''

And then the man turned toward the tea service, walking away as though everything had been said on the subject. Eltrina felt the urge to scream and break something, because Embisson had noticed the mistake he'd made and had quickly repaired it. His first comments had shown that he took it for granted that Edmin would join him, *telling* Edmin what he would do rather than asking. That mistake would have done irreparable harm with someone as stiff-necked as Edmin, trampling as it did on his dignity and pride. But now. . . . There was only one possible response, and Eltrina quickly decided to make it.

"Edmin, my dear, your father is right," she said almost at once, turning to give Edmin a wan smile. "He does need you more than I do, so you really must go with him. I'll . . . be quite all right on my own, you needn't worry about that. If fortune favors me, we'll certainly see each other again.''

"So you really mean to stay," Edmin said, gazing at her with that emotionless look that did so well in covering his thoughts and feelings. "No matter what anyone says, no matter what happens, you mean to stay. The situation has turned into an obsession for you, and you'll sacrifice anyone and anything to that obsession. I'm nothing more to you than a means to an end.''

"Edmin, how can you say that?" Eltrina protested, actually rather upset. His sudden comment had startled her, touching as closely as it did to the real truth. "You know how much you mean to me, and haven't I just proved it by urging you to leave with your father? You can't believe I just said that for effect, not meaning a word? You can't really believe *that* of me, can you?''

"Eltrina, your aspect is Earth magic, but mine isn't Air magic, as I said it was,'' he explained, also getting to his feet. "I'm fairly strong in Spirit magic, and I've learned that people watch themselves a good deal less closely when they don't know a Spirit magic user is about. At first I felt I might be betraying something real by not telling you, but then you began to try to sway me by pretending to things you didn't actually feel. I've found our relationship to be . . . pleasant, but since I abhor people who attempt to use me, you may now consider the time at an end. Do allow me to see you to the door.''

"But where am I supposed to go?" Eltrina demanded as she stood, furious that the man had hidden things from her. "My former refuge must be as empty as your house and this one, and the same is probably true of Grall's house. If you aren't here to use your contacts with those peasants you employed secretly, there won't be anything I'll find it possible to do!''

"I'm afraid you should have considered that sooner,'' Edmin replied smoothly, totally unmoved by anything she'd said. "If you'd kept silent and agreed to go with us, I would have allowed you to do so even though my father obviously had no interest in taking you. Now . . . as I said, I'll see you to the door.''

"Don't bother!'' Eltrina snarled, turning her back on him and heading for the door herself. "I'd rather live on the street than stay here, where people *spy* on you without any warning! And I hope that your precious plans fall down around your ears, leaving you homeless and penniless and wishing you'd stayed in an effort to do *something*! If *I* succeed, you'll certainly never find a welcome in this city again!''

And with that she strode out, caring nothing about whether or not he followed to make sure she actually left— which he most likely would do anyway. She'd wasted her time trying to cultivate him for use in her plans, but maybe not entirely. She *had* met a few of the peasants he'd employed, and they weren't the sort of men to join what the rabble was in the midst of doing. If she found it possible to locate them, Grall's gold would buy their assistance and obedience, at least until she'd completed what she now considered her mission in life. That last member of the five vermin had been taken care of, or at least would be seen to soon. But the disgusting peasants who had been the cause of so much pain and humiliation. . . .

Eltrina smiled as she swung the front door wide and walked out, caring not at all about closing the thing behind her. Those peasants would soon be in the city again, and by then she *would* have a plan in place to see to them. If she survived, she *would* see them destroyed. . . .

Twenty-Eight

Lady Hallina Mardimil woke up slowly, feeling vaguely annoyed. It took a moment or two after her eyes fluttered open for her to understand the annoyance fully, and by then she had progressed to being irate. She was supposed to have been awakened precisely at eight o'clock as usual, but something about the morning sunlight told her it was later than that. A glance at the mantle clock told her it was indeed later, eight thirty-five to be precise, which meant that people were going to be punished for certain!

Hallina threw the covers aside and swung her legs over the side of the bed, and then shock held her still for a moment. For all the years of her life, there had always been a warmed pair of slippers waiting to receive her feet in comfort. It was the one service she required every day of the year, even in summer, and the one her staff always knew was most important. Today there wasn't even a pair of cold slippers, and shock quickly gave way to fury.

"Arwinna! Radli! Sonilin!" Hallina shouted, letting the fury turn her voice shrill. "Get in here, you lazy good-for-nothings! As soon as I've had my breakfast, Hafner will be called in from the stables to see to you three, you have my word on that! Get in here this minute, or the beatings will be that much worse!"

Nothing but silence greeted Hallina's words, nothing of the scrabbling haste she'd been expecting. That was something else which had never happened before, and now indignation settled upon her. If someone had *caused* her servants to be remiss in their duties, it would certainly go ill with whomever the culprit was. She was no peasant who might be trifled with without consequences, and everyone ought to know that. Her servants would still be punished for allowing such a thing, but not until she'd dealt with the fool who had presumed.

Needing to walk barefoot was disgusting to Hallina, even over the softly expensive and exquisitely clean carpeting. Her morning wrap lay draped over a chair arm, a slothful sight which brought back indignation, as did needing to get into it by herself. This entire situation was an outrage, and the sooner it was seen to the sooner she would be able to return to her usual pleasant self. She made a quick stop in her privacy facility, easing herself for the fray, so to speak, and then she marched downstairs.

"Hiding will do none of you any good at all," she announced in a loud voice once she stood at the foot of the stairs. "You will come out now and tell me what caused this—this—outrage, and once I've seen to it I'll then see to all of *you*. Come out, I say, and take your punishments as people who dare not be dismissed from their positions."

That particular truth, that they dare not lose their positions, made Hallina smile. It was the source of one of her greatest amusements, and now would be so again. She stood waiting with her hands clasped together, relishing the thought of how hangdog they would look when they crept out to receive her justified anger, but then her smile faded. Those stupid little nothings should have already appeared, and the fact that they hadn't now turned her anger to twice what it had been.

"I'm going to put an end to this right *now*!" Hallina growled as she stalked forward, heading for the kitchen and pantry, where most of those useless fools often lazed around. It was obviously time to dismiss most of them and replace them with peasants who knew how to keep to their place, and even more importantly, how to value a position. Walking into the dining room brought additional outrage, as not one crumb of breakfast stood ready on the buffet. That was something else the useless rubbish would pay for. . . .

"Now, you listen to—" Hallina began as she pushed through into the kitchen, but the words died on her lips at sight of the emptiness. No one, not one single servant, was in evidence, which was completely impossible. Even if they'd gone insane and had decided not to serve *her* any longer, they themselves had to eat! So where could they possibly be?

Hallina returned to the dining room at a much slower pace, disturbance taking the place of anger. It was beyond belief to think that they'd all deserted her, not when they owed her so much! Most of them had been in her employ for years, and had always been willing to crawl and beg rather than be dismissed. How could they now just pick up and—

The sight of a folded piece of paper on the dining room table halted the ringing questions in Hallina's mind, and she quickly crossed to the table and snatched up the paper. If this was some sort of excuse for the absences, it would make not one whit of difference in the punishments she would hand out. They would all regret having put her through this, each and every one—!

Unfolding the note and scanning it quickly stopped Hallina's thoughts a second time, as the contents were completely beyond belief. It simply wasn't possible, it *couldn't* be! But reading the note a second time, more slowly, did nothing to change the message.

"Dear Bitch," it began outrageously. "This notice of termination of our service is being left with the greatest pleasure, and the word 'our' refers to every slave in the house. Yes, slave rather than servant, because that was what we were to you. You took advantage of our need to keep our families fed and healthy, and treated us like dirt. For that reason *we* now take great pleasure in telling you what you can do with yourself from now on, only without us. But come to think of it, you probably don't even know how to do that much for yourself. Well, we'll certainly think of you in our new positions, picturing you floundering around until you die of starvation, and probably in your night-clothes at that. Most of us don't believe you capable of dressing yourself, and now we'll all learn the truth—especially you. We wish you the worst life is able to provide, and after that a painful, lingering death. The staff."

Hallina let go of the note and just let it drop, too stunned even to be furious. They were *gone*, to new positions? How could that possibly be? No member of the nobility would take on a servant without speaking to his or her former employer, to find out under what circumstances that servant was let go. Because of that, peasants found it impossible to find a new position if they left one for any reason other than a general reduction of staff. It made the service they were given by their staff the best possible, but now. . . . What in the world could have happened?

Suddenly chilled to the bone, Hallina sank down into a chair. This couldn't possibly be reality, so she must be having a nightmare. Yes, that was it, she was having a nightmare. Of course she couldn't see to herself, what true member of the nobility could? She wasn't *meant* to see to herself, not ever, but now. . . .

Hallina's thoughts ended there, and how long she sat staring at nothing was impossible to tell. Time had ceased to have meaning, except for the fact that her hunger began to increase. Then a sound penetrated the stunned fog wrapping her around, a distant thumping of some kind. She had no idea what the sound could be, and truth to tell couldn't have cared less. Her main concern was that she was hungry, and all those miserable ingrates refused to appear to ease that hunger. But she would find a way to get even with them, just as soon as she found out where they'd gone. Having them dismissed from their new employment and then refusing to take them back herself would fix them, that would fix them good and proper—

"So there you are, Lady Hallina," a male voice said, startling her. "Why didn't you answer the door? You must have heard us knocking."

"Me, answer a door?" Hallina demanded, outraged in spite of everything as she turned to look at the brash intruder. "Do you take me for a servant, you fool? But I think I know you. . . ."

"Indeed you do, Lady Hallina," the idiot said with a sarcastic bow. "I'm Lord Rimen Howser, special representative of the Five, and soon to be High Lord. I take it that your servants have already gone?"

"They certainly have, but they're not as done with me as they believe," Hallina growled, beginning to fire up again. "As soon as I learn where they've gone, I'll see to it that they're dismissed immediately. They'll be out on the street with nothing—"

"No, they won't," the idiot had the nerve to interrupt, his expression sourly amused. "They haven't found new positions with someone of *our* class, they've been taken in by the rabble of the city. We've all experienced the same thing, or at least most of us have. Those of our class who made a habit of coddling their staff haven't been completely deserted, but they selfishly refuse to lend out to the rest of us what animals are left. Well, that's neither here nor there. The reason I've come is to take you to the palace."

"Well, at last," Hallina declared with the beginnings of a delighted smile. "Those children have finally understood just who I am, and now they're making sure I'm not discomfited. They're hours too late for *that*, of course, which I'll tell them as soon as I see them, but at least they have the good sense to—"

"No, Lady Hallina, you misunderstand me," the man interrupted again, a habit Hallina found utterly outrageous. "You aren't being honored by the Five, not when you really aren't anyone at all. There may be a need for having you near to hand, which is the reason why you were forbidden to leave the city. It served their purpose to let you stay in your own house in the interim, but now, with your servants gone, it will be best to have you where you won't perish by accident. If it turns out that you aren't needed after all, you'll probably be released to go your own way again.''

That was the point where Hallina really noticed the uniformed guardsmen standing behind Howser. One or two of them wore smirks, amused by her humiliation, but numbness turned outrage thin and tenuous. Her staff was gone for good, she was being all but arrested, and if she managed to live through whatever those vile children had in mind for her, she would be turned out into the street. So how—

''Lady Hallina, go and dress yourself now, and choose no more than three outfits to take with you,'' Howser said, again interrupting her thoughts. ''You'll have to pack the additional clothing yourself, but some of my men will carry it for you. You will do it right now, or I'll be forced to take you as you are.''

Thin and distant outrage touched Hallina again, but that wasn't the overriding thing concerning her now. The one, burning question she had was of vast importance, and could be summed up rather easily. In the midst of all these nightmarish happenings, how was she going to take her just vengeance against Clarion? She didn't know, but one thing was crystal clear: no matter what else she lost, attaining vengeance couldn't be allowed to go with the rest. It just couldn't . . . couldn't . . . couldn't. . . .

''Daddy, I want to go *home*!'' Mirra Agran announced, not for the first time. ''I'm bored absolutely to tears, and now that everyone in the city seems to be goin' insane, even the few parties that *were* bein' held aren't bein' held any longer. We can sue the Ros just as easily and a lot more comfortably in Port Entril.''

''Don't you think I've been *tryin'* to get us out of here, Mirra?'' her father replied from the overstuffed chair he sat in. This was the study of the house they were renting, and he should have been at the desk, working to get her what she'd asked for. Instead he sat in one of the chairs of the room, uselessly sipping tea.

"That insanity you mentioned has spread to everybody, it seems, and gettin' anythin' done is apparently out of the question," he continued. "But don't forget that I wanted to leave a week ago, when I got that message from Jorvin, who's lookin' after the business for me back home. He said things were startin' to get strange, with folk standin' on corners listenin' to men shoutin' about freedom and such, but you wouldn't hear of us leavin'. Now that *you* want to go, you expect everybody to just drop whatever they're doin'...."

"Daddy, how can you speak to me that way?" Mirra complained, using the wounded tone that usually made him understand just how badly he'd failed her. "Haven't you always said that nothin' is too good for Momma and me, and that it's your job to see that we never want for anythin'? Well, now I want somethin', but you're not givin' it to me. I suppose I'll just have to get Momma to ask right along with me."

The threat of getting her mother after him usually worked, as her father actually loved his wife very much. This time, though, the silly man just looked over at her where she stood.

"Your momma is busy in the kitchen," he replied in the oddest tone. "Just before all the servants left, I was told that some of them would have stayed on—if not for the constant demandin' you always do. Until now they had to put up with it, but they were happy about not needin' to any longer. The only reason we had what to eat for lunch was the fact that your momma hasn't forgotten how to cook, but you made no effort to give her even the slightest bit of help. Now you *can* go and talk to her—and ask her to put you to work. That should take care of your bein' bored."

"That craziness must be catchin', if you think *I'll* do any housework," Mirra said with a sound of ridicule, putting her fists to her hips. "I'm meant for much better things, just as you've always said, Daddy. Now, about how soon we'll be leavin'—"

"Damned if he wasn't tellin' the truth," her father interrupted, not quite muttering. "He said I'd spoiled you rotten, and there's no arguin' *that* fact. Now I wonder if he wasn't tellin' the truth about the rest of it."

"If you're talkin' about that Vallant Ro, you can be sure he lied in his teeth," Mirra said at once, beginning to be vastly annoyed. "And he was also insultin', but he'll pay for all that once he and I are married. I *want* him, Daddy, and I don't believe in givin' up things I want."

" '*Things*,' Mirra?" her father echoed, his expression now harder than she'd ever seen it. "He's not a thing, he's a man, but you don't seem to understand the difference. And there's also a difference between wantin' and lovin'. Or don't you know that either?"

"I refuse to discuss things with you when you're bein' unreasonable," Mirra huffed, knowing instinctively that it was time to end the conversation. "I'm goin' to my bed-chamber for a nap, and we'll talk again when—"

This time it was a knocking at the front door which interrupted her, and her father made no useless effort to tell *her* to see who was calling. He rose himself after putting aside his teacup, and strode out to the front hall. Mirra trailed after, curious to see if it might be a party invitation being sent to her, but the man at the door couldn't possibly be mistaken for a servant—not to mention the fact that there were guardsmen behind him.

"Dom Agran?" the stranger said, more a statement than a question. "It seems that you've lost your serving staff along with the rest of us."

"Yes, it so happens I have," Mirra's father replied evenly. "May I ask who you are, and what business is bringin' you here?"

"That's easily answered," the man replied with a smile as his gaze moved to Mirra for a moment. "I'm Lord Ri-men Howser, and you and your daughter and wife are to accompany me to the palace. You'll be given a short time to pack your belongings, but only a *short* time. Whatever isn't packed within twenty minutes will have to be left be-hind."

"The palace?" Mirra's father blurted, obviously shocked. "But why would *we*—"

The rest of his startled protest was lost to Mirra in the

midst of the sudden delight she felt. The palace! They were
going to the palace! Somehow one of the Five must have
seen her, and now wanted to get to know her a good deal
better. One of the Five!

Mirra turned away from the babble of unimportant conversation at the door, thrilling to what lay ahead. One of
the *Five* wanted her, and no matter what he was like he
would *have* her. Of course, once they were married it would
be *she* who had *him*, but that didn't have to be mentioned
at first meeting. She would be the wife of one of the Five,
and Vallant Ro would just die to know that. And he would
suffer before he died, he and that brazen trollop he'd tried
to put in her place, Mirra would make certain of *that.* . . .

TWENTY-NINE

Storn Torgar, master merchant and father of four eminently
desirable daughters—who were considered very much part
of his merchandise—was extremely unhappy. The deal of
a lifetime had been in his hands, completely negotiated and
ready to be begun, and it had all come to nothing because
of a mere slip of a girl. That the girl was one of his daughters made the matter much worse, and certainly would not
be forgotten. He'd given that girl the best of everything,
and she'd repaid his generosity with spite and stubbornness.

"Storn, why are you just sitting there?" his wife demanded, having come into the study without his noticing.
"You know Odrin wasn't joking, so you don't have all that
much time left. Haven't you thought of *anything* to get that
impossible child back?"

"Since I no longer even know where she is, Avrina, how am I supposed to get her back?" Storn responded, automatically turning the words into smooth friendliness. "When I left that high and mighty lord's house, I fully intended to speak to every judge I knew who still sat on the bench. I was in the midst of doing so, you'll remember, when I was brought word that the noble was dead and Tamrissa had disappeared. Since then my agents discovered that she left the city, so what do you propose that I do?"

"There has to be *something*," his wife fretted, pacing to a chair before sitting stiffly. "That arrangement with Odrin Hallasser would have brought us more gold than both of us together would have been able to spend in two lifetimes. It isn't every day that someone finds supposedly worthless land that none of the nobility care to claim, and files on it personally—after which it proves to be anything *but* worthless. If we can start to force people onto that land to work it, the gold will begin to flow in. Why can't Odrin understand that, and simply add his part of the investment without demanding anything else?"

"Because, Avrina, he's a . . . dedicated man," Storn replied, beginning to feel annoyed all over again. "He's wanted Tamrissa since the first time he's seen her, and he didn't acquire as much gold as he has by giving up the things he wants. I agreed to deliver her to him as part of my end of the deal, and now he means to hold me to that. He refuses to understand how impossible that is at the moment, and has even gone so far as to threaten—"

Storn stopped speaking abruptly, belatedly aware that he'd been about to say too much. He hadn't told Avrina everything, just as he never told her everything, but this time she happened to notice.

"Has he threatened to back out of the deal?" she demanded, her face paling. "But he can't finance it alone any more than we can, and the land is already registered to you and him conjointly. If he tries to punish us by backing out, he'll only be punishing himself as well. He can't take anyone else in, after all. . . ."

"No, of course he can't, so you needn't worry on that score," Storn reassured her, using his most charming smile to reinforce his words. "And I'm sure he isn't serious about this deadline he's given me, so let's speak of other things. Have you been able to find any servants to hire? I'm growing extremely tired of having to take all our meals in a dining parlor.''

"No, and I probably *won't* find any," she replied, annoyance strong in her voice even as she looked at him narrowly. "Those stupid low class fools are actually picking and choosing who they'll work for, and the ingrates who *used* to work for us have apparently put us on some sort of refusal list. This is all the fault of the nobility, and they'd better hurry up and get things put back to the way they were. After all, what else are they good for . . . ? Storn, there's something you aren't telling me, and I want to know what it is. All of it, if you please.''

Her voice had turned hard and uncompromising, the ice princess handing out orders. He usually had no trouble handling her, but when she fell into a mood like this. . . . Well, why not? Maybe *she'd* be able to think of a way out. . . .

"All right, I *will* tell you all of it," he agreed, leaning back in his chair. "Odrin Hallasser is sometimes a difficult man to deal with, but this arrangement was one it wasn't possible to pass up on. It's unfortunate that he was the only one who had the ready gold . . . but to get to those details. He and I have indeed registered the land in both our names, but we did something else as well. In order to keep the deal between ourselves, we also named each other as beneficiary of that part of our estates if one of us happened to . . . die.''

"Oh, Storn, you didn't!" she exclaimed with horror, understanding exactly what that meant. "You have to mean it was done without safeguards, the kind you've always used. And without those safeguards. . . .''

"Yes, exactly," Storn agreed glumly. "Without those safeguards, Odrin *will* benefit if I should somehow meet with an unfortunate and unexpected ending. And that's what he's threatened me with if I don't find Tamrissa and turn her over to him in the next two days. I've been looking into the possibility of doing the same to him only sooner, but with the city in such a turmoil, finding the right people is extremely difficult.''

"As if finding people foolish enough to go up against Odrin Hallasser and his group would be easy at any time.''

Avrina spoke the words shortly, her lips compressed with disapproval. "I do wish you'd mentioned this sooner, Storn. Two days. . . . We *have* to stop Odrin from ordering your death, we simply have to."

"Again, I agree," Storn said, not particularly amused. "If you can think of a way I haven't already tried and discarded, please do let me know. Especially if it involves getting my hands on that ingrate daughter of ours. I tried to do the right thing by her and insisted that Odrin marry her, but now I don't care if he does or not. As long as he gets his hands on her."

"And teaches her a good lesson," Avrina said with a nod. "We can't—Oh!"

"What's the meaning of this intrusion?" Storn demanded as he rose quickly to his feet, glaring at the strange man who had suddenly appeared in the doorway of his study. "Who are you, and how dare you enter my house without—"

"Please calm yourself, Dom Torgar," the stranger drawled as he looked idly about. "We did knock, but as no one came to answer the door, we had no recourse but to let ourselves in. If all your servants have left, you should really pay closer attention to the possibility of callers."

"I asked you who you were," Storn repeated coldly, no longer worried that Odrin had decided to act sooner than the deadline. This man was no hired thug, and there were other men in guard uniforms behind him. If they really were guardsmen. . . .

"I'm Lord Rimen Howser, acting for the Five," the man replied negligently, having dismissed everything he'd seen in the room. "You and your wife will now accompany me to the palace, so please pack what you'll need for the stay. But be reasonable about the amount of things you take with you. You have only twenty minutes to pack, so don't waste time on frivolities."

Storn stared at the man as Avrina exclaimed indignantly, naturally refusing to do anything he'd suggested. But for his part, Storn wasn't sure they'd be *able* to refuse. The man was a noble, after all, but what could the Five want with *them*? If there was any chance there would be profit in it, he'd agree without hesitation. But that, of course, remained to be seen. . . .

Hattial Riven was pushed into the room by the oversized bully in guardsman's uniform, the push nearly sending him sprawling. He hadn't meant to stop short in the doorway, but the sight of the room was totally unexpected.

"This is the bedchamber that's yours for right now," the guardsman said as Hat looked around. "If anything ends up broken or dirty you'll be flogged, so you better watch what you do. If you go into the gathering room, don't pester the other people you'll find in it. And if you show up anywhere but in this place or the gathering room, the next thing they'll do is chain you in the pigsty. Too bad they didn't start out doing that."

And with that he turned and left the room, closing the door behind him before locking sounds came from it. Locking sounds had become horribly familiar to Hat lately, but this time they were a good deal less important. This bedchamber. . . .

The room was the sort Hat had dreamed about for years, large and beautifully furnished with a spread on the big bed that matched the drapes hanging where windows should have been but weren't. This chamber was part of an inner grouping in the palace, so the decorators had had to pretend about windows. The carpeting underfoot was beautifully woven and without worn spots, the chairs were upholstered and one even had a matching foot rest, the tables scattered here and there were exquisitely carved, the little decorations looked expensive. . . .

Hat wiped the palms of his hands on the plain blue cotton trousers he'd been given, his tunic a somewhat lighter blue. He'd first been given a bath, though, to get the stink of sweat and muck off him, and then he'd been given the clothing to replace the rags his own clothes had become. That meant he could walk to the chair with the foot rest and sit down, then swing his feet up without worrying about whether or not he was staining the light-colored fabric of the chair. His back twinged a bit as he tried to get comfortable, but the last beating he'd gotten had only been for form's sake rather than punishment. That bastard of an overseer always looked for reasons to beat the workers, and usually found them. . . .

He put his head back and closed his eyes, cringing on the inside over the memory of the beatings he'd been given. The first one had come when he'd tried to explain that they had no right to force him to work on that estate, not when he was a free man and someone who'd had a High position stolen from him. They hadn't cared about any of that, and a group of the guards had kept him from using his ability while the overseer sliced that accursed lash across his back over and over and over. He'd passed out from the pain, and when they'd brought him around again with a bucket of water thrown over his head, he'd almost been unable to move from the agony of the punishment.

But he'd *had* to move, to keep them from doing the same thing to him a second time, and they'd worked him until he was ready to drop. He and the others had been fed on scraps and then were allowed to collapse into sleep, and the next day the same thing had happened. In point of fact the same thing had happened *every* day, and after his second beating Hat had learned to stop cursing the overseer and the guards. But that hadn't stopped him from hating them with every fiber of his being, them and the man who was responsible for his being in that place to begin with. . . .

Hat stirred in the incredibly comfortable chair, anger rising in him at the memory of what one of his fellow slave-workers had tried to claim. The fool had said that nothing had been stolen from Hat because Hat was only fractionally stronger than the rest of them, and a High was *much* stronger than mere Middles. The others had all agreed with that fool and then had told Hat to stop boring them with his imaginary complaints, or they would tell the guards to keep him quiet. They'd refused to believe that Lorand was responsible for all his troubles, but they were stupid slaves who knew nothing. Hat knew the truth, and would never forget it.

It took some effort to calm down again, but once he had Hat realized he was hungry. That was nothing new, of course, not since they'd taken him to that estate to work, but the place he was in *was* new. It was possible that that gathering room had something which would prove edible, even if that turned out to be nothing but the usual scraps. He had no true desire to get out of that wonderfully comfortable chair, but he did so anyway and walked to the second door of the three in the room.

That second door hid access to a comfort facility, a beautifully clean and private one which was apparently all his. Hunger was momentarily forgotten as Hat used the facility, never having had such an opportunity before. What a difference it made, having *private* access like that, just the way a High was supposed to have. It would have been his much sooner if Lorand hadn't stolen his place, and finally finding out what the situation was like added fuel to an already raging fire. Someone had once promised him a chance at revenge; now that he'd been brought to the palace, that chance was hopefully not far away. . . .

The third door led directly into a very large open area, one which had couches and chairs arranged around small tables on the left, and a large dining room table with chairs on the right. The dining room table was being cleared by a single servant, which seemed strange for part of the palace. The first time he'd been brought there, the place had been crawling with servants.

But Hat was still hungry, so he hurried over to the table and thereby brought himself to the servant's attention. He was about to ask that the scraps of the meal be left for *him*, but the servant spoke first.

"Ah, there you are, sir," the servant said cheerfully, pausing in gathering together the remnants of the recent meal. "I'm afraid you've missed sitting down with the others, but a plate has been left for you on the buffet, and the food is, of course, still warm. As soon as I bring this lot to the kitchens, I'll return with a fresh pitcher of tea."

The servant had glanced at a long table beyond the one with chairs as he spoke, a table which held large covered containers. They were the same sort which had been used to provide gruel for the workers every couple of days, a more solid meal than the scraps which they were given the rest of the time. Hat wasn't in the mood for gruel, but it was better than having to beg for scraps. So he took himself over to the other table, and sure enough there were two empty plates standing near the containers. Bowls would have been better, of course, but Hat took one of the plates without complaint and reached toward the first container. He hadn't complained about things aloud since the first time he'd been beaten for the words. . . .

And once he took the cover from the container, he blessed the Highest Aspect for having kept him silent. There wasn't gruel in the container, there was *food*, real food meant to be eaten by people rather than slaves. Hat raised the cover of the second container, found actual meat to go with the mix of vegetables in the first, and because of that didn't fill his plate with vegetables alone as he'd been about to do. Instead he visited all the containers, one after the other, and ended up with a very full plate. Chicken and beef and pork and fish, all with different sauces, and most of the vegetables had the same. He might not be able to finish it all, but he certainly meant to try.

Sitting down at the table alone didn't bother him, not when he had all that incredibly wonderful food to keep him company. The servant was as good as his word and brought a fresh pitcher of tea and a cup when he returned from the kitchen, but Hat was too busy chewing and swallowing to do more than take the pitcher and pour some tea. He needed to wash down the food and make room for more, and that was exactly what he did.

By the time he was forced to push the plate away, he'd eaten most of what he'd taken and was close to being too full to move. And he was no longer the only one at the table, the other occupant of a chair on the other side of the table being a woman. She was older than Hat found of interest in a woman, but she looked as though she'd been fairly attractive at one time.

And she also looked as though she'd been used to living in the sort of surroundings they were now in. She used her fork slowly and gracefully, but her hand shook as she fed herself and her plate was almost as full as Hat's had been. Hat had to look twice, but his first impression of the shadow of dirt on the woman remained. She'd obviously been cleaned up and put into cheap but clean clothes, which meant it was strange that a lingering dirtiness had been left on her skin and hair. Hat extended his senses, the first time he'd done so for his own benefit in quite some time, and then he had the answer. The woman had the residual remains of coal in her hair and on her skin, and it had somehow stained her in what might prove to be a permanent way.

Looking at her disturbed Hat in a way he couldn't define, but he no longer had to put up with disturbing things if he didn't want to. So he rose heavily from the chair and turned away without even a nod to the woman, and then strolled toward the couches and chairs where the people who had eaten earlier now sat. One of them was a really beautiful girl, one with auburn hair and a body to harden any man, and now Hat had the chance to introduce himself. It had been much, *much* too long. . . .

And maybe, if she had the right contacts, she might even be able to help him get back what had been stolen from him. . . .

THIRTY

Allestine Tromin, who had once been the darling of Rincammon and its entire surrounding area, walked carefully into the gathering area of the palace beyond her new bedchamber. Her assigned quarters weren't nearly as nice as what she'd had in her own residence, but after the last—how long *had* it been?—however many weeks, a broom closet of a room would have looked palatial. In the mine, she and the others were locked into the same room for their sleep period, and very often the guards forgot to replace the thin pallets they were supposed to be allowed to sleep on. Forgot on purpose, most of them believed, the lousy, rotten—

Allestine stopped short for a moment, which allowed her to swallow the rage which was with her most of the time. She'd tried to manipulate the guards the way she'd always manipulated men, but they'd actually laughed in her face. She'd been filthy from the coal dust and had been dressed in rags, and one of them said he'd rather do without than use a woman who looked like her. One or two of the men on her assigned gang hadn't felt the same, but the indignity they'd forced on her hadn't been repeated very often. It was almost unheard of for anyone to have enough strength for anything beyond work, food, and sleep, and she'd quickly learned why that was.

There was a man seated at the dining table, and he was so busy shoveling his food into his mouth that he didn't even notice her approach. The buffet table held one last empty plate, so she went to it, chose as much as she would be able to eat from the warming containers, then carried her meal to the table. She was in the midst of salivating at the thought of eating decent food again, and her hands trembled with the urge to take handfuls of it and simply stuff it into her mouth. But that would have shamed her and made her just as low as the peasant gobbling down his food opposite her, a fate she refused to bring upon herself.

So she sat and picked up her fork, then began to eat slowly the way a lady of cultured habits was supposed to. It was very difficult to hold herself back, but she doggedly continued on while paying attention to nothing but the contents of her plate. Or almost nothing. She couldn't help noticing the way the peasant looked at her, as though she were far too coarse to appeal to him in any way. He himself was barely more than a child, and a short, stupid-looking one at that, but he still dared to reject her in his own mind. Allestine felt the rage again, but revenge would have to wait until later. There was still food on her plate. . . .

When the peasant left the table, Allestine's capacity for eating any more seemed to leave with him. But she'd judged that capacity fairly well, and the amount of food left on her plate was just enough to preserve her dignity. She did finish the tea in her cup, though, and then rose to walk over to the group of people the peasant had already approached. If they were all there in the same place, there had to be *something* they had in common.

". . . tell you it can't be anythin' else," one of the men was saying as she approached the grouping of couches and chairs. The peasant hovered uncertainly on the fringes, looking as though he didn't dare choose a chair of his own, but *she* would not be that backward.

"Don't be ridiculous, Daddy," a fairly pretty young girl retorted, tossing her head in a way that told Allestine the girl had practiced the gesture. "We've been invited here to the palace for just a single reason, and that's because one of the Five has noticed me. He'll be comin' by any time now to introduce himself to me, and when he does you'll be feelin' really foolish if you claim we're here for any other reason."

"This is reality we're discussin', Mirra, not your little fantasies," her father returned with a faint sound of scorn. "If you were the only one here, it might be true that you'd been noticed. But your Momma and I are also here, as is Dom and Dama Torgar, not to mention those other folk. Who do you imagine noticed the rest of us?"

"I agree with you, Dom Agran," the other older man said with a nod, looking oddly thoughtful. "We're all here because of our ties with that one group of troublemakers. My daughter is part of it, as is the young man *your* daughter is involved with. If these other people have similar ties, the only question remaining is, what have those ties gotten us into?"

"Nothing good, you can be certain of that," the cold-looking woman beside the man who had spoken said, her sniff full of disdain. "If Tamrissa walked in here right now, I'd slap her face hard enough to leave a hand print."

"Tamrissa," Allestine echoed from the chair she'd taken, suddenly understanding what they were talking about. "She was that friend of Jovvi's, the pretty one with Fire magic. Yes, I think both of you gentlemen are correct. We *are* here because of our associations with different members of that group, but—"

"Well, *I* don't care about that group!" the peasant interrupted from where he still stood, speaking as though his likes and dislikes were of interest to the rest of them. "Lor-and tried to lord it over me as if he was better than me, but—"

"I really do think we need to find out what they intend to do with us," the second, smoother man interrupted in turn, acting as though he hadn't heard a word the peasant had said. That put a flush and a scowl on the peasant's face, but no one cared about that any more than Allestine did. "If we have value to these people we might manage to turn a profit of some kind, but if we mistake their intentions we could end up as damaged goods. Does anyone have any idea how we might find out?"

"I'd say we already know," the woman who seemed to be Dom Agran's wife said mildly when no one else answered. "If that Lord Whoever had brought servants instead of guardsmen to help us move, then we would have had some value to them. But the way he was treatin' us. . . . Was anyone given more than twenty minutes to pack?"

Everyone looked around then, but not even the woman who sat off to one side by herself spoke up to say *they* were an exception to that. Allestine certainly wasn't, as she hadn't even been given that much notice. A guard had come and dragged her away from her work gang, and that had been that. . . .

"So now we know," Dom Agran said as he patted his wife's hand in approval. "We weren't escorted, we were arrested. I didn't know things like this were bein' done here in our wonderful capitol of Gan Garee, but that's beside the point. What needs figurin' out now is just *how* they plan to use us. And if we're likely to survive that usin'."

"Why would anyone care if you peasants survived?" the woman sitting alone said suddenly, cold and distant amusement on her haughty face. "It's fairly clear that I'm the only person of value here, which means I'll certainly survive. What they do with the rest of you. . . ."

"Well, it seems as though I was right," Dom Torgar said, looking at her with distaste. "You *are* a member of the nobility, and you're just as stupidly mindless as the rest of them. If you weren't as unimportant to them as we are, they would have put you somewhere other than here. Since they didn't, you can be certain that if we don't survive, neither will you."

"How dare you speak to me like that, you disgusting peasant!" the woman snarled, her chin rising even higher than it had been. "No one of my class can possibly be anything like yours, not even on the darkest, dreariest day! We are *superior*, fool, and you forget that at your peril!"

"If you're all that superior, why don't any of you have servants any longer?" Dama Agran asked with a snort of ridicule. "Our own servants told us that yours had left you all high and dry, hopin' you all starve to death or break somethin' tryin' to look after yourselves. And I started thinkin' when they said my daughter was just like you. That's the last thing I want her to be, so from now on there will be some changes in what's required of her. I just hope this isn't comin' too late."

"Momma, how can you say that?" the girl all but wailed, looking wounded to the center of her being. "There's nothin' at all wrong with me, and once we're out of this place you'll see that. If one of the Five doesn't come to claim me first."

The last of the girl's words were sleek with conviction, telling Allestine that the little fool still believed she was there because she'd been *noticed*. A bit of wrangling followed, but Allestine no longer paid it any attention. Now that she knew she'd been brought there because of Jovvi, her world had brightened again. Those people had something in mind for her, but that didn't matter in the least. All those times in the mine she'd awakened screaming, horrified to find that she hadn't been having a nightmare after all. . . .

That living nightmare was all Jovvi's fault, and Allestine would make her pay even if it was the last thing she ever did. . . .

Kambil Arstin awoke slowly, having the impression that he'd slept rather than been unconscious. Lack of consciousness had been his only refuge during the past eternity, however long it had actually been. The agony had been constantly with him, and contrary to popular opinion, one did not grow used to being in agony. But now the pain was entirely gone, or at least it seemed to be. If he was in the midst of a dream, it was one he wanted to continue for as long as possible. . . .

"If you need help to sit up, just say so," a voice came, one Kambil would have had nightmares about if he'd been able to sleep normally. "The servant has a tray of food for you, and you'll have to eat as much as you can. You've been missing too many meals lately, and you're thin as a rail."

Kambil turned his head on the pillow to look at Delin, who stood at the side of his bed with the servant holding the tray. It occurred to Kambil that the poison was wearing off and Delin was trying to poison him again, but that didn't make much sense. He'd been absolutely helpless, and the poison could have been readministered in whatever that had been which Delin had been pouring down his throat every day.

"I do need help," Kambil found himself croaking, speaking the truth even though he hadn't meant to. His voice was hoarse and uneven, and his throat still ached from all the screaming he'd done.

"Put the tray down and help Lord Kambil to sit up against his pillows," Delin told the servant without looking at the man. "Then you can give him the tray and leave."

The servant was quick to obey, and in a pair of moments Kambil was sitting propped up. The tray was then put in his lap and the plate covers removed, and then the servant was bowing his way out of the room.

"You may be wondering why there was just the one servant," Delin said once the man was gone, his stare intent on Kambil. "We're experiencing something of a shortage of help, but at least we have *some* servants left. The rest of our peers are having to do without."

Kambil frowned as he chose a spoon to eat with, lifting the utensil with a shaking hand. He would certainly have stabbed himself if he'd chosen a fork, and the cramps in his middle were making him hurry about getting some of that food down his throat. How long *had* it been. . . . ?

"To put it mildly, there's a great deal of unrest in the city," Delin went on, now sitting down in the chair which had been brought close to the bed. "The guard commandant doesn't have enough men to control it, and there have been ugly incidents. I'll tell you about it while you're eating."

The report Kambil heard would have ruined his appetite if he hadn't been on the verge of starvation. Even so he felt disturbed, and happily put his spoon aside as soon as he'd eaten all he could reasonably hold.

"So there you have it," Delin finished up, only a moment or two after Kambil's meal was done. "Not only isn't the guard getting new applicants, too many of their number have taken to deserting and losing themselves among the peasants. For their part the peasants are busily active, having taken over ownership of the businesses belonging to *our* people. Those same people are screaming bloody murder, insisting that we do something to get their property back. I've been thinking about this whole thing, and I've decided that our only option is to go out and destroy a large number of peasants. That will show the rest how helpless the 'usurpers' are, and we won't need to give the remaining guardsmen the knowledge about the tandem linking. What do you think?"

"I think we'd be smarter to hurt rather than kill them," Kambil replied, although he hadn't meant to say anything of the sort. "If people expect to be killed, they can work themselves into believing that they have nothing left to lose. That lets them continue on and on, enlarging the problem you have with them. If they understand that they *won't* be killed but will have to live with being crippled for the rest of their lives, they'll surrender a good deal more quickly."

"You may be right about that," Delin said with raised brows as he stroked his chin with one hand. "I hadn't thought of it, so I'm glad I asked for your expert opinion. And you must be wondering why you're being so cooperative, not to mention why you're free of the pain. Would you care to guess?"

"You've given me Puredan along with the counteragent," Kambil said, speaking the words he'd been fervently hoping weren't true. "I haven't made any attempt to put you under control because you have *me* under control."

"Bravo, Kambil!" Delin exclaimed with a grin, one filled with all the malice the man was capable of. "It upsets me to think of how close I came to letting you die, because then I would have missed the exquisite pleasure of having you obey my slightest whim. How does it feel to be the puppet rather than the puppetmaster?''

"It turns my stomach," Kambil replied, unable to speak anything but the truth. "You're so twisted that you're unable to see your own incompetence, and that chills me to the center of my being. If you don't release me, we'll all be destroyed."

"Considering that everything happening now is the result of *your* being in charge, I don't believe I'll take that piece of advice," Delin said dryly, the hatred flashing only briefly in his eyes. "I've decided that the peasants have to be taught a good lesson, but there have to be five of us doing the teaching or the lesson won't be nearly as effective. You'll spend today regaining your strength, and tomorrow we'll go out and do what we must. You won't spend any time thinking about a way to escape my control, because you've been ordered not to. But I do want you to think about getting the others back under control, Selendi and Homin especially. Every once in a while they flash back to being useful members of this group, but the rest of the time they revert to their old, useless selves. Start on that today, if you can, but plan on doing it tomorrow at the latest."

Kambil found himself nodding to acknowledge the orders, but Delin missed seeing the nod. He had already gotten to his feet and was heading toward the door, secure in the knowledge that he couldn't be disobeyed. Kambil's inward self raged over that, at least as far as he was being *allowed* to rage, which wasn't very far. He'd clearly been ordered not to work on a way to escape, but maybe there was something else he could do. Just maybe. . . .

THIRTY-ONE

"That's the place," Lorand heard Rion whisper, possibly even pointing to the very large house a short distance ahead of where they'd stopped. "It's one of the largest mansions in the city, and should suit our purposes admirably. Can anyone tell if there are people inside?"

"Not even a cat or dog," Jovvi whispered in return, voicing what Lorand had already decided was true. "With the nearest neighbors at least half a mile away in any direction, we should be perfectly safe for a while. But we'll still cover the windows completely before we light any lamps."

Murmurs of agreement came from those who were closest to them, some of the fifty people of the two link groups they now had with them. Most of them had left Colling Green in that arrangement, one Blending with two link groups who could join with each other in the new tandem linking. That hadn't quite exhausted their number of High talents, so the rest had followed with the former guard members. They would all make their way into the city by different routes, and would go to ground in their own chosen locations. By tomorrow morning their full number would be in the city, hopefully without losing anyone to a confrontation.

Lorand sighed as he urged his mount to follow those of the others, pleased that they were still alive but not terribly pleased by the way they'd had to accomplish that end. They'd reached the city in the late afternoon, knowing that any guard groups would be tired and less than alert by then, hoping to slip past them with a minimum amount of fuss. But the guard unit they'd run into had been fully alert and jumpier than anyone had expected, and they hadn't even had time to Blend. The guardsmen had attacked immediately and they and their link groups had responded individually . . . Low and Middle talents attacking more than fifty Highs. . . .

Lorand's mind veered away from the memory of what had been left of those guardsmen, which hadn't been very much. They'd been fools to attack without first finding out who they were attacking, a reckless act so unusual that it hadn't been expected. But maybe reckless acts weren't all that unusual any longer. They'd know for certain once Alsin Meerk came back from speaking to some of his people.

There was a very large stables to the left of the very large house, so half their group dismounted and took the mounts of the other half in preparation for stabling them. The rest would enter the house and start to cover the windows, getting the job done before full nightfall made it that much harder. And some of *those* would see about preparing a meal, using the provisions they'd brought with them if the house proved to be empty of food.

"If anyone had told me a few months ago that I'd be spendin' my time unsaddlin' horses, I would have called them a liar," Vallant said as he walked beside Lorand, leading his own mount as well as another. "If this isn't close to the end of it, I just may take off and go lookin' for the nearest large body of water."

"I feel the same way about being one of those who are leading what amounts to an army," Lorand agreed with a glum nod. "But unfortunately I don't have the sort of temperament that would let me take off, for water *or* dry land. And I wonder why the people who own this house aren't here."

"Rion said there was a good chance that the occupants are at another of their houses right now," Vallant replied with a shrug. "That part of it doesn't bother me, but there's somethin' that does. From other things Rion said at other times, I was expectin' to find at least a small staff mindin' the house. What I'd like to know is where *they* are."

"Maybe they're among all those groups of people meeting on the street corners," Lorand suggested as they entered the stables. "There are a lot more of them than that man Mohr's comments led us to believe, almost as if the people are deliberately flaunting their positions. And did you notice that there wasn't a guardsman near any of them?"

"Maybe all the guardsmen are busy watchin' for *us*," Vallant suggested, obviously looking around for empty stalls. "Mohr and his friends said they would be, but they weren't as disappointed as I expected them to be when we refused to tell them our plans. I have the feelin' we did nothin' to really shake their belief that we're the Chosen Blendin'."

"But we did manage to keep any of them from going along with us, which is a victory in itself," Lorand pointed out. "They were picturing us riding into the city with our full force behind us, banners flying over our heads proclaiming who we were. Or who they thought we were. Then we could have spent our time pushing away the groups of people who believed us and wanted to fawn, fighting those who didn't believe and therefore wanted to put us down, and arguing with any others who decided that *they* were the Chosen. The only benefit in that would have been the trouble the Seated Five would have had getting through the mobs to reach us. By the time they did they would have been exhausted."

"That could be why the Chosen are supposed to have a good chance at defeatin' those five," Vallant said with something of a grin. "I think I'll take these two stalls over here."

Lorand indicated his agreement with that decision by taking the stalls next to those two, and for the next few minutes he was busy stripping the saddles and bridles from the horses. They really could have used a good rubdown as well, but an extra measure of oats made up for the lack, at least temporarily. And the oat bin bulged with its contents, so there was no need to stint.

By the time Lorand had finished, Vallant hadn't yet come out to get the oats for the mounts in his care. So Lorand scooped out what he would need, and went to see how far he'd gotten. The delay turned out to be a snarl up between the bridle of the second horse and the halter Vallant was trying to put on it, something only a novice at horse handling could have managed. Lorand took care of the problem and measured out the oats for both of the horses, and then the two of them were temporarily finished.

, "I owe you for bailin' me out there, brother," Vallant said ruefully as they began to leave the stables. Everyone else seemed to have already left, so aside from the horses they were alone. "It would be nice if I had a real idea of what I was doin', but that sort of thing takes practice. I wonder if the watches I set up are already posted."

"That looks like men on watch to me," Lorand said, pointing out the door into the gathering darkness. "Can't you discern the three of them over there, separated by about thirty feet of wooded land?"

"Yes, of course, now I can," Vallant replied, still sounding rueful. "If I'd just bothered lookin' around . . . I guess what I need is a good night's sleep. As soon as we all finish eatin' I'll assign link groups to stand watch in rotation from the house, and then I'll go and get that sleep."

"Vallant, before we go in there's something I'd like to talk to you about," Lorand forced himself to say. "I know I'm intruding and I hate to do it, but we *are* brothers so I have to. Jovvi told me she spoke to you, and I know that what she said was by way of a quote of what Tamrissa said to *her*. I also saw the way Tamrissa looked at you, which was completely different from any other time."

"Yes, I noticed that myself," Vallant replied as he stopped where he was to run a hand through his hair. "That look was . . . an arrogant, derogatory challenge, worse than anythin' I've ever seen. It told me how little she thought of me and dared me to do somethin' to change the opinion, even though she was certain I couldn't. It was all I could do not to ball up my fists and walk over to tell her to raise her own hands."

"The way we answered challenges like that when we were boys," Lorand said with a nod and a sigh. "But we never did it with girls, and certainly not with girls who were Highs in Fire magic. Have you decided what you'll do instead?"

"Walkin' off to find that large body of water is an idea

that looks better every day,'' he replied, leaning back against the edge of the door and closing his eyes. "It's what any man with an ounce of sense would do, to save his sanity if for no other reason. But there's more than just the Blendin' and the comin' fight holdin' me here, which proves how little sense *I* happen to have. Every time I close my eyes—''

His words broke off abruptly, as though he couldn't bring himself to speak about such private thoughts, but then he shook his head almost savagely.

"Every time I close my eyes I can see myself walkin' up to that woman,'' he continued tonelessly. "First I give her a good shakin' for the way she's been behavin', and then I take the kiss her dagger stare swears I'll never have again. I *want* to do those things, I really do, but something deep inside won't let me. So much of me has already died all the times she ended things between us, that one more time could finish me completely. I suppose once all the trouble is over it won't matter, but for right now. . . .''

Lorand tried to think of something helpful to say when Vallant's words trailed off in another sigh, but the problem was one he could understand all too clearly. When he'd thought he'd lost Jovvi the world and its doings had turned dull and pointless, and so had his entire life. Going on alone had been something he simply hadn't been able to picture, but he'd been lucky in that Jovvi had felt exactly the same. If she ever changed her mind about that. . . . No, Lorand could understand just how Vallant felt.

They stood in the silence of a peaceful night for a few minutes, and then they began to walk toward the house. Not a single glimmer of light showed in any of the windows, which was exactly the way it was supposed to be. Their refuge ought to do for the short time they would be using it, the time between now and when they faced the Seated Five. Which would not be all that long, as they'd decided unanimously on what their stance had to be:

If the Five didn't come looking for *them*, they would have to go looking for the Five. . . .

The meal our people managed to put together wasn't at all bad, not after what we'd learned to eat while on the road. I swallowed down my portion of it with satisfaction, then took one of my link groups on a tour of the house's bedchambers. We were on a hunt for clothes we might wear, while my second link group saw to making the water in the bath house usable.

"If you don't mind the company, I'll come on the 'tour' with you," Jovvi said when I told her what we were off to do. "If I just sit around, I'll start worrying about what's ahead of us and won't get any sleep tonight."

"You know you're welcome," I told her with a smile, then stopped her from reaching for a lamp. "No, don't take that, not when we won't need it. Not all of the bedchambers have had their windows covered yet, so we'll be using very small, shielded glows to light our way. That's why we Fire magic users are doing this, remember?"

"Since I lied and have already started to worry, I'm lucky I can remember my name," she answered ruefully. "But I did ask Naran if she wanted to come with us, and she just smiled and shook her head. I have the feeling she already knows what we'll find, and hasn't said anything because she doesn't want to spoil the surprise for us. As useful as it is, I don't believe I'd enjoy having a talent like hers."

"If I had it, I'd probably end up with everyone hating me," I said in agreement as we began to walk toward the front hall and its grand staircase. "Naran never says anything about what she sees unless there's danger for someone, but I'd probably sound off at every opportunity. Like, 'Don't sit there, someone's going to spill something on your skirt,' or 'Don't bother taking that rain shield, you're still going to get wet in the rain.'"

"I know what you mean, and I'm sure I'd be the same," she said with a chuckle. "The only reason Naran isn't, I'm sure, is because of the circumstances of her childhood. You and I learned to use ordinary talents from childhood, and if someone 'caught' us using them they would probably have been no more than annoyed. With *her* talent, though. . . . She learned not to let anyone know what was going on with her."

"But in a way that does match us," I said, glancing at Jovvi thoughtfully. "I had to hide most of what I was able to do, and from what you've said you had to do the same. All of us, in fact, pretended to be less than what we were, even the men. Lorand and Vallant had the best of it, I think, but even they played down their abilities.''

''Yes, that's true,'' she said, and I glanced at her to see that she regarded me with an odd expression. ''Forgive me for changing the subject, but I couldn't help noticing that you called Vallant *Vallant* instead of *Vallant Ro*. The only other time you did that was when you and he were . . . more friendly than not, shall we say? I wasn't aware that things had changed between you two.''

''That's because they haven't,'' I said comfortably as I raised my skirts in order to climb the staircase. ''If anything has changed, it's the way I'm now looking at things. I wondered why that was, and I finally figured out one cause at least: all that horseback riding we've been doing.''

''Ah,'' she said as she climbed beside me, her smile clear in the light of the glow floating in the air ahead of us. ''I think I understand what you mean. The strength of your talent and its unfettered use started the process, but didn't do anything to free you from dependence on other people. Now that you've learned to ride a horse, you no longer need someone else to take you from place to place. Even if your back still aches, the freedom you've achieved is worth the ache.''

''It certainly would be, but I don't even ache any longer,'' I said with something of a grin. ''I've even learned how to saddle my horse, and although I prefer having someone else do it for me, I *can* do it if necessary. Now if I can just learn to cook, the process ought to be complete.''

''And Vallant doesn't enter into that anywhere?'' she asked, no longer as hesitant as she'd been. ''I'm relieved that I no longer have to shield myself from your agitation, but does that mean you've given up on him entirely?''

''Actually, it means I've stopped worrying about it,'' I said, directing her to the right at the top of the staircase. ''All that agitation you mentioned came from the fact that I didn't know what to *do* about Vallant, and that I felt I had to do *something*. It finally came to me that he's the one who has to do the something, and he's the only one who can. If I'm the one who does it instead, I'll never be absolutely sure of him. And I have to be sure, at least that much hasn't changed. When you get down to it, I'd rather be alone than uncertain.''

"Not everyone would agree with that, but I certainly do," she said, pausing in front of the first door on the left. "I used to think that sharing a man's attention was nothing to get excited about, but that was before I met Lorand. Sharing him with you and Naran isn't really sharing him, not when all of us are so close in that very special way. But if he ever went to another woman. . . . Well, I could never hate him, but the hurt would be so great that our love would never be the same again.''

"That's exactly the way he feels about you and other men," I said with amusement as I led the way into the first bedchamber. "It was the point *you* weren't able to understand, but maybe that was because he didn't voice his thoughts as clearly.''

"And now he doesn't have to, because I'm ruined as a courtesan," she said with a small laugh. "Every client I had would have to measure up to our three brothers, and I *know* none of them would be able to. It seems to be a good thing that we have an alternate career choice—if we live.''

"If we don't live, we won't need any other careers," I pointed out. "I'm not as frightened about that as most people are because I learned an important truth a long time ago. The idea of death *is* frightening, but there certainly are things which are a good deal worse. With some of those things as alternatives, death becomes a friendly, easy means of escape.''

She nodded in agreement, then turned to the wardrobe we'd found in the corner of the bedchamber. The glow I used let us see the men's clothing hung inside, clothing that was a bit too large in the waist and narrow in the shoulders for most of our people. But someone would surely be able to make do with it, so we took two shirts and two pairs of trousers for trying-on purposes, then left to look into the next bedchamber. We got as far as the next door, when Jovvi stopped short and seemed to be listening.

"Ah, it's Alsin arriving," she said, obviously pulling her senses back to where we stood. "He not only has someone with him, he's rather excited about something. We'd better go down and find out what that is.''

I felt the least bit of reluctance over that, but there was nothing to do but agree and go with her. Alsin Meerk had been working very hard to make things easier for me, and what bothered me most was that he'd accomplished his aim. Every time he did something nice I found him just a little bit more attractive, and that was much more frightening than death. Complications in life usually are, which, to my regret, I was certainly finding out. . . .

THIRTY-TWO

''Alsin Meerk has gotten here,'' Vallant heard Lorand say, a general announcement to whoever happened to be in the room. ''One of the Spirit magic users just told me that.''

''Good,'' Rion said from the couch where he sat beside Naran. ''Now maybe we'll find out what's going on in the city. I can't ever remember seeing it like this.''

''Surely we don't *all* need to find out,'' Naran said, pausing an instant before getting up. ''There are still so many things to do in this house, and we've been sitting around not doing any of them. Rion, my love, if you and Vallant would be kind enough to help me, we ought to be able to get to bed at a reasonable hour. . . .''

''I'm sorry, Naran, but hearin' what Meerk has to say is somethin' *I* have to do,'' Vallant said as Rion belatedly began to agree with his woman. ''After all, I can't do much plannin' if I don't know what's goin' on. I'm sure you can understand that.''

"Yes, I'm afraid I can," Naran responded with a sigh, a reaction that was odd enough to have taken Vallant's attention—at another time. Right now there were too many other things screaming around in his mind, including the question of what would happen when the Seated Five knew for certain that they were back in the city. With the help of Naran's talent they'd been able to avoid the rest of the traps along the road between Colling Green and Gan Garee, but as of right now just about anything could happen. . . .

Vallant went to get himself another cup of tea from the kitchen, and by the time he returned with it to the dimly lit sitting room Meerk had come in. Jovvi and Tamrissa, who had both been upstairs searching for usable clothing, had also come into the room, and the very important jobs that Naran had spoken about earlier hadn't taken her or Rion away yet. Some of the link group members were also in the large, plushly furnished room, as was a tall, thin, nervous looking stranger. The man stood close to Meerk, so it was likely that the two had arrived together.

"All right, now your audience is complete, Alsin," Lorand said to Meerk when he saw Vallant walk in. "Tell us what's been going on."

"Apparently a lot more than that Guild man Mohr told us about," Meerk responded, looking around at the others as Vallant found a place to sit. "Biblow here has been filling me in, and I'm finding it hard to believe him. This house is empty now—along with a lot of others—because the noble it belongs to can't take care of it without servants. They no longer have servants because all of them have quit, and those who have been paying their income over to the nobles aren't doing that anymore either."

"The monies are now being used to support the former servants while they build themselves houses and find different means to support their families," the man Biblow put in all on a single breath, obviously finding it impossible to keep silent any longer. "As I told Alsin, I never expected to live long enough to see any of this. The primary reason the people have been able to do this is because most of the guard force was sent out of the city to search for *your* group, and none of them have returned. Have you really come back to challenge the usurpers?"

"That part of the story circulated along with the truth about the competition," Meerk said with a nod. "Mohr was right about how far the word would spread, and there has even been talk about storming the palace. But every time someone suggests doing that, there are two or three people in the crowd who point out that none of them would stand a chance against the usurpers. Mohr's organization is doing everything he said it would."

"And thereby saving lives," Lorand said with his own nod of approval. "Considering what those five have already done, killing half the people in this city would bother them not at all. Is there any chance they'll come out and face us if we send in a public challenge?"

"Well, of course they would," Tamrissa said with a sound of scorn, her words made of sarcasm. "But only if they can face us the way they did the first time, with a victory guaranteed to them by cheating. If they ever do come out to face us, we'll know they have *something* up their sleeves."

"Right now all they seem to have up their sleeves is their arms," Meerk said with a smile for Tamrissa that Vallant didn't particularly care for. "Things haven't been going at all well for them, not since their most influential and effective supporters in the nobility began to die or disappear. Some of our people are still working in the palace as servants, and there's talk of some sort of . . . sickness or something which hit most of the Five. It seems to be under control now, but for a while they were in a lot of pain and none of the physicians was able to do anything about it. And even beyond that, the power in the group has shifted and there's even public disagreement among them."

"*Power* in the group?" Jovvi echoed, her brows somewhat raised. "That has to mean one or more of them wants to be in total control. A Blending doesn't do very well under those circumstances, when hidden—or not very hidden—resentments interfere with the necessary bonding. Resentment is a lot stronger emotion than many people realize, and it can even be more destructive to cooperation than actual hatred."

"I don't doubt it, but what I'd like to hear about is that

sickness you mentioned," Lorand said, looking thoughtful. "Do you have any details about it?"

"We were told that four of the Five fell victim to it," Biblow answered in the rush he apparently used as a usual way of talking. "It happened some hours after they had a private feast, and the one who wasn't affected was the one who had been making a habit of eating gruel instead of food. That night he didn't eat anything at all, so when the others fell ill he was available to look them over. Luckily for them he's the Earth magic member, and he was able to pull most of them out of it. He didn't have the same sort of success with the Spirit magic member, though, not for some time. He gave them all something to drink, and then he sent a message to the Fire magic member about *not* giving him something to drink if he didn't appear immediately at a meeting."

"So that's what the power struggle is all about," Lorand said with a nod. "My guess would be that the Spirit magic member ran things, and the Earth magic member took the first opportunity to change that. The Fire magic member tried to make a change of his or her own, but the Earth magic member still has the upper hand. That means they didn't fall to a sickness, but were probably poisoned. And if they're still being given something to counteract the poison, they're in more trouble than they may know."

"Poisoned?" Meerk and his friend Biblow echoed together, both very surprised. Then Meerk continued alone, "It isn't supposed to be possible to poison a Blending, not without them noticing. And what did you mean when you said they're in more trouble than they may know?"

"There was a poison specialist living in our district when I was younger," Lorand replied, his headshake solemn. "The man had retired to a farm after living and working in Gan Garee, but it was a very small farm and he didn't actually work it himself. He would hire workers every now and then when something had to be done, and I wanted a bit more silver than my father was paying me. So I was one of the workers he hired, but after the first time I wasn't paid in silver. He started to teach me about his specialty in return for the work I did, and that was worth more than the silver."

"But I still don't understand how a poison can get past an Earth magic user," Meerk protested, sounding really disturbed. "I'm just a Middle, but even I can tell if there's something in food that shouldn't be there."

"There's a small class of poisons which have the nasty habit of . . . disguising their presence *behind* food," Lorand said, his voice now distant with memory. "Even a High talent would have trouble noticing one of them, unless the poison was put in something as uncomplicated as . . . plain water, say. Even in a dish with nothing more than a cheese sauce, it would be almost impossible to discern."

"*Almost* impossible," Jovvi repeated, staring at him. "Could *you* tell it was there?"

"Yes, but only because I learned the structure of the poisons themselves," Lorand replied after taking her hand. "Once you study them for a while, you also learn to recognize the . . . very tiny turbulence their presence causes in normal food. For someone who hasn't studied them, it's highly unlikely that they'd notice anything until it was too late."

"So it was probably pure luck which saved the Earth magic member," Meerk mused, also staring at Lorand. "But you still haven't said why they would be in so much trouble."

"It's because they're continuing to take something to counteract the poison," Lorand explained. "An antidote only has to be taken once, but a temporary neutralizer needs to be taken on a regular basis—until it doesn't work any longer. The amount of time varies from poison to poison, but they all end the same way by killing the one or ones who ingested it."

"Then all our problems are solved!" Meerk exclaimed, suddenly in a joyous mood. "Instead of you needing to draw the Five out and being forced to face them, we can just sit back and wait for most of them to die. If only the Earth magic member is left, how much trouble can he be all by himself? Time alone will solve the problem, and none of you has to be risked."

Vallant noticed that Meerk's glance went to Tamrissa when he mentioned the risk, which explained the man's blind spot. His solution just wasn't practical, and he needed to be told that as quickly as possible.

"Sittin' around waitin' for them to die is something we can't afford to do," he said, interrupting enthusiastic comments from Meerk's friend Biblow. "Not at this stage of the game."

"Why not?" Meerk snapped, turning quickly to face Vallant. "Because *you* don't like the idea? Or maybe it's just because you didn't think of it first."

"Neither," Vallant replied, feeling himself stiffen in response to the man's attitude. "It may have escaped your notice, but they're the legitimately Seated authority even if they got to be Seated by cheatin'. If we just sit around and wait for them to die, the power they represent reverts right back to the nobility. Legally it's still *their* place to arrange for a new Blendin', and they'll rally behind the last remainin' member of the old Blendin' to give themselves time to take control again. If we then walk in and try to brush them aside, we'll be the ones breakin' the law."

"I'm afraid Vallant is right," Jovvi said as Meerk began to growl wordlessly. "Right now we're in the midst of a serious social upheaval, with most of the people in the city on our side. That sort of atmosphere tends to dissipate in the face of inaction, and the needs of everyday life will take precedence again. The nobility will be able to go after everyone a few at a time, forcing them back into their old habits and ways. At that point we'll have to choose between taking over by force against more than the Seated Five, and running away again. Don't forget that we've not only broken the law by Blending ourselves, but we've taught others how to do it."

"And don't believe for a moment that the nobility can't regain the standing it used to have," Rion put in in agreement, drawing Meerk's dagger stare. "A private guard force isn't hard to come by when you have the gold to pay out, and Gan Garee isn't the only city in the empire. I'm sure many of those who have left mean to return with such a force, and if everything isn't settled by then we'll have to take them over or destroy them. Very frankly I don't care for either option."

"And if we let them die instead of defeating them, the

rumor of their cheating will always stay that, just a rumor,''
Tamrissa said, speaking more gently than the others had.
"After that it won't matter *who* we defeat, we won't have
defeated the people the nobility have claimed are the
stronger Blending. Even if we manage to be Seated, there
will always be people around who believe we stole our
place rather than earned it."

"Which in turn will mean we'll have to spend a lot of
our time fighting off attempts by people to steal the place
themselves," Lorand put in, clearly in agreement. "We
won't be suppressing the knowledge about Blending again,
so they'll decide that if we did it, they can do the same.
And people will feel free to argue anything we happen to
suggest, because we aren't the 'real' authority in charge.
Personally, I don't care for any part of *that*."

"You're all doing nothing but making excuses," Meerk
bit out harshly, glaring around at them. "You think that if
one of you says something, all the others have to support
that something. But in this instance it's insane, when you
can have everything you want just by sitting back and waiting. If the nobility brings in more guardsmen, why *not* just
take them over? If they try to take control of the Seating
process again, simply don't allow it. And if someone challenges you or refuses to do as you say, just have them
arrested. When you're the leaders of an effort like this, you
can do anything you damned well please without anyone
saying you can't. Don't all those High talent link groups
count for *anything*?"

"Those High talent link groups are made up of *people*,
who count for everything," Jovvi said, just a touch more
sharply than she'd spoken before. "They aren't here as
tools to be used to Seat absolute despots, they're here for
the same reason we are: to *end* that sort of thing. It's pointless for everyone to go through all the trouble they have
just to substitute one set of tyrants for another. You're
thinking with your emotions rather than your mind, Alsin,
and it's doing you not the least credit. Tamrissa can't be
protected by refusing to face reality."

"So that's it," Vallant growled, putting his teacup aside
to get to his feet. "As long as you're busy worryin' about
Tamrissa, everybody else in the world can go hang. For

your information, that woman is better able to take care of herself than you'll ever be, and when you sit around whinin' and tryin' to protect her all you're doin' is insultin' her. She doesn't *need* protectin', as if she were some helpless female off the streets!''

"You *would* think that, because you don't have the stones to protect her," Meerk returned in the same sort of growl, turning now to face Vallant completely. "When you love someone as much as I love her, you can't help but worry over her safety. And when some damned fool tries to put her into danger, you can't do anything but step in and tell him to back off. Maybe *your* life isn't worth anything, but hers is!''

"Yes, her life *is* worth more than mine, but you're not talkin' about love, you're talkin' about possession," Vallant snapped back, moving forward a bit just the way Meerk was doing. "She's not so stupid that she doesn't know how dangerous something can be, but she's entitled to make her own decision about it. You steppin' in says you're tryin' to make the decision *for* her, to force her to do things *your* way. If you loved her the way I do, you'd let her live her own life as she sees fit even if it eats out all of your insides with worry. As a human being she's *entitled* to that, whether you like it or not!''

"What has like got to do with survival?" Meerk demanded, now only a step or so away. "I'd rather have her alive and unhappy than fully satisfied and dead. Only a pitiful excuse for a man would see it any other way."

"She's already been through alive and unhappy, and I'd never let somethin' like that happen to her again," Vallant returned, his tone now very flat. "And if I'm such a pitiful excuse for a man, what are you waitin' for? Show me how big a man *you* are."

Meerk showed his teeth in a feral grin, the expression saying he'd been waiting just as long as Vallant had for something like this to finally happen. Vallant had no need to reach for the power because he was no longer able to release it, so he simply got a tighter grip on it and extended the fingers of his talent toward Meerk. The other man was undoubtedly doing the same with his own talent, and who struck first would certainly count toward eventual victory.

Vallant had no intentions of killing the fool, only of teaching him just how big a fool he was, but his talent suddenly . . . ran into a wall, so to speak. Meerk stood no more than three feet away, but Vallant found it impossible to reach him.

"That's right, we're blocking both your talents," Jovvi said as Meerk's face twisted into an expression of frustrated rage. "The rest of us think you're both idiots for constantly pushing at each other, but if this is what you want we won't try to deny it to you. We just won't let you do it with magic, so if you're going to fight you'll have to do it like the two little boys you are."

Physically, Vallant knew she meant, since it took a while for children to have control over their talents. But that was perfectly all right with him, as the son of a wealthy owner of trading ships often found himself defending against the crime of what family he'd been born into. Meerk, too, seemed to have the same experience in his past, as he put his hands up in a way that said he knew what he was doing. Vallant considered that marvelous, since he hated the idea of beating up on the helpless.

And, happily, Meerk *was* far from helpless. He jabbed at Vallant with his right fist, expecting to connect with Vallant's face, but that hadn't happened often. Vallant tended to move too fast, and his own fist smashed into Meerk's face with satisfying strength. Meerk stumbled back, momentarily off balance, but a moment later he was right back in the fight.

It took an incredibly long time before the fight was over, and by then Vallant's fury was long since faded. Meerk relied on brute strength rather than any sort of technique, and he simply kept throwing punches at Vallant no matter how many times he missed. He actually did connect two or three times, but Vallant knew how to take a punch without folding—a skill often acquired by someone who has worked his way up to captaining a ship. Shaking off the pain of the blow with a sharp movement of his head seemed to also shake Meerk, and when Vallant did it for the third time, Meerk's face grayed a bit.

Not long after that, Vallant noticed that Meerk was doing more stumbling than moving, more panting than breathing evenly. The man was close to the end of his strength, so Vallant hesitated a moment and then stepped back.

"I don't know about you, but I've already proved whatever it was I intended to," Vallant said as he watched Meerk drag in deep draughts of air. "Is there any reason to keep goin' on with this?"

The other man seemed about to refuse to stop the fight, but then he apparently noticed the difference in their conditions. He stared at Vallant for a moment, pain and humiliation and desolation in his eyes, and then he turned and stumbled out of the room. Jovvi gave Vallant a small smile and nod of approval before hurrying out after Meerk, and then Lorand and Rion and Naran were surrounding Vallant.

"Sit down and let me do something about that cut on your cheek," Lorand ordered in a no-nonsense tone as he gestured to a nearby chair. "And I hope you two finally have all that out of your systems."

"We finally realized that you had to be given the *chance* to get it out of your systems," Rion said, his arm around Naran as usual. "My lady kept worrying about the confrontation which refused to become less of a probability, a confrontation in which one of you would have been seriously hurt if not killed. We finally realized that that was so only if you both used your talents, so we joined together with our link groups to keep the fight physical. *Are* you finally over it?"

"Speakin' for myself, I'd hate to go through that again," Vallant said, feeling the gentle touch of Lorand's talent against the cut on his face. "The man had no chance against me, and fightin' someone like that makes you feel as though you're pickin' on the helpless."

"How interesting," another voice said, and Tamrissa appeared between Rion and Lorand. "You consider Alsin helpless, but I'm no longer a candidate for that category. Now, when it's altogether too late, you finally come around to the proper way of thinking. You might like to know, Dom Ro, that I no longer dislike you. Now I hate every inch of you, and I'm never going to speak to you again!"

And with that she turned and marched out of the room, the set of her shoulders and angle of her head shouting out her anger. Vallant's cheek began to sting from whatever

Lorand was doing to it, but Vallant barely noticed. Something inside him had begun an unexpected shift, and his own anger kept his gaze on Tamrissa until she disappeared from sight. This time he had no clear idea of how the woman had challenged him, but he was as certain as possible that she had.

And that something inside him was on the verge of letting him answer her challenge, in the way he most wanted to. . . .

THIRTY-THREE

Kambil sat quietly and watched as the guardsman said nervously to Delin, "Yes, that's right, Excellence, the Commandant feels certain that the fugitives have returned to the city. Two of our patrol groups haven't reported back, and a third was destroyed completely. The Commandant is now in the process of adding all our remaining forces to the palace contingent, which means they'll have to go through us before they can reach you."

"Why doesn't that comfort me?" Delin demanded acidly, glaring at the guardsman. "And if the Commandant was so certain that his new plan would work, why didn't he come himself to tell us about it?"

"As I said, Excellence, the Commandant sends his regrets," the man mumbled, stuttering a bit with fright. "H-he's right in the middle of setting up more guard posts, and means to come in person as soon as everything is done to his satisfaction."

"Does that mean he intends to explain why those miserable peasants were allowed to get back into the city in the first place?" Delin asked much too brightly, which frightened the man even more. "Tell him I'm certainly looking forward to hearing *that* explanation, and the sooner the better. And also tell him that if he isn't here within the hour, he needn't bother coming at all. Or even bother worrying about what to do with the rest of his life, as he won't have a life to worry about! Now get out of my sight!"

The guardsman performed the fastest bow-while-moving Kambil had ever seen, getting himself to the door and out of it even before he'd straightened. Bron, Selendi, and Homin, all back fully under control—as Bron had been since the last session Kambil had had with him—were just as amused as Kambil was, leaving only Delin to rant and rage at the closed and empty doorway.

"They're all a bunch of incompetent fools!" Delin shouted, waving a fist at the closed door. "They were given just one thing to do, but obviously it was too far beyond their ability. Just what do they think they're around for?"

"Actually, I believe they're wondering the same thing about us," Kambil said, able to answer the rhetorical question when he hadn't been allowed to comment at any other time. "You're getting so frantic about all this, you're doing nothing but confirming the rumors about our having stolen the Throne."

"And you *didn't* get frantic?" Delin demanded, rounding on Kambil in his rage. "I seem to recall someone determined to avoid facing those miserable peasants again, and it wasn't me. Surely you haven't changed your mind?"

"Now that they're here, we may not have the choice," Kambil said, and this time he would have stayed silent if he could have. "That message you just sent to the Commandant of the guard—I expect the man will take your advice and not show up at all. He'll pick a direction and start to run, relying on those interlopers to solve his problem for him, and the Highest Aspect alone knows how many guardsmen will go with him. You've just managed to weaken our protection more than the interlopers have."

"In his position, that's what *I* would do," Homin said in support as Delin began to snarl out his disagreement. "He was uncertain to begin with and so sent one of his men to test the waters, and you told the man of your intention to drown him in them. He'd be a fool to do anything *but* run.''

"And it's not as if we've given him any help with what we asked him to do,'' Bron pointed out calmly. "We should have gone out as a full Blending and thrown those peasants back into line, but you refused to do that. The man simply doesn't have a large enough force to cope with what's happening, but instead of supporting him you blamed him for not doing the impossible. So what do you expect we'll do *now*?''

"We'll do whatever we have to to win,'' Delin ground out, his stare at each of them individually filled with the obsession of the extremely unstable. "I don't care what that happens to be or how many people have to die, but we *are* going to win. The only thing we won't be doing is Blending.''

"How can you continue to insist on that?'' Selendi asked with exasperation, shaking her head a bit at him. "*They'll* be using their Blending, they'd be fools not to, so we won't stand a chance against them. We stand little enough chance Blended, but we *have* learned a few tricks they don't know yet. That knowledge could conceivably win the thing for us.''

"And then again it may not,'' Delin countered, calmer now. "It may interest you to know that Kambil disagrees with you about their using their Blending if we don't Blend. Our esteemed Spirit magic user feels that they have what they consider a sense of honor, and they won't take undue advantage of an opponent. As a Blending they're stronger than we are, but that may not be true on an individual basis. We'll each face our opposite number, and if necessary we'll cheat to win. Once they're dead, the rest of the peasants won't have the nerve to mention the word 'usurpers' again. And there's another reason why we won't Blend.''

"What reason is that, Delin?'' Bron asked, his tone no more than curious. "I'd like to know why you refuse to use our greatest, most effective weapon.''

"As if you don't already know,'' Delin replied, scoffing at all of them. "Am I supposed to overlook the fact that I've allowed Kambil to regain control over the three of you? He can't do anything to me directly and by himself, but in the Blending you're four against my one. Overwhelming me would be no trouble at all, and then Kambil would be free and I'd be his slave again. Thank you very much, but I prefer being the master to the slave.''

Kambil very much wanted to use a smooth, persuasive argument on Delin and talk him out of his stance, but he hadn't been allowed the option to do that. Frustration flared high in Kambil, furious frustration in that he *had* expected Delin to have overlooked the fact that the others were back under his control. If they could have Blended just one time, his talent could have freed him as Delin's talent had been unable to do in the same circumstance. He'd expected Delin to look at the situation from his narrow, personal point of view as usual, but Delin hadn't obliged.

"So that's the sum total of your plan to see that we survive this?" Selendi asked Delin, the words still tart. "We face them individually and cheat? What if we can't find a *way* to cheat?"

"Thanks to your friend Rimen Howser, we already have one way," Delin reminded her. "Those hostages he gathered are all here in the palace, so we'll certainly make use of them. And by the way, I gave him the reward he kept hinting he was due—only not the one he expected. I appointed him my personal envoy, and told him he would immediately be given the status of High Lord if he came back with the gold my peasant tenants are so late in sending. He took a small contingent of guardsmen and left the palace, but that was yesterday. If he isn't back by tomorrow, I might have to start worrying about him.''

"So your idea of fun and games has lost us another loyal, competent supporter," Bron said disgustedly, no longer completely sanguine about what Delin said and did. "The man hated peasants so much that he would have done anything to see them put back in their proper places, so you send him into a situation where they probably lynched him. If you're that determined to get yourself pulled down, Delin, why do you insist on taking the rest of us with you?"

"I don't remember asking for your opinion!" Delin snarled, his faintly better mood now completely gone. And that was Delin's major problem in a nutshell, Kambil knew:

the man acted without ever considering the consequences of his actions. Even after the thing was done, his amusement over it continued until someone pointed out what a stupid move he'd made. Instead of seeing the point and learning from it, Delin took the instruction as a personal attack and completely discounted it. He hadn't made a stupid move as far as *he* was concerned, he was simply surrounded by people who were inexplicably grouped against him.

"Since what you do continues to affect the rest of us, you don't *have* to ask for our opinions," Homin said sharply, startling Delin just a bit. "Howser worked for our benefit as well as yours, so you had no right to do what you did to him all alone. I don't care whether you consider yourself our leader or not, Delin, that's not at issue here. If you don't stop doing these imbecilic things, there won't be a group left for you to be leader *of*. Can't you make yourself understand that?"

"Another way we can cheat in the confrontations is by using our special tandem link groups," Delin said after a very brief hesitation, deliberately changing the subject. Kambil had seen that his mind had felt a flash of panic at Homin's question, since he *was* unable to make himself understand what had been said to him. As a child, doubt had been raised about everything Delin had said and done. In order to protect himself Delin had stopped listening to what others said, and now he found it impossible to change the habit.

"We'll know those link groups are there, but our opponents won't," Delin continued, looking at none of them as he fought to regain some inner balance. "They'll think we're alone so they'll come in the same way, and the surprise will be their undoing and ending. Yes, that's what we'll do, without any doubt. We'll stand our hostages in front of us, and while the peasants are whimpering and moaning about putting innocent people in the middle of our argument, we'll reach to our link groups and then destroy them. The plan *will* work, so I don't want to hear any more about it."

Kambil probably wouldn't have said anything even if he'd been able to, and the other three apparently agreed with him. They all exchanged glances which Delin failed to see, glances which made the decision unanimous: no one would access Delin's rage by disagreeing with him, but that didn't mean they meant to obey. There were too many flaws in that so-called plan for it to work as it stood, but that was perfectly all right. The rest of them would come up with their own plan, and Delin would be the only one lost to mindlessness.

"And here's another decision I've made," Delin said, now looking around at them. "The other day I heard a servant wondering aloud to another about when we would go out after those interlopers and finish them off. I decided then and there that we would *not* go out, but would instead make them come in here after us. Having to fight their way through our guards will weaken them, and then they'll be at a disadvantage because we know the palace and they don't. If they bring their supporters with them, the confusion will be even worse—for them. And once we destroy them, their supporters will be conveniently at hand to be destroyed in turn. Do you all understand?"

Kambil joined the others in nodding, which was really their only option. If he'd still been running things, he would have had everyone available searching the city to find out where those five people had gone to ground. As soon as they were located, he would have waited until they were asleep and then would have taken every Earth magic user available to make sure they *stayed* asleep. Then he would have burned their haven down around their ears, ending them in the most practical way possible. For Delin, though, the word *practical* didn't exist any more than the words *sound planning*.

And then a loud, brusque knock sounded at the door, interrupting whatever else Delin had been about to say. None of the servants had ever knocked in just that way before, so Kambil reached out curiously to find out which of them had changed. When he found no one at the door he spread his talent a bit wider, and discovered the guardsman running away up the hall. No one else was anywhere nearby, so when Delin called out permission for the knocker to enter, there was no answer. Immediate annoyance flared in Delin, sending him toward the door with the intention to hurt whomever had caused the annoyance. Kambil wondered why the man had made no effort to reach the person with his talent, but in a moment the question became completely unimportant.

"*Now* what are those fools up to?" Delin demanded when opening the door produced nothing but a folded sheet of paper fluttering to the floor. Obviously the paper had been stuck into the crack of the door, one way to deliver the thing without having to be there in person. Delin bent to retrieve it, unfolded it and read it, and then a ripple of fear danced across his mind.

"What is it?" Bron asked, probably having seen the way Delin's teeth had clenched. "And who is it from?"

"It's from our former guard commander," Delin ground out, hatred flaring in his mind. "This is his resignation, along with the information that he's taking with him any of his guards who want to go. But there's also one other thing as well. The interlopers have had the nerve to send us a message."

No one mentioned that they'd told Delin what would happen with the guard commander, and no one asked the most obvious question. Kambil himself had to hold tight to his balance, and then Delin looked up from the piece of paper.

"Our enemies have given us until tomorrow at this time to surrender to the 'proper authorities' as the usurpers we are," he said in a toneless voice. "If we refuse, they're coming into the palace after us."

Without first having to fight their way through a cordon of guardsmen, Kambil thought but didn't say. Delin had done it to them again, and they might not live long enough to have to worry about another repeat performance. . . .

"But Daddy, I'm bored!" the whiny little bitch complained again, just as she'd been doing for the last two hours. Eltrina Razas, now dressed as one of the palace servants, longed to slap the girl across the face, but couldn't allow herself that luxury. At least not yet, not until all her plans had come to fruition.

"If you say that one more time, Mirra, I'll put you across my knee right here," her father growled, obviously as sick of hearing her whine as Eltrina was. "And you're not to say another word to any of the servants, especially not to give them orders. At the rate you're chasin' them off, we'll soon be takin' care of ourselves."

The girl tried to protest that, but luckily for Eltrina the man stood firm in his decision. Eltrina was now the only servant willing to come into the area where the hostages were, and not just because of the girl. Lady Hallina Mardimil was just as bad, as were the merchant couple who had delusions of nobility. And that ridiculous bumpkin, who had also taken to throwing his weight around. Not to mention that filthy-skinned woman. . . .

But Eltrina wasn't about to be chased off, not when she needed to be there to see how her plans worked out. She'd already made her move against the last of the Five, forcing Edmin's agent to help her. The woman was one of those who had stayed to work in the palace, hoping to earn more of the gold Edmin had payed her. She had accepted Eltrina's gold with very little reluctance, only hesitating when she found out what had to be done for it. But the hesitation had quickly ended, and now that part of it was over. In just a short while, none of the five people who had caused her agony and humiliation would be left alive.

And then it would be the turn of those peasants, who certainly would not fail to appear at the palace: Vallant Ro, a man she'd actually been willing to honor with her use, and that stupid little trollop who had stolen him right out of her hands. The two of them would appear, and then they would pay in the same way the Five had paid, only in a much shorter span of time. Eltrina would stand and watch them die, and then she would smile and turn and walk away.

"You, girl, come over here and fix this pillow!" Hallina Mardimil ordered, once again acting as though she were queen of the world. "I'm not as comfortable as I should be, so get over here and take care of it."

"Take care of it yourself," Eltrina replied smoothly after turning away and heading toward the door out of the area. "I have other things to do, so if you're too incompetent to fix a stupid pillow, stay uncomfortable. And if you complain about *me*, the whole bunch of you will be looking after yourselves, since I'm the only one left willing to come in here. Think about it.''

The Mardimil's sputtering outrage was drowned out by the alarmed comments of the others, so Eltrina left them alone to argue it out among themselves. They'd certainly decide not to complain about the only servant willing to bring them food and drink and to straighten up a bit after them, so Eltrina had nothing to worry about. She would be safe until things began to happen, and then there would no longer be danger from *any* quarter.

Chuckling softly, Eltrina went off to find *herself* something to eat.

THIRTY-FOUR

Considering that our deadline given to the Five was the early afternoon, we didn't have to get up particularly early in the morning. We would have been able to sleep as late as we liked—if we'd been able to sleep in the first place. I'd managed to get in a solid few hours myself, but only by using Jovvi's sleep technique. Even so I hadn't been able to *stay* asleep past a certain point, and since the new day had already started without me I decided not to try to fight waking up. Breakfast would be waiting downstairs, and there was no sense in making it wait too long.

Dressing was no longer very involved, not when I had the choice of wearing my only clean outfit or putting on the dirty one again. Since I'd used the bath house the night before, I settled on the clean clothes and then made my way downstairs. This house was more than twice as large as my own, maybe even three times as large, and that was what made it perfect for us. We hadn't had to put more than two people in a bedchamber, and I'd even been able to get a room to myself.

"Good morning," Lorand said when I walked into the dining room, and I was surprised to see him sitting alone. "Don't bother looking around for anyone else, since the members of the link groups have already finished eating, and you and I are the first of our Blending to be up. Is *our* timing off, or is everyone else's?"

"Since we won't be leaving here for some hours yet, probably ours," I answered, walking over to the buffet to see if there was any food left. "Ah, good. The rest of you *haven't* finished up all our provisions. So, are you looking forward to later, or dreading it?"

"I don't seem to have made up my mind yet," he responded around a mouthful of food, and I had the impression that he wasn't lying. "How about you?"

"Since one way or another this ought to be the end of it, I can't wait to get to it," I responded as I began to take some food, also speaking honestly. "And in this our timing is just right. In a little while the cold weather will start to set in, and that's no time for camping outdoors or extensive travel."

"Not to mention that I'm tired of constantly moving around," he agreed. "My idea of a proper life is to find a place and settle into it, and even Jovvi is weary of all the traveling we've been forced to do. But I'm a little afraid to wonder what things will be like if we win. Will we become the new Seated Five automatically, or will we have to go through the competitions again?"

"You have to *start* things right if you want them to continue on that way," I said, turning away from the buffet to carry my plate to the table. "No one should be able to just walk in and take over, so the competitions—*not* handled by the nobility—ought to be held again. But we're not a Five now, we're a Six. How will any other Blending compete with *that*?"

"I'm happy to say that isn't a problem I have to worry about," he replied, glancing up at me as I settled at the table and began to pour myself a cup of tea. "Naran's mother probably isn't the only one who hid a child with that sort of talent, so there are bound to be others who can do what she does. A year ought to be enough for the other Blendings to search out some of those people, and then they'll be ready to compete against us. But speaking of searching people out, I think there's something you ought to be warned about.''

"Warned?" I echoed, looking at him with the fork halfway to my mouth. "You make whatever it is sound almost dangerous.''

"It *is* dangerous, so forget about the almost," he came back, now also looking directly at me. "Or, rather, I should say *he*. *He's* very dangerous, and if you speak to him again the way you did last night, there will probably be another fight to break up. With two High talents involved it won't be as easy to break up as the last one was, and in fact it might not be possible to break it up at all. With that in mind, my advice would be to carefully watch whatever you happen to say.''

"You can't possibly be talking about our dear Water magic user," I said, heavy annoyance beginning to roll in again. "By his own admission the man is a coward, so what could I possibly have to worry about? Besides, if he stays away from me and anything I happen to be involved in, there should be no problem at all.''

"Tamrissa, you may remember that I was taking care of the cut on Vallant's cheek when you spoke to him after the fight," Lorand responded, apparently catching some of my annoyance. "When I do something like that I also automatically monitor bodily reactions like blood pressure and rate of breathing. Vallant's vital signs were almost normal when the fight ended, but after you spoke to him every reaction shot way up the scale. He'd just fought for you and won, after all—''

"He did *not* fight for *me*," I interrupted at once, refusing to let even Lorand say something like that. "He fought for his own reasons, and I simply happened to be a part of it. If you'll cast your mind back, you'll remember that he no longer wants to have anything to do with me because he's afraid that things won't go perfectly between us. He's right to think that they won't, but that's the only thing he's right about.''

"Look, he has every reason to be afraid," Lorand ground out, now glaring at me. "When something means more to you than your own life, you get a bit crazy at the thought of losing it. It's worse when you keep losing the thing and getting it back, losing it and getting it back, over and over, but now something seems to have changed. It's possible that Vallant has reached the point of refusing to worry about it any longer. He wants what he wants, and if some-one tries to keep him from having it he'll simply shove them out of his way. Do you really want him to treat you like *that*?''

"Let him try—if he wants another really close shave," I said, now having to force myself to sound absolutely con-fident. "I'm tired of playing these games with him, and he'll find that out if he tries to bother me. Aside from that, let's drop the subject. I really don't care to have my appetite ruined.''

And with that I went back to my food, ignoring the glare Lorand continued to send in my direction. For some reason I was more disturbed than I'd been in quite a while, even though I had no time for disturbance. In just a few hours we'd be facing our sworn enemies for the second time, and thoughts about *that* had to take precedence over everything else.

The rest of the meal went by in welcome silence, but it was clear that Lorand still wasn't pleased with me when I got up and left the room. Well, he wasn't the only one who wasn't pleased, I thought as I made my slow way back to the room I'd slept in. I hadn't been lying the various times I'd said how much I loved Vallant, but that love seemed to be firm and sure only when *he* was backing away from it. Hearing that he might become actively interested again had frightened me on some level, throwing me right back to the way I'd been before all the changes. And I didn't *want* to be back there, not for any reason. . . .

I walked into the room and swung the door closed behind me, hating the confusion I suddenly found myself floun-dering around in. It was absurd to think that I still hadn't gotten over being afraid of having a man find me attractive, just as though nothing had—

"Tamrissa."

I whirled around at the sound of my name, actually having to stop myself from using my talent without thinking. He sat in one of the chairs the room held, and when I'd come in I'd walked right past him without seeing him. A small tingle of . . . nervousness rather than fear tiptoed across my nerve endings when he stood up, even though he took not a single step toward me. It was Vallant, of course, and I would have been happier if it had been the entire Seated Five instead.

"I hope you'll excuse my bargin' in, but it's time for us to do some talkin' again," he said, those very blue eyes staring straight at me. "I came here rather than tryin' to speak to you somewhere else so that the conversation can be private. We don't need everyone knowin' what's goin' on between us."

"Nothing is going on between us," I said, having taken a very firm grip on myself. "You decided that you're not in the least interested in me and I agreed that that was best, so there's nothing left for either of us to say. With that in view, I'd like you to leave this room."

"I never said I wasn't interested in you," he disagreed, ignoring the rest of what I'd told him. "I said I couldn't face the idea of havin' you turn your back on me again, not when every time you do a part of me dies. That side of it hasn't changed, but I've recently discovered somethin' I hadn't fully understood: when I'm not near you, I might as well be dead anyway. You bring color and taste to my world with delight and fury, happiness and despair, patience and annoyance, laughter and tears. I wish I'd never met you and I wish I'd known you all my life, and when you feel *that* way about someone you have no chance of ever walkin' away from them."

"I don't want to hear that you've changed your mind again," I said, turning my back toward him as my insides really began to tremble. "You're not the only one who has been dying a piece at a time, and I won't put up with it any longer. We just have to stay together long enough to take care of the Five and get the empire out of the clutches of the nobility, and then we never have to see each other again. Our Blending is needed to win the war, not to rule.''

''Yes, I noticed that myself,'' he murmured, and now he *had* moved a couple of steps closer. ''And it's also likely that we won't be *wanted* to run the empire. There's a big difference between addin' a talent to a group that soothes and balances them, and addin' one that lets them see into the future. A lot of people will be even more afraid of us now, so chances are *we* won't want to stay either. But if you go off all by yourself, you'll be as alone again as you used to be. Meerk left the house last night after the fight, and Jovvi believes he might not come back again.''

That was something I already knew, as I'd tried to find Alsin after the fight to see if he was all right. I hadn't needed Jovvi to tell me how horribly humiliated the man felt after having lost to his greatest rival in the most basic way possible—and in front of so many people. He'd broken his promise about not letting himself be drawn into a fight, and he'd paid for it with the sort of defeat he couldn't have been expecting. If he rejoined our forces at all, it would be among those who weren't part of our immediate group.

''You'd better understand that if you ever took off all by yourself, I'd have to come lookin' for you,'' Vallant said, now no more than a step or two behind me. ''I know nothin' would be likely to harm you, but loneliness is somethin' even the strongest talent in the world can't fight and win against. I'm not tryin' to deny that the trouble between us is mostly my fault, but part of it is yours as well. If we both agree to that, we won't have to face a fight with an opponent we can't best.''

''Better that than constantly wondering when your mind will change the next time,'' I said without thinking, now simply speaking what I felt. ''I know I have my problems and that it's hard for others to put up with them, but that's all part of who I am. I've finally realized that no matter how strong I get I'll never be rid of some of those problems, so to picture me without them is to see someone other than *me*. And that's who you're looking for, Vallant, someone who won't keep getting you upset. Since that someone isn't me, I really would like you to leave.''

''The only reason I keep gettin' upset is because of how

much you mean to me," he replied heavily. "And because we all want to think of the person we love as bein' perfect, you're right about me seein' someone other than the real you. I've been seein' a woman who would understand and put up with my own problems, not another human bein' who had troubles of her own. I can promise that that won't happen again, because I've finally gotten over seein' you as perfect."

I could hear the tentative grin in his voice, a clear attempt to lighten the mood. I felt a pang of memory over the times we'd joked between ourselves, but those times were a long way behind us.

"Then you should understand more easily why I'm not prepared to change *my* mind the way you keep changing yours," I said, refusing to join in the lightness. "Besides, mind-changing is supposed to be a woman's prerogative, not a man's, so you've been stepping over the line in more ways than one. And this is the last time I'm going to be polite about asking you to leave."

"If you're not the stubbornest woman ever to have lived, I'd have to see another one to believe it," he growled, obviously not very pleased with me. "And don't you *dare* try claimin' you haven't been doin' your own share of mind-changin'. Or wasn't that you spendin' all your time on the road workin' to lure me back into your bed? It surely looked like you."

"That was when I still thought you were someone worth *having* in my bed," I retorted, finally turning to face him again despite the warmth I felt in my cheeks. "It took a while to realize I was wrong, but I've finally learned the lesson well enough not to forget it again. Now: are you leaving on your own, or do you need help getting started?"

"The only help I need is with livin', and although only the Highest Aspect knows why, you *are* the one I need that help from."

Those very light blue eyes stared down at me as he spoke, and the strong male beauty of his features brought me another pang. His long blond hair wasn't tied back today, and the faint mark left on his cheek from last night's fight added to his handsomeness rather than detracted from it. But his appearance was only the way I recognized the man I'd learned to love because of what was inside him—and the man I'd also learned to hate *because* of that love.

"Don't try to claim that I didn't warn you," I said, forcing myself to stay with the position I *knew* was best. If I let him get close again, I'd have only myself to blame when the pain returned.

So I reached out with my talent, intending to show him again that I wasn't a woman he could bully and impose upon. A very thin curtain of fire would drive him back a few steps, and if he still refused to leave I was prepared to redden his skin a bit. Not enough to incapacitate him for the coming fight with our enemies, but enough to get him to leave me alone. The curtain flared into being between us—and promptly hissed and sputtered into nothingness.

"I love you, Tamrissa, and I won't give up because I know that you love me as well," he said softly as my eyes widened with shock, his arms reaching out and gently pulling me close to him. "I won't let you drive me away again, no matter what you do."

Panic touched me as his lips lowered toward mine, so I tried to apply my flames to those lips. It would have done the job of driving him back, but this time I could *feel* the water quenching my fire. And then he was in the midst of kissing me, something I'd been dreaming about ever since we'd parted. I loved him so much and wanted him so badly . . . how could anyone human have continued to hold back . . . ?

The kiss lasted an incredibly long time, and for all that time I held to him with every ounce of strength in my body. I never wanted to let him go again, feeling the same thing coming from him in the way his arms crushed me to his chest. We were two halves making a whole again, and when the kiss began to end I was more than ready to go on to other things.

"I have to compliment you on your strategy and tactics," I whispered breathlessly when our lips finally parted. "Starting our discussion here, where there's a bed handy. . . . The confidence you had in yourself was justified."

"It wasn't confidence, it was stupidity," he answered with a groan, still holding me tight. "The men leadin' our other groups began to get here early this mornin', and they're now waitin' for me to join the discussion of how we'll be approachin' the palace. They were takin' a few minutes to have tea and a snack before we got started, but I saw you in the dinin' room and knew you were almost through eatin'. Decidin' to wait for you here in your room happened without my thinkin', and now I'm payin' for bein' an idiot.''

"You deserve it, for making me pay right along with you," I grumbled, pushing back away from him. "You're the most exasperating man I know and I really do hate you, and if you aren't back here the instant that meeting is over I swear I'll roast you alive in your own juices."

"You're already doin' that," he returned with a wry grin, then bent to touch my lips with his. "And if this isn't the shortest strategy session the world has ever seen, it certainly won't be *my* fault. Make sure you don't wander off."

I made a noise to show how likely *that* was, then watched as he forced himself to leave. I knew I was being an idiot for taking him back, but my only hope of keeping him away was also keeping his hands and lips off me. Once that attempt had failed I'd been done for, although the level of his talent strength still surprised me. He hadn't been able to do the same only a very short while ago, and now I had no choice but to take him back.

So I sat down to wait while daydreaming about how wonderful it would be to be held in his arms again while he made love to me, and a certain amount of time passed without my noticing. A knock at the door brought me back to the world, making me wonder why the big fool would knock. I hurried over and opened the door, fully intending to ask the question, but it wasn't Vallant who stood there.

"Are you ready, Tamrissa?" Rion asked with a smile, Naran standing beside him as usual and wearing the same smile. "It's been decided that we'll have to leave earlier than we expected to, if we're to get through the crowds of people who have gathered in front of the palace. Apparently someone spread the word of our ultimatum to the Five, and the entire city has turned out to see what happens."

I felt tempted to say that the Five—along with the entire city—could wait a little longer without it killing them, but that wouldn't have gotten me what I'd been dreaming about. Even if I'd been able to drag Vallant out from the middle of all that planning, knowing everyone stood around waiting for us to be finished would have ruined the mood completely. There was nothing for it but to shrug and say of course I was ready, and then follow Rion and Naran toward where everyone else was.

But considering the foul mood I'd been thrown into, I began to pity those five poor fools in the palace. And also to wonder, now that our reconciliation had been delayed, whether it would be Vallant or me who had a change of mind next time. . . .

THIRTY-FIVE

Lorand sat his horse with as much patience as he could muster, wondering if everyone in the city *had* turned out to watch what would happen. Despite the cloudiness and threat of rain the crowds were enormous, and the guardsman part of their group was having a hard time getting them through those crowds. The guard members had wanted to use the same sort of uncaring force they used to use, and wouldn't have been pleased with the Blending's refusal if they'd been allowed to still have feelings of their own. But at the moment they just obeyed orders, and made a careful way through the throng.

"I think I have a small bit of good news," Jovvi said as she leaned toward him from her own mount. "I can't be certain with this many people around, but I just may have picked up Alsin's trace near another section of our group. I certainly do hope it's him."

"After all he's done for us, it would be a shame if he missed out on the end of this," Lorand agreed with a nod. "It isn't his fault that he couldn't resist Tamrissa, it was just his bad luck. I looked for him after the fight, but he'd already left the house."

"He waited just long enough to see which one of them Tamma would go to first," Jovvi said with her own nod, keeping only half her attention on their rate of progress. "He knew that what she said to that one didn't matter in the least, the important part was which of the combatants she went to. He was just about falling off his feet while Vallant had only a small cut on his cheek, and yet Vallant was the one she went to. That convinced him he really did have no chance at all to win her."

"Maybe he was mistaken to believe that that was important," Lorand ventured, feeling his frown. "Tamrissa and I had breakfast together this morning, and she flatly refused to hear anything I had to say about Vallant. He, for his part, began to run seriously short of patience with her last night, after she told him how much she hated him. Since nothing has changed between them, maybe he has more of a chance than he thinks."

"Lorand, my dear, things *have* changed between them," Jovvi told him gently with a smile. "Vallant was up and around before all of us this morning, and he must have done a lot of thinking. He also must have done some doing, because Tamma's feelings toward him have taken a sudden shift. Couldn't you see the way they kept glancing at each other while we were getting ready to leave the house?"

"I suppose I was too busy with my own thoughts," Lorand said, his brows high with surprise. "I'm glad to hear it, of course, but I really do wish they would pick one way to feel and then stick with it. When you need a High in Spirit magic to tell you what's going on with them at any particular moment, things are definitely out of hand."

Jovvi's laugh tinkled out, but it was clear she agreed with the sentiment. The back and forth between Tamrissa and Vallant could well drive all the rest of them crazy, and probably would have if not for what they still had ahead of them. At the moment they were gently forcing a way through the crowds just in front of the palace gates, and

Nome Herstan, captain of the guard contingent they'd captured in Widdertown, had been perfectly right. There *were* no guardsmen protecting entry to the palace, not any longer.

Once they'd gotten through the gate, progress was a bit easier. Only some of the people had ventured onto the palace grounds themselves, and they now stood in a cluster to one side of the gate. If the rest of the crowd had followed they would probably have stormed the palace yelling and screaming, but with less than a dozen of them in number they didn't quite have the nerve to attack the place where the Seated Five were waiting. They eyed the newcomers as Lorand and the others dismounted, hoping to find something that would send them forward with screams to loot and destroy, but that wasn't going to happen.

"Captain Herstan, take some of your men and get those people back through the gate," Lorand heard Vallant say. Vallant tended to miss very little, and actually did make an extremely good military leader. "Explain to them that we'll be too busy to protect them if the Five decide to destroy them before attackin' *us*, but make sure your men are alert. If those fools try to resist, use whatever force is necessary to throw them out."

Herstan took one section of his guardsmen and headed for the group of people, and Vallant turned his attention to his own group.

"We need to do a bit of reconnoiterin' before we go in there," he said as he glanced around. "The future centerin' around this confrontation was still very unclear this mornin' when we Blended, but maybe it's cleared up a bit by now."

"Are we wise to actually go *into* the palace?" Rion asked mildly with nothing but curiosity behind the question. "The closer we take our bodies, the more our entity will be handicapped by needing to protect them."

"That all depends on how deep inside that place the Five are," Vallant replied, gesturing toward the palace. "The farther our entity has to go, the more strength it will use up before we even get to any fightin'. Let's see if we can locate them, and then we can decide."

That seemed to be the most sensible way to do it, so Lorand and the others quickly agreed. Their link groups had already formed up around them, which meant that in another moment their entity was born again to float toward the palace.

The entity was, as ever, pleased to be cohesive and active again, but this time it felt somewhat perplexed. Most of the many shadows representing the future were still present, but some few had clarified to less than a handful of choices. The entity floated quickly into the heart of the palace, saw what it needed to, then floated out again. On the way it passed a flesh form which had been making its slow way out to the entity's own flesh forms, a newcomer who was extremely frightened. As it carried a small, sealed envelope, the entity realized it would be foolish to stop and question the being. That chore could be safely left to its individual flesh forms. . . .

"I wonder who that is who's creeping toward the front entrance," Lorand said once he was back to himself again. "The poor man seemed terrified, but he's still coming toward us."

"He's certainly a servant," Jovvi said, also looking toward the front entrance of the palace. "But there's still a lot of hall and lawn between him and us, and at the rate he's going he won't get here until nightfall. I think I'll hurry him a little."

"Everyone be very careful when he gets here," Naran warned, her voice trembling just a bit. "There's the possibility of some sort of danger around the man, but not necessarily *from* him. It's more involved than that—But why am I telling you this? You certainly saw it just as clearly as I did."

"Not quite as clearly," Lorand said to her, giving her a smile of reassurance. "The entity puts all of our various talents together, but it still takes practice in using those talents for someone to appreciate everything the entity sees and does. After the Blending is dissolved, I remember more about things connected with Earth magic. For things having to do with seeing into the future, we still need *your* expert interpretation."

"Expert," Naran echoed with a faint smile and a soft sound of scoffing, but it was clear the explanation had relaxed her. "Well, if I'm our expert in that area, let me repeat what I said: be careful with this man whoever he is, as there's something about him that I don't like the looks of.''

Lorand saw that even Vallant nodded his agreement to the caution, all of them apparently wise enough to know when not to dismiss a warning. Then they all gave their attention to the man who now approached at a trot, certainly through the courtesy of Jovvi's talent. She'd clearly taken him over in order to hurry him, and a pair of moments later he stood puffing and trembling before them.

"I—I bear a message from Their Excellencies," the man stuttered, holding out the sealed envelope. "I'm really no danger to you, so please don't hurt me!"

"Wait," Lorand said as Vallant automatically reached for the envelope. "There's something odd here. . . . Jovvi, you usually soothe the people you touch. Didn't you do that with *this* man?"

"As a matter of fact, I did," Jovvi agreed with an immediate frown. "And it usually works a good deal better than this, as you obviously know. Let me see what the problem is. . . . Of course, how could I have missed it? He's been conditioned to continue being frightened. Tell us what your orders were, my friend."

"I—I was s-simply told to deliver this envelope," the man replied, his speech still disjointed and uneven, his arm still outstretched. "I d-don't know *anything* else, I s-swear I don't!"

"He's telling the truth about *that* part of it," Jovvi said, something Lorand already knew. "Whatever the rest is, no one saw the need to let him in on it. There seems to be a trap here, but what *sort* of trap?"

"It has to do with that envelope," Tamrissa said at once, not the least doubt in her voice. "People tend to dismiss those who are frightened, automatically considering them of no threat in any possible way. That would extend to what the frightened offer, so we're supposed to take that envelope without questioning it."

"Which means the danger is in the envelope, not in the man carrying it," Rion summed up, staring at the thing the way they all were. "Why don't you open it for us, my friend, and then we can see what's inside."

"No—oh no—I *can't* open it!" the servant responded,

fear now clearly turning to panic. "I—I'm not supposed to do anything with it but bring it out to *you*, I'm not even supposed to *think* about opening it—!"

"All right, then I'll do it for you," Rion said amiably, and the envelope came free of the man's grip—but didn't fall to the ground. "Take yourself over there to those guardsmen and stay with them, and if we require your presence we'll summon you to return."

The man hesitated for a moment, clearly uncertain about what to do, but fright won over duty and he hurried over to where Captain Herstan and his men were chasing off the last of the people who had come through the gate. Lorand kept half an eye on the man until Herstan had him under guard, and then he was able to give the message itself his full attention.

Rion, using his talent to handle the envelope, broke the seal and opened it. It was now possible to see the paper inside, and one look was all Lorand needed.

"Watch out for that faint, yellowish coating on the paper," he warned sharply. "It's a poison, and a rather nasty one. It works just as well if you breathe it in or get it on your skin, and the antidote for it isn't easy to make."

"Don't worry, I have a bubble of air surrounding the whole thing," Rion said in a distracted voice while the others made sounds of understanding or annoyance, depending on their individual personalities. "I've just discovered that I can work *through* the bubble, even though it's hardened enough to keep whatever is on that paper from reaching us. Now let's see what the note says—if anything."

The paper slid out of the envelope with the same ease as the envelope had been opened, and then it unfolded itself. Inside there was indeed some writing, and Tamrissa stepped forward to read it aloud.

" 'To those who dare to challenge our properly earned positions,' " she recited, scorn in her voice. "Oh, right, properly earned. 'We tell you now that you haven't a chance of besting us any more than you did the first time we faced one another, especially as we've decided not to oppose you as a Blending. If you insist on continuing to break the law, you will have to do it as individuals. That won't be quite as easy as hiding in a group, will it? Of course it won't, which is why we refuse to meet you any other way. If you have the stomach to face the defeat which awaits you, come ahead and meet your fate. If not, just go back to the gutters you came from.' And it's signed, *The Seated Five*. As the old saying goes, they have more nerve than an aching tooth.''

''They're deliberately baitin' us, and I'd like to know why,'' Vallant said, more thoughtful than angry. ''If I had to guess I'd say they don't *want* us to leave, otherwise they would have given us a more dignified way to withdraw. Leavin' now would be 'goin' back to our gutters,' and no one who got this far could be expected to do that.''

''I agree with that completely, but the reason behind it is perfectly clear,'' Jovvi said, a small line of thought between her brows. ''They don't want the threat we represent hanging over their heads, so they've decided to vanquish us right now. There are certain to be more traps waiting for us inside the palace, but what *I* don't understand is this part about us meeting them individually. Why would they insist on something like that, and why would they think we would believe them and do the same?''

''If they're doing it, it's because it gives them some sort of advantage over us,'' Lorand said, offering the only possible—and logical—answer. ''They know something—or believe they know something—we don't, so they're insisting on individual combat. And as far as why we would do the same goes. . . . If we know for certain that they won't be Blending, *can* we Blend against them? It would hardly be fair, and even if the rest of the world believes we bested them fair and square, we'll know better and hate ourselves.''

''So the main question now is, *will* they be Blendin'?'' Vallant said, looking around to see that everyone agreed with Lorand as reluctantly as he clearly did. None of them liked the idea, but none of them was able to argue with it. ''And if they *don't* start out Blendin', how can we be sure they won't change tactics in the middle of those 'individual combats?' ''

''We couldn't be sure, so we'd have to take precautions,'' Jovvi said, obviously as reluctant as everyone else.

"We would keep a light link between ourselves, while one of our secondary Blendings kept a careful watch on the proceedings. If our enemy tried to Blend and attack us without warning, the secondary could delay them while we ourselves Blended. That's if we do decide to go through with this because we believe they'll at least start out facing us individually."

"Do we have a choice other than to take them at their word?" Rion asked, his expression wry. "I would sooner take the word of an animal in a barnyard, but I believe that our aim is to *prove* that their place rightfully belongs to us. How else are we to manage that, save by defeating them no matter *how* badly they cheat?"

"I wish I had an answer to that question," Tamrissa said with a sigh. "I trust them even less than the rest of you, but there doesn't seem to be another way out. Let's admit defeat in the idea department, and get on with telling the other Blendings what we intend to do."

"But let's have *all* the secondary Blendin's watch what happens," Vallant said with one hand raised, his words stopping the general movement which had begun. "That way if one of them is distracted, the others will be there to take over. And we all have to be ready to Blend even faster than we usually do."

Once again there was nothing for the rest of them to argue with, so Vallant had Captain Herstan's men open the gates to let the rest of their people in. Lorand was the first to notice that it had begun to drizzle, which meant they all walked the rather long distance across the front lawns to the palace, went inside, and then had their discussion. Or, rather, their lecture. Vallant told everyone what they were about to do and why, and what they all wanted the rest of them to do. A few members from the other Blendings told them they were crazy, but none of them refused to help and all of them assured the group that they would watch with every ounce of attention their entities were capable of.

"I suppose that does it," Lorand said once there was nothing left to tell or ask anyone. "Now what we need is a guide to where the wings of the palace separate. That *is* where we saw those five, isn't it? In their individual wings?

The entity moved too fast for me to remember what direction it took.''

"I can direct us that far," Rion said, his hand wrapped firmly around Naran's. "I've been here often enough to know that much—but there's no need for Naran to go with us. You can stay here, my love, with the others, and—"

"And keep myself safe while you risk your life?" Naran interrupted, for once not the least softness visible in her expression. "No, Rion, that *isn't* the way it's going to be. I'll be there right beside you, and what happens to you will happen to me. I insist.''

Rion looked at her with raised brows, but Lorand couldn't help grinning. There was really very little difference between Naran and the other women of their Blending, but Rion was only just now finding that out.

"Very well, my love, if that's your wish," Rion surrendered with a sigh. Then he put his arm around her and began to lead off, and Lorand hesitated only a moment before following. Now it started . . . the beginning of the end. . . .

THIRTY-SIX

Jovvi walked close to Lorand as they all moved up the very wide corridor of the palace, feeling better just from being near him. The last time they'd been in that place there had been hundreds of other people around, guests like themselves at the party, servants by the score, guardsmen standing their posts. Now the entire palace felt empty to their senses, the marble halls echoing to the sounds of their footsteps but otherwise silent and dead. There *were* other living beings in that vast and neatly laid out maze, but not close enough—or large enough in number—to make much of a difference.

But Rion was there to guide them through the wide halls, and he did so with an offhand ease that delighted Jovvi. He was well on the way to becoming a marvelous human being, one who enjoyed the strength of his skill but who never flaunted it or used its presence as a claim to superiority. Naran *was* the perfect match for him, and for the rest of them as well. Now that Tamma and Vallant seemed to have gotten past most of their personal difficulties, they all did blend as well in their lives as they did with their talents.

Which added another leg to the claim that they were the Chosen Blending, the ones spoken about in the Prophecies. They'd all tried to avoid thinking and talking about that, but that didn't make the claim go away. Nor did it tell them what they were supposed to do afterward, if they managed to have an afterward. They were in the process of trying to unseat the Seated Five, but not one of them really wanted to take their place. If another group stepped forward to be Seated, that would be perfectly fine with *them*. As long as they could all stay together. . . .

Jovvi sighed as they turned into a cross corridor, fairly certain that if they survived they would not be allowed to live private lives. People were strange when it came to something like a prophecy, most especially when "things" happened to show who the people involved were. Of course there would always be those who doubted, but how much good that would do them remained to be seen. All the rest would insist that they become a traditional Seated Five, doing things in what had become the customary way.

But one of the customary ways entailed there not being any children born to a Five. Jovvi wanted children, and was reasonably certain that Tamma and Naran felt just as she did. If any individuals told them that that couldn't be, those individuals would change their minds just as fast as Jovvi was able to take control of them. But it wasn't possible to take control of an entire city, not to mention an empire, and Jovvi wouldn't have done something like that even if she could have. If people really wanted them to be the new leaders of the empire, those people would have to be prepared to accept change rather than tradition. . . .

Considering the tenor of her thoughts, Jovvi felt the urge to laugh at herself. Although they'd been walking for quite a few minutes, they hadn't even reached the place where the various wings began yet. After that would come the confrontations, and only if they survived those would the questions of change and acceptance become relevant. To think about those questions now was more than foolish, it was downright dangerous. If she let herself be distracted now, she could very well be doing herself out of a later.

So Jovvi made the effort to put all extraneous thought out of her mind, and concentrated on what lay before them. At the moment there was nothing but more empty corridor, but five minutes later that abruptly changed.

"This is the area where the wings of the Five radiate away from the public areas of the palace," Rion said, nodding toward a wide, round lobby with five corridors leading off in five different directions. "The last time I was here, there were a dozen or more servants moving on errands or standing around waiting to do things for those with power and position and access to the Five. There were also guards, and somehow I expected at least that to have remained unchanged."

"They must have done somethin' really good to chase away the entire guard force," Vallant commented as he looked around. "And they *are* all gone, or our entity would have noticed them. So which of them is in which wing?"

"*That* I'm afraid I don't know," Rion admitted, also looking from one radiating corridor to the next. "That woman usually left me here while she called on whichever of the Five she'd come to see, and the servants were kept busy fetching ice cream and sweets to divert me from the wait. And the wait was never less than two hours, many times twice that. I often wondered why she brought me along if all I was permitted to do was to sit twiddling my thumbs, but now, of course, it's perfectly obvious."

"She always needed someone to be impressed with how important she was, even if that someone was only her supposed son," Jovvi said, impressed herself by how far Rion had come with finally seeing the woman he'd grown up thinking of as his mother. "She really is pathetic, Rion, and you're more than fortunate to be able to understand that."

"Oh, I do understand, but I'm not certain that I'm able to forgive her," Rion said, as openly as always. "That old saying which claims that to understand all is to forgive all is nonsense, as it can't possibly apply to human emotions. That woman stole something from me which can never be replaced: the possibility of growing up in a normal way with a parent who really loved me. It's possible that my father *wouldn't* have loved me, that he might even have abandoned me, but because of her I'll never know. Even if the man is still alive and I somehow manage to find him, I'll still never know."

"If we survive this, maybe the Guild will be able to help us locate him," Lorand suggested as he put a hand to Rion's shoulder, and Jovvi could feel the echo of empathy in Lorand's mind. "It's something we'll have to remember, but for right now we need a way to decide who goes to which wing. Of course, we can find out easily enough if we Blend for a minute or two. . . ."

The way Lorand let his words trail off, it was perfectly clear that he already knew the reason why Vallant shook his head.

"If we do that, someone can claim we were cheatin'," Vallant said with a sigh. "If we're goin' to do this we have to do it right, otherwise we might as well just Blend and destroy them from here. Those of the nobility who are left will be lookin' for an excuse to regain their power by puttin' us down, and if we ignore them and just forge on ahead we'll be startin' a habit of people gettin' what they want by breakin' the rules. It doesn't make much sense to go through all this just to have the empire fall apart because of a bad example."

"So how are we supposed to know which way to go?" Tamma asked, somewhat less belligerently than usual. "There aren't any signs over the archways saying which wing belongs to which aspect."

"Maybe I can help," Naran said, her tone odd as she looked from one to the other of the archways. "I've been standing here watching . . . almost-ghosts of all of us, each of them taking a different corridor. The odd thing is that the picture is almost clear, showing that there's very little chance of our doing anything else. We *could* take one direction together or turn around and leave the way we came in, but the probabilities say we're most likely to each take a different direction. Shall I point out who goes where?''

''You might as well,'' Tamma told her with a partial smile, not as confident on the inside as she tried to show on the surface. ''If we don't find some way to make the decision, we could end up standing here until we die of old age.''

''I doubt if that's one of the likelier possibilities,'' Lorand said to Tamma with a grin, then he turned to Naran. ''Why don't you show me my direction, and then I can start us off.''

Naran complied by pointing to the left, so Lorand nodded his thanks then reached over to take Jovvi in his arms.

''I'm rushing things because I want this over with and behind me as quickly as possible,'' he told her in a whisper before touching her lips with his. ''Be as careful as you possibly can be, my love, and don't let them get away with anything. I want *both* of us to survive this.''

Jovvi smiled and nodded, and then joined Lorand in a temporary kiss goodbye. She couldn't have spoken for anything imaginable, not with that terrible burning in her throat, and then, after a final embrace, Lorand was gone. Jovvi watched as he strode into the corridor Naran had pointed to, and after a moment he disappeared into the distance.

''Well, I'm next,'' Tamma announced, glancing around to show that she was definitely not prepared to hear argument on the subject. ''The sooner we begin, after all, the sooner we'll be finished.''

''Don't be in such a hurry that *you* get finished,'' Vallant said after Naran indicated the proper corridor, turning Tamma around to face him. ''We have some unfinished business waitin' for us, and if you don't show up I'll just have to start thinkin' of you as a coward.''

''Anything but that,'' Tamma came back with a grin, putting up one hand to touch his face gently. ''Besides, I think you're getting to the point of needing another really close shave. Just make sure that I'm the only one who gives it to you.''

Vallant matched her grin for a brief moment, and then they were in the midst of sharing a kiss and an embrace. Unfortunately for Vallant the kiss didn't last any longer than Jovvi's had, and then Tamma was hurrying away in the proper direction without looking back.

"All right, it's now become my turn," Vallant said gruffly as he forced himself to take his eyes away from where Tamma had gone. "And the rest of you better be just as careful as I told *her* to be. We still have a lot to learn about Blendin', and we'll only be able to do that if we all get out of this in one piece.''

"In one *live* piece," Jovvi felt compelled to add, not about to let Vallant get away without an extra warning of his own. "Live and undamaged and happy and all the rest of the necessities of life. And now it's *my* turn."

Naran smiled as she showed Jovvi the proper corridor, and then Jovvi kissed Rion while Vallant did the same with Naran. Jovvi then exchanged a hug with Naran while Vallant and Rion shook hands, and lastly she and Vallant gave each other a quick kiss. All this finicky delay was another manifestation of what had sent Lorand and Tamma away without hesitation, Jovvi knew, all of it being reactions of nervousness and tension. If they'd really had the choice they would never have been doing this, but free, uncomplicated choice had been left a far distance behind them—if they'd ever really had it.

Once Jovvi entered the corridor Naran had indicated, she felt slightly better rather than worse. Why being completely alone should make her feel that way she didn't know, unless it was because her mind had flashed back to her childhood. She'd been completely alone most of the time back then, and the state had caused her to do her absolute, utmost best in order to survive. Learning to depend on no one else but yourself can become a good thing—as long as you don't try to carry it too far.

But those were distracting and therefore dangerous thoughts, so Jovvi pushed them away and concentrated on the area she walked through. There were a large number of doors to either side of the corridor at first, at least until she reached the first cross corridor. Then the distance between doors grew larger, and much more expensive decorations hung on the walls and stood on podia and small tables. Priceless tapestries and gold figurines, delicate glass flowers in silver vases, and tiny, exquisite statuettes, they were all marvelous to look at but none of it seemed newly placed. So these things had been left by the previous resident of the wing, and the current resident hadn't added a personal touch to them. Odd, for a Spirit magic user, since the balance of the whole was just the least bit off. . . .

It was possible that this member of the newly Seated Five had been too busy to worry about redecoration, but the situation still bothered Jovvi. That slight lack of balance would have driven *her* insane, and she would have had to stop to fix it no matter what else was going on. It wouldn't have taken long, after all, so there was really no reason for it to be there.

And Jovvi had located the place where the resident of that wing waited, but the woman wasn't alone. Another woman waited with her, and the second woman didn't seem to be a servant. It had been a while since Jovvi and the others had faced the members of the enemy Blending and a lot had happened in the interim, but somehow she didn't remember the Spirit magic user of that other group being female. And there was no indication that the woman was even opened to the power, not to mention touching it. Jovvi knew she was being waited for, but why wasn't there more readiness in evidence . . . ?

If the whole thing was designed to throw Jovvi off guard, the situation accomplished the exact opposite. Jovvi's suspicions grew rather than lessened, and she paused to locate the nearest source of additional power. Her tandem link groups were spread out all over the place against a possible need, and she quickly located one set which wasn't at all familiar to her. Well, some of the people in their very large number of followers weren't very well known to her and the others, especially the ones who weren't Highs. These link group members were no more than Middles, but if a crisis arose they would certainly do.

Satisfied that she was as thoroughly prepared as it was

possible to be, Jovvi continued to walk again. The people waiting for her weren't very far away now, only a short distance up that very corridor. So she walked that short distance, paused in front of the closed door behind which the people stood, then she took a deep breath and plunged in. The sooner begun, the sooner ended. . . .

Opening the door showed Jovvi a rather large and ornate sitting room, one it must have cost a fortune to decorate. Most of the furnishings consisted of antiques, marvelously preserved and lovingly taken care of. But not by the woman—or girl—who shot to her feet as soon as Jovvi walked in.

"What are *you* doing here?" the girl snarled, her stare withering. "You servants were told to stay out of this area, and that disobedience would get you whipped. If you thought I was joking, you'll find out differently as soon as I'm free to give you the attention you've now earned."

"No wonder there aren't any servants left in this wing of the palace," Jovvi commented dryly as she glanced around. "Your winning personality would have *demons* fighting to get away from you. And now I know why your companion seemed familiar to me from a distance. Why is that Mardimil woman here?"

"You can't be one of *them*," the girl returned with a frown and a small headshake. "Your clothes are mere rags, I can't detect any talent in you at all, and you certainly aren't that Mardimil clod. Tell me who you are."

"I'm Jovvi Hafford, and I'm definitely one of *them*," Jovvi answered, suddenly getting an idea. "And now I think I know what's going on. You expected Rion to be here to face you and your Air magic, and that's why you have that woman with you. You expected to use her against Rion, to give you an edge that might let you defeat him. Too bad it wouldn't have worked even if Rion *had* shown up instead of me."

"I expect to see my son this instant!" the Mardimil woman pronounced as she got to her feet, showing the sort of regality which beat you over the head with her presence and importance. "You are and mean nothing, girl, and I demand that Clarion be sent for at once!"

"His name is Rion, and you no longer have any claim

on him whatsoever," Jovvi took a great deal of pleasure in telling the woman. "He knows you stole him from his father when his true mother died giving birth to him, so his last tie to you has been severed. As far as he's concerned *you're* the nothing, the same useless, positionless, nothing everyone else sees you as. You could have had the loyalty and love of a son to sustain you no matter what the rest of the world thought of you, but you threw it all away to *impress* him and cater to your own whims. You really earned what you're getting now, so I hope you enjoy it."

The woman had started to go pale at the first of Jovvi's words, and by the time the speech ended Rion's former mother was as white as a sheet. And her face was twisted with inner pain and torment, not to mention a raging battle of some sort. Jovvi had no idea why that would be—until the woman began to mutter.

"But that *can't* be true, not any of it!" Mardimil husked out, clearly talking to herself. "He's as much mine as he ever was, so when I take my revenge against him it will give him twice as much pain! He *can't* know what she claims he does, nor can he feel as she says. He's *mine*, and I'm the most important woman in this empire!"

"Important!" the Air magic user echoed with a short, derisive laugh, staring at Mardimil with scorn and contempt. "You were good for nothing but to be used as a hostage against that clod you raised, and now you're even useless for that. Keep quiet and stay out of the way, or you'll get what *that* female has earned."

The girl glared at Jovvi as she shoved Mardimil away from her, and the older woman staggered and then fell into the chair she'd been sitting in. Jovvi could tell that she was a good way into shock, but she really was unimportant. It was the younger woman who had to be given full attention, which Jovvi did.

"I'm Selendi Vas, Air magic, and you were a fool to come in here to face me," the girl now said, the words somewhat calm and even—despite the turmoil fighting to begin in her mind. "Didn't you people get the note we sent?"

"Of course we did," Jovvi replied, having a suspicion of what this Selendi Vas was now trying to do. "We all saw it, and we paid it every bit of the attention it deserved—which is to say, none at all. You and your groupmates don't belong here, and you know it as well as we do. If you surrender to me, we may be able to preserve your life.''

"If I were you, I'd be worrying about my own life," Selendi crowed, full delight now on her. "You say you all saw the note we sent, which means most if not all of you touched it. I can tell you now that there was poison on the paper, so in a very short while you'll no longer have a Blending to be part of. Are *you* one of the ones who touched it, or will you just be one of those left alive after the others die?''

"Neither," Jovvi responded pleasantly, probing toward the girl even as she spoke. "I said we saw your note, not that we touched it. Our Earth magic user noticed the poison, so our Air magic user—Rion—opened the thing for us without using his hands. Could *you* have done something like that?''

"I don't believe you," the girl snarled, but her mind said she certainly did believe and would have been devastated—if she weren't under strict control. Their Spirit magic user had been busy, then, doing things he shouldn't even have done to strangers. To put your own groupmates under control . . . ! Jovvi began to unravel his work, but there were still other things to say.

"Yes, you do believe me, and you may not know the entire story," Jovvi said with a bit more sobriety. "We've learned that you and some of your groupmates *have* been poisoned, and you've been holding off the effects of the poison by using a counteragent. Our Earth magic user, who's something of an expert, tells us that the counteragent can't be used for more than a short while before it becomes ineffective. After that you have to have the antidote, or the poison will kill you. As I said before, if you surrender we may be able to save your lives.''

The unraveling of control which Jovvi had done in the girl's mind let Selendi pale and begin to tremble. The girl was now beginning to see the true situation she found herself in, and her thoughts began to turn frantic.

"I knew he was lying to us, I knew it!" she shrilled out,

terror fighting to take her over. "And I'll bet he even has the antidote, which he'll dangle in front of us once the counteragent stops working! I hate him more than I've ever hated anyone except my sister, and *she* stole Father from me! But I can't afford to displease him, or I won't be given the antidote. I hate him, but I still have to do what he wants me to. . . ."

And with that she turned a crazed glare on Jovvi, a completely unstable girl doing what she thought was necessary in order to survive. Jovvi could see that clearly, but what she couldn't do suddenly was breathe. Selendi Vas had taken away the air Jovvi needed to live, and the girl's mindset clearly showed that she would continue on until her enemy was dead.

Jovvi had been trying to unravel the control around the girl's mind in order to establish her own, temporary control, but there were too many layers of command in the way. If she'd had the time she could have gotten through, but now time had run out as quickly as her air supply. If Jovvi didn't do something quickly, she *would* be dead . . . !

In another moment or two, Jovvi knew she would begin to black out. That was inevitable, so whatever could be done had to be done *now*. So she first reached to the tandem link group she'd found earlier and began to draw strength from them, and then turned her talent on the Mardimil woman. Mardimil sat deeply sunk into shock, most of her defenses—and sanity—gone, but it wasn't possible for her to resist Jovvi's commands. The older woman straightened and then stood, turned to look at Selendi Vas, and then she struck the younger woman with a closed fist and all the strength in her round, overweight body.

The blow landed in the middle of Selendi's face, and the pain and surprise threw the girl completely out of control. The air returned around Jovvi as suddenly as it had disappeared, and she bent over to lean against a table and gasp while she fought off threatening dizziness. She'd come *that* close to passing out, and the ringing in her ears said it could still happen. But if she didn't regain control and balance it was still possible she might die, so fainting was completely out of the question.

It took a reasonably short time for Jovvi to pull herself

together, which was fortunate for Selendi Vas. Jovvi had set the Mardimil woman in attack on the Air magic user, and the command continued to hold. Mardimil was beating at the girl who now lay on the priceless carpeting, and when Jovvi canceled the command and sent the older woman back to her chair, Selendi Vas was barely conscious. But she *was* still alive and no longer a threat, so Jovvi found a chair of her own and sat down to finish the work she'd begun.

When all those layers of command had been stripped away from the girl's mind, Jovvi inserted the command for Selendi to stay there in the room and not make any more trouble. Then she got to her feet and headed back to the corridor she'd come in by, anxious to find out how the others were doing. The Mardimil woman had returned to being sunk in shock, but she, too, had been ordered to stay put. Later Jovvi and the others could decide what to do with the two of them, but right now there were much more important concerns—like how the unequal confrontations were turning out. . . .

Selendi Vas lay on her back, her semiconscious mind streaming in all directions. It was almost as though she were half asleep, and the condition was *so* familiar. Pain throbbed in her body and she lay on something hard rather than soft, just the way things had been when she was much younger. Those were the times when Father had come to visit her, to give her all his love and attention. For a long time it had been her sister who had gotten that love and attention, but then it had become *her* turn. She'd hated the pain and that other thing Father did, but it was worth it just to have him be with her so much.

But then she'd gotten a bit older, and one day her sister managed to regain Father's attention. Selendi tried to bring him back to *her* instead, but she'd never been able to accomplish it. He'd never given her that sort of attention again, and she'd spent years going through man after man in an effort to feel that special once more. But it hadn't worked, it never worked, and Selendi hated her sister more

than anyone in the world for having stolen what Selendi
needed and wanted so badly. . . .

A particularly violent stab of pain in her middle brought
Selendi closer to true consciousness, close enough for her
to wonder why she felt that particular pain. She'd taken the
counteragent that morning, after all, and wasn't due to take
it again until tomorrow. So why did the pain feel just like
what it had before she'd been given the counteragent? It
didn't make any sense. . . .

And then a terrible thought came to Selendi, one which
filled her with a great deal of fear. That woman she'd faced,
one of *them*. . . . She'd said that the counteragent would begin to stop working, and then the poison would begin to
kill her. Selendi moaned with terror and increasing pain,
trying to figure out what to do. Delin had to have the antidote she needed, but he was so far away. And she hadn't
done what she was supposed to have, which was kill the
one of *them* she faced. She would have to use her body
again to get what she needed, just as she'd always used
it. . . .

Selendi rolled over onto her stomach in an effort to ease
the pain in her middle, but it didn't help. The pain was
quickly turning into agony, bringing her knees up and putting a scream in her throat. It hurt so *much*, she didn't know
how she was going to give Delin what he wanted . . . even
though she didn't *want* to give it to him. . . . She'd already
had him, and there were so many other men she hadn't yet
gotten to. *One* of them would be like her father, one of
them *had* to be. . . .

The scream in Selendi's throat tried to escape, but she
only had the strength to make it a moan. She now hurt
more and more and more, and the silly thought of what it
might be like to be loved flitted for an instant across her
mind. And then the thought was gone behind the sole
awareness of pain unending, worse than the pain she'd begun to be given at the age of six. It filled her entire mind
and consciousness to the exclusion of everything else—

—and didn't even let her notice it when she slipped over
the edge into death. . . .

THIRTY-SEVEN

Rion watched Jovvi until she disappeared from sight, made sure that Vallant was also definitely on his way, and then he turned to Naran.

"Well, my love, it seems that it's finally become *our* turn," he said with the best smile he was able to produce. "Are you certain I can't talk you into waiting for me here? It would ease my mind a very great deal. . . ."

He let his words end in a half-question, willing to use any means to keep Naran safe, but her sigh as she shook her head contained nothing of doubt or hesitation.

"Easing your mind is my foremost desire, my love, but my remaining behind won't accomplish it," she said with true regret—but no apology. "My talent tells me that I'll be perfectly safe, so you needn't worry on that account. You, however, are another matter entirely, and if I'm forced to wait for you here I'll be out of my mind by the time you return. Do you want me to be out of my mind?"

"You're much better versed at using this kind of tactics, my love," Rion surrendered with his own sigh as he took her hand. "With that in view, we might as well go seeking the one who waits for me. Does your talent have any idea *where* that one waits?"

"As a matter of fact, it does," she replied as they began to walk toward the only unused corridor. "I know just where you're supposed to go, but there's something odd about the location. It isn't a place where only one person is waiting, there are more like three. What sort of trap can *that* be?''

''I have no idea, but we'll certainly find out,'' Rion replied, discovering that he really was a good deal more calm now that he was able to finally get down to it. And he was also finally getting to see the part of the palace which had always been denied him before. How odd that was, to walk these corridors as a man, but not as a visitor. As a child, he'd been more wistful than resentful over having been left behind. . . .

Rion glanced into one or two of the empty rooms they passed, expecting to see superb decoration and taste. These were the precincts of one of the Five, after all, and everyone knew that the Five lived a good deal better than even the highest lord. What Rion saw was certainly beautiful and well kept, but nothing he couldn't have seen even in the houses in which *he'd* grown up. So that was another lie the woman had told him, that he couldn't be permitted to accompany her because of the irreplaceable possessions of the Five. A clumsy child might ruin them, she'd said, and although her Clarion wasn't deliberately destructive, he did have his little accidents every now and then. . . .

''That woman made a point of mentioning how clumsy and awkward *I* was just so that no one would notice her own shortcomings,'' Rion said aloud, finally seeing that part of it more clearly. ''No wonder she took me almost everywhere she went. People were so busy resenting my intrusion, they hadn't the time to see how badly *she* did.''

''People like that aren't really as confident as they pretend to be, my love,'' Naran answered as her hand tightened around his. ''On the inside they're often afraid they aren't as good as they're supposed to be, so they belittle others to disguise their own lacks—usually mostly from themselves. Don't let the thought of her disturb you.''

Considering the situation, Rion decided to take that very sound advice. So he put all thought of that woman aside for later contemplation, and gave his full attention to the areas where they walked. The wing was large and much of it was hidden behind closed doors, but eventually they approached one closed door which made Naran slow and stop.

''I believe that that's the place, my love,'' she said, staring at the closed door. "Can you detect anything your-self?"

"There are three displacements of air inside the room which ought to represent three human beings," Rion replied as he looked around. "You seem to have been correct about that, but I haven't been able to find any other indication of human presence in quite some distance. That makes me curious to learn what sort of trap this might be."

And with that Rion moved ahead alone, telling Naran without words that she was to enter, if at all, only behind him. The sweet girl compromised to that extent, at least, and followed him without protest. What a marvelous thing it was, to have a woman who truly was one with you. . . .

Opening the door revealed a large, well-appointed sitting room, and all three of the people within it came to their feet at his appearance. Rion recognized the two older people as Tamrissa's parents, but it was the one he didn't really know who spoke.

"What in blazes are *you* doing here, Mardimil?" the man demanded, his annoyance obvious. "I've been waiting for someone else entirely!"

"Then that must mean you're their Fire magic user," Rion said with sudden insight, now understanding why Tamrissa's parents were present. "Were you foolish enough to believe that *they* would give you some sort of hold over Tamrissa? Don't you have any idea of how she feels about those two pieces of offal?"

"One of them is less than that," Naran put in suddenly while the Fire magic user—a Lord Bron something, Rion finally recalled—scowled and the two others began to sputter indignantly. "That man is the one I told you about, the wealthy man who decided he wanted me for his use alone. I have no idea *how* much gold he spent sending men to chase after me, but happily every copper of it was wasted."

"He did *what*?" the woman demanded, turning to look at her husband with the deadliest daggers Rion had ever seen. "He spent *my* gold on *what*?"

"Nonsense, my dear, the trollop is lying," the man replied, charm and ease fairly oozing out of him. "They're simply trying to make trouble between us, which will certainly be to their benefit."

"Why would we care about making trouble for *you* people?" Naran countered with a sound of ridicule, more confident and self assured than Rion had ever seen her. "You don't count for anything at all in this, not as unimportant as *you* are. And you needn't take *my* word for what I've said. I'm not the first or only girl he's gone after, so you can ask any of the others."

"The others," the woman growled, not having moved her glare even a single inch from her husband. "And you needn't bother wasting all that charm on me, Storn Torgar. The more you use it the more you're lying, and if *I* don't know that, no one in this world does."

"No, no, my dear, you're quite mistaken," Torgar tried, his smile having turned sickly. "There's not an ounce of truth to what the woman says, so you must continue to put your trust in me. I am, after all, your husband, so—"

"You're my husband *now*," the woman interrupted in frosty tones, clearly not swayed in the least. "If we manage to survive this horrible mess, we'll soon see how quickly that can be changed and I can be gone. And we'll also see how much I can take with me of that fortune you're so proud of."

For Torgar, the true horror obviously lay in what his wife had said. He stared at her with eyes wide and mouth feebly trying to protest, and the man Bron Something made a sound of scornful impatience.

"Now that the truly weighty matters have been settled, let's get back to the negligible reason we're here in the first place," he said to Rion. "You and your friends got our note, I trust?"

"If you're about to break the news about the poisoned paper, you're a bit late," Rion responded with a faint smile, wondering how anyone called noble could ever have impressed him as superior. "Our Earth magic user has already done it for you, happily before any of us touched it. I'm not surprised that your own Earth magic user didn't warn you that that might happen. We've been told that he also failed to keep the rest of you from being poisoned yourselves, and he may not even have let you know how little time you actually have left."

"What do you mean, how little time we have left?" the

man demanded, his frown tinged faintly with fear. "We're perfectly all right—with the help of our Earth magic user—and we're going to stay that way."

"Not with the counteragent rather than the antidote you aren't," Rion disagreed with a headshake. "The counteragent works only for a little while, and then you need the antidote or you die. It occurs to me that *we* might help you get that antidote—if you decide to be intelligent about this confrontation thing. If you refuse, I'll have no choice but to do my best to destroy you."

"*You*, destroy *me*?" the man said with a snort of ridicule, immediately stiffening at the prior suggestion. "I've been given the very pleasant task of killing whomever walked in here, and that's exactly what I mean to do. You'll die like the peasant you've become, Mardimil, and once it's done I'll laugh long and well."

And with that a heavy curtain of fire flared, one which was meant to incinerate both Rion and Naran. Naran gasped and flinched a bit, but when neither heat nor flame was able to touch them, she understood that Rion remained completely in control. He glanced at her with a smile of reassurance, and then returned his attention to the noble.

"I haven't *become* a peasant, you fool, I was born one," he said to the man, pride widening his smile into a grin. "Since you can't possibly understand how marvelous that fact is, allow me to show you."

As it was now Rion's turn to exercise a talent openly, he added to what he'd already done. The wall of hardened air which protected them was more in the way of a sphere, and now Rion reached through that sphere to touch the so-called lord. The instant the man's air was cut off he began to choke, and the flames ravening toward them suddenly disappeared.

"Most nobles are much too good to do more than one thing at a time," Rion said, watching the husky man sink slowly to his knees. "Since I've discovered myself to be a peasant, however, it's no longer shameful for me to practice both defense and attack. What a pity you refused my earlier offer, as now I'm afraid it's been withdrawn."

Rion had added that last because the man seemed to be begging for his life without words, and to grant him the boon now would be pure foolishness. A *noble* will promise anything to save himself, Rion knew, and once that end was accomplished the promise would be promptly forgotten. No, better to let matters continue on to a proper finish, making certain that the Fire magic user never became a problem again.

"I think we can leave now," Naran murmured after another pair of moments, staring at the body of the man who now lay stretched out on the expensive carpeting. "The line of his life comes to a very abrupt end in just a few minutes, so you needn't worry about having to face him again in the future. He no longer *has* a future."

"Very well," Rion agreed with a nod as he released his hold, trusting Naran's advice implicitly, and then he turned to the two people who had cringed back when the confrontation first began. "You two are free to leave now, but allow me to offer a bit of advice. Don't ever let Tamrissa hear from or see you again, or I'll personally find you wherever you may be hiding and I'll do to you what I did to *that* one. Assuming, of course, that my Blending brothers don't make the same effort before me. . . ."

Rion showed the nastiest smile he was capable of as he let his words trail off, and the two paled and jumped a bit. Then the woman glared at her husband and sailed off toward the door, clearly intending to do as she'd promised. Obvious panic sent the man scuttling after her, his words a begging and mewling as they faded into the distance.

"You have my very great thanks for not having killed him, love," Naran said with a chuckle as she took Rion's arm. "Now he'll live to suffer in the same way he's made so many others do, and there's only the smallest, slightest chance that he'll recover from what his wife puts him through. Financially speaking, of course."

"Of course," Rion agreed, putting his hand over hers where it lay on his arm. "Being destitute will do that man no end of bad, and seeing it will do his former victims no end of good. Now let's go and see what bad and good has befallen our Blendingmates."

Naran smiled and nodded, so they headed for the door. Rion would have worried a good deal more if Naran had been upset, but since she wasn't he would do his best to emulate her. But he really did need to *know*. . . .

Bron Kallan regained consciousness slowly, his heart pounding with fear and the efforts of his lungs to resupply him with air. It was something of a shock to realize that he still lived, and the confusion in his mind added to the shock. It was as though something had broken and come loose in there, leaving his mind disoriented and floundering around. And his memories. . . .

"Yes, dear, of course you can do as you please," his mother had always told him lovingly, his father nodding his agreement. "You *are* our son, after all, so no one has the right to deny you. And *of course* it will always be that way, so you just ignore anyone trying to tell you differently."

Maybe they hadn't quite used those exact words, but Bron had known that that was what they'd meant. If his parents denied him nothing, who else would be able to? The point had seemed extremely clear to the child he'd been, but the adult he became hadn't found it to be entirely true. His parents continued to deny him nothing—for the most part—but others didn't behave the same, nor did they change their stance once Bron explained matters. More often those people laughed, and some pointed out that they were raised to expect the very same. How, then, could Bron never be denied if *they* were to be treated like that?

And those who laughed were either more powerful politically or their parents were, so there was nothing Bron could do to change matters. The excellent governmental position he'd taken for granted that he'd be given never came to be, and that had added to Bron's bitterness and resentment—and confusion. He had no idea why his parents had lied to him, but it was beyond argument that they had.

Just as Delin—and Kambil before him—had lied. They'd assured Bron that he would have no trouble besting a silly woman, and not a single word about the possibility that it would be a man he would have to face instead. A man who had had no trouble fending off his fires, a man who wasn't in the least troubled by being called a peasant.

Somehow Mardimil had learned the truth about himself, and rather than being devastated he was delighted. The man must be mad. . . .

Bron made the effort to get to his feet, but his first movement resulted in sudden agony in his middle. His first thought, that he'd hurt himself falling, was quickly dismissed, as he'd only fallen from the height of his knees. No, the pain he felt was more reminiscent of what he'd felt before Delin had given him the counteragent, but it couldn't be the poison troubling him again. He'd had his dose right on time that very morning, and shouldn't need another until—

That was when Bron remembered what Mardimil had said to him, about Delin having failed to tell him the truth. The poison and the counteragent . . . now the poison was winning again, and it would take the antidote to save his life. He had to get up and find Delin, who had probably been hiding the antidote to use as another lever against them—

Screaming agony ended Bron's second attempt to rise almost before it began, tearing him apart and forcing him into a curling on the floor. The pain was worse now, he was certain it was, but that couldn't be allowed to stop him. In a moment he *had* to get up and go looking for Delin, otherwise he might—might—

"Mother, help me!" Bron tried to scream out, but the pain had grown again. The words turned into a choked whisper, his air was taken again without Mardimil even being there, and then—

THIRTY-EIGHT

I hurried into my own corridor as fast as Lorand went into his, fully determined to get all this confrontation business over and done with. Lorand had seemed a bit more edgy than I felt, which was somewhat unusual. During the times of the tests, I'd always been just as jumpy and disturbed as he'd been. . . .

But things did change, I realized as I walked along, at least for me. I'd grown strong enough on the inside to be only a little worried about the rest of my strengths, just worried enough to keep me from arrogance. I'd been on the verge of arrogance when I'd gone out in Widdertown to face those five Fire talents alone, but I'd been saved by nearly getting myself roasted. That sort of thing makes you think once no one else is around—and once you stop not caring whether or not you're killed. I still hadn't *quite* gotten over not caring, and might not for some time to come. . . .

I sighed as I walked through corridors lined with beauty and wealth, paying less attention to the decorations than to my thoughts. Oh, I did make sure to check each room as I approached it to see if there was body heat to show occupancy, but that doesn't mean I didn't also fret about what would happen if we all won over the usurpers. Vallant had tempted me into kissing him again, but did that kiss mean anything? The incredible attraction I felt for him would never change, but what about our relationship? Would there ever really be such an animal, or would we spend the rest of our lives—however long they were—debating proper actions and feelings?

Knowing that things rarely happened just because you wanted them to, I walked along brooding about just how much effort had to be put into a relationship before it worked out. Along with that question came the one asking if I were *capable* of putting out that much effort, and the answer was that I didn't know. I could well decide to try, but would trying count if I failed? What if Vallant tried and failed? How much credit would I give *him* for making the effort? More than he gave me, or less?

It took only a few minutes of that to decide that this wasn't the time to be driving myself crazy with unanswerable questions. It would be humiliating to run smack into the enemy while muttering under my breath about having to find a daisy. The he-loves-me-he-loves-me-not game would do at least as well as I'd done with answering my questions, and right now that seemed the best—and only—way to settle the matter. Pushing it all aside for the moment and thinking about getting attacked was a positive relief, which should give a fairly accurate idea of my state of mind.

Not long after making that very wise decision, I detected two sources of heat in a room just ahead of me. I paused after making the discovery, wondering if two people meant some kind of trap, then shrugged over the matter and started to walk again. Although I hadn't been able to fight back, I'd been able to hold my own against a tandem force of five Highs in Fire magic in Widdertown. Even if there were two people waiting for me here, it shouldn't be more than slightly difficult to defeat them.

The door to the room holding the two people was closed, so I opened it and walked in. I really have no idea whom I expected to see, but finding Lorand's former friend Hat as one of them certainly wasn't part of it.

"I think you've made a mistake, young lady," the other man said as soon as he saw me, both men having come to their feet at my appearance. "One of your colleagues was meant to meet us here, so if you'll just run along and find him and then send him in your place. . . ."

"Making someone feel unwelcome doesn't necessarily

also make them feel inferior,'' I commented as I walked farther into the room. "Sometimes—like now—it makes the person wonder why you're so afraid of them that you're desperate to be rid of them. Do you really think you'll do that much better against Lorand because you have that spoiled little brat to hide behind?"

"He can hide behind me all he likes!" Hat snarled, glaring at me as though I were personally responsible for all his ills. He'd also interrupted the other man, but obviously wasn't aware of it. "I have a score to settle with that so-called friend of mine, and I'm going to—"

"You'll do nothing!" I snapped, sick to death of the little boy's tantrums. "You'll do nothing because that's all you've ever done, that and blame other people for *your* failures. You can't be a High talent just because you want to be, even though you would have deserved it. It would be perfect justice if you got what so many others have."

"What are you talking about?" he demanded, but with less force and more disturbance than he'd shown a moment ago. "Being a High talent is the best thing possible—and I *am* one—so don't try feeding me any bull. They cheated me of my place and gave it to Lorand instead, and he just let them get away with it. That means I owe him plenty, and it's time to pay up!"

"You do owe him plenty, but you're too stupid and self-involved to know it," I countered with a snort. "To begin with, if you really were a High talent, no one would have lied about it or tried to deny it. The nobles *wanted* to find High talents, you see, because they conditioned them with drugs, then sent them out to be part of the empire's armies of conquest, and generally treated them like slaves. Our group missed all that, because they happened to need people for challenging Blendings meant to face their noble Blendings. And they also needed dupes to send against their Seated Highs, people who were either not strong enough or too full of drugs to win."

The frown which creased his face was at least partially one of memory, as he'd been thrown into a competition as one of those dupes. I'd been there to see it so I'd mentioned something he couldn't simply dismiss, and yet I wasn't about to give him the chance to draw the wrong conclusion.

"But don't even *think* about trying to claim that you were drugged," I said at once. "If you had been you would have behaved differently, so that's the second proof you've refused to accept. The Seated High was only a Middle himself, just a stronger, more practiced one than you, and that's why he bested you. So that means you've been pining away for a position that was being held by someone who wasn't a High either, but someone who didn't stand around crying about the lack."

That comment made him look as though I'd slapped him in the face, but only for a moment. People like him always knew what they knew, and getting them to change their minds took more comments than just one.

"That still doesn't let Lorand off the hook," he said after the moment, his face twisting again from that little-boy anger. The man who stood beside him, the one I'd really come to see, simply stood and listened, an expression of droll amusement on his face. After he'd been interrupted that first time he'd made no effort to curtail or join our conversation, but I hadn't dismissed his presence even a little.

"Lorand still owes me for not giving me any help," Hat went on with his huffing. "After they cheated to make me lose the competition, those people gave me to someone who made me into a literal slave! I worked till I dropped and was beaten if I didn't then pick myself up and work some more, and Lorand didn't make the least effort to get me out of there!"

"The first question which comes to mind is, what makes any of that Lorand's responsibility?" I countered, folding my arms. "You were given a coach ticket to get you back home, and you cashed it in and drank up and gambled away the money. When you lost more than you had, you tried to get *yourself* out of trouble by throwing Lorand to the wolves in your place. At the time he didn't even have *copper* to give you, but you demanded gold. When they finally let him earn some gold, he paid Meerk to find you and was ready to finance your trip home out of his own pocket. He tracked you down at the competition, but once again you knew better than to listen to what he had to say, and *that's* why you ended up as a slave. Not long after that we started to have our own trouble, so why don't you tell me what *you* think Lorand could have done to save you from your own stupidity again?''

"That's not fair!" he blurted, his face flushed and his fists clenched. "It *wasn't* my fault, not any of it! Those lousy nobles cheated me, and—"

"And you're the only one who was cheated?" I interrupted, still backing him into a corner. "They cheated everyone who came past them, but some of us were able to blame ourselves for not having done anything about them sooner. You, though. . . . Name one thing in your life that turned out badly because of something that was your fault alone. We all have things like that we can point to, as all human beings make mistakes. But it takes an adult to admit to them, so let me hear you say it. You ignored Lorand's advice, and because of that stupidity you ended up being worked like a slave. Show me that you're finally becoming an adult *worthy* of having someone like Lorand as a friend, and say the words convincingly.''

Instead of saying anything at all, he just stood there staring at me with a frown. Confusion and hurt were clear in his gaze, but even then he found it impossible to admit that the trouble he'd had was his own fault. He'd probably spend his life blaming others for his ills, and die filled with bitterness that people had always let him down.

"Is the entertainment over now?" the other man said with a fey expression, looking expectantly back and forth between Hat and me. "No more accusations and protests of innocence? Isn't it odd that those who are guiltiest are always first to protest how innocent they are.''

"I've been taught that most often they actually *believe* that they're innocent," I said, joining in the game of ignoring what we were really in the middle of. "For one reason or another they can't handle the truth, so they convince themselves that what they're doing is right and proper. People don't do 'evil,' they do what's right and pleasurable and good. The trouble comes in when their definition of those things doesn't match everyone else's.''

"You know, I never thought of that," he replied, now looking interested rather than amused. "I, myself, always do what's necessary, but others rarely agree that those things are needful. So you believe that it's their definitions which are at fault?''

"If everyone disagrees with you, chances are good that it's *your* definitions which are faulty," I said, feeling as though I'd already had that conversation. "I'll grant you that that isn't always so, that it depends on who the other people are, but if you *know* you're always right, you're just as bad off as *he* is. No one is right *all* the time, and if you don't know that, you're out of touch with reality."

"Why *can't* someone be right all the time?" he countered, still speaking calmly and smoothly. "I grant you that most people aren't, but what makes it so impossible for one person out of the general herd to be perfect? Could it be envy and spite which make it impossible?"

"I'm glad we're speaking in general terms rather than talking about someone in particular, like yourself," I returned, my arms still crossed. "If you *were* silly enough to put yourself forward as perfect, I'd have to point out that a perfect man would hardly have groupmates who'd been poisoned. And that same perfect man would now be facing the person he'd expected and prepared for, not someone else entirely."

"Ah, but maybe that perfect person *wanted* his groupmates to be poisoned, so they'd be more easily controlled," he said with a grin of pure enjoyment. "Let's not forget that he himself wasn't poisoned along with everyone else, so that has to count for something. And as far as expecting someone in particular goes, that is surely *your* conclusion, not necessarily the truth. One does what one can with what one has, after all, and to a certain *lower* type of person, one hostage is often as good as another. After all, how would your precious friend Lorand feel if you were to tell him that his bosom companion was dead because of you?"

"He'd probably grieve for a while, and then he'd get on with his life," I replied, fleetingly wondering why we were still just talking. "If you think he'd blame *me* for that man's death, you've probably made the first mistake of your life. I'm not the one who brought him here, after all, and Lorand has no trouble with putting blame where it properly belongs. And as far as your *wanting* your groupmates to be poisoned, that would be your prefirst mistake. It may help you to control them now, but what will happen when the counteragent no longer works and they die? In order to save them you'd have to have the antidote, and you *don't* have it, do you?''

''When the time comes that they need the antidote, I *will* have it,'' he growled, no longer amused or even interested. ''I'm not a High practitioner in Earth magic for nothing, but let's discuss the antidote you and *your* groupmates will need. Since time is very quickly running out, where do you imagine you'll get it?''

''Mistake number three,'' I announced happily while throwing even more strength into the only defense against Earth magic I'd been able to think of. ''I hope you don't mind that I'm now numbering the mistakes correctly, but it has to be done in order to avoid confusion. None of us touched the note you sent, because Lorand saw the poison and warned us. Rion used his Air magic to open the thing and protect us, so any sort of antidote is unnecessary. But that goes only for us. If you don't want to be left without groupmates, forget about this confrontation nonsense and agree to work with Lorand. The two of you can—''

''Nonsense?'' he interrupted with more of a screech than a growl, his face twisting into something grotesque. ''This *nonsense* was *my* idea, and can't possibly fail to win us the day! Once you and the others are dead, all those stupid peasants will understand just how strong we are and will go back to where they belong without any more foolishness. We will *not* lose what we have, we will win even more—starting right here and now!''

And with that he launched his attack at me, the attack I'd been expecting from the moment I'd walked in there. I'd given him a chance to surrender, but I'd first provoked him to what I'd hoped was the point where he would refuse the offer. If any of those usurpers lived, they would be a rallying point for every member of the nobility still eager to run things *their* way. I didn't know if I'd be able to put the man down, but for the sake of all the people who had been and would be hurt, I had to try.

So I'd woven an invisible shield of Fire magic, hoping that it would have *some* effect against Earth magic. A shield like that wasn't supposed to be possible, but I *knew* there was a way for me to touch another aspect *somehow*. The knowledge had been tickling around the edges of my mind for quite a while, but I still hadn't been able to get a grip on it. And then the man's attack crashed in, and I suddenly felt as though my chest were about to explode.

"Isn't it marvelous how another person's heart attack can change a loss to a win?" the man sing-songed, a frightening smile on his face. I'd staggered and fallen to my knees, but the pain in my chest hadn't even let me notice when I hit the carpeting. "I don't know what you're doing to interfere with my talent, but it isn't quite as effective as you'd hoped it would be, is it? You're going to die in another minute or so, and there's nothing you can do to stop it."

I gasped as I began to run out of air, the pain increasing by the minute. But strangely enough that elusive idea had finally come clear, and I now knew what to do to reach the man. The only problem was that I couldn't bring my own talent to bear, not with what he was in the midst of doing to me. I had the answer, but would die before I could use it—!

And then the pain suddenly cut off, not completely but enough to make the growing spots of black in front of my eyes begin to fade a bit. I had no idea what had happened, but even as I heard an agony-filled scream start somewhere, I launched the plan I hadn't been able to use earlier. Woven *power* was the key, not woven talent, not when the talents were so different one from the other. But power was something we all used, so I built a bridge of power to the center of the man's talent, and then sent my fires along it. Why I didn't simply burn him to ash I had no idea, nor was I in any condition to worry about it. I simply did things the hard way, and a second scream sounded in place of the first.

It took some time for me to pull myself together, but the shield I'd used had apparently protected me from lasting, permanent damage. As soon as most of the shakiness left my arms and legs I forced myself to stand, and only then did I understand what had saved me long enough to win the fight. Lorand's friend Hat lay unmoving on the floor, his hands to his head, his eyes wide and bulging, his face still twisted in the scream he'd died with. He must have interposed his own talent between the other man and me, but he hadn't been strong enough to protect himself from retaliation. He'd died before my fires had burned into his murderer, which meant he'd given up his own life to preserve mine.

"It looks like something I said actually reached you," I whispered as I stared down at Hat's body, fighting to keep my emotions under control. "You risked your own life to save mine, and that's what I'll make sure Lorand knows. Now he'll be able to remember you with the love he always felt, Hat, and I promise I'll do the same. Thank you for being a worthy friend."

I couldn't stop the tears trickling down my cheeks, and wouldn't have even if I could. What Hat had done deserved the tribute of tears, so I turned and left that horrible room with a film of wetness blurring my vision, giving tribute to a man who would never again have to worry about admitting that something was his fault. . . .

Delin Moord moaned and moved a bit, then forced his eyes to open. He lay on the carpeting of the room where he'd faced that disgusting slut of Fire magic, and she seemed to have gone. She must have thought she'd killed him with that slicing edge of fire, and something inside his head throbbed with pain. But rather than being dead he was still alive, which meant that he'd be able to find her and pay her back. No slut had ever bested him, and none ever would.

Pushing himself to sitting made him dizzy, but when his vision cleared he was able to see the fool who *hadn't* escaped his just vengeance. And the man *had* been a fool to interfere, as though he were actually the High he imagined rather than the mere Middle he was. Causing a brain aneurysm had settled *his* hash in a hurry, but not soon enough to keep the slut from doing something to hurt him. He'd definitely have to get her for that, her and all her oh-so-special friends—

A sharp, stabbing pain in his middle made Delin gasp, a completely unexpected pain. And with the pain came sweat breaking out on his forehead, a shakiness to his hands, and a swift, invading chill to rattle his bones. He also noticed the dryness in his throat and mouth, and that made the matter certain. Somehow, in some way, an enemy had managed to poison *him*! He couldn't imagine when it could have been done, but the fool doing it had been stupid beyond words. The poison was one Delin was familiar with, and it would be possible to neutralize it without needing to resort to an antidote.

Delin spent a brief moment getting grim pleasure out of the thought of what he would do to the one who was guilty of causing him this extra needed effort, and then he turned to saving himself. The procedure was simple in that the poison was easily identifiable and removable in whatever part of his body it was, and once removed he would quickly return to full health. So he reached inside himself with his talent, and—

The next spasm inside his middle caused him to scream, and this time the sound had an edge of panic to it. He'd reached into himself and should have at least located the poison, but hadn't been able to see a thing. And he hadn't had the *sense* of being inside himself, a practice he was reasonably familiar with. Something was clearly wrong, but what could it possibly be . . . ?

It took a large number of minutes for Delin to finally admit the truth, and by then he lay on the carpeting again, writhing to the increasing pain in his entire body. As wildly impossible as the idea was to consider, that Fire slut had taken his talent rather than his life! She'd burned out every trace of his ability, and even though he knew exactly what could save him, he wasn't able to perform the act! How could anyone be that cruel, that horribly heartless—!

Agony now touched Delin and made him scream mindlessly, at first just with sound and then with words.

"No, Father, please don't hurt me again!" he screamed, terrified and needing to escape but knowing there *was* no escape. "It isn't right for you to hurt me, it isn't *right*!"

"Of course it's right," his father replied, just the way he'd always done. "It was right for *my* father and his friends to do it, and now it's right for me and *my* friends. And if it wasn't right, you'd be able to stop me, wouldn't you? Go ahead and stop me, Delin, go ahead and try."

And the adult Delin tried just as hard as the young Delin

had, but was just as unsuccessful. So maybe his father *had* been in the right after all, and he'd been wrong. Delin screamed again, hating that idea and hating the pain, and then all his hatred was done for all time. . . .

THIRTY-NINE

Vallant fought with himself as he walked along, trying to stop worrying about Tamrissa and simply concentrate on what lay ahead of him. Their timing had really been rotten, but he refused to let that disturb him. He and Tamrissa *would* have the opportunity to hold each other again, to make love again the way they'd done at first. He'd decided to accept no other possible outcome, and he had enough experience with being stubborn to make the decision stick.

As he walked he also examined the various things used to decorate the corridor, beautiful weavings and delicate carvings and castings. Someone with excellent taste had chosen the pieces, but that someone had also had a lot of gold to spend. On the other hand, having a lot of gold to spend doesn't guarantee that a person will be visited with sudden good taste. Tamrissa's late husband was an excellent example of how true that was, as his house had proven that the man hadn't even had taste in his mouth.

But that line of thought was just a sneaky way his mind had found to think about Tamrissa herself, so Vallant pushed it away with the rest. He thought instead about the edginess he could feel working at the back of his mind, a feeling certainly caused by what he now walked into. If there wasn't some sort of trap waiting he would eat his former ship, ratlines, sails, and keel. Their enemies could not be trusted under any circumstances, and he'd do well not to forget that.

It took longer than Vallant liked, but eventually he approached an area containing a room that wasn't empty. The amount and distribution of the water in the room indicated two people rather than one, and that was somewhat puzzling. Twenty or more people would indicate a trap, but what was two supposed to mean? A moment's thought gave Vallant nothing in the way of an answer, so he walked to the door of the room, opened it, and went in to find out the direct way.

"Well, this is a small surprise," the man inside said, smiling faintly as he gazed mildly at Vallant. "I expected your lovely groupmate Jovvi Hafford to come running up to explain that you were in *her* place rather than your own, but she hasn't. I'm Lord Kambil Arstin, by the way, her equal in Spirit magic."

"That's your opinion," Vallant countered with a snort, then nodded to the other occupant of the room, a woman he recognized despite the changes she'd gone through. "Or maybe you bein' Jovvi's equal is simply your boast, as you seem worried enough about her to give yourself a bit of an edge. Was that female over there supposed to rattle Jovvi enough to let you best her? If so, what a shame it isn't goin' to happen."

"Why is it that peasants always presume?" the man asked the world in general with a sigh, pretending that Vallant's words hadn't gotten him angry. "A gentleman speaks to them as though they weren't worth less than dirt, and receives curtness for his trouble. At the very least, another gentleman would have responded with his own name. Or don't you *have* a name, peasant?"

"Since you're so desperate to know, Arstin, I'm Vallant Ro," Vallant responded, wondering what the man was up to—and why he hadn't yet stood. He looked a bit thinner and more frail than Vallant remembered from the competitions. . . . "And don't bother remindin' me about the *lord* part. This empire is about to lose *all* its lords, your lot first and then the rest."

"I'm sure you think so, since all peasants tend to live in

daydreams,'' Arstin replied, that faint smile back in place. ''But you're much better than a peasant, aren't you, Ro? You come from a wealthy shipping family, so you know what it is to have two gold coins to rub together. Merchants do so like to harp on their having gold.''

''And useless slugs callin' themselves lords like to harp on how clever they were in bein' born,'' Vallant returned dryly. ''They sneer at the idea of someone earnin' gold himself, because they know *they* could never do it. That's why it's always *beneath* them, and why someone who does it can never be associated with. They're afraid of bein' shown up for the losers they are. Why is that woman just sittin' there and starin'?''

''Primarily because I grew tired of her insanity,'' Arstin answered, now apparently very pleased about something. ''She's obsessed with revenging herself for what she's been put through, and her not unexpected target is Dama Hafford. It *was* the lady's fault that this one was sent to the mines, after all.''

''The lady had nothin' to do with it, and you ought to know that even if this one doesn't,'' Vallant retorted, unhappy with how satisfied Arstin looked. He was definitely up to *something*.... ''Jovvi didn't even report the matter of the attempted kidnappin', nor was she asked to testify at this woman's trial. She ended up condemned through her own actions and her own admissions, just the way you and your groupmates have been. It's all over, Arstin, and there's no sane reason for not callin' off whatever it is you have in mind.''

''To quote *you*, my friend, that's *your* opinion,'' Arstin said, still smiling that faint smile. ''Since mine is completely different, we'll continue on for a short while yet. I take it that the letter Delin prepared and considered such a good idea turned out to be totally useless? I'll wager not one of you touched the thing, and therefore none of you is dying of poison.''

''This time you're right,'' Vallant agreed, glancing around to see if there was anything he should be noticing but wasn't. ''Our Earth magic user spotted the poison immediately, so none of us touched the letter. But you and your groupmates aren't equally untouched, and we've been told that the counteragent you're usin' won't work for very much longer. You'd better end this, so we can see if there's anythin' we can do for you.''

''A rather tempting offer, but not as tempting as it once would have been,'' Arstin said with a small headshake, something indefinable disappearing from his smile. ''These past few days I've been feeling . . . less strong and capable than I used to, and oddly enough the outlook has very little to do with my physical condition. It's apparently my mind which has lost a good deal of firm support, and that lack of assurance is rather upsetting. I've always thought of myself as supremely capable, and now I find that I must prove the contention even if it happens to be the last thing I do. Do you understand what I'm saying?''

''Frankly, no,'' Vallant admitted, giving the man an honest answer. ''In the last few days I've learned somethin' about myself and others, and that's that the only one who has to believe somethin' about you is you. Other people's opinions don't matter, as long as *you* know the truth and can hold to it. That way you avoid havin' others define you, and you also avoid misunderstandin's over what you are and aren't.''

''In other words, the only one you have to prove things to is yourself,'' Arstin agreed, nodding again. ''Yes, I'm aware of that, so my actions will selfishly be only for myself. And please don't mention my beloved groupmates again, not if you want to continue this conversation. Not one of them has ever been worth anything at all, and I myself was a fool for not having found some way to replace Delin. The only trouble was, none of the other Earth magic users was as strong as he is, so I decided to take the chance that I'd be able to control him. Ultimately I'll pay the price of that stupidity, but not until I've redeemed myself in my own eyes.''

''And how do you intend doin' that?'' Vallant asked, as ready to defend himself as he would ever be. ''You've been pokin' at my mind since I first walked in here, but I haven't had any trouble keepin' you out. Unless you want me to take my own turn at attackin', you'd better rethink your position.''

''No, I have a much better idea than that,'' Arstin disagreed, shifting just a little in his chair. "The first thing I must do is rid myself of this useless female, and then I'll be free to give *you* my full attention. Please don't be upset at what happens, she really is quite mad and therefore useless."

Vallant had the disturbing feeling that he knew what Arstin was about, but before he might move from where he stood, Allestine Tromin gasped where she sat at the edge of her chair, then collapsed bonelessly back. Vallant took an automatic step toward her, but trying to help would have been useless. Even if he'd known what Arstin had done, he couldn't have done anything himself to change it.

"Really, my friend, I told you not to worry," Arstin said, mild rebuke in the words. "She isn't dead, after all, and won't be for a good few minutes yet. I've simply sent her mind down so deep that her awareness is completely buried, and that way she won't be able to manage somehow to interfere. Once I stand—or sit—victorious I'll retrieve her from the depths, but if I don't survive, neither will she."

Amusement returned to Arstin's smile, as though he'd struck a shrewd blow at Vallant. Allestine Tromin's life now depended on Arstin's survival, and if she died it would be directly Vallant's fault. Vallant felt tempted to explain to Arstin that he couldn't have cared less about what happened to the Tromin woman, not after what she'd tried to do to Jovvi and Tamrissa both. He'd mentioned her in the first place only because he thought she might be used against him in some way, not because he was too gentlemanly to ignore the plight of any woman. It would have been satisfying to explain the truth, but at the moment it was much more politic to remain silent.

"Now then," Arstin continued, "I hope you don't mind if I boast just a bit. In a manner of speaking I've been tied hand and foot these past few days, but once you and your friends are defeated I've arranged to have things return to normal. One of my groupmates believes he has the full support of the rest of us, but what we're all supporting is his downfall. With the threat of your five over, the rest will then turn on *him*, destroying him in the fastest way possible. That counteragent you mentioned may not be good for much longer, but we now have the formula for it. We should certainly have enough time to discover the antidote, and then we'll go looking for someone else to round out our Five.''

"You have no idea how insane you're soundin', do you," Vallant remarked, actually more chilled than he felt willing to show. "You've made all sorts of plans and arrangements, and they allow for nothin' but the idea of your group winnin'. Someone would think that the bunch of you didn't know we were stronger."

"Only fractionally stronger, and that as a Blending," Arstin corrected, his good humor unchanged. "It may have escaped your attention, but here and now my people and I aren't *facing* your Blending. And there's something else I really must point out. If you'll look around, my dear Ro, you'll notice that this room has nothing in the way of windows. The nearest windows are quite some distance off, and you'd have to run rather fast and far to reach one. And by the way, thank you for telling me which of those peasants you are. I couldn't have managed without that knowledge.''

The man began to laugh breathily as Vallant looked around again, confirming the fact that there *didn't* seem to be windows in the sitting room. Something stirred at the back of his mind, almost like the beginnings of fear, but that was absurd. There was nothing there for *him* to fear, not even the suddenly stronger probing at his mind by the man who had laughed.

"Not only aren't you gettin' anywhere with that pokin' you're doin', you're workin' on faulty information," Vallant told the man, now seeing all amusement vanish from Arstin. "I'm not the one who worries about not havin' windows handy, I'm the one who plays with water. I'm also the fool who has been waitin' for you to stop attackin', but I can see now that that isn't goin' to happen. So let's see if we can *make* it happen."

"No!" Arstin shrieked, the whites of his eyes showing all around. "You can't do anything yet, not when my link groups have somehow been drained of strength! I have to find more—!"

The man's words broke off when the globe of water surrounded his head, and he thrashed around in an effort to stave off drowning. Vallant had originally intended to pull all the water out of his body, but this way he had more control. He'd let Arstin reach the point of *almost* drowning, and then it would be safe to leave the man and go looking for Jovvi. It ought to be *her* decision whether or not Allestine Tromin was saved, and she was also the only one who would be able to do it.

It took the expected three minutes or so for Arstin to succumb, and once he'd collapsed to the floor Vallant removed the globe of water and left the room. He felt confusion over a number of the things which had happened in that room, but the strangest of all was the way Arstin had made that mistake about Vallant's problem. *He* wasn't the one who feared confined spaces, he was the one who dreaded the thought of burnout. Odd the way Arstin had gotten that mixed up, although Vallant's fear of burnout wasn't nearly as strong as it had once been. Maybe he was finally getting over it. . . .

When Kambil Arstin came back to consciousness, he lay face down on the beautiful carpeting of the sitting room. When he coughed water streamed out of his mouth, and that brought back memory of what had happened. For some reason he hadn't been able to touch the peasant's mind at all, just as though the man had gained three times or more the strength of his own groupmates. He hadn't expected to need the additional strength of the tandem link groups he'd prepared, but when he found he did need them after all he'd been shocked to see that they'd been drained. How could that possibly have happened . . . ?

More water came up with the next cough, along with the question of how he could have been so mistaken. After tricking the peasant into speaking his name, Kambil had known immediately how to reach him even without using his skill. Ro was the Water talent of their group, and the Water talent feared being in enclosed places. Pressing the point should have made the man panic and lose control of himself, and then it would have been pure simplicity to take over his mind.

Once he had one of them, Kambil would then have had the man do away with the woman who had Spirit magic, and then the others would have been taken over just as easily as the first. *That* was his plan, to find himself an entirely new, completely capable group to replace the blemished Blending he'd been forced to work with, and then the entire world would have been his. It should have worked, it *should* have, but why hadn't it . . . ?

A third cough brought up only a little water, so Kambil began to make the effort to force himself to sitting. At least the fool had blundered in not making sure he was dead, and that mistake would cost him dear. His plan would have to be revised, but it was still usable if he acted carefully but swiftly. One of the others in their five—

A gasp of pain forced itself from Kambil's lips, surprising him and bringing a frown. Why in the world would he feel that pain in his middle *now*, after taking the counteragent at the proper time? It was much too soon to need another dose, although he really did have it if he needed it. He'd had Bron steal the formula and take a sample of the counteragent to a Middle practitioner in Earth magic, and then the resulting liquid was brought to Kambil. Afterward he'd made Bron forget he'd done it, as Bron and the others had no place in Kambil's plans. What a fool Delin had been to order Kambil to take control of the others again. He'd made sure Kambil couldn't act against him, but just like the loser he was, he'd forgotten about the others—

A second, harder stab of pain scrambled his thoughts again, telling Kambil that it was time to find and take that newly made counteragent. It took every ounce of his physical strength and store of determination, but Kambil pulled himself up and staggered over to the low cabinet which held a tea service. Opening the door of the cabinet gave him access to his new store of vials, and choosing one then swallowing it down was the work of a moment. It eased the pain immediately just as it was supposed to do, so Kambil took a deep breath and smiled as he straightened. Now on with the plan to make himself the ruler of the entire world—

Another, really hard stab of pain doubled Kambil over, and fear entered him from every pore. The counteragent wasn't working the way it should have, and fumbling out another vial and swallowing its contents also did nothing.

But that wasn't possible. . . . He *couldn't* have been forced to wait too long . . . !

A spasm of agony dropped Kambil to his knees and then to the floor, sending him back to that state of screaming mindlessness that had held him for so long because of Delin. That must be it, the reason why the new counteragent wasn't working. . . . He'd been left to the mercies of the poison too long, and it had eaten its way too far into his vitals. . . . *Damn* that mindless Delin . . . !

"But it can't happen yet, please Grami, don't let it happen!" Kambil babbled, beginning to be beyond knowing what he said. "You told me I'd have it all, and you never lied to me! I loved you so much, even after you stole the life of my sweet, gentle mother. . . . I wanted to cry over that loss, but you made me laugh instead . . . and never ever gave me the chance to mourn. . . . I vaguely remember wanting to hate you, but you never allowed that either. . . . You helped me do it all, and I know now that I can't do anything without you. . . . I admit that, so help me! Don't just lie there dead . . . !"

The pain spread and took over Kambil's world entirely, stealing the ability to speak from him. But in his mind he still cried for help from the woman he both hated and loved, cried and pleaded until he became one with the darkness which had already claimed her. . . .

FORTY

Lorand strode along the corridor at his best speed, determined to get that confrontation nonsense over with so that they could all get out of that place. Palaces were by their very nature large and luxurious, but that particular palace made him feel extremely uncomfortable. Not to mention the fact that he disliked what he would probably have to do.

A lovely tapestry appeared on the wall to his left, a large, wide thing depicting a hunt which made the viewer wonder just what was being hunted. At first glance it seemed that everyone rode horses and some of the riders pointed toward deer and elk and birds, and some of the animals and birds were already on the ground. A second glance showed that only some of the riders were engaged in pointing—the weavers' way of depicting talent being used. The rest of the figures rode double, men with women, and what they were engaged in wasn't a usual part of hunting. At least not on any hunt *he'd* been on. . . .

Lorand sighed as he moved past the tapestry, finding it uncomfortable that he still seemed to be full of the same country naivete which had plagued him when he'd first reached Gan Garee. If some groups of people were supple enough to make love on horseback, who was he to think that they shouldn't be doing it? All too often that judgment came along when someone felt either left out of things like that, or too afraid to try them even if invited. It was so much easier to say that something was wrong, than to admit that you lacked what it took to do that something. . . .

Which brought to mind the main problem bothering him: would *he* be able to do what was necessary? He really disliked the thought of having to kill someone in what amounted to cold blood, even if that someone happened to be a member of the hated nobility—and someone who had conspired to make a slave of him and his groupmates just the way they'd done with others. Not all members of the nobility were directly responsible for the doings of the rest, but when Lorand had once mentioned that to Meerk, the other man had countered that truth without any trouble. *If you know about something that's wrong and don't do anything to stop it*, Meerk had said, *you're just as responsible for what happens as those who are actively producing the wrong. By not opposing it you're condoning it, so guilt can't be escaped with nonaction.*

"And on top of that," Lorand muttered as he glanced around, "if I decide to be softhearted about the one I'm supposed to face, he or she could then turn around and harm one of the others. If any of them was hurt because *I* can't do a job properly, I'd never be able to live with myself. So I have to do it right, but please—*please!*—don't let it be the woman!"

Lorand, not being terribly religious, had no idea whom he might be praying to, but whomever it was he fervently hoped they were listening. Especially since he'd just detected the presence of living beings in a room not far ahead, four living beings in point of fact. That made him feel considerably better rather than more upset, as the more people he faced, the less he would hesitate to defend himself. But that was odd . . . four rather than five? He would hardly have been surprised if the enemy Blending had gathered together to defeat him and the others singly, but with four rather than five? That didn't make much sense.

Even so, Lorand made sure his talent was poised to call to the rest of his Blending if the enemy Five did happen to be there together, and then he strode to the door and threw it open. One of the people inside jumped to his feet, a pudgy young man with fear and nervousness peering out of his washed-out eyes.

"Thank the Highest Aspect you've finally come!" the portly man blurted, sounding for all the world as though Lorand were there to rescue rather than face him. "Another five minutes and I would have been completely out of my mind!"

"Why are you talkin' to *him*?" the girl snapped, a girl Lorand was easily able to recognize. "*He's* not my intended husband, he's some stranger who can't be very important. So where *is* Vallant, I'd like to know! He should be here to rescue me by now!"

"*She's* not the one who needs rescuing," the portly man said with a desperation which confirmed Lorand's earlier impression. "She's absolutely impossible, and I'm sorry I ever went along with this ridiculous scheme. Even if you *were* the man she awaited, I could in no way imagine you wanting to reclaim her. Now that I know you're not and don't, I do believe I'll kill her."

"I'd recommend against that," Lorand said quickly as the other man in the room stopped being quietly amused and got to his feet with an exclamation. "I can understand how much of a trial you've found her, but there's a difference between not being interested in marrying someone and not caring whether they live or die. Vallant has no interest in her, but as he would be upset if she died pointlessly, I must be the same."

"That fat little slug won't do anythin' to *me*," the girl stated to Lorand with her fists to her hips, clearly having no idea how close she stood to death. "I'm much too beautiful to be harmed, everyone has always said so. But how dare you stand there and tell lies like that? Vallant *will* be marryin' me, I've already made up my mind about it. So you just turn around and march right back out, and go and fetch him and bring him here. I—"

"That's enough," Lorand interrupted, putting a harshness into the words that reached through to the girl to some extent. "If you open your mouth even one more time, you'll probably be dead before I can keep it from happening. That's because you *aren't* too beautiful to be harmed, not when the ugliness inside you oozes out to cover any surface beauty. This man you dismiss so lightly has certainly killed before, and you've given him ample reason to do the same again. And as far as lying goes, you're far more experienced at it than I am. Vallant has said more than once that there won't be a wedding, and lying to people—and yourself—won't change that. Now go and sit down and stop bothering us all with the actions of a brat.''

The girl was highly indignant over what Lorand had said to her, but the portly man—and the people who were probably her parents—seemed to agree completely. The portly man now wore an expression of some satisfaction, but that wouldn't have helped the girl. The little fool opened her mouth to retort, most likely in the same obnoxious way she'd *been* speaking, completely ignoring the warning she'd been given. So Lorand had no choice but to touch her vocal cords with his talent, temporarily turning her mute.

''I told you to go and sit down, young lady,'' Lorand repeated with the same harshness as she struggled to speak and—probably—end her life. ''If you don't do it immediately, I'll take the strength from your legs—which will end you up on the floor looking ridiculous. You have five seconds. . . .''

Lorand began to count silently to himself, not about to see the girl die because of her own foolishness. He reached the number four, preparing himself to do exactly as he'd said he would, and then the girl sniffed and flounced over to a chair and sat. She must have noticed that she was about to lose their argument the painful and embarrassing way, and therefore had backed down. If he managed to get through that confrontation, Lorand decided to reward himself with the pleasure of having a long, frank talk with the girl's parents. . . .

''Finally!'' the portly man said, looking away from the girl with the tail end of impatience. ''As though *she* were the important one here. . . . Well, we've established that you're not the Water magic user and I *know* you're not Mardimil, so you have to be the Earth magic user. Am I correct?''

''Yes, that's right,'' Lorand agreed, refraining from pointing out that he would hardly have threatened to take the strength from the girl's legs if he *didn't* have Earth magic. ''And since you were waiting for Vallant, you must be the Water magic practitioner of your Blending. You do realize how little chance you people have?''

"I realize nothing of the sort," the portly man returned, echoing the girl's earlier sniff of disdain. "We are the Seated Five and you and your friends are the interlopers, and I have every confidence that we'll prevail. By the bye, how are you feeling?"

"If you're trying to find out whether or not that poison worked, I'm sorry to disappoint you," Lorand replied wryly, folding his arms as he looked at the man. "I noticed the poison immediately, so none of us touched it. But you can't quite say the same, can you? The poison *you* were given is beginning to affect your entire system. Why not give up whatever your plans are, and let me see if there's anything I can do for you?"

"I prefer to leave things of that sort to my groupmate," the man rejoined, speaking dryly. "I may not be the brightest star in the firmament, but I do know the difference between trusting a friend and trusting an enemy. And besides . . . in order to help me—*or* face me in battle—you would be at something of a disadvantage. In order to be most effective you would have to use quite a lot of the power, opening wide to more of it should the need arise. But you can't do that, not without worrying about being burned out, so I think it should be *you* who surrenders to *me*. Do it now, or face that attack you must be so worried about."

Lorand thought about what the short, pudgy man had said with a frown, wondering how the little man could have made such a mistake. At the words *burned out* Lorand's mind had hesitated an instant, as though expecting to have some sort of memory to bring forward, but there *was* no such memory. There was also no such problem. . . .

"I hate to disappoint you, but you seem to have gotten your facts mixed up," Lorand drawled after the moment of consideration. "I'm not the one with the problem about burnout, so everything you said applies to a different situation. My choices here have been and still are very simple: either I help you, or I destroy you. I tend to prefer to help people, but if necessary I can destroy them. So tell me which one *you* prefer to have done."

"You have to be lying," the small man stated, all of him

covered with an air of confusion and distress. "I can't possibly be mistaken, so you *have* to be lying! Oh, why did Delin insist on doing things *this* way? It's always so much better for all of us when we Blend! Why does he have to continue to be afraid of Kambil—?"

The man had gotten a good start on working himself up into a state of frenzy, but suddenly all that changed. His face paled and he bent double with a gasp, and it took no more than a glance for Lorand to know what was wrong.

"The virulence in your body has now increased alarmingly," he told the man, moving forward quickly to offer assistance. "When are you due to take the next dose of counteragent?"

"Not—not until tomorrow," the man gasped out, crumbling to the carpeting despite Lorand's attempt to help him to a chair. "It's much too soon, but it *hurts*! Make it stop hurting, please, make it stop!"

Lorand went to one knee beside the man, using every bit of his considerable talent to examine the now-writhing body. It took only a moment or two to discover that he *had* been lying, as the poison had spread to an extent which Lorand couldn't possibly do anything about. With or without help this man was about to die, and that fact felt more like a letdown than like a tragedy. Even the counteragent would no longer have been effective, assuming there had been any available to use.

"I'm afraid I have some bad news," Lorand began after his examination, but then discovered that words were now useless. The man had been taken by pain so intense that nothing else penetrated to him, and even suppressing the pain centers in his brain would have been useless. The echo of agony would not have let him know the difference, and in another minute or two it would no longer matter. The poor fool couldn't possibly last longer than that—

"No, please, Mother!" the man suddenly cried out, now moving with fear as well as pain. "I'll be a good boy, I promise I will! Please don't hurt me the way you do Father! I can't bear it, I simply can't bear it!" And then, after a number of heavily panted breaths, "Mother, protect me! She's going to hurt me, I know she is! Please come back and protect me! I don't know how to do it myself, you never let me learn! Please, help—"

The next word failed to come, and would clearly never be spoken now. The man's entire system had collapsed because of the poison, and he'd slid into death in the middle of his appeal to his mother. Lorand had heard every previous word the man had gasped out, but preferred not to think about them as he straightened. It was much too chilling to think about them. . . .

"He's dead?" the older man, the one who was probably the girl's father, said with shock. "I can feel the strength fairly radiatin' from you, but you never used it! And if you never touched him, why is he dead?"

"Didn't you hear me mention poison?" Lorand asked, gently trying to help the man—and his wife, who trembled against him—over his shock. "We learned that most of the falsely seated Five were poisoned, and it might have been too late even for the antidote to save them. This was one confrontation fated to never be, so let's get out of here."

"With pleasure," the man agreed shakily, beginning to urge his wife to walk with him. "I never thought I'd be eager to get out of a palace, but this is one place I never mean to come back to."

"But of course we're comin' back, Daddy," the girl, whom Lorand had been lucky enough to temporarily forget about, put in firmly as she rose from her chair. "I don't believe in givin' up what's mine, and Vallant Ro is *mine*. Especially now, when he and his friends will be takin' over from *this* bunch of nothin's. That will make *me*—"

"The same exact nothin' *they* were," her father interrupted, his voice much more firm than it had been. "I have a lot of unspoilin' to do with you, Missy, and I only hope it's possible. If not, you'll never be fit to associate with decent people. But the fault is mine so I'll do my best with correctin' it, and until then you'll stay at home and do *exactly* as you're told. If you don't, you'll surely regret it. Now let's get ourselves out of here."

The man clamped a big hand around his daughter's arm before starting out of the room again, and she kept up a running protest and a whining all the way back to the beginning of the wing. Lorand kept as much distance between them and himself as possible, and when he reached the area of corridors which led to the public areas of the palace and then outside, they were already gone.

For a moment Lorand was alone in the area, and then a time of confusion and rushing around began. His groupmates appeared one after the other to ask for his help, as none of their opponents had managed to stand against the "interlopers." After his own experience he really didn't expect to find any of the former Five left living, and his expectations proved sound. One wing after the other yielded up death either singly or in pairs, and one of those deaths hit Lorand very hard.

"He sacrificed his own life for mine," Tamrissa told him gently as he stood above the body of the man who had been his friend for most of forever. "He died a hero, Lorand, and I know he did what he did for *you*. In the end he showed that he loved you just as much as you loved him."

"I hate to say and think it, but it's probably better this way," Lorand replied with a sigh. "Hat would never have been happy being anything less than a High, and if he'd lived he would have spent the rest of his life being bitter. But the other one is a surprise. He didn't die from the same poison which killed his groupmates. There's no sign of the other poison."

Lorand had looked at the other body just to distract himself from the pathetically crumpled form of Hat, and had gotten more of a distraction than he'd been expecting. This was the last place he'd been brought, Tamrissa and Jovvi deciding on that together, and their people had long since been sent for to see to the surviving hostages. Lorand was relieved that *they* didn't have to see to that chore, not when he needed a good, stiff drink so badly.

"Well, he's dead no matter what caused it, and no one can claim that we didn't face and best them first," Tamrissa said with a sigh behind the words. "Let's find someplace to sit down for a while, and then we can discuss what we'll do next."

That was the best idea anyone had come up with in a while, and her groupmates eagerly agreed. They might or might not end up living in that palace themselves, but if they did they ought to start getting used to being in it. They made their way back out to the common area, expecting to have to look around a bit to find that place to sit down for awhile, and were surprised to find the crowds that they did. Most of the people were their followers, having come into the palace to offer their congratulations, and the rest were the remnants of the palace serving staff. They'd put cakes and tea—and stronger drink—in a nearby meeting room, and happily urged the victors to partake of it.

Surrounded by friends and supporters and a number of delighted servants, Lorand and the others let themselves be swept into the meeting room. For his part, Lorand would have much preferred if he and his groupmates had been left alone to unwind and talk, but everyone had been under a lot of pressure and now they wanted to celebrate with the people who had freed them from the heavy hand of the nobility. He and the others would have to put up with the partying for a while, and save their conversation for later, when they got some privacy.

More than just a few items of food and drink had been prepared, and one section of the room—right near a dais with five chairs on it—seemed specifically reserved for the heroes. There were five plates near the selection of food, five cups near the separate tea service, and five glasses in case they wanted something other than tea to drink. Once again Lorand would have preferred to join everyone else rather than be set apart, but his groupmates were going along with the thing so he sighed and did the same.

"If we do decide to let ourselves be Seated, we'll have to get used to this sort of thing," Jovvi murmured to him as they walked over to "their" part of the room. "If you're going to rule an empire you *have* to allow a certain amount of pampering, or you find yourself being challenged every other day by people who have been made to think of you as ordinary."

"I suppose you're right," Lorand grudged, then he smiled for how well she'd read him. "And since we might all decide not to go along with this after all, I might as well enjoy it while I can. That food looks delicious and the tea seems to be fresh, so maybe I'll save more serious drinking for later."

"That's what I've already decided about myself," Jovvi

said with a smile of agreement. "And I can't say I'm not a bit hungry, so let's go choose among the goodies."

Lorand had joined her in hanging back a bit to let the others at the food and drink first, but he'd made sure to check all the edibles for drugs and poison. The food and drink was entirely uncontaminated, but suddenly Naran pulled away from Rion.

"Wait, don't anyone eat or drink anything!" she said warningly, especially to Tamrissa and Vallant, who had already filled up plates and cups. "There's something very wrong here, but I'm not completely certain what it is. I've had this terrible flash of danger. . . ."

"I don't understand what might be causing that," Lorand said as he stepped forward to frown at the food again. "I've checked everything on this table, and it's all perfectly safe. It isn't as if—"

Lorand's words broke off as he suddenly noticed something he'd missed earlier, specifically the tableware. The plates and glasses and cups and silverware were top quality and were obviously very expensive and precious, but they were also the least bit . . . dingy. Even without a full staff to do the work, no one should have chosen those things for the new Five to use, not when there should have been other utensils to choose from. And for some reason that dingyness looked familiar. . . .

Automatically reaching for more of the power, Lorand took a really *close* look at the nearest plate and fork. The substance on those things was so diffuse that it was very difficult to perceive it, but a minute examination revealed the substance to be the same poison which had killed one of the previous Five. Each tiny smear of it was harmless all by itself, but even a meal small enough to be called a snack would put enough of the substance into someone that it would quickly turn deadly.

"Naran, it looks like you've done it again," Lorand said once he'd established what was going on. "The food and drink are as safe as I said, but the plates and cups and glasses and silverware aren't at all as harmless. This must be the way the Earth magic user of the Five was poisoned. He undoubtedly examined the food carefully, but forgot about checking what he put the food on and ate it with."

"Naran, remind me to buy you something really nice," Tamrissa said as she and Vallant hastily rid themselves of the plates they held. "And I think it will be a good idea if we go looking for the person or persons who did this. Failing here will probably only encourage them to try again and again until they succeed."

"I agree," Jovvi said, a frown creasing her lovely brow. "We have to find them without delay, since someone innocent could be hurt next time. They can't—"

Whatever else she would have said was drowned out by a scream of rage and insanity. Some of their followers had noticed what Lorand and the others were doing and had passed along the word, and everyone had abruptly stopped reaching for food and drink. It was probably that abrupt change which told the would-be murderess that her plan had failed, so she immediately substituted another. As she screamed she also ran forward with a very long, sharp knife, her targets clearly being Vallant and Tamrissa.

Lorand had already begun to reach toward the sleep centers in the woman's brain, when she came to such a short stop that it was almost as though she'd run into a wall. The crash knocked the breath out of her as well as stopping her in her tracks, and then she dropped to the floor in deep unconsciousness.

"And when she wakes up she won't be able to do something like this again," Jovvi said, joining the others in walking over to look down at the woman. "She may never be completely sane again, but at least she's no longer a danger to anyone."

"She's dressed like a servant, but that has to be Eltrina Razas," Tamrissa said, Vallant's arm tightly around her. "It looks like she bears something of a grudge over the various associations we had with her, but this is really an extreme reaction. There must have been goings-on that we know nothing about."

"And she must have had the same grudge against the Five, since she's obviously the one who finished off the last of them," Lorand said in agreement. "Considering that you took Vallant right out of her hands when she shouldn't have had him in her house, Tamrissa, she was most likely blamed by the Five for Vallant's escape. They may have been confused there at the end, but it's hardly likely they were just as confused all along. And now we'll have to decide what to do with her."

"That can be worried about later, once we've gotten some rest," Jovvi said with a sigh. "But Lorand—what did you mean about the Five being confused at the end? I didn't notice any confusion, just a sense of unbalance that was a very long time in building."

"*I* know what he means," Vallant said before Lorand was able to reply. "I also found confusion, and over what particular problem was supposed to be botherin' me. The fool I faced thought it was closed-in places that I couldn't abide, and tried to take advantage of me by usin' it. What a shame it didn't work."

"That's right," Lorand agreed with a nod. "The man thought that I was worried about burnout, but that doesn't happen to be my trouble. He . . . actually insisted. . . . Why are so many of you looking at me like that?"

Lorand had blurted the question, forced to it by the way Tamrissa and Rion and Naran were staring at him—and at Vallant. Just as though he and Vallant had lost their senses, and the others were simply reluctant to say so. . . .

"Oh, for goodness' sake, I forgot to tell the rest of you what we did," Jovvi said, sounding exasperated with herself. "Lorand and Vallant knew in advance, but now they have no memory of the true situation as it *was*. . . . All right, I'll start from the beginning. We knew the Five would probably try to reach them through their vulnerabilities, so I took control of each of them and then . . . *changed* the memory that caused each of them to have a problem. Without those terrible memories to fuel their fears, they started to get over them rather quickly."

"What memories?" Tamrissa asked, glancing at Vallant. "No one ever told *me* about specific memories. . . ."

"That was because it was very painful for Vallant to talk about," Jovvi said hurriedly, putting a hand to Tamrissa's arm. "He almost drowned while being trapped in an underwater cave as a child, and that's why he couldn't bear enclosed places. Now he remembers only a fun time in that cave, just as Lorand remembers only the punishment given to that girl in his school. She didn't burn out trying to control a thunderstorm, she was caught and stopped before that happened."

"Of course she was," Lorand agreed, wondering why Jovvi was discussing the obvious. "We all have to be cautious at times to avoid burnout, but the rest of the time it's nothing to worry about."

"And closed in places provide *privacy*, somethin' I could use right about now," Vallant said, clearly showing that he, too, felt puzzled. "Right after a decent meal, that is, but I'd rather not try to get one here. Why don't we find a decent eatin' parlor, and give ourselves a reward for a job well and easily done."

"*Too* easily done," Jovvi murmured as the others all agreed with Vallant's idea. "And I can't get past the feeling that we're not quite as through with trouble as we believe. . . . What's all that fuss about?"

The fuss Jovvi referred to was a stir by the door, and then the guardsmen standing there parted to let a small figure hurry in. Lorand was startled to see Pagin Holter, whose Blending had stayed behind to see if they might stop the advance of the Astindan army. Lorand was about to ask if they'd been successful, but one look at Holter's face made the question unnecessary.

"What's wrong?" Vallant asked as he stepped out toward Holter. "Didn't things go the way your Blendin' planned?"

"Not even a little, but that ain't th' problem now," Holter said as he approached, looking around at them. "Th' Astindan army don't wanna hear nothin' about stoppin', but that ain't the worst part. Worse'n thet is tellin' ya m'Blendin' don't have a hope a matchin' th' leader a th' Astindans—and they ain't more'n a day 'r so b'hind us. If'n *you* folk don't do somethin', they's gonna tear down Gan Garee'n scatter th' ashes 'n bricks."

Lorand exchanged glances with his groupmates, realizing that any appetite he'd had had just disappeared. A day or so behind Holter and his people . . . and if Lorand and the others couldn't handle the invaders, they would die along with everyone else. . . .

FORTY-ONE

None of us would have had much of an appetite if we hadn't expended strength, but we had so we did. We found an eating parlor and stopped for a meal, but don't ask me what it was. Rather than paying attention to the food, I couldn't help noticing that we and our people were the only ones in the parlor. Since it was definitely an upper-class establishment there should have been *some* members of the nobility there, but word of what had happened must have already spread. The parlor's serving people were certainly nervous enough, and that despite the fact that they *weren't* nobles. They didn't know precisely who we were, but our escort must have told them we were centrally involved in whatever was going on.

And what was going on could be seen in part on our way back to the house we were using. Ordinary people had come to flood the streets of the former noble neighborhoods, laughing and shouting over their newfound freedom. We'd set Captain Herstan—and any guardsmen in addition to his own that he could find—the task of keeping the celebrations from turning into looting and burning, but there was certain to be trouble anyway. At least until the word spread about the approaching Astindans. Then there would probably be panic and attempts at mass exodus, which might or might not be better than looting and burning.

But *we* couldn't run, not even if most of us would have

354

preferred to do it. Or even some of us. I looked out of the window of the coach which was now turning into the drive leading to the house, admitting to myself that I wouldn't have minded leaving Gan Garee again. Having an actual bed to sleep in was marvelous, but it wasn't worth what we would probably have to pay for the privilege. Pagin Holter and his people were almost as strong as *our* Blending, and they hadn't had a chance against the leading Blending of the Astindans, Holter had said. How much more of a chance *we* would have remained to be seen. . . .

Our entire group was silent as we climbed out of the coaches and walked toward the house, showing that the others were as deeply into their thoughts as I'd fallen into my own. A large number of people moved around the stables and the house, coming and going and generally doing what needed to be done. Most of them were lighthearted and happy, showing that they knew we'd won against the usurpers, but they obviously hadn't yet gotten the rest of the word.

"I'm going to need a few minutes with Lorand and Vallant," Jovvi said as we approached the house. "I suppressed their memories of how they used to react in order to protect them, but suppression never does anyone any good. After I restore the memories, we can all sit down and talk about what to do against the Astindans."

"I'd like to suggest turning Eltrina Razas loose on them," I couldn't help saying. "She finished off the usurpers and almost did the same to us, so she probably has the best chance of winning against them."

"I think I'll second that," Rion said with something of a laugh. "I've always known that the female was the deadlier half of our species, and the former Lady Eltrina simply proves the point."

"The rest of us may end up agreeing with you," Jovvi said wryly as we stopped in the middle of the house's entrance area. "Right now I can't think of anything to better the idea, but hopefully that will change. I'll send someone to find the rest of you once we're done."

We all nodded agreement, so Jovvi took Lorand and Vallant and went off toward the sitting room at the back of the house. I knew Rion and Naran would enjoy being alone, so I went upstairs to my bedchamber to see if anyone had managed to accomplish the request I'd made. Most of our clothing was still at my house, and now there was no reason not to have it brought to us. I'd also asked to have Gimmis's clothing brought, to give Rion and Lorand—and any other of our people who could use the things—something to wear besides what little they had.

It was getting on toward evening and the room was becoming dim, so I lit a lamp and walked to the large wardrobe where I'd put my only other change of clothing. Opening the right-hand door showed the immediate difference, as the wardrobe was stuffed full of dresses and gowns and skirts and blouses. I opened the left-hand door as well and began to search around to see if any of Jovvi's clothing had accidentally been mixed in with mine, and the strangest thing happened. A puff of dust billowed at me, as though the clothing had been left untouched for years instead of days. It was startling as well as surprising, and then—

And then I was suddenly cut off from the power! The world became darker and narrower and much more shallow, as though one entire dimension of it had died and disappeared. And then I began to feel faintly dizzy, just enough so that the thought of going anywhere but to the nearest chair was beyond me. I quickly put a hand to the side of the wardrobe to keep from falling due to the weakness in my knees, and abruptly, frighteningly, a big hand and arm came to circle my waist.

"Let me help you, child," a deep, gloating voice said from my left, making my blood run cold. "I added the dizziness after the hilsom powder did its work in order to keep you from running out of here, but I think I'll leave it in place for a while even though escape is no longer possible for you. You need to be taught right from the beginning who your master is, and the lesson will be sharper if you're unable to be stubborn even a small bit."

Even through the vast confusion in my mind, I knew immediately that it was Odrin Hallasser who held me and now urged me toward the bed. From what he'd said it was clear that his talent was Earth magic, and my being unable to reach the power turned me helpless in his grasp. Deep inside my mind a wail of terror began, but one that would never reach any of my groupmates. It was the power which bound us together, and without that. . . .

"Your father is a fool, and I'm sorry I ever thought it possible to depend on him," the man said as he moved slowly along with me. "These last few days I haven't even been able to find him, so I decided to take matters into my own hands. When I heard that you and your friends had returned to the city, I had your house watched. I expected *you* to return to it, but having people to follow in order to find you was quite good enough. You were off somewhere when I arrived so I waited, and now my patience has paid dividends. We'll leave here together in the same unnoticed way I arrived, and then we'll begin our life together."

"I know you're insane, but are you stupid as well?" I tried to demand, ignoring the way my voice trembled. "Not only will my groupmates come looking for me, I have to be here to help against the Astindan army. We got word not long ago that they're about a day away from here, and they intend to destroy the city when they arrive. That means you can't—"

"Don't even think about telling me what I can and cannot do," he interrupted in an even harsher voice, his grip on me tightening in a way that suggested the action was unconscious. "I'll do exactly as I please, just as I've always done, and no one will change that! Your friends can search for you until they turn old and gray, but you can be certain that they won't find you. And as far as this city being destroyed goes, how credulous do you think I am? No invading force will ever reach our gates; the authorities would never permit it. Now keep silent while I have a taste of you, and then we'll be on our way."

We'd reached the bed by then and he tried to push me down on it, but another strange thing seemed to have happened. Being captured and helpless was terrifying, but the fright wasn't as crippling as it had once been. When he tried to push me onto the bed I struck at him with both fists and all my strength, aiming for his face. He cried out in startlement and pain and backed away a step, so I immediately struck at him again and again. Hurting him wasn't likely to free me, not when he was so much larger than I, but I'd decided to make him pay in advance for whatever he eventually managed to take. I knew I couldn't win, but that was no reason not to fight.

The enraged man bellowed out his anger as he stopped simply defending himself, and the next moment I was thrown onto the bed. He'd shoved me down and away from him, and then he stepped forward to glare down at me.

"There will never be anything like *that* again!" he growled, fury now blazing from those dead black eyes. "My possessions are *mine*, and no one—even the possessions themselves—can deny me! You will be punished for making the attempt, but not in a way that will damage your beauty. You will, however, learn quickly to avoid doing *anything* that will incur that punishment again."

"Wrong," a voice said an instant before I said the same thing in different words. "She isn't going with you, and you aren't going to hurt her. If you don't agree with that, turn around and face me."

Hallasser whirled rather than turned, to see what I already knew he would: Alsin Meerk standing near the wardrobe. The door to the chamber was still closed, which meant that Alsin must also have hidden himself inside before I arrived.

"You don't know me, Hallasser, but I know you," Alsin went on, folding his arms as he stared unblinkingly at the hulking man. "You have a deadly reputation in this city, just like the nobles used to have, but the time has come to get rid of your sort right along with theirs. I saw your people following those who went to Tamrissa's house, so I simply waited until *you* showed up and then came in behind you. The lady isn't going anywhere with you, not now and not ever, so you might as well just leave again."

"Not alone, not this time," Hallasser growled in answer, his hands having turned to fists at his sides. "The woman is *mine*, and I haven't gotten as far as I have by letting people take what's mine. If you think you can stop me, go ahead and try."

And with that they began to fight, but not in a way I could easily see. They both grunted at the same time, suggesting that their talents had clashed, and then they stood braced and glaring at one another. I continued to sit on the bed, fighting with all my strength to reach through to the power, but it was simply no use. If Hallasser was to be beaten with the use of talent, I wasn't the one who would be doing it.

But suddenly it seemed that Alsin would also not be the one. He cried out in pain, his eyes widening in shock, and then he began to fall to his knees! When he hit he also put his palms to the floor, as though trying to hold himself up against enormous weight or pressure, but a final choking sound ended his efforts. He collapsed the rest of the way to the floor, and then lay still.

"And so much for *you*, scum," Hallasser muttered as he panted, obviously having fought hard. "You were stronger than any of the others, but not as strong as I am. You won't ever interfere in the lives of your betters again, and now to go back to what you interrupted."

The man began to turn back to me, but I felt too horrified to really notice. Alsin was *dead*? Another life gone trying to save mine? I put my hands to my head, ready to scream at the top of my lungs, feeling even more dizzy than when Hallasser had been causing it. Wasn't this horror ever going to stop? Did *I* have to die before it would end?

"As I was saying," Hallasser began, then he had to whirl around a second time when the door to the hall flew open. Vallant and Lorand rushed in, realized what was happening in just about a single glance, and then both looked at Hallasser. The bulky man growled and clenched his fists again, clearly intending to fight my groupmates, but this time he didn't stand a chance. First his disbelieving scream rang out, and then most of his bulk was gone. It disappeared just before his clothing fell to the carpeting over the pile of dried ash he'd become, and that part of it, at least, was over.

"Tamrissa, are you all right?" Vallant demanded as he hurried over to me, sitting down beside me to circle me with his arm. I shuddered as I leaned closely into his embrace, needing his warmth to melt the ice inside me. It didn't work all the way, and I felt so terribly confused that I didn't know what I would do.

"Meerk is beyond my help," Lorand said from where he stood looking down at the unmoving body, his voice sad. "He must have thought he'd have no trouble at all against Hallasser, but the man was a potential High. I don't know how Hallasser escaped the net and wasn't put through testing, but he definitely had the strength of a High. But in the end Meerk did what he intended to. If he hadn't fought the intruder with his talent, we wouldn't have known what was going on. He held the man long enough for us to get here, which means he won after all."

"Tamma, Lorand is saying that Alsin gave his life willingly," Jovvi added, having hurried into the room and over to me to put her hand to my hair. "He knew nothing could come of his love for you, but circumstance let him show just how great it was. He would have wanted you to remember him fondly, not with guilt over what he chose to do. Do you understand what I'm saying?"

"I may be able to understand later," I whispered, still clinging tightly to Vallant as both his arms held me close. "Right now I don't believe I can handle any more than this. . . ."

"Of course you can't," Jovvi agreed at once, sympathy and caring clear in her voice. "And you also can't stay in this bedchamber. Vallant will take you to his for now, and later, when you're feeling better, you'll see if you want to change that. I also think you can use a trip to the bath house, and if Vallant isn't willing to keep you company, Naran and I will."

"It will mean forcin' myself, but I think I can manage to do it," Vallant replied with something of a chuckle. "And afterward you can have your choice of a dress to put on. *That* ought to be a pleasant change."

"It won't be very pleasant until we can get rid of all that hilsom powder," Lorand said as he eyed the clothing in the wardrobe. "Now that I see it, I understand how Hallasser was able to get the better of you, Tamrissa. He apparently put it on some of the dresses, and when you opened the wardrobe he must have caused it to blow into your face. But you couldn't have inhaled *that* much, so its effects ought to wear off fairly soon."

"I'm sorry I didn't see this happening sooner, Tamrissa," Naran put in from where she and Rion stood, her voice filled with misery. "By the time it came through to me that something was wrong, we found Vallant and Lorand already hurrying in this direction. If only I'd told Rion sooner. . . ."

"Then Alsin would still be alive, but he would also still be absolutely miserable," Jovvi said when Naran's words trailed off. "I know how miserable *you're* feeling, my dear, but I happen to believe that everything turned out for the best. I *know* Alsin Meerk was happy to give up his life for the woman he loved, since he knew that his love would never be returned. Now let's all go and sit down somewhere together, and talk until the shock of what happened has worn off a bit."

That was a suggestion everyone seemed to agree with, so I let Vallant help me around the pile of mess that had once been a man, and we all went to a sitting room and talked for a while. The talking did help to a certain extent, and after we had some tea Vallant and I were shooed off to the bath house. We were told that no one else was using it and that that would continue while we were still inside, so when the hilsom powder abruptly wore off enough to put me back in touch with the power, I turned to Vallant and coaxed him into making love to me. He didn't really need much in the way of coaxing, and I actually forced myself to tell him how much I'd missed him—and how much I loved him.

"I never thought I'd hear you say that," he whispered as he held me close and caressed me. "I'm tempted to just say the same, but you deserve to hear the full truth. I know Jovvi was right when she said Meerk was glad to give up his life for you, because I've been feelin' the same way. If the man was still alive I'd owe him an apology—and my deepest thanks for what he did. Thinkin' about losin' you. . . . I'd much rather lose my own life, since I'd *have* no life if anythin' happened to you. You *are* my life, Tamrissa, and I'll never love any other woman the way I love you."

I think I cried then, but certainly not for long. Vallant and I shared our love for a very long time, and then we went back to the house and dressed in clean clothing. By then it was dinner time, so we ate with the others and then joined them for a meeting about what we might do against the coming Astindans. There wasn't much we *could* do besides go out and face them, so now I've brought this journal up to date. If I don't get the chance to come back and finish telling the story, maybe someone else will do it for me.

In any event, I intend to sleep in Vallant's arms tonight and for as many nights as we're allowed to be together. That number may come to no more than one or two, but if so, it will still be for the rest of our lives. . . .

FORTY-TWO

The others asked me to finish this narrative, and I suppose it *is* fitting, for a number of reasons, that I do so. So now it is I, Rion Mardimil, who tells of what befell us—but only, as was done from the beginning, as the events occurred.

Our Five had any number of meetings until the Astindan force arrived, and various ploys were thought of, discussed, and for the most part adopted. During this time the city saw the influx of large numbers of refugees, along with the shattered remnants of the army which the Astindans had defeated. At Jovvi's suggestion we set up many units of city people whose task it was to find food and shelter and medical attention for the new arrivals, and those who were physically able were put to work at other tasks.

Quite a large number of nobles still remained in the city, and guardsmen groups—accompanied by volunteer workers—went from house to house confiscating food. In all fairness it should be mentioned that the same was done with nonnoble residences, as the hoarding of food would do no one any good. All arriving shipments of food—what few shipments still came—were directed to central locations where it might be made available to everyone. Rationing was quickly put into effect, and only a surprisingly small number of people complained.

"They're the sort who would complain about the noise if they found themselves in a rainshower of gold coins," Jovvi said with a grimace when the objections were brought to our attention. "It doesn't seem possible to avoid people like that, so you have to find ways to deal with them instead. I think we should have our people tell them that if they don't like the idea of rationing, they're free to go out and find their own sources of food. After all, we'd never want to force people to take what they don't really want."

"But let's make it clear that they can't take what belongs to someone else," Tamrissa added. "If they try it anyway, make sure they know that we'll be the ones who come after them. And let's not forget to tell them that they sound like the old nobility."

"That's adding insult to injury," Lorand put in with a laugh. "But I do have to say I enjoyed the stories about how the nobility took having their mountains of food confiscated. The howling and screaming must have been music to everyone's ears."

"It would have been music to mine," Vallant said with a nod of agreement. "Those people have been due a good takin' down for a long time, and I'm glad I'm around to see it. No servants, no extra food, and no real way to leave the city. Imagine things like that happenin' to people like *them*."

"I believe I'm more pleased to see it than you are," I informed Vallant, enjoying the satisfaction I felt rather strongly. "I've come to the conclusion that every one of those people is a waste of living space, so no one will shed any tears if they don't happen to survive."

"If we manage to have an empire left after the next— and hopefully last—confrontation," Jovvi said, "we'll have to make sure that the same thing doesn't happen to *our* followers. There has to be a way to reward the people who help you, without setting them up in a position where they'll immediately begin to ruin their children. If we bother to look, we ought to be able to find that way."

"I think we can worry about that after we win," Lorand

said after putting his arm around her, softening his words. "Right now we have more immediate things to concern us, like getting the word we've been waiting for about the approaching forces. I just hope that the ones who went are being careful."

A knock suddenly came at the door, and when the door was opened it was as though Lorand's words had conjured the event.

"Excuse the interruption, gentles, but High Master Lavrit Mohr is here and asking to be admitted," Captain Herstan announced. "Do you want to see him?"

"We've been waitin' for him," Vallant confirmed with a nod. "Show him in, and try not to interrupt the meetin' for anythin' but a real emergency."

Herstan nodded and then stepped aside, and High Master Mohr walked in. He stopped to bow to us as the door was being closed again behind him, and then he sighed as he advanced to a chair.

"I can't say I'm completely convinced about your reasons for not moving directly into the palace," he said as he seated himself. "There isn't a person in the city—aside from the nobles—who doesn't agree that the place is yours, and yet you remain here in this house. Surely you know that people would be more comfortable having you there, not to mention how much more comfortable *you* would be."

"We haven't the time to worry about which noble with a grudge might be trying to destroy us the next time," Jovvi answered for us, giving the man one of her incredible smiles. "The palace needs a million people to run it properly, and interviewing them one at a time could take years. It's a good deal easier for us to simply stay here right now, and worry about the palace later—if we have a later. What have your people found out?"

"My people together with yours have discovered the composition of the Astindan army," Mohr replied with another sigh. "Personally, I kept picturing thousands and thousands of troops, all marching vengefully at us, but I'm afraid the truth is worse. There are something like six hundred people in their force, consisting of ten Blendings, each with tandem link groups for every aspect. The rest of the force seems to be two extra members of each aspect for reliefs or replacements in the Blendings, plus a group to see to the horses and preparing meals and such. Do we have enough Blendings to match that?''

"Not quite," Lorand responded after we all exchanged a glance, his heavy tone an excellent indication of how I, myself, felt. "All told we have seven Blendings including ours, and too many of the others have simply practiced as a Blending, not really acted as one. Take our word for the fact that there's a considerable difference in the two situations. Were you able to find out the compositions of their ten Blendings?"

"That's where your people and mine worked incredibly well together," Mohr replied, a small amount of enthusiasm coloring his words. "Yours protected mine from discovery while they rated the members of the Blendings, so now I'm able to tell you that not all of them are Highs. Half of the ten contain strong Middles in one or more of the aspect positions, very strong Middles but still not Highs. That's something of a help, at least."

"Why would they use Middles rather than Highs?" Tamrissa asked, her lovely brow creased in a frown. "It doesn't seem to make much sense."

"It starts makin' sense if you stop to consider what they know about us," Vallant pointed out. "At the time they started movin' on us, our great empire had only one Blendin'. Ten to one make unbeatable odds, even if some of those ten aren't as strong as they might be. But what about the link groups? Are *they* all Highs like ours, or are there Middles mixed in as well?"

"My people hardly had the time to rate all the link group members as well," Mohr said, faintly reproving. "With fifty people attaching to each Blending, it simply wasn't possible. They did, however, spot check the link groups, and had the overall impression of Middles rather than Highs. Strong Middles, to be sure, but Middles nevertheless."

"Which hopefully means our feeble plan might work," Jovvi said, leaning back as she voiced her own sigh. "But that won't eliminate the threat, just make it slightly more manageable. I'm afraid it will eventually come down to which of us has the strongest leading Blending. What did your people have to say about the ones Pagin Holter told us of?''

"As we all suspected, they're third level upper Highs, just like the five of *you*," Mohr said, speaking the words slowly as though he confessed to a terrible crime. "That means rating them precisely is beyond us, as they haven't yet reached their full potential. But neither have you, so the situation is far from bleakly lost. As it would have been with the usurpers, Highs though they were. Their potential was limited by something other than their ability, while yours is not.''

"Potential doesn't mean much if you aren't able to put it into play," Lorand pointed out glumly. "And it doesn't tell you just how far you can stretch yourself before you break. But I have the feeling we'll be finding out about that last part in just a little while. How far away are they from the point where we'll be alerted?''

"As you asked, you'll be alerted when they're half an hour's ride from the city," Mohr responded, now clearly trying to hide a shadow of worry. "They were delayed during their last effort to find edibles, which is naturally becoming more difficult for them. But they aren't destroying the land they've been almost stripping of food and meat animals, and I don't understand that. I thought they were here to exact vengeance.''

"They are, but not against themselves," Vallant responded. "You have to remember that they'll want to retrace their steps on their way home, and if they destroy everythin' now they'll get awfully hungry on the way back. They *are* destroyin' things like houses and personal possessions, but what they'll need to keep them eatin' after they've torn down Gan Garee won't be touched until they don't need it any longer.''

"What a pleasant future we have to look forward to," Mohr said with yet another sigh, then he shifted in his chair. "A pity we aren't able to simply run away, just as the nobles in the path of that advance did. Have you been told that an unexpectedly large number of nobles has *returned* to the city, apparently unaware of what has been happening here? Among them were the owners of *this* house, and the fools actually tried to demand the return of it. Your guardsmen did an excellent job of shooing them off, right after informing their servants about the new arrangements. They ended up having to drive their own carriage, and may not have even made it safely out of the neighborhood. Well, I must be going. If you need me for anything, simply send word to my house."

"We'll do that, High Master, and thank you," Jovvi said, again speaking for all of us. "If things go the way we want them to, your Guild will have a brand new standing in the empire when we rebuild. And you'll never again have to send young men and women to death or slavery."

"That end in itself is worth any effort," Mohr said, rising to his feet to bow. "Needless to say, you have my most sincere wishes for the best of luck."

We accepted his wishes with nods of thanks, and a moment later the man was gone. The news he'd brought hadn't done much to cheer us, and no one seemed prepared to comment until Naran stirred and looked around.

"I've just seen a very small change from what's been shown me until now," she said, her lack of relief a clear indication that not all the answers we sought had been given her. "Our plan to make the confrontation a bit more equal will most probably work, so we definitely have to go through with it. As far as the rest goes, though. . . . Everything will eventually come down to us facing their best, and the outcome of that confrontation is too unsure for me to see anything but multiple shadows. Anything can happen, from all of us as a group to some of us as individuals, living or dying, hurt or unhurt. Everything is still possible, except for one thing: if we decide not to face them, we'll definitely survive. Not many other people will, but we ourselves will be safe. I thought everyone should know that."

"I can't see that it makes much of a difference," Tamrissa said, having borrowed Lorand's glumness. "I, personally, would love to simply pick up and leave, but to go where and do what? And how are we supposed to live with ourselves if we save our own lives at the expense of everyone else's? We'd eventually start blaming each other for having run away, and at the end there would be nothing but self and mutual hatred. Not dying is all well and good, but there's a difference between not dying and actually living. If I can't enjoy the life I'll be living, I'd rather be dead.''

"I'm afraid I have to agree," Jovvi said, her usual smile having disappeared entirely. "I've experienced not dying just as Tamma has, and as I've said before, I refuse to go back to it. If I can't live the way life was meant to be lived, I'll also take death."

I was about to join Lorand and Vallant in agreeing to what our two sisters had said, but Naran interrupted the intention by leaning close.

"It's something of a good thing that they feel like that," she whispered, nodding toward Tamrissa and Jovvi. "I didn't want to say so out loud, but I'm afraid that they have the smallest chance of surviving the confrontation. Do you think I ought to tell them, love?"

Saying I felt appalled is to show the inadequacy of words, and I hadn't the least idea of how to answer Naran's question. A short time went by while I wrestled with the turmoil in my mind, and then the opportunity to reply was taken from me. A knock came at the door, and Captain Herstan appeared again.

"Excuse me, gentles, but word has just come that the approaching host has nearly reached the point of being half an hour's ride from the city. You asked to be informed?"

We agreed that we had, and then we all rose to our feet. No matter whether we lived or died, the time to act had come.

FORTY-THREE

Our ride through the city to the western road was an experience in itself. The weather had turned unexpectedly cool, and yet an enormous number of people stood about in the street watching us go past. Some few tried to cheer when we appeared, but the rest simply stood and stared at us, fear clear on their faces. Word had obviously spread about what we were in the midst of, and above the fear the people showed, putting a very faint light into their eyes, was a glimmer of hope.

"They know about the Prophecy, and are hoping it's true," Jovvi said in a murmur only loud enough to reach our core group. "Beyond that I don't think they know why we have so many people with us, since *we're* the ones who are supposed to fight for them."

"Personally, I think I'd dislike any one person fighting for *me*," I commented, the thought suddenly occurring. "Even a small group of people. . . . If the one or the group is defeated, I'm defeated right along with them even though I haven't lifted a finger. I'm surprised that all these people don't feel the same."

"I'm sure they do, in a manner of speaking," Lorand said, turning his head to briefly give me a smile. "Many of them would prefer it if they were able to defend themselves, but they simply haven't got the strength of ability. That means they have no choice but to let strangers stand their defense, while they do nothing more than sit on their hands and pray. Because of that I feel very sorry for them, as they're the ones who will pay harshly if we fail. Being dead is much easier than living through devastation.''

"And I would guess that running away is simply not possible for them," I replied, having had a second revelation. "They're unable to run and unable to fight. . . . Yes, they've more than earned compassionate pity. But you, brother, surprise me to a small extent. You're no longer mentioning how terrible a fate burnout would be, but instead are simply discussing death. I take it then that Jovvi's ministrations have been completely successful?"

"For the most part, yes," Lorand agreed, Vallant turning his head to add a brief nod of agreement. "I can now remember just how I felt when burnout *was* a serious problem, but the emotional overtones concerning the situation have changed. I'm no more eager to face burnout than I ever was, but now the fear of it has stopped being in control of my life."

"I just remembered a question I had about that," Tamrissa said, mostly addressing Jovvi. "Didn't you say that reaching me was almost impossible because of the strength I'd developed? Lorand and Vallant ought to be just as strong in their own aspects as I am in mine, so how did you reach *them*?"

"Without using tandem link groups and *forcing* them, you mean?" Jovvi said with a better smile than Lorand's. "For a long while I couldn't see any other way to accomplish what needed to be done, but then I had a . . . revelation, sudden insight, inspired guess? Call it what you will, but one day I abruptly found myself wondering about those woven patterns we've been using for almost everything. We've all been weaving our various *talents* into the patterns, but no one has tried to weave the power itself. So I decided to try it, and it actually worked."

"I—ah—think I ought to mention that I should have . . . mentioned something sooner," Tamrissa said with what looked like painful embarrassment while I and the others were in the midst of exclaiming over Jovvi's discovery. "What you just said about weaving the power itself. . . . I did exactly that back in Widdertown, but somehow forgot to tell all of you about it. I suppose it was the way you all kept yelling and screaming at me that drove the memory out of my head.''

"That was because you *were* out of your head to do that in the first place," Vallant told her dryly. "You deserved gettin' yelled at, but right now we're discussin' weavin' the power itself. If you two ladies have done it, the rest of us ought to be able to do the same."

"Assuming the need arises, which it might not," Lorand said with a doubtful look. "We'll be operating as a Blending, remember, so individual actions probably won't enter into it. I'm assuming that that's why Jovvi hasn't discussed this sooner, but it certainly can't *hurt* us to know about it. . . ."

The note of doubt continued in Lorand's voice as his words trailed off, and I must confess that I agreed with him. Circumstance had had us face the usurpers as individuals, but this current situation was hardly likely to turn out the same. It was Blendings which the Astindans brought toward us in attack, and that, therefore, was the method we would need to use to reply. As well as we were *able* to reply. . . .

The rest of the ride was a fairly quiet one, making it impossible for me to miss the fact that Naran's face remained as drawn and worried as it had been all morning. The vision of our future still hadn't resolved itself then, and my beloved merely forbore mentioning that unpalatable fact. A gust of wind and a few drops of rain blew across us, bringing a reminder of winter, causing us all to draw our cloaks more closely about us. And yet people still stood in the streets, refusing to return to the shelter of their homes. Could they truly be there in support of us? Or were they merely there to learn at once whether they were to live or die?

It seemed wisest to push questions such as that from my mind, most especially as we had reached the outskirts of the city. Our allies had, in accordance with our plan, placed themselves a bit farther along the road, approximately half way between us and those who approached. We rode to the spot where we had chosen to make our stand, dismounted along with our tandem link groups, then chose places to sit once our mounts had been led away. Our escort of guardsmen then moved to surround us protectively, as though they would actually be able to stop the doings of a fully active enemy Blending. The concept was more pitiful than laughable, but none of us mentioned that fact.

"We'll first have to make sure that everyone else is in their proper position," Jovvi said as she settled herself, then she turned a faintly worried expression to my brothers. "Lorand, Vallant—From which direction is this rain coming? We're only getting a few drops right now, but if it happens to be coming from the same direction as the Astindans. . . ."

"We've already thought of that, so we checked," Lorand answered for the two of them. "The actual rainstorm is passing to the northeast, which means we shouldn't get much more than this drizzle. It's possible the Astindans won't get even this much."

"But they most probably *will* get the winds," I added, to keep anyone from being overly optimistic. "Those who are lying in wait will need to be extremely cautious in order to do as they've been instructed, not to mention in protecting themselves and their people."

"And they may even have already started," Tamrissa pointed out, looking at the rest of us. "Let's stop talking and find out."

That seemed the most sensible course of action, so we all prepared ourselves for Blending. I naturally took Naran's hand to hold, but not simply for the pleasure I always felt from her touch. She alone still had nothing in the way of supporting link groups, and I thought that perhaps, if we were in contact, she might share some of the strength of my own groups. . . .

And then the entity opened its perceptions once again, to look about itself in preparation for doing what was needed. The first item on its agenda, so to speak, was to see how the lesser entities were doing with the chore given them, and so the entity floated quickly in the direction of where they would be.

Three of the lesser ones—the newest, most inexperienced three—had been sent to perform a specific act, and even as the entity reached their position it saw that the action had already begun. The approaching enemy rode in the expected way, with each entity's flesh forms surrounded by those who formed their link groups. Earlier investigation had shown, however, that no more than one entity was called forth at a time, and that one was merely to be on the alert against attack.

For that reason one of the three of its own lesser entities had been given the task of masking the presence of the others, which it had apparently done. The enemy was none the wiser—or had been until the remaining two entities began their efforts. A large amount of the substance known as hilsom powder had been prepared and positioned along the road, and while the third entity continued to shield the others, the remaining two formed chutes of hardened air which stretched above the column from one end to the other. Into those chutes went the hilsom powder, and the entire column should have been liberally sprinkled with it.

Should have been. As the entity watched the wind playing havoc with its plans, it understood more fully why the success of the ploy had been so completely surrounded by uncertainty in its future vision. A good half of the column was coated with the powder which immediately severed their connection with their aspects, but the other half, the first half, was left virtually untouched. The lesser entities' own flesh forms were protected from having a like fate thrust upon them by the presence of moistened kerchiefs over their noses and mouths, which was a fortunate thing. The entities of the leading flesh forms in the column appeared immediately, and a moment later every grain of the hilsom powder had been burned to nothing.

And then, of course, those avenging entities began to search for the ones responsible for halving their numbers. But that possibility had been anticipated, and so the entity brought *itself* to the attention of the enemy and then quickly returned in the direction from which it had come. The enemy followed a short time in pursuit, which allowed the flesh forms of the lesser entities the opportunity to take themselves quickly off. When the enemy entities returned, their attackers would hopefully be well hidden from their perceptions.

It was necessary to inform its allies of what had occurred, and then the entity was able to return to its flesh forms.

Just before it separated, the entity reflected that its inner balance was now substantially improved, and yet there was still that one definite lack. It was possible that that lack would soon be remedied, but if not. . . . The leading enemy entity had seemed far stronger than any other the entity had come across, which could well make for difficulties when they two faced one another. . . .

"Well, at least we cut them down to half," Jovvi said while I adjusted to being my own self again. "It's now their five against our four, or possibly even better odds if one of those three ambushing Blendings manages to make it back here in time."

"That didn't seem very likely," Lorand responded with a sigh. "With the help of their tandem link groups they can hide where they went to ground, but if they try to come back here they'll probably be spotted—and destroyed. If we have to do without their help, I'd rather it be because they're hiding, not because they're dead."

"I'm afraid Lorand is right," Naran said, sounding and looking a bit drained. "The probability is very small that they'll try to rejoin us, which is a lucky thing. If they do try they'll be discovered and killed."

"That means we need another plan," Vallant said, looking more thoughtful than disturbed, "and I may just have one. When I was a boy, my brothers and I got into an argument with a larger group of boys. They should have been able to beat us down and then beat us up, but my oldest brother did somethin' that kept it from happenin'. He ducked aside from the other leader's attack—mostly physical with a bit of talent added—and threw all his ability into helpin' the rest of us one at a time. In effect we went two against one with those other boys, and once the last member of his group was down, the other leader took to his heels. He had no stomach for facin' my oldest brother all by himself, even though they were the same age and size."

"That's a very real part of the bully syndrome," Jovvi said with brows raised while the rest of us made sounds of pleased surprise. "There's nothing to say that the invaders suffer from that, but at the worst we'd then have to face only their leader. Yes, I certainly do like it."

"And I like it even more," Naran said, her gaze clearly on something other than what was before the rest of us. "The probabilities have just shifted rather dramatically, and it's now virtually certain that we can cut their numbers again in just that way. After that things are still hazy and unformed, but we're close enough now to this particular future for the details to begin to turn into reality. But we have to do it as quickly as possible."

Everyone nodded their understanding, and then it was the entity who hummed approval to itself. Its flesh forms were certainly doing their part by being creative, and the new plan was rather amusing. It would not have occurred to the entity to face a lesser entity in cooperation with its allies, not when logic said *it* was fully capable of besting that lesser entity alone. In point of fact it would have simply stood in challenge against the strongest of the enemy entities, leaving it to a matter of greater ability to decide which of them would stand victorious.

Now, however, that would no longer be the case, and the entity suddenly became even more aware of the lack of time involved in which the ploy must be used. It therefore floated very quickly to its allies, gathered them together, then explained what would be required of them. There were, of course, no voices of dissent, and they moved in a body in the direction of the enemy.

An enemy which had already begun to move in *their* direction. Five entities, tinged with anger, floated along the road, clearly having decided to keep their flesh forms back out of danger. Their intention to attack and destroy any opposition was more than obvious, and when they perceived the entity's force they hesitated not at all. The enemy came directly for them, the leader clearly intending to stand alone against the entity, which certainly would have come to be only a short while earlier. Now the entity slipped around the leader, and more quickly than thought assisted its lesser entities in overcoming those behind the leader. Those lesser enemies were not completely destroyed, not with the short amount of time available, but they were certainly rendered incapable of standing in challenge for quite some time to come.

One of those lesser entities had an extremely strong ability in Fire magic, and without the entity's assistance its ally would have surely been destroyed. The entity stood its own ability in opposition, and an instant later it was cold fire which consumed the enemy. Cold fire required more effort than the ordinary sort, but the effort was put forth without hesitation. The others had need of the entity's protection, but even having used all due speed, one of the entity's allies was destroyed before it was able to stand itself before the others.

—Your actions are despicable!— the last remaining enemy entity all but spat, hatred pouring forth from it. —But the same has been true for years now, so this being is unsurprised. You may now find it possible to destroy me as well, but the action will avail you naught! Should we fail to return, others, in greater numbers, will follow behind us! Your depredations will not go unpunished!—

And then the enemy entity took itself off at great speed, returning to where its flesh forms and link groups waited. The entity would have been easily able to match that speed, but not so its allies. And perhaps pursuit was not the wisest course in any event. The matter must be thought upon after it had returned to its own flesh forms. . . .

For the enemy entity moved in a righteous cause, after having been seriously harmed by those flesh forms formerly in charge of the entity's homeland. At one time that would have made little difference to the entity's intentions of victory, yet now. . . . Maturity apparently brought more than greater ability and clearer memory, and each time the entity formed it found itself a bit more mature. And now it found itself faced with a dilemma: Defeat could not be countenanced, and yet victory would be truly honorless. What, then, could the proper answer possibly be . . . ?

FORTY-FOUR

The amount of strength we'd expended wasn't excessive, so we merely had a light meal once Jovvi dissolved the Blending. It seemed obvious that not one of us would have eaten anything if we hadn't had another battle to look forward to, not after having lost one of our supporting Blendings. We hadn't known the people in the lost Blending all that well, but we *had* known them. They'd been living, breathing, *High* practitioners, and now, because of the leader Blending from Astinda, they were dead. Our entity had felt only mild regret, but we ourselves felt considerably more.

"Yes, Rion, I'm just as disturbed about it as you are," Jovvi said once I stumbled through an inadequate explanation of how I felt. "But I have to admit that I'm equally disturbed about what *we* did. Those people came here with a legitimate complaint and I can't blame them for wanting vengeance, and yet we destroyed some of them as well. That cold fire thing. . . . Is that something you only just recently thought of, Tamma?"

"I suppose it's related in some way to invisible fire," Tamrissa replied, weariness apparently still covering her. "That enemy entity was so horribly *strong* in Fire magic. . . . Our own entity held the memory of cold fire, and I was able to produce it so I did. But once again I was almost an individual inside the entity, and the effort was . . . somewhat harsh. I also had to draw in more of the power to do it, or the enemy would have bounced the effort back at me and gotten me first. They have a *lot* more experience with Blending than we do. . . ."

That utterance of truth silenced us all for a time, as I had gained that very same impression. Even if the strength of our Blendings turned out to be equal, our opponents had the advantage of . . . better training? More practice? A clearer grasp of what it was they did? Possibly all of those things, and if so then we were very much risking defeat if we faced them directly.

"Why do I have the feelin' that we can't use any more clever plots?" Vallant asked after a time, looking around at us in an obvious request for an answer. "I'm sure I could come up with somethin' to win this thing for us, but a part of me deep inside won't even try."

"It could be because our future shows eventual destruction along just about every possible line of that sort," Naran replied, nothing left of the diffidence she'd once shown—but weariness etched more deeply into her lovely face. "We *can* destroy them, but if we do it will mean our own destruction as well. Just as they said, others will come after them and in even greater numbers."

"How can that be?" Lorand asked, disturbance clear in his eyes. "If we *don't* defeat them, they'll tear down Gan Garee and probably kill hundreds of people at the same time. Now you say that we don't dare defeat them, so what are we supposed to do?"

"Apparently we're supposed to do as the Prophecy demands, and *face* our greatest enemy," Jovvi said, faint annoyance in her tone. "It would have helped considerably more if that prophecy had suggested *how* we're to face them, as it can't be in victory nor in defeat. When you can't afford to win and you can't afford to lose, what in the name of reason *can* you do?"

"The answer to that question is rather simple," I said, wondering why none of the others was able to see the obvious. "The time reminds me of my young manhood, and the various occasions when I ran across certain members of my supposed peer group. If I had allowed them to best me in some way they would have left me in peace for a time, but then that woman who called herself my mother would have subjected me to an endless lecture on the subject of losing face. The lecture would not have been given if I'd bested *them* in some way, but then they would have spent all their energies trying to regain their own lost face. My only course of action turned out to be a balancing act, wherein neither I nor they lost any face whatsoever.''

"You made the contest a draw!" Vallant exclaimed, speaking the words a heartbeat sooner than Lorand. "Of course! Why didn't I think of that?"

"Possibly because that still leaves us nowhere?" Tamrissa suggested with a pained look. "I'm sorry, Rion, I don't mean to insult your idea, but we aren't dealing with a group of teenage noble fools. The people in that Blending we'll be facing have probably lost friends or relatives—or both—to the depredations committed against them, and they won't be in the mood to let the confrontation end in a draw. Just consider how reasonable *we* would be if people we loved had been horribly and uselessly killed by *their* countrymen."

"Your point is very well taken," I replied with a sigh, now seeing my mistake. "A draw is possible only when both parties are willing. So what are we to do?"

"We might—just *might*—be able to end the confrontation on our own terms," Jovvi said slowly after a long moment of silence. "I've been thinking and digging at the question, and it just occurred to me that their greater experience with Blending just *might* be offset if we had much greater strength. If they find themselves about to be destroyed, they could well decide to listen to reason."

"But . . . how much more of the power can we reasonably be expected to take in?" Lorand asked, his brow furrowed. "I know what that question sounds like coming from *me*, but it isn't fear talking this time. I remember when our entity hesitated to draw in more power, so we all must be very close to our limit. And didn't Tamrissa say she had to draw in more in order to do that cold fire thing? How much farther can she push herself before we lose her?"

Vallant voiced his immediate concern just as I did the same, and Jovvi put a hand to her throat as she paled a bit. The light drizzle of rain which had bothered us to begin with had now stopped, but none of us felt in the least more comfortable. I, personally, would have been happier in a downpour, if the lives of my sisters and brothers were no longer in jeopardy.

"Wait, everyone, wait," Naran said, her stare once again on the elsewhere. "After Jovvi made her suggestion, a large number of shadows disappeared into greater solidity. Unless I'm completely misreading what I see, that *is* what we all have to do. And I think I can help to keep us from going too far."

"Are you sure, Naran?" Jovvi asked, her color still not completely back. "Are you certain you can make it less of a danger?"

"In my vision, all of us are represented by various numbers of shadows," Naran replied, her tone oddly distant. "As I look at you now, Jovvi, I'm able to see most of the possible actions you'll take in the next . . . oh, say, in the next hour. By limiting it to that time frame, we also limit the number of possibilities—which range from you surviving easily, all the way to you suddenly ending your time as a viable human being. That last possibility is now rather faint, but if you were to begin drawing in more power, the closer you came to your limit, the stronger that possibility would grow. By watching that possibility closely, I *should* be able to tell when you need to stop."

"And if I draw in the power slowly, I should also be able to stop in time," Jovvi said, now considerably brightened. "I really do think it will work, so I'll go first. But Naran . . . you look very tired. Are you sure you're up to doing something like this?"

"At the moment I'm not, so that means *I'm* the one who gets to go first," she replied, sending an immediate chill through me. "But don't worry, my love, I won't be in any danger. At the moment I can see myself just as easily as I see the rest of you, so everything will be fine."

Her last words were spoken with warmth and a smile as she touched my hand, giving me reassurance and the support I needed to remain silent. I knew well enough that Naran must face what the rest of us faced, and for that reason would do nothing to shame or embarrass her. And yet, if it had been possible for me to face the danger in her stead. . . .

But of course it wasn't, so it was necessary for me to sit

and watch while the reason for my continuing to live attempted to add to her strength. Long, silent moments went by as she sat motionless, and then, abruptly, it was over.

"All right, that's all for *me*," she said more briskly than she'd been speaking, smiling around at all of us. "I had no idea I'd be able to handle *that* much power, so I suppose I've been operating at something of a handicap. But now I'm filled with as much as my talent can safely process, and I feel as though I've had a full night's sleep. Are you ready to go next, Jovvi?"

"I certainly am," Jovvi replied with a smile of her own. "In point of fact I'm now looking forward to it, as I could use a good night's sleep myself. Tell me when you're ready."

"Go ahead," Naran said after a brief hesitation, and again I saw that distant look in her eyes. "But go slowly, and stop as soon as I tell you to."

Jovvi nodded and fell silent, and another timeless time dragged past. I pictured her opening herself to more and more of the power, slowly filling with that substance which wasn't a substance at all. . . .

"Stop," Naran said suddenly, the word hard and commanding. Jovvi jumped the least little bit, but then Naran smiled. "You did it just right, my dear, and stopped at precisely the right time. How do you feel?"

"Better, but not a full night's sleep worth," Jovvi responded with amusement. "I must have been working at a point closer to my full capacity, so don't be afraid that I'll try for just a *little* bit more. I'm perfectly happy to leave any small sliver of difference right where it is."

"I'm glad to hear that," Naran replied with a small laugh. "All right, who's next?"

I answered just the least bit faster than Lorand, so I became the next to go. It felt rather odd, opening myself by increments no wider than the thickness of a fingernail, feeling the power pour in at an ever increasing level, then stopping instantly when Naran called out. I, too, felt more that I'd taken a nap than had a full night's sleep, and Lorand and Vallant, at the end of their turns, also agreed.

"Now it's your turn, Tamrissa," Naran said gently once Vallant had settled back down. "Or would you prefer to stay as you are? You did open to more of the power only recently, so it might be best if you waited a short while before—''

"All right, Naran, what have you seen?" Tamrissa interrupted to ask, her stare rather penetrating. "Under other circumstances I'm certain you would have suggested that I go before the men, but you jumped to answer Rion's request so fast that it made my head spin. There should be no danger at all for me to do as the rest of you have, but everything you've done tells me that that isn't true. So I repeat: What have you seen?"

"It's . . . a more complicated arrangement that I honestly can't interpret," Naran admitted after a short hesitation, worry now wrinkling her brow. "For some reason your stance in the near future isn't all that solid, but I can't tell what might be causing the problem. *Something* will put you in added danger, and I'm just afraid that opening to more of the power is that something."

"Shouldn't you be able to tell?" Tamrissa asked with her own frown. "I mean, I've just decided and announced that I'm going to try opening to more of the power anyway. If that's what's causing the problem, shouldn't the danger become more certain with the decision firmly made?"

"Not necessarily," Naran denied with a sigh. "If it was almost a certainty that you would decide that way—and it just might be—then the announced decision would make no difference. I strongly suggest that you change your mind—and mean it!—so that I can check the thing from the other end, so to speak."

"All right, then I've changed my mind," Tamrissa said, turning to put a hand to Vallant's arm. "Yes, my love, I know what you're about to say, so you needn't say it. I will *not* go off and leave you unprotected against all those women who will certainly throw themselves at your feet once this is all over. If I'm all that close to my top limit where opening to the power goes, I'll simply have to continue as I am. After all, I haven't done too badly *so* far."

"Yes, for a helpless female, you aren't doin' too badly at all," Vallant agreed with a grin, then exchanged a kiss with her. I, personally, was intent on watching Naran, who frowned a frown which slowly grew deeper.

"This is beginning to be very frustrating," Naran said with a small headshake after another moment. "Jovvi, I dislike doubting Tamrissa's word, but I really must ask: Was she speaking the truth, or only what she knew we wanted to hear?"

"No, she *was* speaking the truth," Jovvi said with her own frown. "Actually, it was the truth both times. Does your question mean that there's been no change?"

"That's exactly what it means," Naran replied, now looking at Jovvi rather than at the unformed future. "So what are we supposed to do?"

"That question sounds familiar, but this time I believe I know the answer," Jovvi said with a shrug. "If there's a chance that Tamma's . . . shadows won't change if she starts to take in more of the power, then she'll have to stay as she is. Doing anything else is an unnecessary risk."

"How do we know that *that* isn't the source of the problem?" Tamrissa asked, an undirected annoyance now in her voice. "If it is and we do nothing, we could be precipitating the trouble. If we have to err, I'd rather do it on the side of additional power."

"I'd recommend against that," Naran said, now speaking to Tamrissa. "It's possible that you're opened as widely as possible to the power right now, and even one more attempt to increase that will instantly burn you out. Considering how you feel about strength, it's to be expected that you might insist on taking the risk no matter what the rest of us said. That could explain why nothing has changed: Ultimately you may talk yourself into trying."

"Which means that you really need to be distracted from making that decision," Jovvi said, her tone now a good deal more brisk. "We've gone to a lot of trouble to isolate that one Astindan Blending, but that isolation won't last forever. The others will begin to recover in just a few hours, so if we're ever going to find a way to make this come out right, we have to do it now. We won't find a better time, so why don't we go looking for a fight?"

That question seemed to refocus everyone's attention, most certainly including mine. We'd eaten and had tea, walked about and stretched a bit, and now there was nothing else left to do. It was time to face "our greatest enemies," but my own observations of the event are far from complete. Jovvi's give a much wider perspective, so the next segment will be narrated just as she related the happenings to me.

FORTY-FIVE

Jovvi waited until everyone nodded their agreement, then she initiated the Blending. She expected the time to be the way it usually was, her identity merging with those of the others to produce the entity, but this time an odd thing happened. The entity most certainly appeared at once, but the Jovvi part of it was *not* completely submerged. It felt more as though a larger, much more strengthened Jovvi began to float along the road, heading toward the place where the enemy entity would be found.

The experience was unusual, but not enough to distract the Jovvi entity from what she was about. The invading force had made a temporary and very much emergency camp right there on the road, with quite a lot of their flesh forms hurrying back and forth. The ones who had inhaled the hilsom powder were quite beside themselves with agitation, and others apparently attempted to calm them. Those who had been disabled earlier by the entity and its allies lay stretched out on makeshift pallets, attended to and hovered over by other flesh forms. At first there was no sign of the main invading entity, but after no more than a moment it appeared.

—So those who are honorless have returned, —the invading entity sneered, hatred fairly pouring forth from it.

—Is it now that you will claim all our lives?—

—Had this entity wanted your lives, it would hardly have come here unaccompanied,— the Jovvi entity replied. — This being has come instead to speak with you, in an attempt to—

—In an attempt to gull, cozen, and destroy us!— the other interrupted, anger blazing hot. —Once before those from your empire came with sweet words of friendship, and those who believed them are long since dead! As I sense that you were indeed foolish enough to approach this entity alone, you may now pay for the deeds of those who came before you as well as for your own!—

And with that the entity attacked, all its strength poured into the boiling cloud of incandescent destruction which raged at the Jovvi entity. And that strength was enormous, just as the Jovvi entity had known it would be. Had her flesh forms not added to their own strength they would have been quickly overwhelmed, and even so raising the necessary resistance was no simple matter. But it *was* done, and the attack was deflected.

—It grieves this entity that one of yours was destroyed,— the Jovvi entity sent, adding a full measure of compassion. —Just as it grieves this being that one of our own was done the same. But this being's flesh forms and those who support them were not responsible for what was done to your homeland. They, too, were victims of the same authority, an authority which has now been overthrown. Join us in sitting down together in the manner of rational beings, and—

—No!— the other entity denied harshly, fury still blazing hot. —False words are too easily spoken by those who stand behind you! This being will listen to none of them, not now and not ever!—

And again an attack came ravening in, one which combined every aspect available to the entity. Just as it began, the Jovvi entity noticed something odd: she was able to anticipate what would happen a measurable amount of time in advance of its actually happening. Then the Jovvi entity realized that that must be the contribution of the Naran flesh form, a talent which the opposing entity did *not* display. The added talent allowed the Jovvi entity to block or avoid the opposing entity's attacks, but even so the matter could not be allowed to continue as it had been going. Too much of the Jovvi entity's strength was being used up in defense, leaving less and less should an attack of her own become necessary.

And it seemed that an attack might well have become necessary. Holding off the maelstrom of hatred and destruction accomplished nothing in the way of changing the opposing entity's intentions, therefore a different tactic now seemed indicated.

—For an entity who is more mature than this being, you behave in an exceedingly foolish manner,— the Jovvi entity remonstrated once the second attack had ceased.—This being has come to offer true friendship, and yet you refuse to listen. Are you unable to *tell* that this being speaks the truth?—

—Truth is an elastic substance, stretching in the direction of choice designated by the one who speaks it,— the entity replied with impatience. —It may be true friendship which you now claim to seek, yet in a short while that could easily change. This entity has no cause to believe your truth, and many reasons to doubt it.—

—You mean to force us to destroy you?— the Jovvi entity inquired, definitely perplexed. —Such a course of action has no logic to it whatsoever, instead being related only to emotionalism. Is that what greater maturity brings? An abandoning of logic for emotionalism? Do you *wish* to be destroyed?—

—The logic you value so highly should bring the proper reply to that inquiry,— the opposing entity responded with harsh intolerance. —It should by now be quite clear that this entity does not intend to be destroyed, rather that it means to *do* the destroying. Once that small chore has been accomplished, the rest of its vengeance will be taken!—

For the third time the opposing entity launched its attack, allowing no further discussion. It was now beyond doubt that simple defense would never suffice, therefore the Jovvi entity followed the demands of logic and deflected the attack, then countered with an effort of her own. As had been previously noted, the opposing entity had nothing of the talent to anticipate what the future would bring. The Jovvi entity's own awareness was growing fainter as its Naran flesh form lost more and more strength, but that slender advantage still remained.

As did another advantage, one which more than one of its flesh forms had learned to accomplish. The opposing entity shielded itself—and its flesh forms—with its enormous strength, a shield which was impossible to penetrate. No single entity ever formed would find itself able to generate enough power to force a way through, and yet the Jovvi entity knew that force was unnecessary. It had proven possible in the past to *go around* such a shield, which the Jovvi entity quickly did.

Striking at both the opposing entity and its flesh forms at the same time was extremely difficult, most especially as the Jovvi entity had no wish to destroy either target. The situation demanded that her touch be exactly right, neither too hard nor too soft, so that the opposing entity might be shaken into a more reasonable state of mind. The sense of a scream came from the opposing entity, most likely due to the fact that it had believed its flesh forms disguised and impossible to locate, but the Jovvi entity knew that trick as well and had been able to negate it. The opposing entity and its flesh forms were now literally *down*, and the Jovvi entity deliberately loomed over them.

—This being feels foolish repeating words already rejected by you, and yet the words *must* be repeated,— the Jovvi entity sent slowly and clearly. —We come in friendship to *aid* you as best we may, yet not at the expense of those who are blameless. You may take your vengeance upon those who earned such treatment if you wish, but not upon those who have been victimized far longer and more harshly than you and yours. Should you find this offer impossible to accept, this being *will* have no choice but to destroy you. Give this being your thoughts, and let all consequences be on *your* head.—

—It . . . cannot be true,— the opposing entity all but gasped, shock and confusion clear in its being.— Those in this land are enemies to us, yearning for nothing but our destruction. It cannot be true that *our* well-being is desired. . . . —

The next happening came horribly fast, and yet the Jovvi

entity saw it all with a clarity which made the horror even worse. First an awareness touched in, an awareness of suddenly much clearer vision. Before the Jovvi entity might wonder about the change, she became conscious of the presence of those lesser entities which had spread the hilsom powder among the invaders. Those lesser entities had left their places of hiding and had neared the makeshift camp, and now they had gained the wrong impression. Seeing that the Jovvi entity had not destroyed her opponent, they apparently believed that the Jovvi entity was *unable* to destroy it. With that in view, they realized their duty at once. If the Jovvi entity lacked the strength to complete her task, it was up to them to assist her.

For that reason the two lesser entities attacked simultaneously, unable to link and yet more than able to attack together. Their combined strength was certainly enough to destroy the now weakened opposing entity, but that could not, under any circumstances, be allowed. There was only one action open to the Jovvi entity, therefore she immediately attempted it. With a wordless cry of —No!— she threw herself before the opposing entity and its flesh forms, shielding them from the attack of her own allies. They were the newest and weakest of the allied entities, after all, and she the strongest. . . .

The Jovvi entity screamed with pain, suddenly realizing that she *had* been the strongest, *before* facing the opposing entity. Holding off that being's attacks had taken its toll, and now the Jovvi entity's vast store of strength was nearly depleted. There remained just enough to deflect the double attack until the lesser entities realized their mistake, and then—

And then Jovvi came out of the Blending with a scream of her own, turning immediately to Tamma. Before the bond had broken she'd felt Tamma collapse, the effort to deflect those last attacks just too much for the girl to bear. It was *Tamma's* strength which defended the Blending, and that strength had been taxed far beyond even *her* incredible limits.

"No!" Vallant cried, pulling Tamma's limp body to him and rocking her as he held her close. "No, my love, don't leave me! You promised, you promised!"

"Lorand, do something!" Jovvi sobbed, despite the fact that Lorand already bent over Tamma. "Please don't let her die, please! The rest of us—*and* the Astindans—are alive because of her! We *can't* let her die!"

"But the thread of her life is so thin and far away!" Lorand whispered, tragedy twisting his features. "I'm putting everything I have left into it, but I can't get a good enough grip to pull her back! She needs *support* to fight her way back, but I don't have enough left to give it to her! She's slipping away.... I'm losing her ... !"

Even as the tears of agony flowed down Jovvi's face, she suddenly became aware of something ... different and powerful. She had no idea what it could be—and then Lorand cried out in sudden delight.

"It's working!" he told them, his face, too, covered in tears. "There's something there, helping me pull her back with the strength and support she needs. If it only keeps on for another few minutes, she'll be out of danger!"

—The effort will continue,— Jovvi heard inside her mind, immediately recognizing the mental tones of the opposing entity.— The flesh form knowingly emptied itself to protect this being's own flesh forms and existence, enemies though we supposedly were. How might this being allow it to die, and continue to consider itself honorable?—

"You're *very* honorable," Jovvi answered aloud with a laugh of delirious relief. "And we mean to prove that we're the same, just as soon as we can all sit down together. We *will* do all we can to help you bring life back to your land, as we feel responsible even though we weren't the ones who caused the destruction."

—The devastation will take years of backbreaking effort to repair,— the opposing entity replied. —With the large number of flesh forms destroyed along with the land, there is but one way it may be done. Let those who are responsible for the thing now be set to repairing it.—

Jovvi exchanged a glance with the others, their expressions telling her that they understood exactly what the entity meant. It was harsh and cruel, but a perfectly fitting punishment to suit the crime.

"We'll have to discuss how it's to be done, but we have no objection to your idea," she said with a sigh.

The entity sent an indication of its satisfaction, and then continued to help Lorand strengthen Tamma. Jovvi simply closed her eyes, wondering if guilt would set in once she'd had enough sleep to turn her human again. The threat of war seemed to be over, but the price of peace would be the enslavement of every member of the former nobility.

FORTY-SIX

I thought I wanted nothing more to do with this journal, but now that I've finally had enough sleep and a few decent meals, I've agreed to finish what I began. But I couldn't have done the parts where I came so close to dying, so it was a good thing Rion rode—or wrote—to my rescue. It *was* proper that he be the one, as he and I were the two who were most changed after joining the group. In that way he and I have something of a closer bond than the others do, a positive accomplishment we share in that both of us are better people for the change. Or at least I hope I'm a better person than I was. . . .

When I finally woke up, it was to find the entire group clustered around my bed. Every face wore the silliest smile I'd ever seen, but at least no one asked me how I felt.

"Well, now we know why I saw what I did about you," Naran said instead, her own expression wry. "How much power you were able to handle had only a little to do with it."

"That last effort drained you too far," Jovvi amplified when I looked at Naran with confusion. "You were able to shield our former enemy as well as the rest of us from that mistaken attack, but in doing so you were taken right up to the brink of life and death. If the Astindans hadn't made the effort to help.... Well, I'd prefer not to even think about it.''

"None of us wants to think about it," Lorand said, his arm around Jovvi. "If I'd had to stand there and let you die.... I never would have gotten over it, and neither would any of the rest of us. The Astindans saved more lives than just yours.''

"Which is odd, when you consider what they came here to do," Rion put in, his own arm around Naran. "But you look as though you could use more sleep, just as soon as you eat the food we've brought. We can talk about this again once you're more like your usual self.''

Through the confusion and vagueness surrounding me, the word "food" had no trouble getting my attention. I did feel absolutely hollow, so I ate the meal they'd brought— with Vallant's arm firmly around *me*.

The next time I awoke it was the following day, and I finally found it possible to remember everything I should have. I knew Vallant had spent most of the time in the bed next to me, holding my hand, but right now the room held me alone. So I got up and washed and dressed, then wandered downstairs to find something to fill the new hollow nesting in my insides. When some of our people noticed me, I was whisked to the dining room, seated at the table, then stuffed to bursting with what seemed like everything the kitchen must have held. Only when I could barely move did they relent and let me go, telling me that the others were outside overseeing what was going on.

Since I had no idea about what *was* going on, I went outside to see what could be taking everyone's attention so thoroughly. I remember walking out the front door, expecting nothing but the sight of the large and pretty grounds around the house—but found utter chaos instead of peace and quiet. There seemed to be hundreds of people standing around in small groups with guardsmen ranged everywhere to watch them, and most of the people in the groups were hysterical in one way or another.

"I'm almost tempted to feel sorry for them," Vallant's voice came, and I turned to see him approaching me from the direction of the stables with a tender smile on his face. "You're lookin' a lot better, love. Are you sure you're strong enough to be out here?"

"I was just wondering that myself," I replied, immediately stepping closer to the arm he was in the midst of putting around me. "I don't understand what's happening."

"We've begun to make good on the agreement we have with the Astindans," he answered, just the flicker of unease in his light and beautiful eyes. "Their country is in ruins because of what our armies did, and too many of their people were killed along with the land. If they have to work to bring the land back alive by themselves, a lot more of their people will end up dyin' before they'll be able to do it. That's why we've agreed to let them have the people responsible for their trouble as workers, to use them in the rebuildin' and get it done that much faster. And in a manner of speakin', the Astindans are doin' us a favor by takin' them."

"Of course," I breathed, finally making sense of what I saw. "Those people are our former nobles, and that's why so many of them are having hysterics and trying to demand their *rights*. But why are they *here*? Is this the only place anyone can think of to put them?"

"We brought some of the Astindans here as our guests, so it's as good a place as any," Jovvi said as she and the others came up in time to hear my question. "We offered to let them use the house to ... interview their newest workers, but they decided that the stables would be more fitting. They feel that these people need to get used to the conditions they'll be working under as quickly as possible, since they aren't being put under *total* control. The Astindans are simply making them obey any orders given them by proper authority—meaning someone other than each other—and also making it impossible for them to run away. Aside from that, they'll be fully aware of what they'll be made to do."

"It's really too bad that Meerk isn't here to see this," Lorand said, his gaze moving around the milling crowds. "He would have appreciated the justice of—"

"See here, you people, this is absolutely intolerable!" a high-pitched voice interrupted as the closest group of nobles—about six or seven in number—began to stride toward us. "As you seem to be in charge, you may now tell these—these—ruffianly bullies to step back from their betters and allow us to leave!"

The man wasn't very old, but from the extra weight he carried and his imperious manner, he must have been somewhat important. Or at least he must have been important at one time. . . .

"You're right, we *are* in charge," Lorand told him, faint annoyance in his voice over having been interrupted. "We're the ones who defeated that marvelous noble Blending you fools had Seated—through the usual trickery. But you mentioned something about people who are better. . . . Surely you can't be referring to yourselves?"

"Of course he means *us*, you peasant fool!" the woman beside the man snapped, her nose so high in the air it was a good thing for her that it wasn't raining. "We are important people of *quality*, and once the proper authorities hear about this, all you criminals will be sent to the mines where you belong! You will release us at *once*, and then we *may* say a few words in your defense at your trial. We'll require carriages or coaches, of course, and—Oh!"

Some of the scattered guardsmen had come over, and the group was abruptly shoved to a stop about six feet away from us. They were all outraged at being treated like that, of course, but Lorand let them know how the rest of us felt about it.

"Since you've obviously missed the point, let me spell it out for you," he said, addressing the two people who had spoken. "Your sort has never been anything but *poor* quality, and as far as importance goes you'll never be thought of—or treated that way—again. We and our followers are the new proper authorities in the empire, so you may take it as official that you and your precious group are now about to pay for every criminal act and outrage you've ever committed. Your worst failure, of course, is being stupid, but where *you're* going that won't matter. You won't have to give any orders, just take them, which is really all you're good for. A lot fewer lives would have been wasted if you and your ilk had been stopped sooner."

"Wait!" one of the other men in the group protested as

the guardsmen began to prod them back toward the place they'd come from. "I don't know what you mean to do with us, but it can't possibly be fair! *I* didn't do anything to hurt you or the rest of the commoners, so why do I have to suffer along with everyone else? You have to believe that I didn't *do* anything!"

"Oh, we do believe it," Jovvi said, her tone rather dry. "You and quite a lot of your equals never did do anything, which is another point you've obviously missed. If you *had* done something you might have made the situation better, but you chose not to get involved. That's almost as bad as what your friends did by actively participating, so you can't complain about having to pay right along with the rest of them. From now on you *will* do something, but you've lost the right to have it be by your own decision."

That brought out more sputtering and protests, but none of us was interested in listening any longer. We all turned away and walked into the house, then headed for the sitting room where we might have some tea while we talked.

"The Astindans have already started the first group of converted nobles on their way back to Astinda," Lorand said as we approached the sitting room. "One of their Blendings along with their link groups is in charge, and we arranged a few provision wagons to go along with them. They're making the nobles walk, of course, so they'll be in decent shape for hard work by the time they get to where they're going."

"And we've sent our own Blendings along with theirs to search the rest of the empire," Jovvi added. "Too many of the most prominent nobles—meaning the ones really responsible for what was done—left Gan Garee before all this started, and it would hardly be fair if they weren't found and sent after their class equals. It would also be foolish on our part to leave them wherever they happen to be, giving them the chance to make trouble once most of the confusion is over and the last of the Astindans has gone home."

"And now we have to decide what *we're* going to do," Rion said as we began to enter the sitting room. "Master Mohr keeps asking when we expect to move into the palace, as do all the other people he's brought along with him. They really think we're—"

Rion's words broke off abruptly, and with good reason. Five people stood waiting in the sitting room, four of them grouped behind a jolly-looking man of middle years, and of those we were able to see, not one of them was someone we'd met before.

"Who are you people, and what are you doin' in here?" Vallant demanded as we all came to an abrupt halt, his tone a growl. "And while I'm askin' questions, how did you get in here?"

"Getting in here wasn't very difficult, Dom Ro," the man replied, his smile making him look even friendlier and more . . . lacking in danger, might be the best way to put it. A frolicking puppy gives you no sense of personal danger even if you don't like dogs, and that's very close to the impression the man gave off.

"Unless you've been brought by someone we know, you shouldn't be anywhere near this house," Lorand said, standing shoulder to shoulder with Vallant and Rion. "We aren't quite up to accepting strangers as friends yet, so you'd better tell us who got you through all the guards and the rest of our people."

"The answer to that is what's known as a long story," the man said, his tone and manner now apologetic. "We really do understand the reasons for your disquiet, but we aren't here to cause harm. It just happens to be time to answer some of the other questions you've undoubtedly been asking, so we've come to do it. The process will be quite painless, I assure you."

He beamed around at us as though he were our teacher and we his prized honor students. I joined the others in exchanging perplexed glances, but still didn't relax my guard. Naran's expression said she had no idea what was going on, which made things even stranger. Jovvi wore a frown, and after a moment she stirred.

"He believes he's telling the complete truth," she said with a small headshake. "The feelings of the others support that, but I can't imagine what he's telling the truth *about*."

"Oh, certainly you can, Dama Hafford," he chided gently, but in a humorous way. "For instance, I'm sure you'd

Sharon Green

like to know how it came to be that your Blending *knew* about that mistaken attack just before it was launched against the Astindans. By then, Dama Whist should have been too exhausted to function properly.''

That time all of our mouths must have fallen open, judging by what happened to mine. It wasn't possible for the man to have known about that, not unless . . . what?

"Please do sit down with us now," the man coaxed, his amusement gone, with gentle patience and understanding replacing it. "I'm Ristor Ardanis, and to prove you really can trust us, we've brought along someone you all ought to know."

The one person we hadn't been able to see clearly until then, caused by her standing behind others of the group, stepped forward, and I couldn't hold back a gasp.

"Warla!" I exclaimed, staring at the girl who had been my companion for so long. "I had no idea where you'd gone . . . or if you were all right. . . ."

I added that last because of the way she looked, which was subtly different from what I'd grown used to seeing in her face and manner. She was definitely the same person, but the usual . . . nervousness and uncertainty were gone.

"I'm perfectly all right, Tamrissa," she said with a warm, supporting smile, and even her voice had lost its usual hesitance. "Actually I'm more than just all right, now that I don't have to play that part any longer. Won't all of you please sit down and talk to these people? They really do know things *you* need to know."

We exchanged glances again, but short of asking Jovvi to put them under control, we had little choice. If we wanted to know what was going on, we'd have to sit down and listen.

"Thank you," Ristor Ardanis said as we wordlessly began to take our places on chairs and couches. "And I believe that this confirms *my* opinion in the matter?"

He'd looked to one of the men with him as he'd said that, his brow raised in faintly amused questioning. The man nodded wryly and grudgingly, and Ardanis chuckled as he took his own seat.

"Why don't you begin by explaining that very odd exchange," Jovvi suggested from where she sat beside Lorand. "*What* confirms your opinion on *what* matter? I'd like to know why that man was more nervous than he is now."

"I suppose we might as well start with that," Ardanis agreed with a nod, his expression still amused. "It should do well with introducing the main topic. My friend was nervous to begin with because he believed that you would give in to temptation and put us all under control in order to find out what you want to know. I, on the other hand, firmly believed that you would not do such a thing unless you felt yourself and your groupmates to be in danger. You might say that *my* sight was a deal clearer than his in this instance."

"Your sight," Jovvi echoed, looking at him with her head to one side. "That word has special significance for you, so I'm going to make an educated guess: Naran was strong enough to warn us during the last of the confrontation because she finally had tandem link groups of her own to draw strength from. Am I wrong?"

"No, you're perfectly correct," Ardanis agreed with a chuckle for the way some of us gasped—especially Naran. "We are indeed just like her, and are overjoyed that we can finally admit it. We've waited centuries for the opportunity, knowing it *would* come, but not precisely when."

"Then you must be the ones responsible for the Prophecies!" I blurted, visited by sudden inspiration. "No one ever said where they came from, but it stands to reason. . . . What I don't understand is why there's so much secrecy involved here. If your people went so far as to make Prophecies, why didn't they come completely forward into the world?"

"They did, right after the Prophecies were made," Ardanis said, and this time it was heavy sadness which replaced his amusement. "Too many of our brothers and sisters of that time were sure we would be fully accepted, and in a manner of speaking we were. The new ruling Five greeted us warmly and offered us their protection until people . . . grew *used* to those with Sight magic, was the way they put it. And at first they were perfectly serious in their intentions, otherwise our people would never have been taken in. But then they began to think about the benefits in knowing about what was to happen, and realized how truly beneficial it would be if they were the *only* ones who knew."

"Oh, dear," Jovvi said, an understatement if ever I'd heard one. "They must have had in mind any plots against them, just as they'd plotted against the Four. So what did they do to your people?"

"They enslaved them, and hid them away from the knowledge of the rest of the world," Ardanis replied with a shrug that seemed full of horror rather than indifference. "Happily, the strongest of our people hadn't joined the others in coming forward, and by the time a search was made for them they were long gone. The Five tried to use some of their enslaved Sight magic users to find them, but those who had escaped had a stronger talent and were able to avoid being found."

"But if the first Five knew about you, why didn't the next, or their nobility?" Lorand asked. "I'm assuming that they didn't, of course, but it makes sense that way. If the nobility had known, the present generation of them would never have been surprised the way they were."

"The first Five held the secret very close, intending to make their reign a good deal longer than twenty-five years," Ardanis said with a sigh. "They were *very* ambitious people, and knowing what the future holds tends to ... *change* even those who aren't that ambitious to begin with. They intended to rule for the rest of their lives, and would have made the Four's despotic rule look like a pleasant family picnic. They thought it was their destiny to accomplish that, not realizing that those of us who had escaped were *really* High talents."

"So they ... clouded the future for those who were enslaved," Naran said suddenly, surprising me. "I've wondered for some time if that was possible, and now I know it has to be. It made the Five rely on a false picture of what was coming to be, so they must have failed. What happened to them?"

"They were maneuvered to a place where they were exposed to Fire Fever," Ardanis replied, the look in his eyes grim. "As I'm sure most of you know, Fire Fever killed hundreds and thousands of people before High practitioners in Earth magic finally found a cure for it. Once the Five came down with it nothing could be done for them, and their secret died with them. Our people were rescued, and then they went about hiding their presence in a much more thorough way. They'd learned a hard lesson about how people would view their talent, and had no intentions of repeating the episode."

"So they hid out in homes for the 'talentless,' those who were called nulls," Vallant said from next to me, his expression as disturbed as mine probably was. "No one likes talkin' about that subject, and undoubtedly likes bein' near the homes even less. Instead of havin' to search out those who were born with your talent, your people just sat back and waited until those poor, talentless children were brought to *them*. Does that mean no one is born talentless?"

"I wish it did," Ardanis said with another sigh. "I grew up in one of those homes, just as all of us here did, and being talentless doesn't also make someone other than human. I felt delighted when I was told I had a talent after all, but it was rather painful when it became clear that not all of my friends were in the same position. Our people helped those 'useless' children to grow up with the least amount of bitterness possible, and many of them were able to rejoin the society which had rejected them—without anyone being the wiser. After all, some people's talent is so weak they might as well not have it. Those who didn't care about the outside world stayed at the homes, helping out with the constant new arrivals."

"And some of them married, and had children of their own," Warla put in, her smile gentle and her expression calm. "Only a few of those children shared their parents' affliction, the rest being perfectly normal in their respective aspects. It was possible for a High talent to tell which of those children would never want to join our secret community, so those children were given up for adoption in the outside world. The rest were raised with love and a full awareness of what the community was all about, and some even established themselves in the outside world in order to keep the home community fully informed. Or to do special jobs that needed doing."

"Like being a companion to someone like me?" I asked with all the confusion I felt. "And not just an ordinary companion, but one who was frightened of her own shadow? What possible good did any of that do for anyone at all?''

''Before Warla answers that question, you need to hear a few more facts first,'' Ardanis interrupted apologetically. ''Those first Prophecies which were made so long ago weren't real, legitimate prophecies, but were a collection of common sense warnings which our people had learned to notice. History has shown us that when a new social system is established, it thrives for about a hundred and fifty years and then begins to slide downhill. After two hundred years many people are dissatisfied with the system, but it continues on because no one is dissatisfied *enough* to try changing it. At the end of two hundred and fifty years things are really in a mess, and somewhere around the three hundred year mark the old system falls apart by itself or is pulled down by those who no longer find it possible to live under it. The first Five ennobled their supporters and put all power and property into their hands, and that action alone immediately indicated disaster at some future time.''

''Is that what multiple shadows around a particular event means?'' Naran interrupted to ask. ''That the action will cause disaster at some time in the future?''

''Sometimes, but not always,'' Ardanis replied with a warm, caring smile for Naran. ''Don't worry, my dear, you'll learn everything you need to, and in just a little while. In the interim, I have to finish my explanations. Is that all right?''

Naran nodded with a sigh, obviously knowing there wasn't much else she could do, and Ardanis smiled his thanks.

''I'll try to be as brief as possible,'' he said after taking a deep breath. ''After our experience with the first Five we kept our existence a secret, but we also kept a close watch on the world about us. After all, we had to live in the same world as everyone else, and the better the world, the better off *we* were. Quite a lot of time passed with things growing worse and worse, but when we reached a particular time our High talents told us that we could no longer just stand by and watch what happened. We had to become actively involved, otherwise our communities would go down right along with the rest of the empire. That time was a little more than twenty years ago."

He paused at that point to look around at us, and I doubt whether any of us missed the significance of what he'd said. They'd decided to take a more active role in the world just about the time that the members of our group were being born.

"Yes, it was your births which triggered the need for our activity," he agreed, showing a smile again. "Even then our people were able to tell that a devastating crisis was in the making, but not like the crises spoken of in the original Prophecies. Those crises were described in the most general terms, so that they would match whatever general crisis arose during the reign of each of the Seated Fives. And of course more than one crisis arose in each twenty-five year period, something that was only natural and to be expected. It was hoped by the people who circulated the original Prophecies that those in power would hesitate a long while before trying to control the selection process for the Five, and for quite some time the ploy worked. But it had stopped working approximately seventy-five years earlier, and now a real crisis loomed in our future which only the strongest of the strong would be able to face and best."

"Which the chosen noble Blendings weren't," Lorand said with a nod. "Are you telling us that your people knew we would enter the competitions and lose, then manage to come back and win? How could they have known so far in advance, and what exactly did they do for us?"

"My people *didn't* know any of that," Ardanis denied with a short movement of his head. "They were only able to tell that certain people would be involved in the crisis, and that you were some of those people. And as for what was done for you, not all of you were given help. You, Dom Coll, along with Dama Domon and Dom Ro weren't given immediate assistance because you didn't require it. Dom Mardimil and Dama Hafford did, so it was supplied. There was a servant in your mother's house for a time, Dom Mardimil, who took more than a slight interest in you. Do you remember him?"

"Of course I do," Rion answered with a frown. "Are you saying that *he* was one of you?"

"You needed someone to teach you certain things and to be a friend of sorts," Ardanis confirmed. "Just as Dama Hafford needed a warm, loving family to be a part of. They grew to consider you one of their own, Dama Hafford, and I'm delighted to tell you that they're very proud of the woman you've become. If you like, I'll carry a message back to them for you. They're no longer living where they were, you know."

Jovvi nodded to show that she did know, and the surprise on her face said that she probably *would* send a message. I, however, still hadn't had my question answered.

"What you've said doesn't explain why *I* got a scared-to-death Warla," I pointed out. "That was your idea of help?"

"Of course," Ardanis responded with a grin. "Didn't you use Warla's presence as an awful reminder of what could happen to *you* if you faltered in your resolve? That was what we were told you needed the most, so that was what Warla gave you. Are you saying it didn't work?"

I couldn't say anything of the sort, and both Ardanis and Warla seemed to know it. Warla's gentle laugh was a sharing rather than ridicule, and realizing that finally let me give her a return smile.

"And last but not least we have Naran, who should have been brought to our community but wasn't," Ardanis continued, gazing at Naran fondly. "We knew her mother would refuse to bring her, of course, and when something like that happened we usually used one of our people in an official position to force the parent to part with the child. This time, however, all indications showed disaster if we interfered, so we merely followed and watched and helped when it became necessary. Naran was the one all our hopes hung on, for once she joined you it wasn't possible for her to use her talent and yet keep it a secret. With the example of the first Five hung vividly before our eyes, we had to know how *your* Five would react when you learned about the sixth aspect."

"So how did we do?" Vallant asked, an edge to his voice despite the very neutral tone he used. "Since you're here and talkin' to us, are we to assume that we passed the test with flyin' colors—or that we have to be put out of the way as the first fivefold Blendin' was? I take it you *are* strong enough to keep Naran from knowin' about any danger ahead of us?''

"Actually, no single one of us *is* quite strong enough for that,'' Ardanis replied, pretending he noticed nothing of the way we all tensed. "Your lovely Naran Whist is truly the strongest among us, especially now that she's opened herself so fully to the power. Just as the rest of you are the strongest and best in your various aspects, not to mention much more honorable than the average. If you weren't, you would already have engineered your own downfall.''

"Would you care to explain that?'' Jovvi asked, the only exception to the general air of tension. "It's not difficult to tell that you're still speaking what you consider the truth, but I don't understand what you mean.''

"It's perfectly simple,'' Ardanis said with his usual smile. "The time during that last confrontation was the true crisis point for you, and because Naran was so tired we *were* able to hide sight of the possibility from her. When your other two Blendings mistakenly attacked the Blending from Astinda, your own Blending had the choice of protecting only yourselves, or protecting people who were supposed to be your enemies as well. If you had chosen to protect only yourselves despite the warning that the Astindans had to survive, two of the other Astindan Blendings would have destroyed you on the spot. They had just enough strength to do it, and seeing their leader struck down completely after already being bested would have triggered that final attack. There was a very strong possibility that that was what would happen, and if it did then we would have had to wait for our next opportunity to rejoin the world.''

"And it didn't matter that we would be dead?'' Lorand asked, clearly as upset as I felt. "All that mattered was that *your* people would be all right?''

"You miss the point,'' Ardanis said, his face and voice a study of calm. "If you were the sort to think only of yourselves, it was made very clear to us that you would be just as bad as the first fivefold Blending. But if you went so far as to put your own lives in danger to protect people who were still your enemy, then we could safely trust the secret of our existence to you. And it all links in with the fact that you haven't moved yourselves to the palace yet, which you have every right to do. If you were likely to betray us the way the first Five did, you'd already be there.''

"We aren't there because we don't yet know if we want to *be* the Seated Blending," I said, needing to disagree with him in some way. "Doesn't *that* fact change your reasoning just a little?"

"No," he denied, his smile changing to a grin. "Actually it reinforces the theories, since you're not grabbing for the reins of power the way almost anyone else would. When you finally do let yourselves be Seated, you'll be the best rulers this empire has had in five hundred years or more. And you'll be Seated on the Sixfold Throne, which is really the clincher for us. Once you introduce Naran to the world, the rest of us can come out of hiding.''

"No, don't bother arguing with him," Naran said as Vallant, Rion, and Lorand all began to speak at once. "The possibility of our not being Seated has all but disappeared, so he's not guessing. I think what he said about all of us really being the strongest has chased away our doubts, so now we're ready to do as we're supposed to. And since everyone already considers us the Chosen Blending . . .''

"Everyone will simply go along with it," Vallant said in a sour—but defeated—tone. "But at least now *we* know that we're not Chosen, since the original Prophecies were just general warnings. Isn't that true, Dom Ardanis?"

"Certainly it's true," Ardanis agreed with his grin still in place. "It was a useful ploy to have people think the Prophecies were real, so we encouraged that belief. And I, for one, can't wait to see what a Sixfold Blending will do for the empire. Things are going to change very radically, but certainly for the better.''

"Just a moment," Jovvi said slowly while everyone else began to comment about that aloud. "The thought of a Sixfold Blending is exciting and all, but I'm afraid I still have a question. If all that noise about the Prophecies was simply a ploy, then what about the signs that would indicate to the world that the Chosen Blending had come to be? Was that also supposed to be a ploy?"

"Of course," Ardanis said, but his grin had faded quite a bit. "I see something that I don't in any way understand, so I must ask what you're talking about, Dama Hafford. There's something . . . *looming* in the future, but I can't tell what it can possibly be—except that it's related to the question you just asked. What *about* the signs that were supposed to be manifested?"

This time we all looked at one another rather than just glancing about, and no one answered Ardanis. I'd been expecting the man to say that *his* people were responsible for what we'd experienced, but it was obvious they weren't. And yet those incidents *had* happened, something none of us could deny.

So if the Guild people weren't responsible for the manifestations, the hidden people weren't, and we certainly hadn't imagined them. . . . *Something* had caused them, and I couldn't help wondering just when in the future we might manage to find out who that was—

And did we really want to know . . . ?

If you've enjoyed the adventures of Tamrissa, Vallant, Lorand, Rion and Jovvi in The Blending *series, watch for the exciting new trilogy by Sharon Green coming soon from Avon Eos!*

The Chosen Five have become Six, and the gifted Naran joins her mysterious, powerful Sight magic to the Earth, Air, Fire, Water, and Spirit magic of the fivefold Blending to form an unprecedented Sixfold Blending to rule the country.

But claiming their birthright and gaining the throne as the Seated Blending was only the beginning for the brave heroes . . .

A new trilogy from Sharon Green, coming soon from Avon Eos.

World Fantasy Award-winning Editors
Ellen Datlow and Terri Windling
Present Original Fairy Tale Collections for Adults

"Unusual and evocative . . . [the] series gives the reader a look at what some of our best storytellers are doing today."
Washington Post Book World

RUBY SLIPPERS, GOLDEN TEARS
77872-6/$6.99 US/$8.99 Can

Original stories by Joyce Carol Oates, Neil Gaiman, Gahan Wilson, Jane Yolen and others.

BLACK THORN, WHITE ROSE
77129-2/$5.99 US/$7.99 Can

Featuring stories by Roger Zelazny, Peter Straub and many others

SNOW WHITE, BLOOD RED
71875-8/$6.50 US/$8.50 Can

Includes adult fairy tales by Nancy Kress, Charles de Lint, Esther M. Friesner and many others.

Avon Books Presents
Science Fiction and Fantasy
Writers of America
Grand Master

ANDRE
NORTON

BROTHER TO SHADOWS
77096-2/$5.99 US/$7.99 Can

THE HANDS OF LYR
77097-0/$5.99 US/$7.99 Can

MIRROR OF DESTINY
77976-2/$6.50 US/$8.99 Can

SCENT OF MAGIC
78416-5/$6.50 US/$8.50 Can